To my children—
For believing in me
And to my mother who was always there for me

1

Drenched in sweat, she jolted awake. She sat for a moment, dazed. Beneath her blouse, the sweat trickled down her sides. Wiping away the moisture from her brow with the back of her hand, she quickly scanned the room. What had happened? Why was she on the attic floor? Her eyes dropped to the album lying open next to her. The picture! She had been studying the couple in the picture, and the woman's eyes, a deep violet-blue, when she started feeling dizzy. Had she fainted? She picked up the leather-bound album again, running her hands softly over the surface of the faded print. She could have sworn the woman's eyes had been blue, but how could that be? It was a black-and-white photograph. A tingling feeling rippled through her body, and her mind drifted back to a few weeks ago, to that first weekend in the house. Hadn't she seen something in one of the attic windows?

Clad in her white eyelet nightgown, her mass of unruly blonde curls framing her face, Libby stood in the archway that looked onto a massive dining room with large Palladian windows. Their first night in the house. She'd woken up before Josh, eager to start the day unpacking. Padding across the bare wooden floor, which was in desperate need of a good waxing, she admired the ten-foot high ceilings bordered with elaborate molding, details rarely seen in houses nowadays. Opening the French doors wide, she breathed in the aroma of lilacs mixed with sea air and stepped out to the brick patio to peruse the gardens, if one could call them that. Though more a conglomeration of densely overgrown weeds, Libby liked to imagine what they had looked like in their glory days.

Libby and Josh had purchased this *find*, as Josh's friend in real estate had put it, just two months ago. It had been on the market for only a few weeks, but it had sat abandoned for the past sixteen years. The house was located in a small fishing and oyster town on Maryland's Eastern Shore halfway between Easton and Cambridge.

Libby inhaled the rich earthy smells and exhaled all the tensions of the past few weeks. She had felt a connection here from the minute she first laid eyes on the house; this was somewhere she could finally call home. She made a mental list of the work that needed to be done in the yard, but after walking the grounds, the items on the list became too numerous to remember. She pulled a few weeds as she walked down to the water and studied the pier. It reminded her of an old roller coaster track. A hurricane had swept up the bay several years ago, lifting some of the pilings out of the water, which had caused the boards to buckle, creating a waving pattern.

"I guess that will need replacing," Libby said aloud. The only response was the lapping of the bay water. The cost was mounting rapidly as she mentally calculated the repairs and renovations. This so-called find was turning out to be quite expensive, but she wasn't going to let that upset her. Today was going to be a new beginning, *the first day of the rest of her life*. She laughed at the cliché. She'd recently turned thirty, and the milestone had planted a seed of discontent, giving her the feeling that something was lacking in her life. It wasn't her six-year marriage to Josh; there were no real problems there, and she loved her job as a seventh grade English teacher. From the outside, everything appeared perfect, but lately a nagging feeling tugged at her; her life, it seemed, was passing by uneventfully, almost too smoothly. She shook her head and took a deep breath, releasing the unwanted feeling, telling herself she was being silly. She should be happy. Things would be different now that they were in this house. As she turned to go back inside, her eye caught sight of something in the third-floor window, a movement. She placed her hand over her eyes to block out the sun and looked again. Nothing.

The search for houses began almost a year ago. They had been living in a tiny walk-up apartment outside of Fells Point, a section of Baltimore near the Inner Harbor and within walking distance to the prestigious law firm where Josh worked. He kept promising Libby that as soon as he started making decent money, they would get out of the city and move to wherever she wanted, as long as it was within commuting distance. When Abbott & Peterson offered him a partnership, she immediately began checking out information on the surrounding areas of Baltimore and, after much research, decided on the Eastern Shore.

The Shore, as the locals referred to it, was a unique area, cut off from the rest of the state by the Chesapeake Bay, a large estuary that provided much of Maryland's industry. Rivers and creeks spurred off from the bay and, from an aerial view, it appeared there was more water than land. This disconnect from the rest of the state rendered the area an anachronism. The small towns still moved at a slower, pre-superhighway pace. The locals even had their own accent. Libby, having grown up in a small Connecticut town, loved the quaintness and charm of the Shore towns, something she had missed while living in Baltimore.

Finding the right place hadn't been as easy as she'd expected, and after months of searching, she became discouraged, thinking they were going to live in the city forever. Josh didn't mind city life. Having grown up just outside Baltimore, he was used to the congestion and detachment from one's neighbor. But Libby missed the connectedness of a small town, where everyone knew each other by name and said hello when passing on the street.

Then one afternoon, just when Libby had given up hope of ever finding a house, they got a call from Rick, an old college buddy of Josh's who now had his own real estate business.

She had just walked into the apartment after an exhausting day teaching twelve-year-olds at Harrison Park, the Baltimore City middle school where she'd worked for the past five years. "Challenging" was not the word for what she did. Some days she wondered why she'd ever wanted to be a teacher. She'd envisioned standing in front of a classroom with all the students listening intently, soaking up knowledge like sponges, but in reality, she spent most of her days as a disciplinarian or referee. Breaking up fights, sending children to the principal's office after they had disrupted class for the umpteenth time, ruining it for the few who did want to learn, had become frustrating to say the least. That day, which started off with Bobby Guidotti's supergluing Angela Boswell's hair to the back of her chair, had been particularly draining, and all Libby could think of was getting home and soaking in a hot tub while drinking a glass of wine.

Entering the apartment, she threw down her keys, removed her hat, coat, and scarf, and then yanked off her snow boots. She hit the button on the message machine with its blinking red light. The first message was from a telemarketer; she erased it, letting the tape move on to the next. She walked into the bedroom, unbuttoning her shirt as she went. She could hear the next message from the dentist's office reminding Josh of his upcoming appointment. Libby thought how crazy the world had become—no one talked to each other anymore, just recordings talking to other recordings. She was about to run the bath water when she heard Rick's voice on the machine, and she ran into the living room to listen to the message. All she caught was "...so I think you better act quickly because this place won't last long." She hit the rewind button and listened from the beginning.

Libby grabbed the phone and punched in the numbers, her excitement bubbling over while she waited for him to pick up. As soon as she heard his voice, her words spilled out, "Honey, guess what?"

"I give up, what?" Josh replied.

"I think we may have found our house!"

"Really? Where?"

"I'm not sure. I have to call Rick and get more details, but I just had to tell you first."

"You haven't even seen it yet?"

"Well, no, but Rick left a message and said it was really great, and it won't last for long."

"Look, Libby, don't get your hopes up too high. Rick's a salesman; of course he's going to make it sound great."

Josh's ever-present voice of reason made her feel like a balloon slowly deflating. "You never know, Josh. This could be the one. I can get a substitute for tomorrow. Can you take off so we can go look at it?" she pleaded gently.

"I've got meetings all morning, and it's going to get pretty hectic. Why don't we go this weekend?"

"We can't wait until then! Rick said it won't last long on the market." She fumbled at the undone buttons of her shirt as she stared out the window at the dismal gray sky. She felt he didn't care; she was in this alone.

"Well, then, why don't you and Rick go look at it, and if you really like it, then put down a deposit and I'll go this weekend to see it."

She wanted Josh to be there, too. It was something that they should be doing together, but it was stupid to wait until Saturday; it could be gone by then. "All right," she replied weakly.

It was a bitter cold March morning, but the sky was a brilliant blue, and through the car window, Libby imagined it was a warm spring day. She and Rick were driving down a partially paved road scattered with water-filled potholes. The property was much farther away than

Libby had expected. Maybe Josh was right. She shouldn't have gotten her hopes up. She was about to tell Rick that maybe this was a little too far out of commuting distance for Josh, when they rounded a bend and she caught sight of the house. Rick slowed the car down as they turned into a driveway bordered by two brick pillars covered with brown vines, the only remnants from something that had bloomed at one time. A gold plaque inset in the pillars read "HAVERFORD HOUSE." The tall pine trees lining the drive swayed in the winter winds. Even though the grounds were a tangled mess of brown weeds and overgrown shrubs, Libby felt something stir inside her that made her feel as if she were coming home after a long absence. They parked in the circular drive in front of the ivy-covered brick Georgian-style house. Behind some trees to the left, the drive split off, leading to a three-car garage that Rick informed her had once been a stable. Libby had not spoken a word since turning up the drive. As she opened the car door and stepped out, the frigid air hit her face, taking her breath away and sending a shiver up her spine. The only sound was the crunch of her footsteps as she walked across the crushed oyster shells that covered the drive. "It's beautiful," she whispered.

"It'll require a bit of work," Rick said as he followed Libby to the house. "The agent listing it said she tried to talk the owner into fixing it up before putting it on the market, but apparently he just wants to be rid of it. Let's get inside out of the cold."

They stepped through the large oak door but found no more warmth inside. "The house has a lot of history." Rick started in on his sales pitch, his breath making puffs of air as his voice echoed through the empty rooms.

"In 1859, an Englishman, who was in the shipping business, built this for his wife as a summer home. They lived the rest of the year in Annapolis but eventually moved here because his wife loved it so much..." Libby was half listening to Rick as she moved through the rooms, taking in the intricate detail of the trim work, the sweeping staircase to the second floor, the delicate crystal chandelier that hung from the ten-foot ceiling.

"Haverford descendants lived here for years. The current owner had the whole place modernized years ago, putting in central heat…" Rick's words remained distant to Libby. She loved everything about the house and had already decided this was the place.

They climbed the dark wood staircase to the master bedroom that faced the back of the house, overlooking the water. Libby stepped out onto the balcony. Flecks of white sparkled on the water from the sun. A warm feeling filled her from head to toe, despite the chilly wind whipping around her face.

She remembered as a child how she would spend afternoons winding her way down the dirt path through the woods to the small creek that bordered their property to find the perfect rock to sit on. There she would daydream about her future. Some of the days, she would get so lost in her dreams, her mother would have to send her older sister, Emily, out to look for her and bring her back for dinner.

Something about the house made Libby feel as if she had been here before. "I want it," Libby blurted out, as she swung around to face Rick.

"OK…" Rick paused, then added, "I'll get the papers drawn up, but don't you think you better check with Josh first?"

"He said I could put a deposit on it if it was what I wanted."

After heading back inside from her inspection of the yard, she stood at the white-tiled counter in the kitchen. Libby poured the coffee, remembering Josh's reaction when he'd first seen the house. He had no vision, she thought; to him the place had looked like a dilapidated wreck. It took many nights of pleading and cajoling to convince him that this was the place. Nor was he keen on the commute, an hour and forty-five minutes on a good day. Eventually Libby convinced him that someday this would be a showplace where they could entertain all his bigwig lawyer friends.

She placed the two coffee mugs on a tray and headed up to the bedroom. Setting the tray on the dresser, she pulled back the curtains she'd hung the day before, bathing the room in sunlight. She opened the window, letting in the fresh May air, and looked out at the bay. Colorful sails dotted the horizon as an oyster trawler slowly chugged past.

Josh rolled over in bed and moaned, "Turn off the light."

"Time to get up, sleepyhead. We've got a lot of work to do today." They had taken the three-day Memorial Day weekend to move in.

The chattering of birds sang through the bedroom. "Doesn't that sound great? No more truck engines and horns blaring outside, no more diesel fumes, just sea air." Libby inhaled deeply as she stood at the window. She grabbed a mug of coffee and headed over to Josh. "Here, have some of this. It'll wake you up."

Josh leaned up on one elbow. The sunlight streamed through Libby's thin nightgown, silhouetting her long, lean limbs. Josh reached out, took the coffee from her hand, and set it on the nightstand. "I think this will wake me up better." He grabbed her arm, pulling her down on top of him. "Besides, we haven't officially christened the new house."

2

⦿

School was about to end for the summer, and Libby was eager to have her days free to work on the house. In one more week, her commute to Baltimore would be over. When she got home, she planned on going over with Josh projects for the weekend, one of which was re-tiling the master bathroom. But as she merged onto the Bay Bridge, traffic was at a standstill. Because it was the only way over to the other side, she had no choice but to sit.

The Bay Bridge was actually two bridges side by side—one for westbound traffic, the other for eastbound—that spanned the Chesapeake Bay from Sandy Point on the Western Shore to Kent Island. When it was built in 1952, it was the longest continuous over-water steel structure in the world, running over four miles from point to point. The first bridge consisted of two lanes, which had been adequate back in its day, but with the increased traffic heading to Ocean City and the Delaware beaches in the summer, a second bridge was needed. Now, forty years since the completion of the second bridge, they had again reached capacity. A push was underway to build a third bridge farther down the bay.

Libby felt sorry for Josh who would have to put up with this commute every day, but he hadn't complained. In fact, he hadn't said much about anything the last few weeks. The law firm was keeping him preoccupied.

Creeping along the bridge, she turned off the air conditioner and rolled down the window. The temperature had climbed into the high eighties, but a cool breeze blew into the car. She glanced out at the sailboats dotting the water as she recalled the early times in their relationship when they had spent summer days sailing on the bay. She was still in college, and Josh was studying for the bar and working as a paralegal for the Justice Department. Life had been fun and spontaneous. She could remember Josh calling her unexpectedly and telling her to grab a bathing suit and meet him out in front of her apartment. He would pull up in his beat-up old VW Beetle, and they would take off for the water. As the years passed, that spontaneity had died. Now, even a dinner out required a week's notice.

The car behind her beeped its horn, telling her to move on with the traffic on the bridge. She jumped out of her thoughts and hit the gas. Once over the bridge, it was smooth sailing the rest of the way.

The phone rang as she walked into the house; she quickly dropped her purse on the foyer table and ran into the kitchen to answer it. It was Josh. He was tied up in a meeting, he said, which would probably run late into the night. Since he had another meeting first thing in the morning, it made sense just to stay in town. The law firm kept an apartment near the Inner Harbor for clients or partners working late. Libby said she understood, but after hanging up she felt dejected.

She had been looking forward to fixing a nice dinner and discussing the plans for the house. She sighed, feeling sorry for herself, and headed upstairs to change. So many things needed to be done, so she decided to make a list to sort them all out. She loved making lists. Though a lot of the time she never finished the list, she got great satisfaction in being able to cross something off once it was completed.

Libby poured herself a glass of wine, made a quick salad, grabbed her notepad, and strolled out onto the brick patio. Bordering the patio was a low brick wall with large planters set on top. Libby pictured them filled with red geraniums and wrote, "Pick out plants for planters," neatly across the page. Gazing out past the porch to the stone path leading to the water, she visualized perennial borders lining each side of the path. She added to the list, "Book on perennials." Realizing how much work needed to be done on the yard, she then added, "Call a landscaper?"

After finishing her salad and wine, she decided to go through the house and write down what needed to be done in each room. She climbed the curving staircase all the way to the third floor, thinking she would start at the top and work her way down. The landing opened onto a wide hallway with doors to four bedrooms, two on each side. Each side shared an adjoining bathroom. She imagined the rooms filled with children someday. She and Josh had been trying for two years, and she worried that she might not be able to get pregnant. Her sister Emily had three kids, but then her sister had started right out of college. Had Libby waited too long? Were her eggs no longer viable? She put the thought out of her mind; everyone told her the more she worried, the harder it would be for her to get pregnant. Easier said than done.

At the end of the hallway was a door that led to the attic, which ran the length of the house. She had walked up there once, before buying the house, but had only stuck her head in at the top of the stairs and glanced around. She remembered some items had been left over from the previous owners. She decided to go up and explore the possible treasures left behind.

Libby loved exploring. As a child, she would create make-believe mysteries. Her mother used to say she'd make a great detective, but her sister just made fun of her. Libby used to wear her father's hat and trench coat hiked up under her arms and go around asking questions, trying to solve imaginary cases.

She tugged on the crystal doorknob to the attic several times before it finally released. The door squeaked lightly on its hinges as she pulled it open. Was she walking into a trap? She laughed at her childish imagination. A light switch at the bottom of the staircase was wired to single bulbs hanging on either end of the attic. She flicked on the switch. The steps creaked underfoot as she climbed up. The musty smell of old books and stale air hit her as she cleared the landing to an expansive room with a high ceiling that sloped on both sides to a peak. The temperature was at least ten degrees warmer up here. Sneezing a couple of times from the dust, she strode across to one of the four large dormer windows that faced the front and back of the house and released the latch in the center of the vertical panes. It took several pushes before they opened with a cracking sound of dried paint breaking free. Leaning out, taking in the sea air, she spotted a tugboat at the curve of the bay and a colony of seagulls soaring along the water's edge. From this height, she could see the huge expanse of the bay. She smiled, feeling exhilarated. This was their house now. She wanted to pinch herself to prove it wasn't all a dream.

She opened a another window then turned and surveyed the assortment of cardboard boxes and odd bits of furniture—a rocker, several lamps, an old bed frame. There was more stuff up here than she had remembered. She spotted a trunk at the opposite end and crossed the wide plank floor to examine its condition. Maybe she could use it in the bedroom. She used an old rag to wipe the dust off the trunk. With a little polishing, it was actually in pretty decent shape. The wood grain had a beautiful whorled pattern.

Libby lifted the top with both hands. The items inside looked to be very old. She carefully lifted a blue and green silk shawl embroidered with an intricate scrolling design. Red and gold flowers were woven into the pattern, and a delicate blue fringe hung from its border. She set it aside. Underneath the shawl were hand-stitched pillowcases made of the softest cotton, the initials JJH sewn onto the edge in an interlocking script. She removed the pillowcases to find a leather-bound album, which she took out of the trunk. She unbuckled the leather clasp that held it shut.

Sitting down cross-legged on the floor with the large album in her lap, she opened it to the first page. Neatly written across the yellowed, brittle page in a fine script most likely from a quill pen were the words, "The Haverfords." She turned the page to find a listing of births and deaths with dates going back to the 1600s. The pages crackled as she turned them. On the next page was an oval-shaped, tintype photograph of a man and a woman with three children and the caption "James, Elizabeth, James Arthur, Benjamin, and Lily, June 12, 1868." The woman, seated in a chair, wore a dress with long sleeves and a high collar, her hair piled up on her head; the man stood behind her, his hand on her shoulder. The two boys were on the floor by their mother's feet, and the small girl sat in her mother's lap. The woman's deep violet-blue eyes mesmerized Libby; it was as if the woman were calling to her from the photo. It sent a chill down Libby's spine. Suddenly she began to feel light-headed and dizzy. Her cheeks became flushed and hot. She needed some air. She set the album down on the floor and tried to stand, but as she did, the room started to spin.

When she came to, she was on the floor, her body drenched in sweat. How long had she been there? The leather-bound album was next to her on the floor, open to the photo of the couple. She slowly sat up, touching the page softly, her fingers stroking the woman's face. That's funny, she thought. She could have sworn the woman's eyes had been blue, but it was a black-and-white photograph. Across the room was a loud *bang*; she jumped at the sound. The window had slammed shut. Maybe it was time to go back downstairs; it was getting a little creepy up here. She carefully placed the things back in the trunk and went over to latch the window.

The gusting wind blew whitecaps on the water, and the sky had darkened to a threatening indigo. Her hair whipped around her face as she pulled the other window shut. Streaks of lightning shot across the sky followed by a low rumble of thunder. "It looks like a storm is brewing," she said out loud to the empty room. She almost expected to hear a response, suddenly feeling as if she wasn't alone. She raced toward the staircase and quickly ran down, shutting off the light and slamming the door behind her. She shuddered, brushing off the feeling that someone was following her, and then ran down the next two flights of stairs.

The warm glow of the lamp on the table in the kitchen eased her nerves. She poured another glass of wine, spilling some from her shaking hands. She sat down at the kitchen table, breathing heavily. Why had she fainted? It must have been the heat, she thought. She shook her head, trying to rid her mind of the strange sensation. On the notepad in front of her she wrote in bold letters "GET A DOG." She hadn't even thought about a dog before, but if she was going to be spending nights alone in the house, she decided she could use the company.

3

Astreak of sunlight shone through the partially opened curtains onto the bed. Libby stirred. What day was it? Friday she was taking the day off work to go to the permit office in town. She stretched her arms over her head and spread her legs out across the bed. No Josh. He must have already left for work, she thought. Then she remembered he had spent the night in Baltimore. She glanced at the bedside clock. The green digital numbers read 8:05 a.m. Wow, she had slept in. She got out of bed and headed over to the window, pulling back the curtains and opening the panes. The storm from the night before had cleared the humidity from the air. For Libby, that meant a good hair day.

Tying up her unruly blonde hair with a big clip, she studied her reflection in the bathroom mirror. Her hair always drove her crazy. No matter how hard she tried to straighten it, if she walked outside into the humidity, the stubborn coils sprang forth on her head.

Heaven forbid she went out on a misty day; she would end up looking as if she had stuck her finger in an electric socket. She battled with gels, creams, and irons to no avail, finally giving up. The hair had won.

She leaned in closer to the mirror, running her hand over her face, inspecting her skin; she had a fair complexion with wide cheekbones. She smiled, her full lips revealing large white teeth. She was pretty in an odd way. Not cutesy pretty—her features were too large. When put together, though, she was quite striking.

Staring into her ice-blue eyes, she watched as they transformed into a dark violet-blue. She jumped back, blinking several times, rubbing her hands over her eyes. What was that? She looked again in the mirror, half-afraid of what she would see, but her eyes were their normal color. She shuddered, remembering the woman in the photo whose eyes had been that same violet-blue. My mind is playing tricks on me, she thought. She needed to get out; she'd been alone too long.

Driving through town was like a scene from a movie. As she drove down the tree-lined streets, she marveled at the stately Victorian homes, with their stained-glass windows and wraparound front porches. The main part of town consisted of four streets: a North Main Street and a South Main Street, which ran parallel to each other and were intersected by two streets running east and west, Commerce Street on the south end and Liberty Street to the north. In the center of town was a large square with the courthouse at one end. Corsica was the county seat and boasted one of the oldest continuously used courthouses in the country. Shops and offices lined the courtyard. The permit office was at one corner of the square. Libby pulled her car into a parking spot right in front. She chuckled; if this were Baltimore, she would have spent half the day driving around looking for a place to park.

Inside the permit office, Libby was welcomed by a petite middle-aged woman with a tight perm. She smiled from behind the counter as Libby walked in. "Good morning," she said.

"Good morning." Libby smiled back. "I need to get a permit for a pier we're re-building."

"Why sure, I can help you with that." The woman opened a drawer and pulled out a piece of paper. "Just fill out this application."

Libby wrote down all the pertinent information and handed it back to the woman. The woman glanced over the application. "So you bought Haverford House. Finally, someone will be living there; it sat dormant for so long. I thought no one would ever live there again. But I guess after what happened, some people may be superstitious."

"Superstitious? About what?" Libby asked apprehensively.

"The death of Cecilia Reynolds." The woman stated it as if it were common knowledge and was surprised that Libby had had to ask.

"I'm afraid I don't know anything about the previous owners."

"Oh." The woman acted a bit flustered and then said, "I forget not everyone is familiar with the goings-on of Corsica. I shouldn't have said anything; that was ancient history." She looked down at the application and then patted her permed hair, her cheeks turning slightly red. She looked back up at Libby. "Mr. Reynolds is a state senator now. In fact, he's running for the US Senate this year."

Libby had heard his name mentioned before. Senator Cardiff, the incumbent, was retiring after this term, and the race was between two new candidates. "Was she his wife?"

"Pardon?"

"The woman, Cecilia Reynolds, who died. Was she his wife?"

"Oh yes, I'm sorry." She smiled, her eyes drifting past Libby. Then she added, "It really was tragic."

"What happened?"

"She committed suicide."

There was a pause in the conversation. The woman noticed Libby's furrowed brow. "I didn't mean to upset you. I'm sure you'll love living there. I always thought that was a beautiful place. I'll get your papers processed and have the permit ready for you this afternoon." She smiled kindly at Libby, trying to make up for what she had said.

"Thanks." Libby turned to go and then, without knowing why, she turned back and asked, "You don't by any chance know anything about the original owners?"

"Oh my, that was a long time ago, way before my time." She paused for a minute. "But I can tell you who might know: Tassie Jackson. She lives over to Millers Road down by the bend. If anyone knows anything, it would be Tassie. Not only has she lived here her whole life, but her family goes back generations. No one knows exactly how old Tassie is; she's been around for as long as anyone can remember. They even say Tassie is one of those gifted people—you know, can see the future and the past. Now I don't know if I believe all that." The woman pursed her lips and shook her head.

"Interesting." Libby's curiosity was piqued.

Libby decided to stop at the library. Maybe there she could find some information on Haverford House. Rick had said something about the original owners, but she couldn't remember any details. After seeing the photograph in the trunk, she needed to know more about the history of the house. Although she had a million things to accomplish on her day off, she felt compelled to learn more about the Haverfords.

The smell of books hit her as she walked in. She loved that smell. The brick building was old, and the dark wood floors creaked underfoot. It claimed to be the first free library in the state. There were floor-to-ceiling shelves lined with books, and Libby noticed they still had card files. Not a computer in sight.

The library was empty except for two elderly men reading the paper. Libby walked up to the front desk. The librarian sat on a stool behind the counter, reading a book. The woman couldn't have looked more like the classic librarian if she had been cast by a Hollywood agent, right down to the small jeweled clasp that held her cardigan over her shoulders. When Libby approached, she glanced up over her half-glasses. Libby asked if there was a section on local history. Without speaking, she led Libby to a back corner of the library. She pointed to a lower shelf and whispered, "These books are all about this area. Is there something in particular you're looking for?"

Libby whispered back, feeling a little silly about the hushed tones considering they were the only ones there besides the two old men.

"I wanted to find out about the old Haverford House out on Poplar's Point."

The librarian pondered for a minute and then selected a small book from the shelf. "This one might be helpful. It's a book on all the historical homes in the county." She glanced through the index. "Ah yes, here we go, Haverford House, page thirty-six." She flipped back to the referenced page. There was a paragraph written about the house along with a picture.

"Thanks," Libby said as the librarian handed her the book. "But I really wanted to learn more about the Haverfords themselves."

"I'm not sure if there would be much written about them in these books. But I'll tell you who would know—Tassie Jackson. She's been around forever, and her family goes way back."

"That's funny; you're the second person to mention her name. She must be pretty famous around here."

"She is unique to say the least. But when it comes to the history of this town, she is the one to go to."

"I guess I'll have to look her up."

"Well, you won't get her by phone. Tassie doesn't believe in all the 'newfangled gadgets' as she calls them. She thinks they might try to steal her spirit or something silly like that."

Libby was forming a mental picture of this "Tassie" woman, and it was becoming more and more colorful.

The librarian set her up with a library card, and Libby checked out a couple of books with references to the house.

※

The noise must have been a door slamming. Turning the crystal knob, she felt her heart beating in her throat. A sense of excitement mixed with fear shot through her. Why did she always like to imagine something eerie?

Like the time they had just moved into their apartment in Baltimore, and she'd awoken to a knocking sound. She'd shook Josh, telling him that someone was in the other room. He'd roused slightly, leaning up on his elbow, listening. Then he'd lain back down saying it was just the radiator rattling. She'd sat in bed staring into the darkness. Then she got up, grabbed Josh's old baseball bat from the corner, and tiptoed into the living room, her heart pounding, sure she was going to find someone. She loved the adrenaline rush that had coursed through her veins, but Josh had been right, it had been the old metal radiator by the window.

After returning from the library, she was putting some canned goods in the cupboard, when a waft of cool air had brushed across her face. She didn't make much of it until she heard a loud bang from somewhere upstairs. Maybe a window was left open and a breeze had blown a bedroom door shut. But when she'd rounded the corner from the kitchen to investigate, she'd caught sight of a figure crossing the hallway at the other end. Her neck hair had bristled, and her heart beat a little faster. Her mind must be playing tricks on her again. It was probably just a shadow through the window.

She crept down the hall, telling herself she was being silly, but at the same time, her senses were in overdrive. At the end of the hall to the foyer, she peeked around the corner. Nothing. Her pulse went back to normal, and she chuckled inside at her overactive imagination. After checking the windows and doors on the second and third floor, she found herself staring at the attic door.

As she slowly climbed the attic steps, a rush of blood pumped through her, like a child in an amusement park entering the house of horror, knowing it was make-believe, yet filled with fright. When she reached the top, she saw that one of the windows was open. She must not have latched it tight enough last night. She walked over to the window, exhaling the tension that had built up inside, saying out loud, "See, I told you there was nothing to be afraid of. It was just the wind."

She pulled shut the window and securely latched it, giving it a few jiggles to be sure. But as she turned to leave, she felt the hair on her arms prickling her skin. She shuddered and rubbed her arm. Suddenly a bright light shone from across the room. She blinked. Was it coming from something outside? She glanced back at the window. Nothing but blue sky and a few puffy white clouds. She looked back at the light and stood frozen as it transformed into the shape of a woman.

Her heart pounded. What was happening? It was the woman from the photograph, wearing a long dress with what appeared to be the silk shawl from the trunk wrapped around her outstretched arms. The woman's eyes pleaded at her.

There was another loud bang and Libby screamed. She ran across the dusty floor. Clambering down the steps, she lost her footing and slipped, hitting her hip against the hard wood. A jarring pain shot through her. She glanced back and saw the shimmering light floating toward the stairs. She scrambled to her feet and continued down the steps. But the attic door had closed. She grabbed the knob with shaking hands and pushed, but it wouldn't open. The woman was now on the steps above her. Feeling as if her air supply was cut off, Libby gripped her throat. She heard the phone ringing in the distance. With all of her strength, she thrust her body against the door and it gave way, swinging open so fast, she nearly fell onto the floor. She slammed it shut behind her and flew down the rest of the stairs to the first floor, afraid to look back.

She grabbed the phone off the wall in the kitchen. "Hello!" she shouted, gasping for breath.

"Lib, are you OK?" Josh asked.

"*no!* I mean yes…I don't know."

"What's wrong?" Josh asked anxiously.

"I just saw a ghost!"

He laughed. "Oh, is that all? You had me worried for a minute."

"No, Josh, you don't understand. I *literally* saw a ghost."

"Have you been painting or something? Maybe the fumes have gone to your head," Josh joked.

"I'm not kidding! Listen, I know this sounds crazy, but I think this house is haunted. I found a picture in this trunk in the attic last night, and it was the woman in the photo. I saw her in the mirror this morning and then again just now." Libby's words spilled like marbles from a jar.

"Whoa, slow down." Josh sensed the panic in Libby's voice and knew he had to calm her down. "Look, Lib, you've been alone in that house for a while. Maybe your imagination is conjuring things up. I'm sure there's a good explanation for all of this."

"I don't know." Libby felt confused. Listening to Josh's reassuringly calm tone made her think that maybe she had imagined it all.

"I'll try to get out of here as early as I can. I was calling to tell you that I might be home sooner than I thought."

"OK, see you tonight. I love you," Libby replied weakly.

"I love you, too."

Drained physically and emotionally, she slumped down at the kitchen table. The birds chirped outside the open window over the sink. She glanced around the kitchen, feeling confused. Everything appeared normal. The newly painted peach-colored walls, the warm wood plank flooring. The white-painted cabinets with the antiqued handles. Josh had to be right. There was no way she'd actually seen a ghost. Her crazy imagination had finally spun out of control.

She spotted the library books on the table. Picking one up, she flipped through the pages until she came to the picture of the house. Underneath the photograph was the caption, "Haverford House built in 1859." She read the small write-up about James Haverford, a shipping magnate based out of Annapolis, Maryland. He was married to Elizabeth Cornwall, whose father had been a prominent landowner in Virginia. James Haverford had been a sea captain, but after marrying Elizabeth, he was able to use her family's fortune to buy a fleet of ships and start his own business, which became very successful. Not much more was said about the family; the rest was on the architecture of the house. Libby closed the book. Had she seen Elizabeth in the attic? The name "Tassie Jackson" popped into her head. Maybe she should go find this woman.

She grabbed her purse and keys off the table, needing to get out of the house. She drove to the end of the driveway and stopped the car. What was the name of that road the woman at the permit office had told her? It started with an *M*. Mitchell Road? No, Millers Road. She pulled her cell phone out of her purse and punched the map icon. According to the map, it was located on the other side of town.

Libby pulled out onto the road and hesitated. Was she really going to go see her? Her foot punched the gas pedal. She had to learn more about the Haverfords.

4

She found Millers Road easily enough. She remembered the woman had told her Tassie lived by a bend. Hopefully, the road didn't have too many bends in it. About a mile and a half down the road was a sharp turn to the right. A rusted-out mailbox leaning to one side had the name "JACKSON" in black letters. Dense brush lined both sides of the road, blocking any view of the house. I guess this is the place, she thought. As she turned down the lane, she began to wonder what she would say to this woman.

It took some serious maneuvering in the Volvo station wagon to avoid the potholes on the dirt drive. She finally rounded a corner after about a quarter of a mile to find a tiny ivy-covered cottage set in a small clearing in the woods. A white picket fence, which had seen better days, bordered the property. The sun shone through the break in the trees onto brilliantly colored wildflowers so bright they didn't look real.

Libby parked the car on the dirt lane and got out. The little gate was barely hanging on the hinges, and it squeaked loudly as she opened it. She stood at the front door, her hand up ready to knock, when the door opened and a tiny woman stood before her. At first glance, Libby thought she was a child. At five-nine, Libby towered over the woman who couldn't have been more than four and a half feet tall.

"I'm looking for Tassie Jackson."

"That's what they call me," the woman drawled in a soft voice.

"Sorry to bother you, but some people in town said you were the one to come to for town history."

"I guess you could say that." The woman laughed. "If you live long enough, everything is history. Come inside, dear, and have some tea with me." Tassie motioned for Libby to follow her. The cottage reminded Libby of a dollhouse; everything appeared to be in miniature. There was a small sofa on one wall and a little black rocker with a calico cat curled up in it on the opposite side. White tie-back curtains adorned the windows.

"I don't want to put you to any trouble," Libby said. "I just wanted to ask a few questions."

"It's no trouble. I was makin' a pot anyway. And as I always say, you can't have a good conversation without a pot a tea." Tassie's voice belied her age; there was a soft singsong lilt to it.

Libby followed Tassie into an even tinier kitchen with a bay window overlooking a massive garden. A small round table covered in a flowered tablecloth and two antique-looking wooden chairs with cane seats filled the nook. Libby sat down in one of the chairs, hearing it protest from her weight, feeling like Alice in Wonderland after she had eaten the cupcake. The smell of lavender blew in through the open window, and visions of her grandmother's house flashed through her head.

Tassie brought over two cups made of delicate bone china, so thin the sunlight streaming through the window passed right through them. She poured the tea from a matching teapot into each cup. Her fingers reminded Libby of a spider's legs, long and thin, arthritically bent and black as night. It was hard to determine Tassie's age; her face showed not a single wrinkle. Her coal-black complexion contrasted sharply with her white teeth and closely cropped, tightly curled silvery hair.

"You said you had some questions? I'm sorry I've forgotten your name." Tassie sat down in the chair across from Libby.

"No, I probably didn't tell you. I guess I'm a little nervous." Libby snorted a laugh. "I'm Libby Langston. My husband and I recently moved into Haverford House. I was hoping to find out more information about the previous owners—actually, the original owners." Libby decided not to mention seeing the woman in the attic; she didn't want Tassie thinking she was some kind of nut.

"The Haverfords, they were one family with a history of misfortunes." Tassie closed her eyes and sat for a few minutes. Libby thought maybe she had drifted off to sleep, she sat so still. Libby was about to reach over and wake her, when Tassie popped open her eyes and Libby jumped back in response. "I remember tales from my grandma about the original Haverfords. They were a very prominent family in this town at one time. They's all gone now. They owned quite a bit of land back then, though. Over the years, they lost some of it, mostly during the Great Depression."

"What about the woman, Elizabeth? Do you know anything about her?" Libby stared into Tassie's mesmerizing black, liquid eyes.

"I do remember my grandma saying when she was a young girl she used to go to the big house with her daddy. My great granddaddy wasn't a slave, you see; he was a free man. He was freed when he was a boy, and he was able to make his livin' as a blacksmith. He took care of the horses at Haverford House. Some days he would let my grandma come along." Tassie picked up a silver teaspoon and rhythmically stirred her tea as she talked.

"She told me about one a them times she went there; she got bored and started wandering around the grounds, somethin' she'd never done before. Usually her daddy made her stay right with him in the stable, but this day he was real busy, so he didn't notice her slippin' out. She discovered a stone path that led down to the water. There were tall reeds on either side of the path, she said, higher than she was. When she got to the shore, she could hear someone crying. She stopped on the path, holdin' her breath, makin' sure her bare feet were silent as she tiptoed on the rocks. She peeked out from the reeds where the path opened and saw a woman standin' by the water's edge, sobbin'. I remember she described her as a beautiful woman, one of the prettiest women she had ever laid eyes on. She said she wore fine clothes with her hair swept up on her head, and a beautiful silk shawl wrapped around her shoulders, lookin' so outta place standin' there on the rocky beach. My grandma slipped back into the reeds, not to be seen. She said she wanted to go to the woman and ask her why she was cryin', but she knew her daddy would beat her good if he found out."

Tassie shook her head and sipped her tea before continuing, "A tall man came walkin' along the beach toward the woman. My grandma wondered if he was Mr. Haverford; she had heard he was real tall. She sunk back in the reeds a little more, but my grandma could still make out their voices. I remember she told me she would never forget what she heard them say. The man had a very deep voice, and he told the woman that he had been searchin' for her and that she shouldn't have left the house, that the doctor told her she needed to rest. She heard the woman cry back to him that she couldn't stay in the house *one more minute*. He asked her if she was takin' the medicine the doctor had given her, and my grandma said the woman just started crying with her head in her hands. The man told her she had to think about the *boys*. Then the man put his arm around her and gently led her back up to the house as if she were a small child. My grandma wondered who 'the boys' were, and she wanted to know more, but she knew she couldn't ask her daddy." Libby watched Tassie's spidery fingers moving while she talked, as if she were playing out the scene with her hands.

"That night my grandma asked her mama if she knew anything about the Haverfords. Her mama laughed and told her, 'Child, they *is* this town. Without them, half the people would be outta work.' My grandma asked if they had any children, and her mama told her that was a mighty sad story. They lost their baby daughter who was no more'n four years old. From what they says in town, she went out on her daddy's boat when a storm came up. She got drenched on the boat, and when she got back home, she'd caught a chill. It went straight into pneumonia, and she never did recover. She passed away a couple of weeks after that. My grandma said to her mama that Miss Haverford musta been real sad, and her mama said she was sure she was. And then her mama wanted to know why she was asking so many questions. She didn't ask anymore; she was afraid her mama would find out about her sneakin' away."

Tassie stopped talking and poured herself and Libby another cup of tea. Her soothing voice had lulled Libby into a dreamlike state. Libby sat up in her chair, bringing the cup to her lips, and she inhaled the sweet aroma. Cinnamon. "Did she tell you anything else?"

"Oh yes. She said for days after that, she could not get that lady outta her mind. She was hoping her daddy would take her back to the big house so she could find out how Miss Elizabeth was doin'. But weeks passed, and he didn't go back there. One night she woke up in bed. She said she sat straight up, as if she were jolted by a bolt a lightning. Her heart was a pounding, and she felt a terrible ache in her chest. She thought she'd had a nightmare, but she couldn't remember what she had dreamt. She got outta bed and went over to the window. The moon was shining bright in the night sky. Somethin' bad had happened. She just knew it." Tassie smiled, shaking her head. Her gaze went out the open window to the garden. Libby's eyes followed. There were rows of herbs and flowers, some that Libby had never seen before. Everything was lush and full. Libby wanted to ask her what her secret was.

Tassie looked back at Libby. "My grandma was like that; she had a sense about some things. She used to tell me I had it, too. It was a gift that was more like a curse, she would say." Tassie sipped her tea and then continued: "The next morning the town was a buzzin' with the news that Elizabeth Haverford had gone and killed herself. The talk was, she had gotten up in the middle of the night, walked down to the water's edge, and just kept on walkin'. Her body had washed up with the tide that morning. My grandma said when she heard the news in town, she just sat down and started cryin'. Her mama could never figure out why she took the news so bad. Grandma never told anyone about seeing Miss Elizabeth on the beach that day until she told me."

Libby was so caught up in the story, she blurted out, "I saw her. Elizabeth came to me."

Tassie was silent, staring into Libby's eyes. "Do you have the gift, too?"

"No. I mean I've never experienced anything like this before. In fact, talking about it now, it sounds kind of crazy, I know." She laughed nervously.

"Did she talk to you?" Tassie asked, not seeming the least bit surprised.

"No, I only saw her for a second, and then she disappeared. But she had this pleading look in her eyes. I can't get it out of my head."

"She's trying to reach out to you, child. Next time you see her, ask her what she wants."

Libby's eyebrows shot up. "*Next time?* You think she'll come back?" Libby rubbed her hands together, feeling like she was in the twilight zone. "You make it sound like it's perfectly normal having a conversation with a dead person." She snorted a laugh.

"One person's normal is another person's crazy. It's all in how we choose to perceive things. I'm telling you, she wants to tell you somethin'. Don't be afraid. From the way she sounded in my grandma's stories, I think she was a nice lady."

※

Libby had dinner laid out on the black wrought iron table on the back porch. It was a beautiful evening; the temperature had cooled down to the mid-seventies, and the setting sun painted the sky with brushstrokes of pink. She'd lit candles all around the porch and opened a bottle of wine. Josh walked out onto the patio still dressed in his suit, minus the jacket, his tie loosened around his neck. "Wow, you really went all out. Smells great." He wrapped his arms around her and kissed her on the cheek. Libby hugged him tightly, inhaling his familiar Acqua di Gio cologne.

She didn't want to let go, drinking in the warmth of his body. "I missed you so much."

"I wasn't gone that long." Josh chuckled.

"I know. It's just good to have you here."

"Have you recovered from your ghost episode?" Josh asked with a hint of sarcasm.

Libby rolled her eyes at him. The wrought iron chair scraped against the bricks as she pulled it out. "Don't make fun of me. It really freaked me out." On her way home from Tassie's, she'd pondered what had transpired in the attic. The memory had a dreamlike quality. Had it been her imagination? Had Josh been right? But Tassie's matter-of-fact manner about the ghost return- ing- niggled at the back of her mind. She started dishing up the food, which consisted of roasted pork with rosemary, roasted baby potatoes, and fresh, locally grown green beans sautéed with slivered almonds.

"I'm starving!" Josh said as he cut into the pork.

Libby poured the wine. "So how was your day?"

"Insane. This Tolman case is a bear. If everything comes out right, I could be the rising star in that firm. But if things don't, I may be looking for another job."

"Just from one case?" Libby noticed the small lines around Josh's green eyes that seemed to have cropped up overnight. She hoped his making partner wasn't too much stress on him.

"This could be a precedent case if we win, and it could help a lot of our other clients. And I think I've come up with a strategy that just might get us to win."

"That's fantastic. I knew you were brilliant. That's why I married you." Libby leaned over and kissed him on the cheek.

"You never know, though. A judge could shoot me down in a heartbeat. What about your day?"

"I've decided we need a dog."

"A dog? What brought that on?"

"If I'm going to be alone in this house at night, I need someone to keep me company. And besides, you love dogs."

"I didn't say it was a bad idea; it just came out of the blue."

"This would be the perfect time, since I'm off for the summer. I could be here to train it every day." Libby jabbed a forkful of beans. "I went in to town today to get the permit for the pier."

"How'd it go?"

"Fine. I also found out a little more about the house. It turns out one of the previous owners committed suicide in the house."

"Really? Who?" Josh took a sip of wine and twirled his glass. The deep red color burnished against the setting sun.

"A woman named Cecilia. She was the wife of that guy Reynolds, who's running for the Senate."

"*John* Reynolds? He's a friend of Peterson," Josh said, referring to the head partner in his firm. "Peterson's been trying to get Reynolds as a client." Josh looked puzzled. "This used to be his house? I just saw him the other day at the office." He brought his wineglass to his mouth and then hesitated. "I guess one of his LLCs arranged the settlement—I don't recall seeing his name on any of the papers." He took a sip of wine. "So, his wife committed suicide. It's funny that Peterson never mentioned that."

"It happened a long time ago. Maybe he doesn't know."

"Maybe not." He looked out toward the water.

"I also found out about the original owners. I told you about the trunk in the attic and the woman I saw."

"Lib—"

Libby put her hand up. "I know, I know, it was probably my imagination, but I couldn't get her out of my mind, so I went to see this woman, Tassie Jackson. She's incredible. She's probably close to a hundred years old, and she knows everything about this town. She told me all about the Haverfords."

"How'd you meet her?"

"The lady at the permit office told me about her, and then the librarian mentioned her, too, so I decided to go see her. She told me some fascinating stories. In fact, Reynolds' wife was a direct descendant of the original Haverfords and the last; there were no more heirs after her. We're the first people outside the Haverford family to own this house, other than Reynolds, but he was married to a Haverford." She didn't mention the part about Tassie telling her to talk to the ghost.

After dinner, Libby and Josh walked down to the water hand in hand. The sun had dropped below the sea, replaced by the full moon that shone a wide path across the bay, narrowing at the horizon. The current sent small rippling waves onto the shore, making a gentle lapping sound. Libby stared out at the dark water. "I feel so badly for that woman. She must've been in so much pain to take her life that way."

"Reynolds' wife?"

"No, Elizabeth Haverford. She had a daughter who died of pneumonia when she was only four years old, and Elizabeth couldn't handle the grief, so she killed herself by drowning. She stood right on this beach and just kept on walking out to sea. It's so sad."

"It's also ancient history," Josh said as he stood behind Libby with his arms around her. "Why don't we make some history of our own right here on the beach?" He turned her around to face him and kissed her softly on the lips. The past began to slip away with the tide, but a thought crept into Libby's head: two women had committed suicide here. Was there a curse on this house?

5

After dropping off Josh's suits at the dry cleaners, she strolled down the sidewalk in town. Beside her was the new addition to their family. She'd contacted a dog rescue center several weeks ago after finding a black Lab puppy on their website. But when she'd gone to the center, the woman showed her a mother dog who'd recently weaned a litter of puppies. At only a year and a half, she was practically a puppy herself. She'd been abused, tied on a short chain, and kept outside with no shelter. Libby had fallen in love with her the minute she saw her. The dog's name was Stella, a honey-colored Lab with green eyes—a rare color according to the woman at the rescue center. Something about her eyes, when she looked at Libby, told Libby this had to be her dog. That had been almost two weeks ago, and they'd been inseparable ever since. Stella slept in the bed with her when Josh wasn't home and followed Libby everywhere she went.

Libby had spent every day working on the house now that school was out. Summer had exploded with the temperatures soaring into the nineties. She'd hired a landscaper to do the heavy work in the yard, like preparing some of the beds, pruning the bushes, and installing an irrigation system. But she left most of the planting to herself. She loved working in the garden, and she was beginning to see it take shape. She'd been worried Josh would get upset with how much she'd spent on the yard, but he hadn't complained; in fact, he'd hardly said anything at all the past few weeks. His case was all-consuming. Most of Libby's days were spent alone, not even any visits from Elizabeth Haverford since that day in the attic, and Libby was convinced it had all been her imagination.

Two men were unfurling a big red, white, and blue banner in the courtyard in preparation for the Fourth of July celebration. A poster in the window of the cleaners had displayed the events for the day: a parade through town, a band on the square, and a fried chicken dinner sponsored by the fire department, followed by fireworks at night.

Libby sat down on a bench in the shade of a large oak tree to watch the men hang the banner on the front of the temporarily erected pavilion on the square. She noticed across the square that Mr. Tompkins, who owned the hardware store, was out front talking to Mrs. Tidwell, the librarian. Libby was beginning to know people in the town. Down from the hardware store was Edward's Pharmacy, where she spotted a tiny lady. It was Tassie Jackson. She hadn't thought about her for quite a while.

Tassie, dressed in a flowered shirtwaist dress with a small cornflower-blue pillbox hat on her head, walked down the sidewalk with a large patent leather purse hanging on one arm. She turned at the corner, heading in Libby's direction. Her gait was slow but spry.

Libby stood up and waved as Tassie drew closer. "Hi, Miss Jackson." Tassie stopped and peered at Libby. "Do you remember me? Libby Langston."

Tassie squinted and then smiled, her eyes crinkling up at the corners. "Why sure I do, child. You're the one who seen Miss Elizabeth. You talked to her lately?" Tassie sat down on the bench, and Libby sat back down next to her.

"No, actually I haven't seen her since that day I came to your house. I guess she changed her mind about wanting to tell me something." Libby laughed.

"No, I doubt that. Those that have passed don't try to reach out unless they have somethin' very important to say. She'll be back."

Libby shuddered involuntarily at Tassie's words, which were spoken with such conviction. "It still freaks me out to think that I may have a ghost in my house. My husband thinks I imagined the whole thing, and I'm beginning to think maybe he's right."

"I told you, you don't have anything to be afraid of. I don't think she's an evil spirit."

Libby chuckled. *Evil spirit?* Was she really having this conversation? She had to remember this woman was close to a hundred years old; maybe she was getting senile. Libby changed the subject. "Are you coming to town for the parade on the fourth?"

"I don't think so. Too much commotion for me."

"You sound like my husband. He says he would rather spend a quiet day at home, but I really want to come. I think it might help us get to know people better. I still feel like such an outsider here."

Tassie opened the gold clasp on her pocketbook and extracted a folded paper fan on a black metal frame. Libby hadn't seen one like that since she was a child. She'd loved playing with one her mother had with a Chinese print on it. Tassie spread open the fan, displaying a floral design, and began waving it back and forth as she nodded her head slowly, listening to Libby. "Give it time, child. Some things you can't rush no matter how badly you want them."

"I guess you're right." The humid air clung to Libby's blouse as beads of sweat trickled down her sides.

Tassie pointed out various people she saw on the square and gave Libby a little background on each one. There was Pearl who had the coffee shop on the corner and knew all the gossip in town. Her family had been farming in Corsica for years.

"Poor Pearl; she's had a troubled life," Tassie said. "She'd been a beauty in her day and could've had the pick of any boy in town, but she'd got pregnant her senior year of high school and had to drop out. Her daddy made her marry Tommy Dean, the father of the baby, but the marriage didn't last long. Pearl had a string of beaux after that." Tassie shook her head. "But then she took up drinking, and her only daughter, Kelly Ann, moved away when she turned eighteen, leaving Pearl all alone." Tassie smiled, exposing her white teeth. "The good Lord decided to shine his light on Pearl and about ten years ago, Kelly Ann came back and helped her Mama get off the drink. They opened up the coffee shop, and the two have been running it ever since."

The short plump woman heading into the sheriff's office was Margaret Porter, but everyone called her Maggie, Tassie told her. She'd worked for Sheriff Tucker for years.

Listening to Tassie's tales, Libby wished she had a pen and paper to remember the details. She loved hearing her talk; even Stella was fixated on Tassie. "It looks like Stella is quite taken with you." Libby pointed at the dog whose eyes were half-closed staring at Tassie.

"I have a way with animals, even the wild ones. They come right up and sit in my lap. Animals have a special sense; they can feel things most people don't." Tassie gently stroked Stella's head, while the dog sat trance-like. Libby knew what Stella was feeling. Tassie had a peaceful, soothing way about her that made one feel completely at ease.

Libby gazed at the banner now draped on the front of the pavilion. A lawn mower hummed in the background and the smell of freshly cut grass wafted across the square. "Why do you think Cecilia Reynolds committed suicide?"

Tassie waved her fan slowly back and forth. "Cecilia was a sweet girl. She was the only child of Francis Haverford and lived a very sheltered life. I don't think she ever went to public school. I remember her daddy got a tutor for her due to her frail constitution. Cecilia's mother had died in childbirth, and Francis had never remarried. He raised Cecilia by himself."

"How did she end up married to John Reynolds?"

"Everyone in town was quite surprised when Mr. Reynolds showed up and started courtin' her. He swarmed into this town like a fly to a honeypot. The talk was that he was trying to buy some of the land from Francis Haverford, and the next thing we knew, he was makin' eyes at Cecilia. You see, the Haverfords still owned quite a bit of property. They had acres and acres of farmland and most of the land in town as well. So, I guess he figured if Francis wasn't interested in selling his land, he'd just marry Cecilia. You see, Francis was an only son of an only son, and that left Cecilia the only remaining heir."

"Do you think that was the only reason he married her, or did he really love her?"

"It's hard to say, but it wasn't long after he breezed into town that they were makin' announcements of a wedding. Everyone was shocked, considering Cecilia had never even had a boyfriend before, much less a fiancé, but Cecilia was a beautiful girl. She had honey-colored hair and the bluest eyes you ever saw. She was so delicate looking, like a bird." Tassie stopped waving her fan and looked off into the distance. "Her daddy Francis was born with a weak heart. He suffered his first heart attack at forty. I think he worried about what would happen to Cecilia after he was gone. He knew she would never be able to survive on her own. When Mr. Reynolds came along, it was like an answer to his prayers. I don't think he ever considered why Mr. Reynolds wanted to marry Cecilia; he was just glad she would be taken care of."

"Then why'd she kill herself?"

"Well, it wasn't two years after they married, her daddy had a massive heart attack and died. It hit Cecilia real hard. She'd been so close to her daddy that people believed she killed herself because she couldn't handle him passing—but I never believed that."

"Why?"

"I remember one day—it was about six months after her daddy died—I ran into her in town, right over there on the corner." Tassie pointed with her fan to the far-left corner of the square. "We had a little chat. I can picture it like it was yesterday. She was beaming from ear to ear, a big old smile on her face. I asked her what was makin' her so happy, and she said nothing but the beautiful spring day. Then she asked me if I thought yellow was a pretty color for a nursery. She never said she was expectin', but I knew just by looking at her she was with child. Now why would a woman who seemed so happy about having a baby kill herself not a month later?"

"Did you ever tell anyone about it?" Libby wiped perspiration off her brow with the back of her hand.

"I surely did. Sheriff Tucker patted my hand and said thanks for givin' him the information, but I knew he didn't care what I had to say. I never heard anything said about her expectin' no baby."

They talked for several more minutes, and then Tassie said she needed to head back home. She told Libby if she ever wanted to come for tea and talk again, she was always welcome. Libby thanked her and said she'd take her up on that.

Libby walked through the square over to the farmers' market that was just on the edge of town. Every Tuesday, the local farmers and fishermen would bring their wares. Rows of brightly colored vegetables along with homemade jams and jellies filled the aisles under the large white tent.

Strolling through the stands, picking out zucchini and yellow squash, with Stella by her side, Libby placed the vegetables in the small basket provided for shoppers. At one end of the tent was the seafood section. The smell of fish mingled with the scent of cut flowers that sat in buckets along the aisle.

Libby eyed the assortment of rockfish, bluefish, and crabmeat on the trays of ice, pondering which to buy for dinner when she noticed out of the corner of her eye someone standing next to her. She glanced over. A man about six-two with a slim yet muscular build in a tan police uniform was staring at Stella. He was nice looking, Libby thought.

The sunlight streaming through the edge of the tent shone on his blonde hair. Brushing his collar, his hair was longer than typical for a police officer. He reminded Libby of an actor from a sixties beach movie.

"You have a beautiful dog. What's her name?" He stooped down where the dog sat by Libby's feet. Her tail began thumping the ground.

"Stella. We got her from the local rescue."

"My wife and I are looking for a dog." He ruffled Stella's neck fur. "With three kids, they won't stop bugging us. We promised them when we moved over here they could get one."

"Where'd you move from?"

He stood back up. "Baltimore."

His name tag read "Deputy Sheriff Seevers."

"We just moved from Baltimore, too. It seems everyone in this town has lived here forever. I feel like we're the only ones who don't know everyone. Have you been here long?"

"A little over a year. When we found this town, my wife immediately fell in love with it."

"I did the same thing. It seems like a great place to raise kids."

"That's why we're here. I'll have to tell my wife about the rescue. I know I can't put it off any longer." He extended his hand to Libby. "I'm Will. Will Seevers."

"Libby Langston." She paused. "So you work for Sheriff Tucker?"

"That's right. You know him?"

Libby shook her head. "His name came up recently."

Will raised his eyebrows. "What's being said about him now?"

"Nothing. Just something about an old case." She opened her mouth to say something and then stopped.

"What?"

She waved her hand. "Never mind, it's probably nothing."

"Now you've got me interested. What is it?"

"We moved into Haverford House. You heard of it?"

Will shook his head.

"Well anyway, the woman that lived there before us commit-ted suicide, but Tassie, the woman I was talking with, said she didn't believe it was a suicide."

"Why?"

Libby explained Cecilia's possibly being pregnant and Tassie's tell-ing Sheriff Tucker about it. She then added, "Who knows, maybe she lost the baby, and that's why she killed herself. I'm sure an autopsy would've revealed everything."

"Most likely."

Libby laughed. "I'm sorry for going on like that. I've always had a habit of playing detective. I'm sure it was nothing."

Will nodded. "Good luck with the dog."

"Thanks." She watched him walk on through the market, thinking he seemed like a nice guy. When they'd lived in the city, she'd felt iso-lated around her neighbors in the apartment, and she hadn't expected that here. Growing up in a small town, she'd never had that outsider feeling, but moving to a small town was another story. It might take years before she was accepted as one of them. Maybe it wasn't going to be so hard after all.

Stella's head stuck out the half-open window of the car with her ears flapping in the wind. Libby turned up the radio, which was play-ing an oldies tune, and she sang loudly, feeling happy. On the winding, two-lane road out of town, she passed the numerous chicken houses, the long white buildings with large fans that emitted a smell she still hadn't gotten used to. Farther down she drove by a horse farm. White rail fencing stretched along a pasture where bay-colored horses fed in groups of two and three. Off in the distance she saw a man riding in a sulky around a dirt track. A whiff of horse manure blew into the car. Now that was a smell she liked; it reminded her of her summers in Connecticut.

From ten to sixteen, she'd been obsessed with horses. She'd even worked at a stable for two summers. She loved the smell of the horses, how they'd rumble their low whinny, greeting her when she'd walk into the barn. But she hadn't had the same passion as her mother, who'd almost made the Olympic team in dressage years ago, and by the time Libby went off to college in Maryland, her horse days were over.

She reached over and stroked Stella's fur. Things were going to be OK. She'd begun to doubt her decision to move, but driving by the beautiful landscape reassured her she'd made the right decision. The song "Surfin' Safari" came on the radio, and she thought about her encounter with the deputy, Will Seevers. She smiled, feeling less alone in the new town.

6

Will Seevers set his thermal coffee cup on his desk at the station. The sheriff's office was a small square room with three desks: one for Maggie, the receptionist/dispatcher; one for Will; and one for Sheriff Tucker. Maggie, who was all of five feet-two, had worked for Sheriff Tucker since high school, more than thirty years ago. What she lacked in stature she made up for in attitude. The term "spitfire" came to mind whenever Will thought of Maggie. But she liked Will; in fact, she would do pretty much anything he asked. She treated him like the son she never had.

The building sat on the corner of Main and Commerce and had been there for almost a hundred years. In the back were two holding cells that remained empty the majority of the time, as they were now.

Will pulled up his swivel chair to the old wooden desk that he'd inherited from the previous deputy, who'd probably inherited it from someone before that. He sorted through the few papers on his desk.

Maggie was busy working her daily crossword puzzle, and Sheriff Tucker was down the street at the coffee shop having his morning pastry and chatting with Pearl or her daughter, Kelly Ann. Will leaned back in his chair and stared at the old case file he'd pulled out after talking with Libby Langston.

"Hey Maggie."

"Yes, Will?" She erased a word from her puzzle and brushed the newspaper with the back of her hand.

"You remember the death of Cecilia Reynolds?"

"How could I forget? The whole town was in shock, poor child."

"So you believe she killed herself?"

Maggie looked up from her puzzle. "Of course she did. There were little innuendos at the time about her being murdered, but that was just town gossip. No, that poor girl just never got over the death of her father. She'd been so close to him." Maggie stuck her pencil in her heavily-sprayed beehive hairdo she'd worn for decades and scratched a spot on her head.

"Do you remember if an autopsy was performed?"

"An autopsy?" Maggie made a humph sound. "Why would they have done that? She drowned herself, pure and simple. You don't need an autopsy for that. I mean, there was no struggle or anything like that."

"Maybe she was drugged; an autopsy would have shown that."

Maggie laughed and waved a dismissive hand at Will. "Honey, you watch too much of that *CSI* on TV. I remember Sheriff Tucker investigating that case, and he had no reason to believe anything but suicide." Maggie gave Will a quizzical stare. "What makes you so interested in that old case anyway?"

"I don't know. I just heard some talk in town about it, and it made me curious."

"You can't believe what you hear in town. Some people just love to make up stories just to hear themselves talk. You would be best to just ignore them." Maggie went back to her crossword.

Will picked up the manila folder labeled "C. Reynolds—Closed." He'd taken it from the old case file box in the storage room. Things had been slow and after meeting Libby the day before, he kept thinking about what she'd told him. He leafed through the few pages that were in there. On one page were notes in Sheriff Tucker's handwriting from his interviews with John Reynolds and others who had been close to Cecilia. One thing he didn't find was any mention of a suicide note. From his experience, people rarely committed suicide without leaving something behind.

Will slipped the folder inside his desk drawer when the door to the office opened and Sheriff Tucker walked in, just like clockwork. Every morning at nine o'clock, he came to work after stopping by Pearl's. Sheriff Baynard "Bubby" Tucker was on the far side of sixty and could have retired years ago, but this was the life he loved. He enjoyed the status it gave him in town, and since he had no hobbies, what would be the point of retiring? His wife of thirty-nine years, Myrtle, had died two years ago after her battle with cancer, and his only child, Mary, lived in Idaho and rarely came back for visits.

"I tell you, this may go down on record as being one of the hottest *Julys*," Sheriff Tucker said, emphasizing the first syllable and drawing it out. He wiped the back of his neck with his handkerchief. "I would guess it's already in the nineties, and it's only nine o'clock." Patches of sweat had formed under his arms, but his rotund figure may have had something to do with that. At five feet eight, he weighed over two hundred seventy, proof that he loved his sweets. He also loved his cigars; Maggie always teased him that one day he would be found dead with a Twinkie in one hand and a stogie in the other. She constantly nagged him about getting into shape, but his comeback was always the same: What would be the point in living if he couldn't have the few things that made him happy?

"What's new today, Will?" He asked this same question every morning, and Will usually responded with the same answer: "nothing much." Today, however, Will decided to shake things up a bit.

"I was looking into some old case files, and I came across one that caught my eye."

"Which one would that be?"

"Cecilia Reynolds."

Maggie looked up from her crossword to catch Sheriff Tucker's reaction.

"Now why would an old suicide case catch your eye?" Tucker asked, setting his heavy frame down in his chair, which nearly buckled under his weight.

He had to be careful in his approach. Will didn't want to insinuate the sheriff hadn't done a thorough job. "I just heard some talk of the possibility of murder instead of suicide."

Tucker laughed, his belly heaving up and down. "Listen son, I know all about that talk, and that's all it is. I think you need to let this one go. John Reynolds is a good friend of mine, and he surely wouldn't want his wife's suicide dredged up so many years later. He's running for office; we don't need no mention of scandal that could ruin everything for him."

"Scandal? What do you mean by that?"

"Oh, there was talk long ago about some woman, but it was all rumor. John assured me there was no truth to any of it. I hear it may be a close race for him, and that is all it would take for some nosy reporter from Washington to come snooping around and making a mountain out of a molehill. John Reynolds is an asset to this town, and we sure don't need to be looking into his past. Why, he has plans to build a whole new development in this town." Sheriff Tucker motioned with his cigar toward Will. "You know he owns half the land around here, and he told me himself that if he gets into office, he'll make sure we get the funding for a new road that will come straight here from the main highway, making it much easier for people to get here. He has plans for houses and shops. Why, you never know, we could get a whole new office with two or three deputies."

"Growth is not always a good thing," Will said.

Growth was exactly what Will had been trying to get away from. Julie and he had left the Baltimore area for that exact reason. They had both grown up in Essex, a blue-collar community on the outskirts of Baltimore City, and had started dating after attending a pep rally in eleventh grade. They became inseparable and were married right after high school graduation. They lived with Julie's parents while they both attended community college. Will took classes in law enforcement—his dream had always been to work as a police officer—while Julie studied to become a paralegal.

After two years of college, Will applied to the police academy. Six months later, he graduated and started his field training. Julie went on to graduate, securing a job with a law firm in the city. They eventually moved out of her parents' house and rented a tiny apartment in the city. Will joined the Baltimore City police force and moved quickly up the ranks with the help of his sergeant, who saw his potential.

When Julie became pregnant, Will didn't want her to have to work after the baby was born, so he took a second job as a night security guard. After several years, he was able to quit the second job. By the time he was thirty, he had made detective, but by then they were already hating the city.

By the time Wyeth, their oldest, had started school, Julie begged Will to move out of the city, but it took five more years for it to actually happen. Will learned of the deputy sheriff position from an old friend of his that knew he was looking to move. He'd heard of the possibility of the sheriff's retiring soon, or at least that he should be, considering his age. After many sleepless nights wrestling with the decision, Will finally accepted the job. It was a large cut in pay, but his family's happiness mattered most to him, and he prayed their move would work out for the best.

A year later, he had no regrets other than missing his old job occasionally. In Baltimore, he'd been assigned to murders cases, mostly drug related, some complicated, but he loved dissecting the puzzle, and he was good at it. Ever since coming to Corsica, the most interesting case he'd had was trying to find out who had broken into the high school and stolen the football team's prized nine-foot plastic statue of an Indian, the Corsica High Warrior's mascot, that stood in the stands for every game.

But he hadn't moved here for his career. The school system was much better, and he could tell Julie was happier—or at least he hoped she was. Lately, she'd been out of sorts, but with three children and one on the way, he attributed her moodiness to the stress of motherhood.

Will had turned thirty-six a month ago. Age wasn't something Will thought about, but ever since his birthday, an undercurrent of restlessness rumbled inside him, and he wondered if it had to do with getting older. He kept remembering his surfing days. His family had lived in Southern California when he was young. From the time he was eight years old and could pick up a surfboard, riding the waves had been his passion. At fifteen, when his father was transferred to the East Coast, Will sulked for months, but he eventually resigned to surfing the Atlantic, even though the waves didn't compare.

He loved Julie and the kids, but there were times he longed for those untroubled days of his youth.

7

Libby was fixing up one of the guest rooms on the third floor in hopes that her parents would come and visit or possibly her sister Emily, who lived near Chicago. Emily and her kids usually spent a week every summer at the beach with Libby, but they hadn't made any specific plans yet.

Libby had ordered a few things for the bedroom and bath from a catalog. She placed new pillow shams on the bed, giving them a good fluffing, and laid out a flowered quilt at the foot of the bed. Stella was lying on the floor, basking in the sunlight that streamed through the window.

Libby opened another packing box, took out a white shower curtain embroidered with tiny roses, and went into the bathroom to hang it. Stella got up and followed Libby, but as soon as Stella stepped into the bathroom, the dog stopped in her tracks and let out a low rumble of a growl.

Libby turned around. "What's the matter, girl?"

Stella ignored Libby and stared straight at the bathtub, continuing her growl, the fur on the back of her neck raised. Libby walked over to the big claw-footed tub to see if maybe a mouse or something was in it, but it was completely empty. "Stella, come here; it's OK," Libby said in a soothing voice, but Stella took a few steps back from the doorway. Libby walked over to Stella, and the dog wagged her tail excitedly, rubbing up against Libby's legs. Libby knelt down, gave her a hug, and reassured her everything was all right. Then she went back into the bathroom and called for Stella to come. Stella took a few tentative steps forward but stopped at the threshold and began growling again.

"What's going on?" She searched the bathroom for something unseen that maybe Stella could smell, but she couldn't find anything unusual. She finally gave up and hung the shower curtain while Stella remained in the bedroom.

Josh called at half past four. He had left the office early and was already halfway home. She was excited he was coming home so early. His normal time, lately, was more like nine o'clock. She couldn't wait for this case he was working on to be over.

Libby folded some towels from the dryer and carried them upstairs. She stacked some in her linen closet and then took the rest up to the third floor guest bathroom. She stopped in the bedroom and admired how the room had turned out. Lemon-scented furniture polish still lingered in the air. The old wrought iron bed accentuated the antique dresser she'd found in a shop in town. The new blue and yellow shams brightened up the room.

After hanging the folded towels in the adjoining bathroom on the brass towel rack that stood in the corner, she turned to leave and something caught her eye. The newly hung shower curtain was pushed back to reveal the tub filled with water. She stiffened. The tub had been empty just a few hours before. Could the faucet have somehow broke and leaked into the tub? She checked the valves, but both the hot and cold spigot worked fine. She pulled the stopper out of the tub and stood perplexed, wondering how it had happened. She left the bathroom again to find Stella waiting outside. She looked back into the bathroom. Could there be a connection?

Having put the tub incident out of her mind, she went out back to water the planters on the patio. The planters, now brimming with red geraniums and white impatiens, added some much-needed color to the porch. The stone walkway down to the water, now free of weeds, was lined with lavender, sage, and hydrangeas. The place was finally beginning to look like a home.

Stella, who'd been lying in the shade of a maple tree, began barking furiously. Libby glanced over in her direction. Stella was on her feet, staring up at the house. A cloud passed overhead, casting the rear of the house in shadow. Libby followed Stella's gaze—the shimmering image of Elizabeth Haverford was in the upstairs bathroom window. Libby gasped and jumped back. She squinted through the glare of the sun, which had just broken through the clouds. When she peered back at the now-darkened window, she saw nothing.

Thoughts raced through her mind. Had she really seen the woman? She remembered what Tassie had said, that Elizabeth just wanted to tell her something. She headed toward the house, with Stella at her heels, to find out what was going on. Was her mind playing tricks on her, or was there really a ghost in the house? She walked briskly through the French doors, on a mission, not really thinking what she would do if confronted by the woman. Her heart beat fast in her chest, but her curiosity overshadowed her fear. She had to find out what Elizabeth wanted.

She rounded the corner of the hallway into the foyer and ran smack-dab into someone. She let out a bloodcurdling scream, and Stella barked loudly. Then she heard Josh's voice.

"Hey, calm down. Weren't you expecting me? I called and told you I was on my way home."

"Oh thank God, it's you."

"Who did you think it was?"

"You're not going to believe this, but I saw Elizabeth again. And I know it wasn't my imagination this time because Stella saw her, too." Libby's hands shook. This time she needed to be believed.

She explained the water in the tub and Stella's reluctance to go into the bathroom and then about Elizabeth standing in the window. They went upstairs to solve the mystery. Reaching the third floor, Libby slowed her pace, letting Josh go ahead.

"I don't see any ghosts," he called to Libby. He pulled back the shower curtain and added, "No water in the tub either."

Libby rounded the corner of the bathroom door. "Josh, I know what I saw. Just because she's not here now doesn't mean she wasn't here earlier. And watch this." Libby called Stella into the bathroom. Josh watched as Stella approached the doorway and stopped, smelling the air with her nose up. "See what I mean?" Libby said defiantly, relieved that at least Stella was on her side.

"Maybe it just smells funny to her."

"Or maybe she can sense things we can't. Maybe she knows there are spirits here. You have to believe me, Josh, or otherwise you have to think I'm crazy."

"I believe that you believe you saw someone standing in the window, but there's always a good explanation for things. Who knows, maybe it was a shadow falling on the window that made it appear to be a figure."

"I know what I *saw*!" Libby stormed out of the bathroom.

"OK, OK, so you saw a ghost," Josh said with frustration as he ran after her. "What do you want to do about it? Sell the house?"

"Of course not." Libby spun around to face him. "I love this house. I just wish I knew what she wanted."

"Maybe we should have a séance and see if she'll come and tell us."

"That might not be a bad idea," Libby said, holding up her finger.

"I was *joking*!" Josh shot back. "Look, Libby, you know you've always had an overactive imagination. You said as a kid you were always living in some fantasyland, making up stories. Maybe you've just been spending a little too much time alone, and your imagination is taking over."

"I'm not a child anymore. I know what I saw, and I'm not in some *fantasyland!*"

Josh raised his hands in front of him. "OK, I'm sorry. But there's probably a perfectly logical explanation for what you saw. I just don't want you to be afraid to live in the house." He kissed her cheek.

"I'm not afraid." She turned away from him. "I need to find out what's going on, and I want you to believe me." Tears welled in her eyes.

"OK, I believe you." He grabbed her shoulders and turned her to face him. "Don't be upset."

"I wouldn't be upset if you'd just *believe* me."

"I said I did!"

"OK." She hugged him, not wanting to fight, but she had a nagging feeling he hadn't meant what he said.

❧

Libby was able to cajole Josh into going to the Fourth of July festivities in town. They made a compromise; they would go in town for the parade and chicken dinner but come home before the fireworks. Around noon, they packed Stella into Libby's old Volvo station wagon and headed out. They pulled up to the outskirts of town and parked on a side street. The parade route had all the main roads closed off.

They walked with Stella toward the town square. The streets were crowded with children and adults eagerly awaiting the parade. It was a warm day, but a constant, gentle wind warded off the oppressive heat from the previous days. The red, white, and blue banner proudly displayed on the front of the pavilion billowed in the breeze. Vendors selling cotton candy, lemonade, funnel cakes, and other treats lined the square. The smell of popcorn and hot dogs permeated the air.

Josh stopped to buy a drink. While Libby waited, she noticed Will Seevers and his family walking across the courtyard. She called out, "Hey, Will!" He turned in her direction and waved. He said something to his wife, and then the whole family came over. One of the kids was carrying a puppy in his arms.

"You found the rescue?" Libby nodded toward the puppy.

"Yeah. I told Julie about it, and the kids wore me down. We just got him yesterday." Will introduced Julie and the three kids—Wyeth, who'd just turned ten; eight-year-old Nathan; and Sara, who was three and a half. He tapped each of their platinum blonde heads as he said their names.

Libby introduced Josh.

"I want some cotton candy," Sara whispered to her mom, tugging on Julie's dress. Julie had short brown hair cut in a bob and was petite except for her stomach, which stuck out so far Libby wondered how she didn't topple over.

"We'll get some soon, honey, but we don't want to miss the parade."

Libby thought how lucky Julie was to have three children and one on the way. It wasn't fair; she couldn't have even one.

"Will's the deputy sheriff in town," Libby said to Josh. Will was out of uniform, dressed in a pair of jeans and a polo shirt. "And they moved here from Baltimore."

"How do you like it over here?" Josh asked Will.

"We love it," Will said.

"My dog's name is Milo," Nathan said proudly. Then he added, "He's only nine weeks old, and he's part German shepherd."

Libby knelt down to see the puppy, while Stella investigated with her nose, sniffing the puppy all over. "He's very cute," Libby said as she rubbed Milo's brown and black fur. Milo eagerly licked her hand.

"He's a handful, but we're working with him," Julie said.

"I have a great training book, if you want to borrow it. It has a lot of good tips."

"Thanks, I may take you up on that. With this baby coming, I don't know how much time I'm going to have to train him, but Will swears he and the boys are going to do all the work. But you know how that goes," Julie raised her eyebrows at Will.

He shrugged and then looked at Libby. "Oh, I checked out that case you mentioned. It turns out there was no autopsy done."

Libby nodded.

"Case?" Josh frowned at Libby.

"It's nothing. I was just curious about Cecilia's death."

"Mommy! I want some cotton *candy*," Sara whined.

"Well, I guess we better pick out our spot for the parade," Julie said, as Sara hung on her arm.

"Maybe we could get together for dinner sometime," Libby added before they'd walked away.

"Love to," Julie said over her shoulder as Sara pulled her away.

"What exactly did you ask him to do?" Josh asked Libby.

"What?"

"Will Seevers. What did you ask him to look into?"

"Nothing. I just told him what Tassie had said about Cecilia being pregnant. It was nothing." Libby waved her hand at Josh. "Do you think I sounded too desperate?"

Josh frowned, puzzled.

"When I said that about dinner. It would be nice to finally meet some friends in this town, but I hope I didn't come across too pushy."

"You were fine." Josh took her hand as they continued their stroll.

The sound of a marching band reverberated in the distance. They headed to a spot along the sidewalk. As the parade approached and the music got louder, the beat of the drums resonated in her chest. Libby felt tears sting her eyes. She couldn't help it. Ever since she was a child, there was something about a parade that made her cry. The Corsica high school marching band passed, dressed in their green and gold uniforms, followed by several fire trucks ranging from antique to new, farm tractors pulling floats, and riders on horseback waving the

American flag. As they turned the corner, the sound of the horns and the thumping of the drums faded in the distance.

After the parade, people started congregating around the pavilion. Libby and Josh walked over to the folding chairs set up in rows in the courtyard. A heavyset man dressed in a light seersucker suit strode across the platform and stood in front of the microphone. "Ladies and gentlemen, it's wonderful to see so many of you today." A loud screech of feedback emanated from the speakers. The man fidgeted with the microphone and tried again. "As mayor, I am very proud of the great job everyone did on the parade. I think this was one of the best yet, and I hope everyone has an appetite today because I know the ladies have been working real hard baking pies and making mashed potatoes for you all." There was applause from the crowd, and then he continued, his voice echoing over the loud speaker.

"Today is a special day, a day for us to celebrate our great country, and I think Corsica represents what America is all about. A lot of hard-working family people with faith in the Lord. Today, on this special day, we have the privilege of having one of our town's prominent figures with us. He would like to say a few words to you all. Ladies and gentlemen, Senator John Reynolds." The mayor waved his hand to the side, and John Reynolds walked onto the stage. The crowd clapped again, and the small band that sat at the back of the pavilion played a patriotic tune as he walked up to the microphone.

"What a beautiful day!" He paused for a minute before continuing: "I could have been many places today, but I said to myself there is only one place I would like to spend my Fourth of July celebration and that is in my favorite town, Corsica!"

The crowd cheered. Libby studied the man, trying to picture him living at Haverford House with Cecilia. She wondered how he had taken his wife's death. He was dressed in nicely tailored navy blue slacks and a sky-blue polo shirt. His hair was silver-gray, and his face was tanned with the look of someone who spent his days sailing on the water or playing a lot of golf. He was an attractive man, and Libby could see how he had made it in politics.

"As Mayor Hopkins said," Reynolds continued, "it is a great country we have, and as you all know, I'm running for the US Senate, and I want to preserve that greatness we all love and cherish. Many Washington politicians have forgotten what makes this country so great. The backbone of this country is made up of fine people like you. And if I am elected, I intend to make sure that our freedoms and rights are not taken away. That our children will be able to grow up and have the same opportunities that we had. I will fight for the farmers; I will fight for business owners; and I will fight for each and every one of you." The timbre of his voice intensified as he continued. "So please remember to vote this fall, and if you are there for me, I will be there for you. Thank you, everyone. It's great to see you all, and I can already taste that fried chicken." He waved to the crowd now standing on their feet, applauding him. The band resumed their song as he exited the stage.

Libby turned to Josh and said, "Is *he* ever a politician."

"I think he's a genuine guy. The few times I've met him, I got the impression he sincerely wants to fight for the people."

"He just seems a little too smooth for me."

Libby and Josh milled about the square, stopping at the little tables set up along the way displaying various handmade goods from pies to quilts. Libby was inspecting a crocheted table runner when she heard someone say, "Well, Josh, fancy meeting you here." She turned to see Senator Reynolds shaking hands with Josh.

"Nice to see you again, Senator," Josh replied. "Sir, I would like you to meet my wife Libby. Libby, this is Senator Reynolds." Libby smiled and shook Reynolds' hand.

"What brings you to these parts of the woods?" Reynolds asked them.

"It's ironic, really. I recently discovered we purchased your property, the Haverford House. I had no idea that had been yours," Josh replied.

"What a small world. Yes, that had actually belonged to my first wife's family. After her death, I had it added to the estate's holding company. It was hard living there after she passed away. I stayed for a few years, but there were too many memories."

"I'm sorry to hear that," Josh said.

"It was a long time ago." There was a slight pause in the conversation, and then Reynolds added, "Well, I'm sure you'll enjoy living there. It's a beautiful place."

A woman who looked to be in her early thirties sauntered over and linked her arm onto Senator Reynolds'. He turned toward her. "Ah, Cynthia, I was wondering where you had gone off to." Reynolds introduced his wife to Josh and Libby, explaining to Cynthia that they were living at Haverford House.

"Really? How nice." She smiled, exposing a perfect set of sparkling white teeth. She had to be almost twenty years younger than Reynolds. He didn't do so bad on wife number two, Libby thought. She made the perfect politician's wife: not too flashy, not too chic, but striking, with perfectly styled, bleached-blonde hair and well-cut clothes. Libby noticed her jewelry, which was understated but very expensive—small diamond earrings, a gold bracelet, and a beautiful emerald and diamond ring on her finger. "How long have you lived at Haverford?" Cynthia asked.

"A little over a month. We did some renovations before we moved in," Josh replied.

"Yes, I'm sure it needed some work done," Reynolds said. "The house sat for many years. I couldn't bring myself to sell it, but I couldn't live there. With this campaign, as tight as this race is, I needed to liquidate some assets. I couldn't take the time to fix it up; I just wanted a quick sell. Cynthia and I live over in Annapolis now. I love it over here, though, and I still have many interests in this town. I like to get over here as much as I can."

"Well, we love it," Josh said.

"I hear you're the boy wonder on the Tolman case. How's that going?"

"Pretty well, I think. We're getting close to closing arguments."

"That's good. Listen, tell Peterson I said hello and that I'm still considering his offer. I think I'm ready for a change of counsel."

"Great, I'll let him know. Nice meeting you," Josh said to Cynthia.

"My pleasure," Cynthia replied.

Libby said good-bye to both of them and watched as Reynolds walked past them, schmoozing the crowd.

"That guy is too slick for me. Maybe he's genuine, but he seems to have the act down just a little too perfect."

"You better keep that to yourself, because he may become a pretty influential client of ours, especially if he wins the election."

8

Thinking about the night before, Libby rolled over and hugged Stella, who was in the bed curled up beside her. Libby had woken up a little after midnight with thoughts of Elizabeth and Cecilia. After tossing and turning, she'd eventually gotten up and gone downstairs for a glass of milk. Sitting at the kitchen table, she'd wondered when Elizabeth would return so she could find out what she wanted. She had even closed her eyes, trying to will Elizabeth to appear, but nothing happened.

"What do you want to do today, girl?"

Stella cocked her head to one side, looking at Libby, waiting to hear a word that would require an action from her. Libby found herself having conversations with Stella when she was alone, and even though the dog couldn't respond verbally, she was a good listener. As soon as Libby put her feet on the floor, Stella was at her side. She was her shadow, and Libby loved it.

She spent the morning working in the garden. The sky was a brilliant blue with just a few wisps of clouds passing by. A cool breeze blew off the water, keeping the heat at bay, and sending a marshy smell across the lawn. Libby wore a big straw sunhat to protect her fair skin. Dressed in a pair of shorts, an old T-shirt, and hiking boots, she concentrated on a section of the yard that needed clearing, tossing the weeds into the wheelbarrow. Stella was lying in her favorite spot under the maple tree. After clearing the weeds and raking the area, Libby stepped back to survey her progress. Not bad, she thought, as she wiped the sweat off her forehead with the back of her arm.

Libby had bought some petunias, verbenas, and vincas at a local nursery and stored them in the boathouse to keep them cool before planting them. She walked down the stone path with Stella at her side to retrieve the plants.

The boathouse, a stone structure located near the pier, had a small window on one side and an old weather-beaten door on the front. Libby opened the door and stepped in, adjusting her eyes to the darkened room. Immediately Stella started her low growl, the fur on her back raised.

The room was crammed with assorted boat items and boxes of junk. Libby and Josh hadn't had time to clear the place out. A long table in the middle of the room was littered with buoys, ropes, fishing nets, and rusted tools, and along the walls were some old shovels, a broken-down lawnmower, and other discarded items in boxes. As her eyes came into focus with the light change, she looked around the room to see what was causing Stella's growling. She shuddered; maybe Elizabeth was haunting the boathouse, too.

"All right, Stella, what is it this time?"

She hoped it wasn't a rat or some other creature hiding in a corner. She fumbled with the switch on the wall to cast more light on the unlit room, but it did nothing. The wiring must be bad, or maybe it just needed a new bulb. She bent down to pick up one of the flats she had set on the floor when something to the back of the room moved, making a noise. She dropped the flat and stood up. "OK, who's there?" she asked in the most commanding voice she could muster. If it was a ghost, she was ready to face her, and if it was a rat, she was ready to run. She walked toward the back where the sound had come from. "Come out, come out, wherever you are," she said in a singsong voice. A flash of something streaked by the other side of the table, and Libby screamed, tripping over an old watering can and almost falling on her rear. She caught sight of what looked to be a child running out the door. "Wait!" She regained her footing and followed him.

A boy ran down the beach with Stella at his heels. Libby chased after them, but they were too fast. She stopped and bent down with her hands on her knees, trying to catch her breath. She called after Stella, not wanting her to go too far away. Stella turned in Libby's direction, saw that Libby was not in on the chase, and ran back toward her.

Libby had gotten only a glimpse of the child, a boy who looked to be about ten or eleven, barefoot, wearing a pair of baggy shorts and a torn T-shirt. His black hair was closely cropped to his head, and his skin was as dark as ebony. What had he been doing in her boathouse, and where did he come from?

Libby walked back to the boathouse and looked around inside; there was nothing of real value in there, nothing worth stealing. She wondered how long he had been hiding. She looked down at the flat she had dropped to the flowers and dirt strewn about the floor. She put the plants back in the flat and then swept the concrete floor with an old broom against the wall by the door. She went back to her planting and put the young boy out of her mind.

Later that day she sat on the patio, enjoying a ham and cheese sandwich and a glass of iced tea. She thought of the Fourth of July and their meeting with Reynolds. He was definitely charismatic. He appeared to be the perfect politician; he had looks, money, and a beautiful wife. She wasn't sure what it was about him that she didn't like. Josh liked him; maybe she shouldn't have judged him so quickly. She recalled Reynolds saying how hard it had been to stay in the house after his wife died. Libby wanted to know more about Cecilia. She had planned on going into town to pick up some picture hangers at the hardware store; maybe she'd stop by Tassie's afterward.

The door made a ringing sound as she entered the hardware store, where the air was heavy with the smell of lumber. Mr. Tompkins was stocking paint cans on a shelf. He looked up and said, "Mrs. Langston, how good to see you."

Libby said hello in return, surprised he'd remembered her name. She chatted with Mr. Tompkins briefly as he led her to the aisle with the picture hangers. Libby loved small hardware stores as opposed to the big box chains that had cropped up everywhere. She felt short of breath with the enormity of them and found herself wandering around forever trying to locate something. Mr. Tompkins' store reminded her of the small shops in Connecticut, of going with her dad on a Saturday morning to pick out materials for some project of theirs, like building a birdhouse or tree fort.

Standing at the checkout counter Libby asked Mr. Tompkins if he had known Cecilia Reynolds.

Mr. Tompkins smiled. "She was a sweet girl."

"What did you think about her suicide?"

He frowned and shook his head. "I guess we never know the troubles some people have. On the outside everything had appeared normal, but she must've been wrestling with demons none of us knew about."

The bell jingled and Libby turned to see a man dressed in overalls come into the store.

"Chester," Mr. Tompkins nodded in the man's direction. "I got those hooks you were looking for."

Leaving the hardware store, she smelled a wonderful aroma that emanated from the bakery several shops down; the smell was enough to entice her inside. Her mouth watered at the sight of the freshly baked pies and cookies; maybe she would pick up a pie for dessert tonight. Her stomach was rumbling, and she felt famished even though she had just eaten lunch about an hour ago. Mrs. Jenkins, who owned the bakery, came out from the back. She wore an apron dusted with flour over her plump torso and a big smile on her face.

Libby had met her before; she was one of those people who seemed to be always cheerful. Libby said hi to her, and they exchanged some small talk about the weather. Libby then asked for an apple pie. After Mrs. Jenkins boxed up the pie, she let her sample some blueberry pastries that had just come out of the oven. Libby couldn't resist buying those, too, and thought they would be a nice treat to take to Tassie's house.

Libby was amazed at the size of the flowers in Tassie's yard. She had to remember to ask Tassie what kind of fertilizer she used. She walked up the tiny path to the front door and knocked, hoping Tassie was at home. There was no car parked in the driveway, but she didn't remember seeing one the first time she was there either. She wondered how Tassie got around.

Tassie opened the door within seconds after Libby knocked; it was almost as if she knew Libby was coming.

"Well hello, dear, it's good to see you again."

"Hi, Tassie. I hope I'm not bothering you. I wanted to ask you some more questions, if you have the time."

"Of course, my child. I have all the time in the world. Would you like some tea?"

"I'd love some, and I brought a little something we could have with the tea," Libby said, holding up the bag of pastries.

They walked back toward the kitchen. Libby loved the smell of the house, fresh cotton mixed with lilacs. The sound of birds singing came through the open windows along with the humming of a fan from somewhere in the house. The house remained cool from the shade of the large oak trees that surrounded it.

Libby sat in the tiny cane-seated chair. Tassie took the pot of water that was already hot from the stove and poured it into the teapot.

"I guess I picked the perfect time to come. It looks like you had already started to make the tea."

"I had a feeling someone would be dropping by. Don't ask me how I knew; I just did. So, is there anyone in particular you wanted to know about?"

"I can't seem to get Cecilia Reynolds out of my mind. You know they never did an autopsy on her. I guess we'll never know for sure if she was really pregnant."

"I'm never wrong about those things. Just like you, child, I could tell the last time I saw you. I knew you were expecting."

Libby looked puzzled. Did she hear her correctly? It sounded like she said she thought Libby was pregnant. "I'm sorry, Tassie. What did you say?"

"I said I knew you were with child when we met in town the other day. Have you not told anyone yet?"

"Told anyone? I didn't even know myself! Why would you say that? Are you sure?"

"I've never been wrong yet. I'm sorry, child. I don't usually blurt things out like that. I just assumed you already knew."

"Well, we've been trying, but it's been so long I was beginning to think it would never happen. I gave up buying the at-home tests because the results were always depressing." Libby couldn't stop smiling. Excitement rose up inside. She wanted to jump out of her seat and scream. She had to tell Josh. But wait—she really didn't know for sure. She had only the word of this old woman whom she hardly knew. But she said she was never wrong. "You know, now that I think about it, I have been having weird food cravings lately, and I did have those dizzy spells. I thought it was because I saw a ghost, but maybe it was because I was pregnant. I can't believe this; I have to go. I have to get a test at the store to be sure." Libby almost knocked her chair over backward.

"Hold on, child." Tassie placed her hand on Libby's arm. "You need to calm yourself down. That baby isn't goin' anywhere. It can wait a few minutes while you sip your tea. I think maybe I better go with you to the store. I wouldn't want you to be so distracted you can't drive properly."

Libby thought about it for a moment and agreed that she needed to calm down. She had to think rationally. Until she took the test, she wasn't going to get her hopes up.

They drove into town, stopped at Edward's Pharmacy to buy the pregnancy kit, and decided to go to Libby's house. Tassie said it would be better for Libby to be in familiar surroundings when she did the test.

Libby reflected on the past month, and it all started to make sense. There had been signs that she was pregnant, but they never registered with her. Maybe all the strange happenings in the house had just been her hormones in a frenzy.

When they pulled into the long drive, Tassie muttered, "My, my, this does bring back memories." Tassie had explained to Libby on the drive over how, when she was a teenager, she would go to Haverford House with her grandmother. Tassie's mother, Sally, did the laundry for Miss Annabelle, the wife of Benjamin Haverford. At the time, Miss Annabelle had no children, though they had been trying for some time.

Tassie's grandmother specialized in medicinal herbs and had a special knack for fertility potions, so Miss Annabelle asked for her help. Tassie came along because her grandmother was training her in the art of herbal medicine. Tassie would help concoct various herbs to make fertility elixirs for Miss Annabelle. The herbal treatments took a while, but eventually they worked. After two years, she became pregnant with Archibald, but he remained her only child.

"This place hasn't changed," Tassie said in a quiet voice. "It's still as beautiful as I remember."

Stella greeted them at the door. She was just as excited to see Tassie as she was to see Libby. Libby led Tassie into the kitchen and told her to make herself comfortable while she went to the bathroom.

Within minutes, Libby returned with a giant grin plastered to her face. "I'm pregnant!" Libby shouted, so excited she hugged Tassie. She wanted to thank Tassie, as if Tassie had been a part of the reason she was pregnant. "I have to call Josh!" Libby ran to the phone and began to dial but then stopped midway. She hung the phone back on the cradle. "I think maybe I'll wait. I really want to tell him in person. I can't wait to see his face."

"I think that is a good idea," Tassie agreed.

Libby couldn't stop smiling. She hadn't been this happy for as long as she could remember.

"Why don't you show me around the house," Tassie suggested. Libby had been nervously pacing back and forth in front of the kitchen table.

"Sure," Libby replied, glad to have something to focus on. Her mind was racing with all sorts of thoughts. How far along was she? Were there any decent doctors in the area? She needed to call her parents.

Libby gave Tassie the tour of the first floor, and then they stepped out back. Libby wanted to show Tassie her work in the gardens and get some advice on how to get her plants to look as beautiful as Tassie's.

Tassie told her how she had a compost pile in the back of her house that she mixed with horse and cow manure. It was the best manure, she said; you didn't want to use chicken manure because it was too high in nitrogen and could burn your plants. Her neighbors kept her supplied with the manure. She said it was all in the mixing and balance of what you put in the compost. She also sprinkled used tealeaves on the ground around some of her plants, like hydrangeas and azaleas to brighten their colors.

They walked the grounds and then ended up at the boathouse. Libby told Tassie how she had found the boy in there that morning. She described him to Tassie, and Tassie said it was probably Trevor Clay. His family lived just on the other side of Poplar's Point. The Clay family had lived there for years and had worked at Haverford House doing various odd jobs.

"Trevor's mama has been quite sickly these past few months, and I think Trevor has a lot of time on his hands," Tassie explained. "He's the youngest of the family; all his brothers are out working their summer jobs. I'm sure he meant no harm when he was here. He probably just got bored and was lookin' for something to do. If you see him again, ask him if he'd like to help you with your gardening or some other tasks around here. You know, now that you're with child, you shouldn't be lifting or bending over so much."

Libby agreed that would be a good idea. They made their way back into the house and finished the tour upstairs.

As they approached the attic door, Libby turned and looked at Tassie, hesitating before placing her hand on the crystal knob. "It's OK, child. There's nothing to be afraid of. I don't feel anything evil in this house, only love. Believe me, I've been places that I can tell right away bad energy is around. I don't feel that now."

They walked slowly up the stairs, followed by Stella, into the warm attic. "It's a little stuffy in here, but I wanted to show you the trunk I found." They walked over to the trunk and Libby lifted the lid. She carefully removed the silk shawl from the top and showed it to Tassie.

"This looks just like the shawl my grandma described Elizabeth wearing the day she saw her on the beach." Tassie gently caressed the fabric.

Libby then picked up the album. "This is what I really want you to see." She turned the page to the picture of James and Elizabeth with their children. Libby bent down so Tassie could see the picture. Tassie touched the photo, lightly drawing her finger around the outline of Elizabeth's figure. She closed her eyes and started humming a soft tune. Libby wondered what Tassie was doing. After a few minutes, Libby felt the hair on her arms begin to rise, and she got that same dizzy feeling as before.

"I think I need to sit down," Libby said. Afraid she would faint again, she immediately sat on the floor.

"Yes, child, sit down. She's here with us," Tassie replied, her eyes still closed.

Libby looked around the room but didn't see the woman. "I don't see anyone."

"Just be patient, child. She will come."

A few minutes later, an apparition appeared across the room. She was dressed the same as before. Libby gave a short gasp, and Tassie grabbed her hand and held it tightly. Libby took deep breaths, squeezing Tassie's hand. Then Tassie opened her eyes and smiled at the image. Libby was suddenly aware of an intense energy in the room. She stared hard at Elizabeth, willing her to come into focus, hoping the strength of her stare would keep Elizabeth visible.

Elizabeth raised her arms and reached out to them. Then she mouthed the words, *save her*. Libby wasn't sure if she had said it aloud or if her mind had just perceived it that way. Again, Elizabeth repeated the words, *save her*. Tassie and Libby were side by side, hands gripped, with Libby sitting on the floor and Tassie standing beside her. After what seemed like an eternity, the figure dissipated.

Libby turned to Tassie but didn't know what to say. A ghost had just spoken to them, or at least had tried to speak.

"Do you think she's talking about her daughter? That she wants us to save her somehow?" Libby asked Tassie.

"I don't think so. I got no vision of a child."

"Then who?"

"That I can't say, dear."

9

After driving Tassie back home, Libby stopped by the market for some crab cakes. Chesapeake Bay blue crabs were considered the best-tasting crabs in the world, and she loved that she could pick them up in season right at the local fish market. They sold live crabs for steaming, tubs of lump crabmeat, and already-prepared crab cakes. She wanted to have a special dinner ready for Josh when she surprised him with the news, and crab cakes were his favorite.

Seated at the table on the back porch, Libby poured Josh a glass of wine. Josh took a bite of the crab cake, savoring the taste. Then he noticed she had poured only one glass. "Aren't you going to have any?"

"No, I thought I should probably refrain for a while."

"Why?" Josh appeared puzzled.

Libby had a Cheshire cat smile. "You know what they say: women shouldn't drink alcohol when they're pregnant." Libby watched Josh's expression go from puzzlement to realization. His eyebrows shot up.

"Are you serious? You're pregnant! Are you sure? How did it happen?"

Libby laughed as Josh sputtered one question after another. "Yes, I'm serious and yes, I'm sure, and I think you know how it happened. We're going to have a baby!" Libby clasped her hands in front of her face and jumped out of her seat.

Josh stood up and gave Libby a big hug, sweeping her off her feet. Then he quickly put her down saying, "I'm sorry." He gently stroked her stomach.

"It's OK, Josh; I'm not going to break."

They sat back down. Josh ran his hand through his hair. "I can't believe it. How long have you known?"

"Just today. In fact, I still wouldn't have known if it wasn't for Tassie."

"Tassie?"

"I went over to her house today to get some more background on the Haverfords. Tassie has this weird sense, and she can tell when someone's pregnant. She said she knew I was expecting the day she saw me in town. I was totally shocked. I had no idea."

"You mean you think you're pregnant because some old woman told you so?" Josh looked incredulous.

"Of course not!" She frowned at Josh. "I took a test."

"OK, I was just wondering."

Libby swatted at a fly hovering over her plate. "Do you really think I'm that stupid?"

"I didn't—"

"I sometimes feel that you think I'm not all there."

"Don't be ridiculous. It's just you get a little swept up in things without thinking them all the way through."

Libby fought back tears. Things weren't going the way she'd planned.

"So what else did Tassie have to say?"

Libby sat silent. She knew Josh was trying to make up for what he'd said. She shook off the hurt feeling, not wanting to ruin the evening. "She told me more about Cecilia Reynolds."

"That reminds me. John Reynolds is one of our clients now. He came to the office today and had a meeting with Peterson; he wants me to handle his affairs personally. Can you believe that?" Josh took a sip of wine. "He said he was so impressed with my work on the Tolman case, and he was ready for a fresh start with a new counselor. After he left, Peterson practically kissed my hand. I mean, this is a huge amount of work for the firm. Reynolds has considerable assets and holdings, and they say his campaign is really taking off. He's ahead in the polls now. If he gets in, he could have a lot of power in Washington someday."

"That's great. I'm proud of you." Libby's voice lacked enthusiasm.

"What's wrong? You don't sound very excited."

"I'm sorry. I think it's great," Libby smiled. She was happy for Josh, but she didn't want to talk about work. She wanted him to be more excited about the baby.

Josh sensed Libby's change but wasn't quite sure what it was he'd done wrong. He tried again to cheer her up. "So what else happened today?"

"Nothing." Libby twirled her fork on her plate, telling herself to snap out of it. She wanted this to be a happy dinner, something she'd always remember. She looked out at the sun hanging on the horizon, a huge coral-colored ball, ready to slip below the sea, trying to think of something to say.

She told him that she'd run into Julie Seevers at the fish market and they'd exchanged phone numbers. Julie had invited them for dinner Saturday night. There was a pause in the conversation, and then Libby said, "I saw the ghost again, and this time I wasn't alone. Tassie was here, and she saw it, too, so I'm not crazy." She wanted Josh's approval. He didn't want to accept that the house was haunted, but he was going to have to.

Josh nodded but didn't say anything.

Taking his silence as a sign he was beginning to believe her, Libby continued: "We went up to the attic so that I could show her the trunk, and while we were up there, Elizabeth appeared. She even spoke, or at least it appeared she was speaking. But I couldn't really tell if she was talking out loud or if it was in my mind. It was really weird."

"Libby, listen to yourself. It's more than just weird."

"I know, but if you'd been there, you would understand. It seemed natural at the time. I really had no fear. Tassie definitely helped; she assured me there was nothing evil about Elizabeth. She wasn't there to hurt us, just to tell us something."

"So what did she tell you?" Josh asked. Then he shook his head. "I can't believe I'm even asking."

"Just two words—'Save her.' That was it. I thought she meant her daughter who had died so young, but Tassie didn't think so. I really want to figure out what she wants."

Josh shook his head with his lips pursed shut. "Do you think hanging out with Tassie, who may be off her rocker, is a good thing?"

"Tassie is *not* crazy. A little eccentric maybe, but she's perfectly sane."

"OK. No more talk of ghosts. This is a night to celebrate!" He held up his wineglass. "A toast to our new baby!"

"And to my brilliantly successful husband!" Libby added, holding up her glass of water. She leaned over and kissed Josh.

Libby was at the library in search of baby books. When she called her parents the night before to give them the news, her mother suggested getting some books on pregnancy. "You can never be too prepared," she'd told Libby over the phone.

It's just like my mother, Libby thought. Super-organized. The queen of planning and order. Libby loved her mother, but Libby had a more laid-back approach, like her father. She'd hesitated about giving her mother the news so soon, worried that if she told her mother now, she would arrive with a whole nursery suite of furniture. But her eagerness to share the news had won out.

After talking to her parents, she thought maybe getting some books on pregnancy wasn't such a bad idea, considering she had no clue about what to expect, except for maybe her feet swelling, a fact she'd learned from Julie.

She found several books that looked to be very informative, maybe a little too informative. One had a whole chapter devoted to hemorrhoids. This isn't good, she thought. After choosing two out of the stack, she noticed a wall lined with newspapers on wooden rods. An idea popped into her head, so she approached the counter.

"Would you by any chance have newspapers that go back twenty years?" she asked the librarian, who was sorting a pile of books on the counter.

"Well, we don't have the actual paper, but we do have everything on microfiche." Mrs. Tidwell spoke in her librarian whisper. Libby wondered if the woman ever spoke normally. "We're in the process of getting computers for the library; in fact, we recently received a large donation from Mr. Reynolds to modernize the library. He's such a generous man, thinking of our community like that. But for now, we make do with what we have. Here, let me show you how it works."

She led Libby to an old school desk in one corner of the library. Next to a machine on the desk was a wooden file cabinet with small drawers labeled with dates.

"We have the Corsica Times going back to the forties here. What year were you looking for?"

Libby performed a quick mental calculation. She remembered that Rick, their real estate agent, had told her the house had sat empty for sixteen years. Reynolds had said he'd stayed a few years after Cecilia's death before moving.

"I guess around the early nineties," Libby replied.

Mrs. Tidwell tilted her head back to see through her half-glasses as she scanned the rows of drawers. "Let me see…here we go." She opened one of the drawers and pulled out a roll of film. "This one is from 1990 to 1993."

"That's good; I'll start with that."

Libby watched as Mrs. Tidwell showed her how to load the film into the machine. She then flipped on a switch on the back of the machine, which lit up a screen on the front. A knob on the front turned forward and backward, scrolling the paper across the screen.

"Thanks," Libby said. "I think I've got it."

"Just be sure to put the rolls back in the correct drawers when you're finished," Mrs. Tidwell instructed, walking back to her counter.

Libby sat down in front of the machine and began scrolling. "JANUARY 1, 1990" appeared at the top of the newspaper page. She quickly scrolled through, mainly concentrating on the front page of each edition. News of Cecilia's death, she figured, would have been front-page news.

After about fifteen minutes, she sat back against the wooden chair and rubbed her eyes. Staring at the small screen illuminated by fluorescent lighting had strained her eyes. She wished she could pinpoint a date. Maybe she should have found out exactly when Cecilia died instead of wasting all this time. At least the local paper was published only once a week—and wasn't very big. Just as she was ready to give up, scrolling past "MAY 16, 1992," a headline caught her eye: "TRAGEDY STRIKES HAVERFORD HOUSE," written in bold and spanning the top of the page. Libby rotated the knob and centered the article on the screen. There was a picture of Cecilia, probably from her wedding day, with the caption, "Cecilia Haverford Reynolds, July 15, 1968– May 14, 1992." The article read as follows:

Cecilia Haverford Reynolds, twenty-three years old, was found dead Wednesday in her home on Poplar's Point. The Sheriff's Department is calling it a suicide. Investigators say that her husband, John Reynolds, discovered the body early Wednesday morning floating in the bathtub located on the third floor of the home. He attempted CPR, but she had already died, EMT Ron Talbot told reporters. "By the time the paramedics arrived on the scene, Mr. Reynolds had moved the body out of the tub and covered it with a large bath towel," Sheriff Tucker said. Initial reports conclude that she died from drowning. Close friends of Cecilia Reynolds say that she was a very fragile person, but they are shocked that she would have done something like this. The sudden death of

Francis Haverford seven months ago was said to have been very hard on Cecilia. John Reynolds was not available to give a statement. A spokesperson for the family said he was too distraught to talk to the press.

The article provided a brief summary of the history of Haverford House, naming Cecilia as the last remaining heir of the Haverford estate. John Reynolds, it seemed, would inherit the entire family fortune.

Libby re-read the article, stopping where it said Cecilia was found in the third-floor bathroom, the one Stella had refused to enter, the one where she'd seen Elizabeth in the window. Was Elizabeth trying to tell her something about Cecilia?

Libby's curiosity was piqued; she wanted to find out more on Cecilia's death. She scrolled the papers for more articles on Cecilia, but she didn't learn much more about her death. One article detailed the arrangements for the funeral, while another speculated on what John Reynolds would do with Haverford House. The police, it said, had officially closed the investigation and ruled it a suicide. There was no mention of Cecilia's being pregnant. Had Tassie been wrong?

She turned off the machine, placed the roll of film back in the correct drawer, and then checked out the baby books. Exiting the library with her head down, consumed with thoughts of Cecilia Reynolds, she collided with Deputy Seevers. He grabbed her arm to steady her.

"Excuse me," Libby said and then looked up. "Will! Hi. I'm sorry; I guess I wasn't paying attention to where I was going."

"You look like you're on a serious mission. What's with all the books?"

"I'm taking a crash course on having a baby. I just found out yesterday. In fact, I called Julie this morning to ask her about her doctor."

"Congratulations! I bet Josh is walking on cloud nine."

"He's a pretty excited father-to-be." Libby started to walk away and then turned. "I just went through the old newspaper clippings on Cecilia Reynolds' death. There wasn't a whole lot of detail, though." Libby looked across the street at an elderly man riding a bicycle. "I wonder why an autopsy wasn't done. Would that be normal?"

"Not usually. I know in Baltimore, a case like that would've had an autopsy." Will took a step toward the door and then stopped. "Hey, I just have to drop this book off. If you have some time, maybe we could get a coffee. I'm on break right now."

Libby hesitated and then said, "Sure." While she waited for Will to come back out, she thought maybe she could convince him to open the case back up.

They sat across the booth from each other at Pearl's Diner. The lunch crowd had dwindled, and there were only a few patrons left. An old man, who, judging from the elevated pitch of his voice must have been partially deaf, sat on one of the stools at the counter, relaying to Kelly Ann his problem with birds nesting on his porch and making such a mess. A man and woman in their mid-forties sat at a booth catty-corner from Libby and Will. Libby wondered if they were married or just co-workers.

"I just can't get it out of my head that anyone who was pregnant and happy about it would kill herself. It just doesn't make sense," Libby said as she lifted a forkful of blueberry pie to her mouth.

"Does seem strange. I can do a little more digging, but I'm not sure if I'll be able to find anything. Sheriff Tucker may not like me snooping into a closed case of his. He's been around for I don't know how long, and I'm still considered the new kid on the block. When I mentioned the case to him, he did say something curious."

Libby leaned forward. "What?"

"He said it was just rumor, but there was talk of a possible affair the husband was having. It may be nothing. But Tucker also said something about being good friends with Reynolds. I wonder if that had anything to do with why there was no autopsy done. The good-old-boy system is alive and well, I believe."

"I don't want you to get into any trouble looking into the case."

"I can handle Tucker, and I know how to be discreet." Will took a sip of his coffee and leaned back against the booth. "So, have you adjusted to the culture shock? Moving from Baltimore."

Libby smiled. "It's different. But I love it. I know most people would go stir-crazy without the activities you have in the city. I guess it reminds me of my childhood. I grew up in a small town."

Will nodded.

The couple had left the diner. Glancing out the picture window, Libby watched as they walked arm in arm. She assumed they were married, but then thought, maybe not. She looked back at Will and caught him studying her face. She quickly averted her eyes to her half-eaten slice of pie. His gaze made her cheeks flush slightly.

"Where'd you grow up?" Will asked.

"Connecticut." She smiled and placed her hair that had fallen forward behind her ear. "A little town called Bantam. I'm sure you've never heard of it."

Will shook his head.

"Home of the Bantam Cinema." Libby laughed. "We had the oldest running movie house in Connecticut." Libby watched Kelly Ann clean the counter in circular swipes as she nodded to the elderly man who was still complaining about his bird problem. The smell of bacon grease hung in the air. "I noticed an old drive-in theater on the north side of town the other day. That's something you don't see anymore. Do you know if it still plays movies?"

Will nodded. "Only in the summer on the weekends." He smiled. "I've had to drive out there a couple of times, breaking up fights. But mostly it's just young kids going out there to make out. Remember those days?"

Libby felt her cheeks get hot again. She remembered her huge crush on Billy McKay in ninth grade. The first boy she'd ever kissed. She'd been a late bloomer. Tall and lanky her whole childhood, it wasn't until high school she finally began to look less like a boy. "Where'd you grow up?"

"I was born in California. I moved to Essex when I was fifteen. I remember thinking my life had ended."

"I take it you liked living in California."

Will told her about his surfing days and how he'd competed in tournaments. Libby asked him what made him want to go into law enforcement, and he told her that he'd been obsessed with detective shows on TV and detective books as a kid.

"Did you ever read any of Gertrude Chandler? *The Box-Car Children?*"

"Oh, yeah. Wasn't there one called *Mystery Ranch* or something like that?"

Libby nodded. "I remember I had this favorite spot I'd go to when I was a kid. It was out behind our house through this path in the woods that led to a small creek. There was this perfect rock, long and flat, that jutted out over the water. I'd take whatever book I was reading at the time and head out to that rock and sit for hours, reading and conjuring up mysteries of my own."

Libby was shocked when she noticed the hands of the round clock on the wall read ten of three. They'd been talking for over an hour. Will said he had to get back to the station. They stood on the sidewalk, and Will told her he'd let her know if he found anything interesting with the Reynolds case. She walked away feeling happy. It had been so long since she'd had a normal conversation with anyone.

10

Will was out on a call that had come in from a woman who claimed her husband was a no-good drunk, and if someone didn't come over right away, she would beat him sober with an iron skillet.

As Will drove along Foxhall Road about five miles out of town, he noticed a large tract of land that had white pipes protruding from the ground. Someone had been doing perc tests to see if the land could be subdivided. He wondered who owned the land and who was developing it. Sheriff Tucker's words replayed in his head about John Reynolds' wanting to bring growth to the area. Could the land belong to him? If what Tucker had said was true, it would be a huge conflict of interest for Reynolds to use his Washington influence to get a highway into town so he could benefit from it. Will wondered how many people knew about Reynolds' plan.

The tires on the patrol car crunched against the gravel as Will pulled into the driveway of the Thompson house. The lawn, made up of overgrown weeds, was cluttered with various pieces of farm equipment, a rusted old tractor, and other nondescript items in declining stages of disrepair, now permanent fixtures in the yard. The sun glinted off a large metal blade that stood above the tall grass surrounding it, an attachment to one of the tractors. Will swatted at the flies that buzzed around his head.

He saw no sign of either of the Thompsons, and the house was quiet as he approached the front door. He wiped the sweat from his forehead, thinking about the background he'd learned about the owners of the farm from Maggie. Jimmy and Ada Thompson had lived for over forty years in the house. Jimmy Thompson had inherited the property from his father who had farmed it, as did his father before him. What had once been over a thousand acres was now only twenty. Jimmy had long ago given up farming and instead raised chickens and hogs, which yielded a modest profit.

Will knocked on the weathered wooden door. After a few minutes, the door opened to reveal Ada Thompson clad in a flowered cotton housecoat with snap buttons up the front; tiny curlers adorned her gray hair.

"Well, it's about time," she said as she swung the door wider for Will to enter.

"Is everything all right, ma'am?"

"It is now. You took so long, the damn fool's passed out." She gestured toward the small living room right off the foyer entrance. Jimmy was sprawled out on the sofa in a pair of faded overalls with no shirt. The sound of snoring resonated from the room. Will was surprised to see how spotless the house was compared to the way things looked outside. The old, wide, plank pine floors were swept clean; white-fringed curtains hung at the windows; and everything was neatly in its place.

"Come on into the kitchen. I got a pot a beans on the stove I need to check on." Will followed Ada, who walked with an arthritic gait in her slippered feet down the hallway to the kitchen. The house smelled of mothballs.

"Have a seat."

"Ma'am, is everything OK? Is there anything you want me to do?"

"I'd love for you to kick some sense into that lump of a husband, but I know you won't, so why don't you just have a seat. I'll fix you a slice of my peach pie and a glass of lemonade."

The kitchen was just as tidy as the living room. A white metal table with four white wooden chairs around it stood in the center of the room. Red and white checked curtains were at the window, and Will spotted the pie sitting on the gold-flecked, white Formica countertop. Will quickly surmised that Ada Thompson was the driving force in this marriage.

He reluctantly sat down after Ada kept insisting he have some pie. After all, he drove all the way out here; it shouldn't be for nothing. Will sensed the woman was desperate for company and wanted someone to listen to her troubles.

"So, what exactly was your husband doing when you called?" Will bit into the homemade peach pie, thinking to himself it was some of the best pie he had ever eaten.

"It's what he wasn't doing. His drinking has gotten so bad. I have to do everything now. He won't even take care of the chickens or hogs anymore." Ada shook her head slowly and then continued, "All I said was to go down and check on the fans in the chicken house. We've been having trouble with the circuits out there, and if the fans blow out, the chickens will surely die in this heat. It wasn't even noon yet, and he had already been hittin' the sauce. He hides it from me, but he's not fooling anyone." Ada gave Will a look, her hazel eyes revealing years of love that had now turned to frustration. "I know when he's been drinking. So, I was bakin' my pie and in the middle of canning beans when he comes weaving into the kitchen, mumbling some nonsense. So, I said to him, 'Make yourself useful, and go check on the fans.' I don't know what got into him, but he started yellin' at me and telling me no woman was going to boss him around, and I needed to know my place around here." Ada imitated Jimmy's deep, gruff voice. "I just laughed at him and told him I didn't want any drunken fool in my kitchen, and he could just hightail it out of here right now. But he was a fired up, and he starts yellin' that he wasn't drunk, but if he was, it was because he was married to such a mean woman who drove him to drink."

Will watched as Ada dabbed her handkerchief at the corners of her eyes. He felt sorry for her and pictured that at one time they'd had a happy marriage. He could never imagine Julie and him becoming like this. He wondered if it was the alcohol that caused the problems. Or, were there problems that caused him to drink? Either way, the situation was not good.

"How long has your husband been drinking?"

"Oh, off and on for as long as I can remember. But it's gotten worse these past few years. I remember when we were kids"—Ada's face changed completely; a smile came to her lips, and her eyes crinkled at the corners—"Jimmy was so *handsome*. I had the biggest crush on him in junior high. It wasn't until junior prom in high school that he actually noticed me. We didn't go to the prom together, but we ended up dancing practically every dance together, and boy could he dance." She sat there for a few seconds reminiscing, and then she sat erect at the table. "The trouble with Jimmy is he's had it too easy all his life. The kids in school always liked him; he was good in sports; and he always knew he would have his daddy's farm. The one thing he didn't have was gumption. We got married right out of high school, and I moved into this house with him and his parents.

"After we had our two kids, the house got too crowded, and Jimmy's parents decided to move to Florida, which had always been a dream of his dad's. But that left Jimmy to run the farm all by himself. We had around a thousand acres back then. Farming's hard work, you see, and a lot of it is out of your control. We had a few back-to-back bad years with the weather, and that's when Jimmy began selling off some of the land. He just kinda gave up on farming. I was real worried back then. I mean, we had kids to raise and send to college. Money had never been an issue, but I knew it would be if we had no income. I was the one who had suggested we get into chickens and hogs. I thought maybe something different would spark his interest and get him to doing somethin'. But he had already started his binges. He would drink sometimes for days in a row and just sit in front of the TV, and then he would eventually sober up and be real good for weeks at a time. In fact, there were times I thought things would be OK. He got into raising the livestock and did a pretty good job. We were able to send both of our kids, Jenna and Jack, to college." Her eyes sparkled when she mentioned their names.

"Where are your children now? Do they live close by?"

"Oh, no, you know how it is; they got a taste of that city life and didn't want any part of farming. Jack lives outside of Atlanta, and Jenna is living in Alexandria. I know that's not far away, but she's got one of them important jobs in politics and hardly has the time to come back home. I do get to see her from time to time and on holidays." She stopped for a minute, turning the handkerchief around in her hand. "Jack is real busy with his job, working for some investment bank down there. But I do have three beautiful grandchildren from him. Here, let me show you." She jumped up from the table and went into the other room.

Will glanced at his wristwatch. He really should be getting back to the station. After a few minutes, Ada returned carrying a silver framed photo of the three grandchildren, all dressed up and posing for the studio shot. "Aren't they beautiful!" Ada exclaimed, holding the photo in front of Will and sitting back down at the table.

"Yes, they are," Will replied, noticing they were close to his own children's ages. Will stood up and pushed his chair in. "I'm sorry, ma'am, but I really need to get back. If you want me to say anything to your husband, I will."

"No, I'm fine. He'll sleep it off. Tomorrow's another day." She set the photo on the table but continued studying the children's faces.

"No need to get up; I can find my own way out. And thanks for the pie. It was the best I've ever had."

Ada beamed. "Why, thank you."

Will drove back to town, his mind on the Thompsons and all the other families he had come across in his line of work as a police officer. He thought of his own family growing up. The youngest, with four older sisters, he remembered his father always had several drinks in the evening, but he'd never missed a day of work.

Family dynamics and their complexities had always fascinated him. He had yet to come across a "perfect family." He thought about his own marriage. Julie and he had been together so long he couldn't remember a time without her. They'd had their ups and downs over the years—the usual things, like money problems and juggling their schedules with the kids—but the past few months, tension was mounting between them. Julie would snap at him and the kids with barely any provocation. He kept telling himself that once the baby was born things would get better, but he was beginning to wonder if that was true. He thought about the Thompsons again. At least their children had turned out fine.

Will passed the drive-in theater. The giant white screen loomed over the now-empty parking lot. His mind drifted to Libby and the lunch they'd had together. He hadn't laughed that much in a long time. Then he thought of the manila folder still in his desk drawer. C. Reynolds—

Closed. Was there anything he could do with that case?

11

J osh walked into the kitchen covered in grease. He had been working on the lawnmower, which was sputtering black smoke. He told Libby he would have to go into town to pick up a part. He was wearing a pair of torn jeans and a worn-out University of Maryland T-shirt from his college days. His normally neatly combed dark hair was disheveled, and his face was smudged with dirt. Something stirred inside Libby. She got up from the kitchen table where she'd been making her list for the day and gave him a kiss on his cheek. He smelled of Old Spice deodorant mixed with sweat.

For the past couple of weeks, her libido had been in overdrive. She'd read in one of her library books that it happened to some women during pregnancy. Was that why she had visions of Josh grabbing her and pressing her against the kitchen wall, his hands caressing her while his mouth explored her body? She squeezed his arm, but instead of the fantasy that played in her head, he patted her on the shoulder and then grabbed the car keys, heading for the door.

She slumped down at the table. Ever since she'd told Josh she was pregnant, he'd been treating her differently, like he was afraid to touch her. After several minutes of brooding, she looked down at the to-do list sitting in front of her and tried to focus on the chores she'd planned for the day. It was Saturday, and they were going to the Seevers' for dinner. She thought about Will. They had a lot in common. She smiled thinking about their conversation at the diner the other day. She was looking forward to the visit.

She was kneeling down, yanking on a stubborn weed in one of the beds, when she heard Stella barking at something in the tall reeds near the water. She looked up from her gardening, glancing in Stella's direction. "What is it, girl?" Hearing a rustling in the reeds, she stood and walked toward Stella, who was still barking and wagging her tail. Just then, she saw the young boy from the boathouse, Trevor Clay, dodge out of the reeds.

"Wait! Trevor, come here!"

When he heard his name, he stopped, surprised, and turned toward Libby. "How'd you know my name?"

"A friend told me. I'm Libby Langston. My husband Josh and I live here now. I hear your parents used to take care of this place for the previous owners."

"Yeah."

"I take it you like to come here. I saw you the other day in the boathouse. You didn't have to run away."

"My mama would get mad if she thought I was over here."

"Why is that?"

"She says now that people is living here, I shouldn't be trespassing."

"I don't mind. In fact, how would you like to help me with some odd jobs around here? I could pay you."

"I would have to ask my mama. If she says it's OK, then I guess I can."

"Great! I tell you what. Why don't you run home, ask your mother if you can help out, and then come back. I've got a few things you could do today."

"My mama's sleeping right now, but I can help you today. I'll ask her tonight if I can come back."

"OK, that sounds like a deal. Come over here, and you can help me haul away these weeds." Libby led Trevor over to where she'd been working. She asked him to get the wheelbarrow out of the boathouse and roll it over. He took off running barefoot down the stone path and was back in minutes with the wheelbarrow.

"Why don't you pick up all the weeds in these piles and put them in the wheelbarrow. Then, while I plant these flowers, you can weed further down the garden."

"OK," Trevor said enthusiastically. He worked quickly but carefully, scooping up all the pulled weeds, making sure he left nothing behind. For about an hour, they worked side by side in the garden.

"So, I guess you're too young to remember the previous owners."

"Yes, ma'am, but I heard stories from my mama and daddy."

"What kind of stories?"

"There were all sorts. I know my mama loved Miss Cecilia. She said she was one of the kindest women she had ever met. She always treated my mama like she was one of the family."

"What about Mr. Reynolds?"

"I don't know much about him." Trevor sat back on his haunches and thought for a minute. "But I know my mama didn't like him like she did Miss Cecilia."

"Why's that?" Libby asked.

"I don't know if I should be repeatin' this stuff," Trevor said, looking uncomfortable.

From the corner of her eye, Libby caught sight of Josh coming through the French doors, walking toward them. She stood up and brushed the dirt off her shorts. "Josh, I want you to meet Trevor; he lives around the Point. I've hired him to help me with the gardens."

"Hi, Trevor. Nice to meet you," Josh said, extending his hand. Trevor quickly wiped his hands on his shorts and gave Josh a firm handshake.

"Trevor's parents used to work for the Reynolds when they owned the house."

"And you're going to carry on the family tradition. Well, it's nice to have you here. I know Libby could really use the help."

"Thank you, sir."

"Call me Josh."

"Thank you, Mr. Josh."

Josh chuckled. It was refreshing to meet a young person wanting to work and having such good manners as well. "How old are you, Trevor?"

"I'm ten. My birthday was last week. My parents gave me a big party now that I'm double digits."

Libby and Josh both laughed.

"I tell you what, Trevor. Why don't we take a break and have some lemonade," Libby suggested.

"My mama wouldn't want me to be a bother."

"You're no bother. You've worked hard; you deserve a cool drink in this heat. Come on up to the house," she said.

Josh and Trevor sat out on the back porch while Libby went inside. She returned carrying a tray with three glasses and a pitcher of fresh lemonade. She poured Trevor a glass, and he finished it in three gulps.

"You must've been thirsty. Have another," Libby said as she filled his glass again.

"I was asking Trevor if he knew anything about lawnmowers, and he said he's watched his father work on his," Josh said. "Would you mind if I borrowed him for a little while? I could use some help getting this new part installed."

"That's fine. I think we've done enough in the yard today. I need to do some things inside. How long can you stay?" Libby asked Trevor.

"I don't have to be back home for a while. My mama sleeps a long time; she doesn't feel so good lately."

"OK. I'll pay you when you and Josh are finished with the lawn-mower. How does eight dollars an hour sound?"

"That sounds great!" Trevor said, his eyes as round as saucers.

On the drive over to the Seevers', Libby glanced down at her blue flowered sundress. She'd tried on at least ten outfits before picking the soft cotton sundress, an old standby. Though it was too soon for maternity clothes, her stomach was already fuller, making her clothes tight around the waist. Lately, she'd found herself unbuttoning her shorts because they were getting uncomfortable. Not only did her dress complement her eyes, making them look even bluer, but it also had an empire waistline and flowed loosely down to about mid-calf. She'd been surprised to see how snug the bodice was when she put it on. She'd thought her bustline had increased, and after studying her reflection in the mirror, her A-cup breasts had definitely grown. She hoped they'd stay that way.

Her arms were warm from the slight burn she'd gotten working in the yard, even though she'd loaded on the sunblock. She rarely wore makeup, but she'd applied mascara, some blush, and even a hint of lipstick. The effect had been dramatic, accentuating her large eyes and lips.

She glanced over at Josh. He'd hardly said two words to her when they were getting ready. He'd barely even looked at her when she asked him what he thought of the dress. "You look nice" had been his only reply. *Nice.* Just what she wanted to hear. Why not beautiful or glowing? Did he not find her attractive anymore?

Libby looked at the clock on the dashboard. She'd been anxiously prodding Josh to hurry up before they'd left the house. She wanted so badly for them to become friends with the Seevers, and she intended to make a good first impression. The Seevers' house, a two-story Victorian, was on a tree-lined street just outside of town.

When they rang the bell, Sara, the youngest, greeted them at the door. "My mommy's in the kitchen," she said before running off into another room. Josh and Libby entered the house and looked around for Will or Julie. A children's television show played loudly from another room.

They stood in the foyer, wondering if they should just walk on in, when Nathan flew around the corner with the barking puppy hot on his trail. Nathan crashed straight into Josh's legs. "Sorry," he shouted, before continuing on his flight. "Oh, hi," Wyeth said rounding the corner in pursuit of Nathan. "My mom's in the kitchen, and my dad's out back. You can go on back there."

"Thanks," Josh replied.

Josh and Libby picked their way across the living room floor littered with toys and made their way to the kitchen.

"Hello?" Libby called out as they entered the room. Julie was taking something out of the oven.

"Hi! Come on in. Dinner's almost ready."

"I brought a pie," Libby said and set it on the counter.

"Great! Thanks. Will's out back grilling, if you'd like to go back there. I'll only be a few more minutes in here."

"Do you need any help?" Libby asked.

"If you don't mind taking that tray out back, I thought we could eat out on the patio; it's such a nice evening."

"Sure." Libby grabbed the tray of plates, silverware, and napkins, and she and Josh went through the back door to the patio. Will, clad in an apron, was basting the barbequed chicken on the grill.

"Smells great!" Josh said.

Will turned around. "Hey! Hope it tastes as good as it smells." He reached out and shook Josh's hand. Libby placed the tray on the large round table. "I see Julie has already put you to work." Will gave her a hug and then stood back. "Wow, you look fantastic! Pregnancy must agree with you."

"Thanks." Libby's cheeks burned as she glanced over at Josh.

"Can I get you a beer or something else to drink?" Will asked them both.

"I'd love a beer," Josh replied.

"Ice water is fine for me."

"After tonight I hope you don't regret what you're getting into."

Libby frowned, and then it dawned on her that he meant having kids. "Never," she replied with a laugh. She began arranging the plates around the metal patio table sheltered by a red umbrella. Just then the boys came running out into the backyard, the screen door slamming behind them.

"Hey, slow down, guys. What did I tell you about slamming the door?"

"Sorry, Dad," they yelled as they ran past them into the fenced-in yard filled with a swing set, sandbox, bikes in various sizes, and more toys scattered about.

"I've got some beers in that cooler, Josh. Help yourself," Will said, pointing to a Styrofoam cooler on the ground. He turned to Libby. "Let me get you an ice water."

"I can get it," Libby said. She went back into the kitchen where Sara was sitting on the floor with a baby doll, attempting to wrap it up in a blanket. Julie was in the process of tossing a salad.

"Mommy, I can't get it right!" Sara said, frustrated.

"You're doing fine, honey. Just keep trying."

"Would you like some help?" Libby asked as she knelt down next to Sara.

"OK," Sara replied.

"Here, you hold her while I get the blanket laid out." Libby handed the doll to Sara, laid the blanket on the wood floor, and then folded it into a triangle. She then took the doll from Sara and placed her on the blanket. She took the point of the triangle, folded it up toward the baby doll, and then took each corner and wrapped it snuggly around. Libby handed the doll back to Sara. "There you go, a nice and cozy, bundled baby."

"Thank you," Sara said as she got up and ran out of the room.

"She's going to have an adjustment when the baby comes," Julie said. "She's been the baby for so long. I've been trying to explain things to her. You know, what to expect. She's gotten very attached to her baby doll lately."

"I can't wait to be bundling a baby for real."

Julie laughed. "I remember those days. But I wouldn't rush it if I were you. Cherish the time while the baby is still inside and contained." Julie brushed her hair back from her face. Libby noticed she was sweating, and her face was slightly flushed.

"Are you OK?" Libby asked.

"I just need to sit down for a few minutes. The heat gets to me."

"Sit down. Tell me what needs to be done, and I'll do it for you."

"Oh, thank you! What a great hostess I am. I invite you over for dinner and then have you do the work."

"Don't be silly. It looks like most of the work is done." Libby poured two glasses of ice water.

Julie sat down at the kitchen table and put her feet up on one of the other chairs. "I had these big plans for a nice dinner party, with the table set and the food all ready before you got here, but everything just fell apart. You all are the first people we've had over since we moved. It's been so hard to meet people."

"I know the feeling. Coming from the city to a small town is an adjustment. You'd think in a small town it would be easier to meet people, but it isn't." Then Libby added, "Well, we can stick together."

"Yeah, we can start our own little group. Oh, I wanted to ask you, did you call Dr. Crawford?"

"I have an appointment next week. I can't wait to find out how far along I am. I have a guess, but I'm not sure."

"Well, like I said, enjoy the serenity while you can." Julie watched Libby dishing the asparagus into a serving bowl. "Libby, I feel bad; let me get Will to finish this up."

"I don't mind. Looking at those feet of yours, I think you need to be queen for a day and just rest."

Julie snorted. "I feel more like QEII right now."

The conversation flowed at dinner in between interruptions from Sara's spilled glass of milk and Nathan's being caught feeding Milo his chicken under the table. They talked of raising children and training dogs. And how the two were somewhat similar, unanimously agreeing that consistency is most important. When the kids had finished their dinner, Will excused them from the table and said they could go in and pick out a DVD to watch. All three went running into the house, each shouting out a different movie title they wanted. Will added before they got to the door, "And if you can't agree on a movie, then you all can just get ready for bed." They didn't say another word after that.

Will got up from the table and got two more beers from the cooler, handing one to Josh.

"Thanks. The food's fantastic. This chicken was done perfectly; I need to get your secret," Josh said as he helped himself to more of the macaroni casserole.

"The secret to the chicken is the brining; it keeps it moist. You just soak it in salted water for about six hours before you're ready to cook it," Will said as he sat back down at the table.

"I'll have to remember that trick," Josh replied.

"Oh, Libby, I wanted to tell you I think there might be some things I can look into with the case."

Josh glanced over at Libby.

Libby recognized that look in Josh's eye. He didn't like it when she meddled in things he felt was none of their business. "There's things about Cecilia's death that don't add up," she said to Josh, trying to explain the situation.

"What's the point in bringing all this up now?" Josh asked.

"There's no statute of limitations on murder," Will replied.

"*Murder?* What makes you think she was murdered?" Josh set his fork down.

"I didn't say she was. It's just, from glancing at the case file, it didn't look to me like there was enough information to rule either way. There really wasn't any kind of an investigation done at all."

"I can't imagine taking your own life. How desperate she must've been," Julie said, shaking her head.

Libby thought about Elizabeth. "Ironically, another woman who lived in the house years ago committed suicide as well, but we know why she did. She'd lost her daughter."

"Don't you find that creepy? Two people killing themselves in your house?" Julie asked. "Did you know about this before you bought the house?"

"No."

"How'd you find out about the other woman?"

Libby's eyes darted toward Josh. She wondered if she should tell them about the ghost. Why not? If they're going to think she's crazy, she might as well find out now. "I don't want to sound like a nut, but I believe our house is haunted."

"Haunted?" Will and Julie replied in unison.

Libby nodded.

"Why do you think it's haunted?" Will asked.

"Because I saw her—Elizabeth. She's the other woman who killed herself."

Josh was staring at his beer bottle, turning it slowly in his hand.

Libby continued, "Josh thinks I'm insane, and I know it sounds crazy, but seeing is believing. Before I moved into that house, I probably would've told you there was no such thing as a ghost."

Julie and Will glanced at each other, and then Julie said, "You hear about old houses being haunted all the time. Right, Will?"

Will raised his eyebrows.

"Well, not *all* the time," Julie added. "But it happens. I remember reading an article about a house in Gettysburg that was so haunted no one could live there."

"Sometimes our imagination plays tricks on us," Josh said, still staring at his beer.

"It was *not* my imagination," Libby shot back at Josh.

"You even said so yourself, that maybe your hormones from the pregnancy altered what you saw."

Libby inhaled and exhaled with measured breaths, her eyes staring down at her lap to a barbeque stain on her dress. She rubbed her hand over it. "I said maybe that was possible. But I don't think that's the case. Even Tassie saw her."

"Tassie?" Julie asked.

Libby told them about Tassie. "She knows all about ghosts." Libby saw the strained look in Josh's eyes and then glanced over at Will who was fidgeting with his beer, his eyes averted. She felt her cheeks get hot. They all thought she was a lunatic. "Maybe I shouldn't have mentioned this. I don't want you to think I'm weird or something. I really am a normal person." She was sounding even weirder now, she thought. She stopped talking, feeling as if she might cry. She was ruining their evening. These people were never going to want to be friends.

Julie reached over and patted Libby's arm. "We don't think you're weird at all. Do we, Will?" She looked over at Will.

"No, of course not." Will smiled.

"Go on, Libby. I want to hear more about what you saw," Julie said, encouraging Libby to continue. Josh sat in silence, looking down at the table.

"Maybe we should talk about something else," Libby replied.

"No, I'm really interested. I love watching those shows on TV about paranormal stuff."

Libby smiled at Julie. At least she had one on her side. She glanced back at Josh with a look asking for his OK. He shrugged and said, "Go ahead."

She relayed the progression of events from finding the album in the attic to Elizabeth's cryptic message, "*Save her*."

"Interesting," Will said as he sipped on his beer.

"I wonder if it has something to do with Cecilia. That's why I was hoping you could open up the investigation again," Libby said to Will.

"Libby, that's ridiculous. I'm sure Will has more important things to do than dredge up old case files," Josh said.

"It's no problem, as long as the sheriff doesn't put a stop to it," Will said. "It might be fun. My usual day consists of calls for a missing bicycle or a cow that's gotten loose on the road. This case looks interesting."

"Look, Will," Josh replied, "We don't want you to stir up trouble with your boss. I think it would be better for all if we just left this thing alone." Josh's jaw twitched.

"Josh, I'm sure Will won't do anything to jeopardize his career," Libby said.

"Who wants dessert?" Julie interjected. "That pie you brought, Libby, looked delicious."

Josh slammed the car door and then jammed the keys in the ignition. He was fuming, but he kept his words steady: "You've got to stop playing amateur detective. If you're bored, try doing something else around the house. God knows there's a million things that need fixing."

Libby stared out the car window, hurt by his words. "You don't know what it's like. I really have seen this woman, and I think I'm seeing her for a reason. I just have to find out what that is."

"Lib, the past few months have been pretty hectic. We moved to a new place; I've been really busy at work; and now you find out you're pregnant. Did you ever think that maybe you're under a lot of stress? Listen to what you've been saying. I mean, you even told the Seevers that ghosts are talking to you. Does that sound rational?"

"Only if it's true. I don't know how I can convince you this is really happening."

"All right, maybe it is true. But can you look at this from my perspective? I'm about to take on one of the most influential clients I've ever had, and you want to investigate his wife's death that took place twenty years ago. Do you see how crazy that sounds? I can't believe you got Will involved with this as well. Hopefully he'll drop it."

Libby was silent as she watched the haze of passing streetlights. The evening hadn't gone as she had expected. They pulled into the driveway, neither one saying anything, each in their own thoughts. Libby didn't want to fight, and she felt that lately that's all they'd been doing.

She sat at the foot of the bed, the first to break the icy silence. "I'm sorry. I know Reynolds is an important client. I won't pursue this if you don't want me to."

"Thanks," Josh said as he walked past her to the closet, not even looking at her. He took off his shoes and put them away. He then pulled his polo shirt over his head and threw it down on the floor.

"Do you still find me attractive?" she asked in a barely audible voice.

"What did you say?" Josh turned around.

"I feel like you don't even look at me anymore. Ever since you found out I was pregnant, you've changed. You've been treating me as if I were the Madonna or something. Like you're afraid to even touch me." Tears spilled down her cheeks.

Josh walked over to the bed. "You can't be serious," he said with surprise, but the look on her face told him she was. He hated seeing her upset. She got up from the bed and started to walk past him. He grabbed her arm before she got too far and spun her around. Without saying a word, he put his hands on both sides of her face, forcing her to look at him. He kissed her. His fingers moved from her face to her hair, entwined in her blonde curls. He picked her up, laid her on the bed, and then slowly began to undress her.

12

L ibby and Josh spent Sunday boat shopping in Annapolis. Now that the pier renovations were underway, Josh was eager to buy a boat. They looked at small skiffs all the way up to large sailing yachts. Josh had fallen in love with a 38' Sparkman & Stephens sloop, but the price tag was a bit steep. After going to several dealers, he decided to go online and see if he could find a used one for a better price. He'd spent the last hour in the den on the computer.

Libby was in the kitchen making dinner and talking with her mother, Diana, on the phone. Diana had caught Libby up on all that was happening with her sister. Emily was three and a half years older than Libby and a clone of their mother, not only in personality, but in looks. Libby had always been envious of their straight auburn hair that always cooperated.

Emily had married her high school sweetheart, Michael, right after graduation from Northwestern where they'd both attended;

he'd received an MBA while she a degree in Fine Arts. They immediately went on to have three children, who were now twelve, ten, and seven. Michael worked at an investment firm in Chicago, and they lived in a large home in Evanston, Illinois, on a beautiful tree-lined street. Emily had never worked outside the home.

Libby missed her sister and wished they could see each other more often than the usual twice-a-year visits. Libby and Josh went to Evanston for Christmas, and Emily's family spent a week with them every summer at the beach in Ocean City. It was hard to find the time for any other visits. Emily had a busy life, chauffeuring kids from sports practices to art and music classes. Diana told Libby that Lindsay, the oldest daughter, was still playing the flute at the Music Institute of Chicago. She'd performed in several recitals and was getting recognition from some important people in the music industry. Diana went on to tell her how she hoped Lindsay would still want to go to Bryn Mawr, Diana's alma mater, when it came time for college; since neither of her daughters had followed in her footsteps, at least her granddaughter could.

Emily had to be the best mom on the planet, Libby thought. She'd made her own baby food and joined all the right playgroups when the kids were young and school groups when they got older. She had everything prepared for them right down to the college she wanted them to go to someday. Libby knew she'd never be as organized as her sister, but maybe she could get some pointers from her now that she was going to have a child of her own. *A child of my own.* Just thinking about it made her feel ecstatic.

"I told Emily you were expecting. I hope you don't mind," her mother said over the phone.

"I figured you'd tell her. I called her the other day, and she said you'd already told her the news. She still might try and bring the kids out before the summer is over." Libby sprinkled oregano into the big pot on the stove. "I wanted—"

"Wait until you see Jonathon; he's shot up like a weed," Diana said, cutting Libby off. "He's taller than Lindsay now. And Becca's taking riding lessons. Emily says she's a natural; takes after her grandmother."

Libby thought about her riding days. She hadn't stuck with it. A twinge of regret swept through her. Was there anything she was good at?

Her mother asked her what she'd been up to, and she started to mention the ghost but then changed her mind. She wasn't sure how her mother would take it. Instead, she told her about the work she'd done in the gardens and around the house.

"Your father and I were at Emily's last month," Diana continued. "Michael was away on business. His new job involves a lot more traveling. I hope it doesn't put too much of a strain on their marriage."

Libby stirred the sauce for the pasta as her eyes focused on the afternoon sun that shot through the stained glass window over the sink, creating patterns of light on the large stainless steel stove. "They've always been the perfect couple. I can't imagine them having any problems."

"Raising kids is a lot of work, and it's hard to do it alone," Diana said.

Libby tasted the sauce off the large wooden spoon. "I worry. Josh has been working long hours lately. I keep waiting for the case he's been on to be over so things can get back to normal. But what if they don't?" She shook some salt into the pot. "What if he always works this much?"

"I'm sure Josh will be a devoted dad."

Libby turned the light down on the gas stove and went outside with Stella to sit on the back porch while the sauce simmered. A breeze coming off the water brought the scent of marsh grass mixed with a hint of jasmine.

Diana added, "What do you plan on doing about work? Are you still going to teach in the fall?"

"I haven't even thought about it. I want to teach, but if I have to take off in the middle of the school year, it may be harder for them to find a replacement."

"Do you plan on going back to work after the baby's born?"

"I don't know." Libby realized she hadn't even thought that out.

"Well, I think you should have some kind of plan in mind. If you go back, you need to decide if you'll get a nanny or take the baby to daycare."

A low fog hung along the edge of the shore. Libby stared out at the murky water. Nannies, daycare...Why hadn't she thought of any of this? All the time they'd been trying to get pregnant, they'd never even discussed it.

"How does Josh feel about it?" Diana asked.

"I don't know."

"I think this is something the two of you should discuss. Don't you agree?"

"Yeah." Thoughts swirled in Libby's mind while she watched two geese land silently onto the dark water. What did Josh think about her going back to work? Did she want someone else raising their child? She hadn't even gone to the doctor yet. Her appointment was Tuesday. Once she knew when the baby was due, then she could make concrete plans. She still had plenty of time, she told herself.

The obstetrician's office was located in a medical office park not far from the hospital and only two blocks from historical downtown Easton. Libby entered an office filled with women in various stages of pregnancy. Pastel shades of pink and blue made up the color scheme, with one corner designated as a play area. Four little ones were busily stacking blocks and putting together puzzles.

Libby approached the sliding window. The woman behind the glass smiled and slid the window open. She asked Libby if she was a new patient and then handed her a clipboard with several pages that needed filling out. She marked the spots that required Libby's signature and told her to have a seat.

Her hands were tightly clasped together as she glanced around the spotlessly clean reception area. A fluorescent light flickered and buzzed overhead. She was excited but also anxious. Her periods had been so sporadic; she dreaded that maybe something was wrong.

The hands on the large, square clock on the wall ticked loudly. She'd been waiting for half an hour. Where was Josh? A nurse came to the door and called Libby's name. She stood motionless for a second. She didn't want Josh to miss this. She wondered if she should ask the nurse to skip her and take the next person so she could wait for Josh. "My husband's supposed to be here."

The nurse shrugged and smiled. Libby anxiously looked toward the entrance and then reluctantly followed the nurse, who directed her to a bathroom. After Libby provided a urine specimen, she was ushered into an exam room.

The paper gown made crunching sounds as she adjusted her position on the table. The room was cold. She ran her hand down the goose bumps on her arm. She was irritated with Josh for not being there. He could have called at least. She jumped off the table and rooted her cell phone out of her purse. Josh picked up after two rings. "Hey, Lib, what's up?"

"Did you forget?"

"Forget?—Oh my God! Your appointment. I'm so sorry. I've been tied up with this client all day, and I totally forgot. Where are you?"

Libby forced back her tears. "I'm at the doctor. Where do you think I am?"

"Look, I'll make it up to you. I really am sorry. Call me after you get out, OK?"

Libby heard a knock, and the door to the exam room opened. "I've gotta go." Libby hit the end button on the phone.

Dr. Crawford introduced herself. She was dressed in a flowered lab coat with a stethoscope around her neck. With thick, curly red hair pulled back in a ponytail, she looked to be in her early forties. She shook Libby's hand. They were warm and dry against Libby's sweating palms.

"So, this is your first pregnancy?" Her soft voice put Libby at ease. Libby nodded.

"And it says here you're not sure when the baby was conceived?" The doctor glanced down at the clipboard in her hand.

"That's right," Libby replied. "I mean, I have an idea, but I'm not really sure." She giggled nervously.

"That's fine. It happens more often than you'd think. When was your last menstrual cycle?"

"That's the problem. I'm not sure. About a month ago, I had what I thought was my period, but it only lasted for a day. And before that, I can't remember." Libby went on to explain their recent move and how things had been hectic, so she sort of lost track.

"Well, you're definitely pregnant. The urine test proved that. We'll do an ultrasound, and that will tell us how far along you are."

"OK."

She had Libby lie back on the table and opened the front of Libby's gown. She squirted a cool blue gel on Libby's stomach and then pressed the transducer across her abdomen. Immediately a screen lit up on a machine next to the table. To Libby it looked like an underwater film of abstract objects in motion.

Dr. Crawford continued to move the wand around her abdomen, eyeing the screen. A thumping sound echoed from the machine. She slowed her movement as an image formed. "Here we go. Look at that." She pointed and, at the same time, captured the image, freezing it onto the screen. "It looks like you are at least three months pregnant, maybe closer to four. See this right here?" She circled a small object on the screen with her finger. "That's the fetus. It's hard to tell from this position if it's a boy or girl. Let me see if we can get a better image." She began to move the wand around again, and the screen went into motion. Libby strained to see what it was she was seeing.

Dr. Crawford slowed the wand again and captured another image. "This one is better. I'll print this out for you to take. See? You can even see the arms and legs. I'm afraid it's still too hard to tell the sex from this view, but I'm sure on the next visit we'll know. The heart seems to be beating fine."

"Are you sure I'm that far along?" Libby asked.

"Oh, definitely. The CRL is the best indicator of fetal age, and, looking at this length, I'd say you're fourteen to fifteen weeks. The heartbeat sounds strong. I think everything looks good, so whatever you've been doing keep it up."

"I can't believe I didn't have any symptoms. I never really felt sick." Libby calculated back to when she would have conceived, March, around the time she found the house. Had she done anything she shouldn't have during that time? She couldn't remember taking any medications, and she never drank very much. "I was drinking wine. Is that OK?" she asked, suddenly worried.

"How much?"

"Maybe a glass or two a week."

"I wouldn't worry about it. A couple of ounces of wine now and then won't hurt the baby. You're really fortunate. Some women are extremely sick the first trimester." The doctor wiped the gel off Libby's stomach and told her to get dressed and to meet her in her office where they would set up an appointment schedule. She'd also give Libby some information on birthing classes. After Dr. Crawford left the room, Libby lay there staring at the tiled ceiling. FOUR MONTHS PREGNANT! She quickly did the math. The baby was due in December.

Walking past the shops on her way back to her car, she spotted a pink and white dress hanging in the window of a children's boutique. She paused for a few seconds and then went inside. Hand-crocheted items, hand-sewn quilts, knitted attire, and clothes filled the space.

Looking at a beautifully stitched quilt, she thought about her mother asking her if she'd decided on a color for the nursery yet. And then Tassie's voice popped into her head: *"and Cecilia asked me if I thought yellow was a pretty color for a nursery."*

Yellow is a nice color, Libby thought. Bright and cheery. Maybe she'd do yellow.

Libby picked up a tiny crocheted jacket of the softest yarn. Her fingers caressed the little pearl buttons on the front. She could picture the baby wearing the jacket. She smiled—*her* baby! Again, Cecilia came to mind; how could she have killed herself? But she had to forget about that; she'd promised Josh she wouldn't pursue it anymore.

❧

The house had two identical master suites on either side of the second-floor hallway. Originally, each side had two adjoining rooms, one for the bedroom and one for a sitting/dressing room. In Libby and Josh's bedroom, the sitting room had been converted into a master bath and walk-in closet. The two rooms on the other side of the hall had remained unchanged and Libby thought they'd be perfect for the nursery.

The evening light from the long windows bathed the room in a golden light. Empty, except for a few boxes they'd stored from the move, the room needed little work. The walls could be painted. Wide crown molding ran along the ceiling. The smell of cedar hung in the air.

She pictured the room with a crib, a changing table, and a rocker, and excitement welled inside. She felt giddy. A baby! They were going to be parents. She imagined a mural painted on the wall opposite her. A nautical theme? Or animals? Maybe her mother could do it. Diana had been painting watercolors for years and belonged to an artist's group.

She walked into the adjoining room, thinking it could be a playroom one day filled with toys. She and Josh lying on the floor with the baby, watching him or her crawl for the first time. A wave of sadness washed over her. She suddenly felt all alone. She sunk down on the warm wood floor and rested her head in her hands. Why couldn't Josh have been there today? And why couldn't he be here now? He'd called her on her way home from the doctor's and told her he was going to be late again.

Stella came over to her, nudging her head under Libby's arm and licked her face. Libby lifted her head and hugged Stella, but she couldn't shake the sullen feeling. She fought back tears but then finally gave in, as she sobbed into Stella's warm fur.

13

Libby bolted upright in bed, drenched in sweat. Disoriented, she glanced around, adjusting her eyes to the dark. Josh was snoring softly beside her. Had she had a bad dream? What time was it? Her clock glowed 1:48 a.m. Then it came to her. She'd gone to bed early to read her book. She must have fallen asleep shortly after that because she didn't remember Josh coming home. She flipped the covers back to cool off. Stella lifted her head off the floor, ears perked, her eyes locked on Libby.

Starving, Libby padded down the stairs. After a thorough search of the refrigerator turned up nothing, she decided on a bowl of cereal. Stella scratched at the door to go out. "Stella, it's not really time to get up. You don't have to go out," Libby scolded her gently. Stella's eyes pleaded with her. "OK, maybe you do have to go."

Libby opened the back door and Stella ran out, wagging her tail. Libby stepped out onto the small back porch off the kitchen. A soft breeze blew, lifting strands of her hair, cooling her neck. Libby's nightgown clung to her legs. The almost-full moon shimmered on the water, casting a pale light over the yard. She walked down the steps of the porch and followed Stella, cereal bowl in hand, around to the patio. The night air felt refreshing. She sat down at the table and tried to recall what she'd been dreaming, but nothing came to mind. The day's events replayed in her head. She needed to decide what she was going to do about work. If the baby was due in December, she'd have only three months of teaching. And would she want to go back to work right away? Josh had said he would leave it up to her. The extra money would be nice, but did they really need it? If she didn't return to work after the baby, then would it make sense to even start the school year? She was plagued with indecision. After weighing the pros and cons, she decided to put it out of her mind until tomorrow. She would make a list—that always helped her focus. She finished her cereal and decided to head back to bed.

"Stella," Libby called in a loud whisper. "Come on, girl. Let's go back inside." She looked around the yard but didn't see her. Where had she gone? Libby followed the stone path down to the water. As she neared the beach, she could make out Stella's silhouette. "What are you doing down there?" Stella was wagging her tail but growling a soft, low growl at the same time. Libby's voice grew firmer: "Stella, come on, let's go inside." An eerie feeling crept over her, and she didn't want to be outside alone anymore, but Stella wasn't budging. Libby took a few more steps down the path, nearing the end of the tall reeds. As she got closer to Stella, she noticed the shape of a woman standing on the beach. Her heart jumped, and she let out a small gasp. She saw the distinctive shawl and heard Tassie's voice, telling her not to be afraid. She took a deep breath and spoke, "Elizabeth?" Her voice cracked as the word came out.

The woman slowly turned toward Libby with the same pleading look in her eyes. Libby's eyes locked with hers for several seconds, and then Libby said in a voice just above a whisper, "What do you want?" The image began to flicker, and Libby was afraid she would disappear altogether. "Wait! Don't go. Tell me, what do you want me to do? Why are you here?"

A small smile formed on the woman's lips, and then softly she spoke the same words as before: "Save her."

"Save who? Your daughter? Cecilia? But they're already dead."

"The hummingbird."

Libby was puzzled. Had she heard her correctly? Did she say "the hummingbird"?

"The *hummingbird*? What does that mean?" Libby stepped toward the woman, but as she did, Elizabeth's image began to fade and then was gone completely. Stella came running over to Libby, jumping up and barking. Libby felt as if she'd been suspended in time, as if she were waking from a dream. She searched the beach for any remaining sign of her. Why did Elizabeth keep tormenting her? If she wanted something, why not just tell her? And what in the world did "the hummingbird" mean? Did she want her to save a hummingbird? Libby was getting frustrated; she couldn't stand this guessing game anymore. Anger rose up inside, and she called out in a loud voice, "Fine, don't tell me anything more, but don't expect me to help you either!"

Her words were lost to the lapping water as it ebbed back and forth against the shore.

The next morning, Libby woke to the smell of bacon. Her mouth watered. There was nothing more delicious to the senses than the aroma of bacon, she thought. It was already 9:15. She couldn't believe she'd slept so late. Why did she smell bacon? Was Josh still here? Events from the night before came back to her. Had that been a dream, or had she actually seen Elizabeth down on the beach? Stella was on the floor beside her bed in her usual spot. "Did we really go outside last night, Stella?" Stella cocked her head to one side in her typical response, her tail thumping the floor.

Libby jumped out of bed and headed downstairs, curious as to why Josh was still home. More of the previous night flashed through her head. It wasn't a dream, she was sure; it all seemed too real. She could remember eating the cereal. The cereal! If there was still a bowl in the sink, then she would know for sure.

She breezed into the kitchen. Josh was at the stove, an apron tied over his dress shirt and tie, cooking eggs and bacon. He looked up. "Ah, you're up. I was going to bring this to you in bed."

"What are you doing home still?" Libby padded over to the counter and popped a piece of bacon in her mouth.

"I told you I'd make it up to you for missing the appointment. I canceled my meetings this morning. I don't have to go in until eleven." He leaned over and kissed her cheek.

Libby walked over to the large, white porcelain sink. It was empty. "Did you wash any dishes this morning?"

"What?"

"The dishes—did you wash anything this morning in the sink?"

"I don't know. Why, what's wrong?" A worried expression flickered across Josh's face.

Libby realized she was sounding panicked and steadied her voice. "Nothing." She didn't want to mention Elizabeth to him. She was tired of his doubtful looks.

"Why'd you ask?"

"I woke up in the middle of the night and came down and got a bowl of cereal. I couldn't remember if I put it in the sink or not."

Josh nodded.

Maybe she had imagined the whole thing last night. Was Josh right? Was Elizabeth just some figment of her imagination? She plopped down in one of the kitchen chairs and ran her fingers through her thick hair.

Josh brought a plate of bacon and eggs over to her. "You know, come to think of it, I did put a bowl in the dishwasher."

A smile spread across Libby's face. Aha! She wasn't crazy after all.

"I really like the idea of a nautical theme since you're on the water, but the animal one sounds cute, too. Which one do you like better?" Diana waited for Libby's response on the other end of the phone. "Lib? Did you hear me?"

"I'm sorry, Mom. What'd you say?"

"Is everything OK, dear?"

"Yeah."

"This is your mother you're talking to. I can tell when something is on your mind. Why not talk about it? Is it something between you and Josh?"

"No, not really." Libby hesitated before continuing. She was sitting on the back porch. Josh had left for work. "This is going to sound insane, and I've been debating whether to mention it or not, but I don't want you to think it's anything horrible."

"I'm listening."

Libby knew she had her mother's full attention. "This house is haunted." Libby paused for a second waiting for a reaction, but there was silence on the other end. "I told you it would sound crazy, but hear me out." She told her mother everything. When Libby finished she waited, holding her breath, hoping her mother didn't think she'd completely gone off the deep end.

"Have you told anyone else about it?"

"Just a few people. I don't want anyone to think I'm a nutcase. Josh knows, but he's never seen the ghost himself, so I think he's having a harder time believing it. You know Josh, the pragmatist; he has to have a reasonable explanation for everything, and talking to ghosts is not one of them. He even had me thinking that maybe it was my hormones affecting me, and I was just imagining it all, but someone else saw her, too." Libby told her about Tassie.

"The thing that's really troubling is I don't know what she wants me to do. I asked Elizabeth last night if she was referring to Cecilia, but she wouldn't tell me. All she said was, 'the hummingbird'— whatever that's supposed to mean. I tell you, this ghost thing is exasperating. Every time she appears, instead of giving me answers, she confuses me more. Why can't she just come out and tell me what she wants me to do?"

"I don't know."

"To make things even more complicated, Cecilia Reynolds was the wife of one of Josh's clients." Libby twirled her finger around one of her long curls.

"What?"

"Yeah, can you believe that? I mean it's crazy."

"Yes, it does sound strange."

"The only thing I can think of is Elizabeth wants me to look into Cecilia's death. Maybe it wasn't suicide. Maybe someone murdered her."

"*Murder?* Libby…"

"I know. Don't worry. I've promised Josh that I'll stop looking into it. But I have a friend who's the deputy sheriff in town, and he's going to do some digging. I really want to find out what happened."

"Please don't take this the wrong way—but it seems that you're basing this whole murder thing on the fact that this woman was pregnant, and the only person who says she was pregnant is this Tassie woman. I don't know if you should get mixed up in this. And besides, you told Josh you'd leave it alone. You can't very well go back on your word."

"I know, but maybe I can figure out what Elizabeth wants. I wonder what she meant by 'the hummingbird'? It must be some sort of clue."

"Whatever you do, be careful. You remember the trouble you used to get into as a child."

"Mom, I'm not going to do anything stupid." Libby sighed. She remembered having to defend herself as a child. Like the time she'd convinced herself that Mr. Garrison from across the street had murdered someone. She'd just finished reading one of her mystery novels, and then she'd seen Mr. Garrison packing some boxes in the trunk of his car. And the next day, she'd seen him with a shovel. When she'd told her mother that she'd snuck into his garage looking for more clues, her mother had chastised her and told her to stay away from the Garrisons and that her mystery books were just fiction. People didn't go around killing other people and stuffing them in the trunk of their car.

14

Josh stared at the skyscrapers outside his office window on the twentieth floor. The view of the Inner Harbor cost the firm dearly, which motivated him even more. The buildings made of steel and glass represented power, and he felt a part of it when he gazed out at them. He loved his job; this had been his dream since his early days at law school.

He had grown up in Catonsville, a suburb on the outskirts of the city. Both his parents worked when he was growing up. His father had been a professor of history at UMBC, while his mother worked as a nurse in the public school system. His family had lived in a cookie-cutter house on a street with sidewalks out front, where the kids rode their bikes and skateboards. An only child, he'd had a good childhood. His family lived comfortably and, by most standards, one couldn't ask for anything more, but to Josh that was all he could think about.

He remembered the first time he set foot in a courtroom on a class field trip in middle school, and they were allowed to sit in on a trial. The attorney mesmerized him during his closing arguments to the jury. The timbre of his voice echoed from the dark-paneled walls lined with paintings of historical figures. This was power; this was where he belonged. From that day forward, he knew he wanted something different from what his parents had, and practicing law would be his ticket out.

His rise in the firm might be considered meteoric; at thirty-three, he was already a partner at Abbott & Peterson. Although his name was not on the plaque just yet, he knew it wouldn't be long. It wasn't luck that had gotten him there, though. It was his hard work and his innate ability when it came to trial work. He knew how to connect with a jury and win them over to his side. Most of the firm dealt in corporate law, which was Josh's specialty, but he had the added asset of being an exceptional trial attorney as well. The case he had just finished had saved his client millions of dollars in suit money. Corporate law could be tedious, and to the average person it was boring, but he had a way of breaking it down to a level any layperson could understand. That factor allowed him to bond with the jury, convincing them to rule in favor of his client.

He brushed his hair back from his face and laced his fingers behind his head as he leaned back in his leather chair. He swung back around from the window to face his desk and glanced at the brochure open to the sailboat he'd selected: a new Catalina 250 MkII. It had been a little more than he'd planned on spending, but business was good, so why not? It was scheduled to be delivered in a month, and by that time, the pier would be finished.

Life was good. He would soon be a father, and his career was taking off; he just wished his dad could have been there to witness his accomplishments. His dad had passed away seven years ago from liver cancer, and his mother had died shortly after that from complications after heart surgery. His parents' early deaths were another reason for his ambition. Life was fleeting. He wanted to live his life to the fullest, and money was one sure way to do that. If he kept going at this pace, he could retire by the time he was fifty, maybe even forty-five.

His buzzer went off on his desk, and his secretary's voice came over the intercom: "Mr. Reynolds is on the line. Do you want to take the call?"

"Yes, thanks Stephanie. Put him through." Josh picked up the phone. "Mr. Reynolds, how is everything?"

"Everything is great, and call me John. If we're going to have a working relationship, we should be on a first-name basis."

"OK, John, what can I do for you?"

"I have this little matter I'd like for you to make go away. I was wondering if we could meet this evening at Dominick's for drinks and discuss it?"

Josh glanced at his calendar and saw he had penciled in "Don't forget dinner with the Seevers!" He had written it down that morning when Libby called to remind him of their dinner plans. He hesitated for a second before replying, "Sure, what time?"

"How about half past six?"

"Sounds great. I'll see you then." Josh hung up and stared at the phone. He dreaded calling Libby, but he couldn't blow Reynolds off this early in the game. His hand rested on the receiver before picking it up. He quickly dialed the house. Libby answered after the first ring, her cheerful voice making it that much harder for him.

"It's about tonight."

"Josh, no. Don't tell me you're canceling dinner."

"Hon, I'm sorry, but something has come up, and I can't get out of it. I hate to do this to you, but you can still go without me. I'm sure you'll have fun." He tried to sound upbeat, hoping she'd go along.

"Sure, it's lots of fun to be the third wheel. Josh, I know you're busy at work, but just once it would be nice if I could count on you to be there for me."

"Come on, Lib, you know I would be there if I could. Please don't make me feel any worse than I already do. I promise to make this up to you."

"I'm keeping track; you've got a lot of making up to do, you know."

No sooner had he hung up with Libby, his cell rang on his desk. He looked at the caller ID. It was Diana, Libby's mom. He wondered why she was calling him. When he heard her tone of voice on the line, he knew something was wrong.

"I'm worried about Libby, Josh."

"What do you mean?"

"I spoke with her the other day, and she told me some strange stuff about a ghost and a murder. What is going on?"

Josh leaned back in his chair and ran his hand through his hair. Air blew through his lips. "Listen, Diana, I'm concerned, too. But I'd chalked it up to her hormones, and I think it's all in the past now. She hasn't said anything more to me for a while."

"I don't think she's through with it. It sounded to me like she was still seeing this ghost."

He rubbed his knuckle over his eye. A headache was coming on. "I don't know what to do, Diana. I really don't. Every time I try to tell her how crazy it all sounds, she just gets mad at me. I know there's a logical explanation for all of it, but I can't convince her of that."

"What about a doctor?"

"What?" Josh leaned forward in his chair. The afternoon sun cut a swath of light onto the floor-to-ceiling bookcase across the room.

"A doctor, a psychiatrist, or even her gynecologist. You may be right about the hormones, but maybe it's something else."

"How am I going to get her to go to a doctor when she believes what she's seeing is real? I feel like part of this is my fault. I've been leaving her alone a lot in the new house. And I worry about this woman she met, Tassie or something..."

"She mentioned her to me. You think she's dangerous?"

"No. Not dangerous, just maybe leading Libby down a path she shouldn't be going."

"Do you want me to come there? I can talk to her."

"You don't have to. I'll talk to her. Maybe I can persuade her to get some help."

He hung up the phone and searched in his drawer for the bottle of Advil he kept there. His headache had exploded to a migraine.

He arrived at Dominick's at six-thirty sharp. The exclusive club was an old Baltimore establishment frequented by politicians, lawyers, and judges. On any given night, one could find a Who's Who of Baltimore seated at one of the tables. Even a few prominent sports figures were known to drop in.

Josh opened the heavy oak door out front and stepped into the vestibule. Stopping at the gilt-edged mirror hanging on the wall, he checked his tie, and smoothed his suit jacket. He wore a dark gray Italian suit that he had recently purchased, a burgundy-striped tie, and a gold tiepin. His dark hair was stylishly slicked back, and he felt confident he looked the part as he sauntered across the plush carpet; an official player in the game. He was one of them; he had made it.

Soft jazz music played in the background, and blue pendant lights shone onto the rows of bottles stacked against a mirror behind the bar. Josh searched the room to see if Reynolds had already arrived. He spotted him seated at a booth, talking to a judge that Josh recognized from the courthouse. His polished shoes strode across the dark carpet toward the booth. Reynolds waved to him and motioned for him to sit down. The judge was standing beside the table, and Josh slid in on the side opposite Reynolds.

Reynolds smiled. "Judge Sanders, this is Josh Langston."

"Josh, nice to meet you." They shook hands.

"Nice to meet you, too, sir," Josh replied.

"Josh is my new counsel."

The judge's eyebrows rose as he looked back at Josh. "Is that so?"

Reynolds chuckled. "I know he looks too young to be any good, but don't let that fool you. This guy is going places, I guarantee you; you will be hearing his name a lot."

"Well, that's some endorsement. John doesn't give out too many of those. Good luck, son. You'll need it working with this guy." The judge squeezed Reynolds' shoulder, said good-bye, and then headed back to his own table.

"So, what's your poison?" Reynolds asked Josh as he motioned for the server.

"I'll have a scotch on the rocks."

"Good choice. Is Glenfiddich OK with you?"

Josh nodded, thinking, why wouldn't it be?

Reynolds lifted his empty glass toward the young, attractive server. She smiled and took the glass away. The eye exchange between her and Reynolds suggested this was not their first encounter.

Josh settled back against the thickly padded leather seat. "So, what is this matter you would like to have disappear?"

The dimly lit booth cast a shadow across Reynolds' face. "As you know, the campaign is revving up, and we're doing great in the polls. But in politics, that's when you have to worry. The opposition will be driven to dig up anything they can on me to make things swing the other way, and I'm afraid if they find out about this, that is exactly what will happen. It's really just a nuisance, and normally it wouldn't even be worth my time addressing, but I can't let even the hint of impropriety come out now."

The server returned with the drinks, and Reynolds leaned back in the booth, eyeing her as she set the drinks on the table. He picked up his bourbon and took a slow swallow. He had the smooth self-assurance of a man who has gotten what he wanted for a long time, Josh thought.

He continued, "Several years ago, I purchased some property in Annapolis in a section that, let's just say, was not very desirable. I got the property for a song, tore down the old rundown stores, and replaced them with a brand new shopping center."

"I don't see any harm in that." Josh brought the pale golden liquid to his lips, breathing in the malty smell of the scotch.

"No, but here's where it gets a little sticky. After I was elected to the state Senate, a bill was passed that would stop the funding of low-income housing surrounding that area and basically used the eminent domain factor to condemn the houses and allow a developer to put up luxury condominiums. The area is on the water, and it was just a matter of time this would've happened anyway. Now, out of the blue, the guy I purchased the land from is saying I had knowledge of the eminent domain deal prior to the transaction, and he says he wants to sue me. All I need right now is for some reporter or snoop in the opposition to get a hold of this and say that I used my influence on the legislature for my own advantage. I can't afford any bad publicity right now."

"What exactly did you want me to do?"

"I thought maybe you could meet with the guy and spin some legal bullshit at him and maybe offer him a little something to make the whole thing go away."

"Is there any evidence that you did have prior knowledge of the eminent domain going through?"

"Of course not! But that's not the point. Don't you see? Even the speculation of that would make people unsure about me. I have my guys working on trying to find something on Jamison because then we could use that to shut his side up. But I can't count on that before the election."

"Give me all the paperwork you have relating to the transactions, and I'll see what I can do. I'll have my secretary schedule a meeting with this guy. I wouldn't try and hide it, though. I think you'd be better off coming out with whatever settlement we can get with the guy, and explain that even though you did nothing wrong, you still thought it was the fair thing to do to allow him to gain something from the deal. That way, there would be no point for the other side to leak the story out. There would be no shocker for them to dump on the media. And you may come out looking like a very generous guy."

"I like the way you think." Reynolds held up his bourbon and tilted it toward Josh. "I knew I made the right decision in hiring you. I'll have my people send you all the documents tomorrow." Reynolds leaned back in the booth, flashing Josh his million-dollar smile. "So, how are the house renovations coming along? And how is that pretty wife of yours?"

"Libby's great and so is the house. The renovations are moving pretty well. We also found out we're expecting our first child soon."

"Congratulations! Give my best to Libby. She struck me as a very intelligent woman. I never had any children myself, never really had the time. I've been too busy building an empire." Reynolds chuckled at his own words. "Maybe it's something I should think about now. It would be nice to have someone to leave it all to."

Josh nodded. As he listened to Reynolds, he wondered how much time he'd have to spend with his own baby. Should he have waited, too?

"We should get together sometime," Reynolds continued. "I'll get Cynthia to give Libby a call. We can take you out on the yacht."

"That would be wonderful. I just recently bought a boat myself. It's nothing in your league, but you have to start somewhere."

Reynolds laughed. "Just wait, son. Stick with me, and you'll have your own yacht before you know it."

15

Libby decided on dinner with Julie and Will even though Josh had canceled. At first, she wasn't going to go, but then thought—Why not? She could use the company. Julie and Will were already seated when Libby arrived at the Sunset Grille, a little restaurant in town known for its cream of crab soup. The smell of Old Bay seasoning wafted through the air. A baseball game aired on the television over the bar, and a group of men were shouting at the screen.

"I'm sorry again about Josh, but work has been pretty chaotic for him," Libby apologized, pulling out the wooden chair and sitting down.

"Don't worry about it. We're glad you decided to come anyway," Julie answered with a smile. "I'm just so thrilled to have a night out without the kids. We finally found a babysitter; she's a girl down the street who just graduated high school. The kids love her." Julie fanned her flushed face with the plastic menu. Her stomach had gotten even bigger.

Libby studied the menu. "So, have you been working on anything exciting?" she asked Will.

"Not really. Just the usual domestic disputes and traffic incidents. But I've done a little more research on your case. The sheriff hasn't been very helpful. In fact, he insists the case was investigated properly, and there was no cause to suspect anything but suicide. I re-read all the notes. It's a shame no autopsy was done. Any evidence may be permanently gone now. Nor was there any reference to a suicide note being left behind. And in my experience, there almost always is one." A loud shout erupted from the group watching the game, and Will glanced over at the television. He turned back to the table and took a sip of beer. "I also wanted to read the coroner's notes, just to get an idea of what he saw."

Libby replied, "Didn't you mention something about Reynolds having an affair?"

Will nodded. "It would be pretty hard to prove, though, after twenty years."

"Wouldn't an affair mean there was more reason to suspect suicide?" Julie asked. "I mean, if this woman had been mentally unstable and she found out her husband was cheating on her, that might make her want to kill herself."

Libby handed her menu to the server after he'd taken their orders. As the server walked away, Libby said, "Or maybe her husband wanted people to think she was unstable, so it would appear to have been a suicide, when in fact he killed her."

"Hmm. I never thought about that," Julie said. She took a sip of her water and glanced around the restaurant. "What about the ghost? Has it come back?"

Libby leaned into the table and nodded. "I haven't told Josh about it. He doesn't want to believe any of this, but I know what I saw." She looked at Will and then back at Julie. "I hope you all don't think I'm crazy." She paused, brushing some crumbs with her fingers across the red and white checked tablecloth, her eyes averted, wondering if they didn't believe her either. But when she glanced up, neither one appeared skeptical. She continued: "Elizabeth mentioned again *saving her*. It's frustrating. I feel like there's something I should be doing, but I don't know what."

"Do you think she wants you to probe Mrs. Reynolds' death?" Julie asked. She tore a hunk off the warm bread that sat in a basket on the table. The aroma of it made Libby's mouth water.

"Maybe." Libby jabbed a tomato wedge with her fork. "She also mentioned something about a hummingbird, which really makes no sense to me." She waved the fork in her hand and shrugged. "Maybe she's just playing games with me and wants to drive me crazy."

"I think Reynolds is worth looking into," Will said. "The sheriff also mentioned something about Reynolds having big plans for this area. I'd like to know more about that. One of the reasons we moved here was to get away from the crowds. I'd hate for this town to be turned into some kind of tourist attraction or big development site."

"I don't trust him either. He's too slick. But he's Josh's client now. Maybe I should leave it alone, but that doesn't mean you have to stop, Will." Libby grinned at him.

"Who knows? It could be nothing, but it can't hurt to do a little digging," Will replied.

By the time Libby got home from the restaurant, Josh was already there. He was in the kitchen fixing a turkey sandwich.

"When'd you get here?" Libby asked, setting her purse on the table.

"Just a few minutes ago. How was dinner?"

"Great. We missed you."

"I missed you, too." Josh gave Libby a kiss and a hug. "You smell good."

"Thanks. It's eau de crab soup."

He laughed. "So how are the Seevers?"

"Fine." Libby pulled out a kitchen chair and sat at the table. The sun had almost set, and Libby switched on the small lamp, casting the room in a rosy tint that reflected onto the weathered oak table. Josh brought over his sandwich on a plate with a glass of milk.

"Josh, we really need to talk."

"Uh-oh, I don't like the sound of this."

Libby rolled her eyes at him. "I think we need to discuss what's going to happen when the baby comes. Your hours are crazy, and I'll be starting a new job. Why hadn't we thought about who's going to watch the baby? I hate to think of a nanny or daycare raising our child."

"So what are you saying?"

"I think maybe I shouldn't go back to work. I mean, we've waited so long to have the baby. I want to be there to raise it."

"I agree; we don't need your salary to get by. And besides, you'd probably be spending close to that in daycare anyway."

"What about you? Am I going to be a single parent in this?"

"Libby, somebody's got to bring in the money. What are you suggesting? That we both quit our jobs and stay home with the baby?"

"Of course not. I just don't want to be alone all the time."

Josh thought about his conversation with Diana earlier. "Maybe going back to work would be better for you."

"What makes you say that?"

"Well, you just said you don't like being alone. Maybe if you got out of the house, you'd feel better."

"What I meant was I feel like we never spend any time together. Going to work isn't going to change that."

"It's not always going to be this crazy, but right now there's a lot going on."

Libby studied Josh's face. He looked tired. The long hours were taking their toll on him, she thought. She hoped he was right about work not always being so busy. "I guess I'll call the school tomorrow and tell them I won't be able to teach. I feel bad leaving them in the lurch. I was looking forward to a new class, but I really want to stay home with the baby."

Josh's mind raced with ways he could bring up the topic of seeing a doctor. "Libby…"

"What?" She smiled at him.

He chickened out. She looked so sweet. He didn't want to upset her. He knew that whatever way he presented it, a fight would ensue. "Nothing."

Libby took a sip of his milk. She began pulling dead leaves off the ivy plant that sat at the base of the lamp on the table. "How many kids do you want to have?"

"I don't know. How many do you want?" Josh asked, taking a bite of his sandwich.

"Two or three?"

"Sounds good to me. It wasn't fun being an only child."

"It's too bad we can't take turns carrying them," Libby joked.

Josh laughed. "Hey, I was thinking on my way home tonight that it would be fun to have an end-of-summer party, maybe on Labor Day weekend. By then the pier should be done and most of the renovations. Would you be up to something like that?"

"Sure. Who would we invite? We don't have many friends around here."

"We could invite our old friends from Baltimore and some of the people from my office. And we could even invite some locals and maybe get to know them better." Josh thought maybe a project like this would keep Libby's mind off the ghost and Reynolds's dead wife.

"I can get some invitations and start sending them out. You'll have to get me a list of names from work."

"I could invite some of my clients as well."

"Like Reynolds?" Libby said with a skeptical tone.

"Libby, he really is an OK guy. You just need to get to know him better. In fact, he invited us to go out on his yacht."

"Oh boy, I can't wait." When she saw the look on Josh's face, she added, "I promise I will try and enjoy myself for you. I can turn on the charm like the best of them." Libby batted her eyes at Josh.

"All right, smart aleck. Just remember, he could be my path to a full partnership."

Libby smiled at Josh and wrapped her arms around his neck. She knew how much this meant to him. Stroking his hair, she thought about her conversation with Will regarding Reynolds. Was she being deceitful by not telling him?

16

The dense fog hung like a blanket, obscuring the horizon. Libby gazed out at the murky water, and a chill ran up her spine. She wondered how something that appeared so tranquil and inviting one minute could look so menacing the next. It reminded Libby of an old Sherlock Holmes movie she'd seen as a child. She could visualize the Loch Ness monster rising out of the water, or maybe Chessie, the local version of the legendary creature that people had spotted years back in the Chesapeake Bay. She remembered the grainy photographs supposedly depicting the monster. Most likely, it was just a floating log in the water.

She'd woken at 5:30. Unable to fall back asleep, she'd taken Stella outside. Sitting at the porch table, she pictured Elizabeth standing on the beach over a hundred years ago. How desperate she must've been to have walked out into the water and not looked back. Losing a child had to be the hardest thing a person could endure. She reflexively placed her hand on her belly and gently stroked it back and forth. How ironic that Cecilia had died of drowning as well. Again, a curse was called to mind. She shivered as she imagined the cold, black water filling her lungs.

Deep in thought, she flinched, nearly spilling her orange juice, when she felt a hand touch her shoulder.

"Sorry, I didn't mean to scare you." Josh stood behind her.

Libby breathed deeply. "I didn't hear you come out."

"I've been looking all over for you." He was dressed in a navy blue suit with a gold and blue silk tie, his hair neatly combed. She smelled his cologne as he bent down to kiss her cheek. "When I got up and saw you weren't in bed, I just assumed you'd gone downstairs to get a drink. I was beginning to get worried when you hadn't come back up."

"I woke up early. I guess I got lost in thought out here. What time is it?"

"Seven thirty."

"Want some breakfast?"

"No, I've got an early meeting this morning. I have to run."

"Don't forget to get me that list of addresses for the party."

"I'll have Stephanie get something together and e-mail it to you."

"Great."

"See you tonight." He leaned down and kissed her again, this time softly on her lips.

Libby, dressed in a sundress with her blonde curls piled up in a big clip—the only way to combat the humidity—was out back watering the planters along the border of the porch. Tassie sat in a lawn chair under the shade of the big maple with Stella at her feet. The fog from the morning had completely lifted, and the sun was shining bright in the sky. Libby had picked up Tassie earlier in the day and brought her over for company.

As she poured from the copper watering can, her eyes were drawn to the bay. A transformation had taken place in just a few hours. The water had gone from black and ominous to a deep, clear greenish-blue that shimmered with sparkling flecks from the sun. The temperature had already reached the high eighties, and the cool water beckoned at her.

Stella let out a bark, and Libby saw Trevor Clay coming up the beach. He was dressed in his usual attire—cut-off baggie shorts, a torn T-shirt, and bare feet.

"Hi, Trevor," Libby called in his direction as he got closer.

"Hi, Miss Libby. I come to see if you need any help today."

"Sure."

Trevor had been coming over a couple times a week. He'd told Libby that his mother said it was OK as long as he didn't wear out his welcome.

"The beds out front need weeding. Do you think you could do that for me?"

Trevor nodded. "Hi, Miss Tassie." He waved in Tassie's direction as he walked toward the front of the house.

"Afternoon, child," Tassie answered.

"We're going to have lunch later. Would you like to join us?" Libby asked Trevor.

"Sure." He turned and gave her a big grin.

"I guess I had this fairy-tale picture of what marriage would be like." Libby sat in the white Adirondack chair next to Tassie. The heat had finally gotten to her, and she'd had to rest. She took a sip of lemonade. "I imagined we would always do things together. Josh would come home from work, and we would play with the baby together, and feed it together, and take walks together."

Tassie chuckled.

"I know, it sounds silly when I say it out loud. And the way Josh has been working lately, I'll be lucky if he even gets to see the baby before it's asleep at night." Libby felt the sting of tears in her eyes. She knew it was her hormones, but lately she'd found herself crying for no reason, like the other day when she was watching television and an ad came on for some credit card where it showed a couple going through life, getting old together. And she sat on the couch with tears streaming down her face.

"I don't know what's wrong with me lately. I mean, I know it's the pregnancy, but I guess I'm afraid I'm going to be raising this child alone. When we lived in the city and both of us were working, we constantly did things together. We went out to movies, took walks in the park. When Josh was a law clerk and then a new lawyer, I still felt I was the most important thing to him. Now that he's become a partner in this firm, I feel like I'm losing him to his career. I can't really put it into words. Saying this out loud makes me sound like I'm some kind of spoiled child. Josh hasn't done anything wrong. After all, I'm the one who pushed him to move over here. And he does have a long commute every day." Libby looked down at her hands, feeling embarrassed for having said so much. "I'm sorry. I shouldn't have gone on like that."

"What you're feeling, child, is perfectly normal when you're pregnant." Tassie reached over and squeezed Libby's hand with her tiny spidery fingers. "You're the one carrying the baby and connected to it from the beginning. Josh doesn't have that. This baby is already a part of you, but to Josh it's still an abstract thing. It's natural for you to feel that he's not as involved because he's not—no man is. I guarantee you once that baby arrives, he will be a changed man."

A bee buzzed around Libby's head as she swatted it away. "I hope you're right."

Seated at the wrought iron table on the porch, Trevor shoveled forkfuls of seafood salad into his mouth—a recipe that Tassie had given Libby.

"Now slow down, child. You're going to give yourself indigestion eatin' that fast," Tassie clucked her tongue at Trevor.

"Yes, ma'am," he replied, wiping his face with his napkin.

"Trevor's told me so many stories of when his mother worked here. I told him he should start writing some down," Libby said to Tassie. "He's a good storyteller, just like you."

"My mama likes telling me stories," Trevor said after taking a huge gulp of his lemonade. "She said she always loved Miss Cecilia, that some people are just born with a kind soul, and she was one of 'em."

"Your mama and she were close. Yes, they were," Tassie said nodding.

"My mama said Miss Cecilia didn't have many friends, and she didn't go out much. My mama knew her since she was a little girl, and my mama was about the only one she ever talked to."

"I wonder what Cecilia did all day in this big house alone?" Libby asked.

"I know she liked to write. My mama said that she wrote poetry in a book. She would read to my mama some of her poems."

"Really?" Libby pictured Cecilia sitting out back in a lawn chair with the birds chattering in the trees, the sweet smell of lilacs in the air, while she read to Trevor's mom.

"Yeah, she said they were real good. She always told Miss Cecilia that she should get them published. Miss Cecilia kept that book with her like it was her Bible. She always had it with her; my mama said her daddy gave it to her for her birthday one year. It was a real pretty book, prettier than any other book she ever saw."

"How so?" Libby asked.

"She said it had tiny jewels on the front of it in beautiful colors." Trevor waved his hand in a sweeping motion in front of him. "And they were put together in the shape of a bird."

"That does sound pretty."

"It was one of them tiny birds, you know, the kind that hang in one spot." Trevor thought for a minute. "I forget the name."

"A humming*bird*?" Libby asked.

"Yeah! That's it," Trevor said with a big smile, pointing his finger at Libby.

Tassie looked at Libby, her eyebrows raised. She'd told Tassie about the encounter with Elizabeth on the beach. Libby's pulse quickened. "I wonder what happened to the book," Libby pondered.

"I don't know. My mama said she came over to the house after Miss Cecilia passed to help Mr. Reynolds box up her things, but she never came across that book. My mama thought that was strange since it meant so much to Miss Cecilia. The only thing my mama could figure was maybe she kept it in a special secret place so no one would ever find it."

Tassie and Libby glanced at each other again. Could the book still be in the house? Libby wondered.

Just then, a clap of thunder rumbled loud in the sky, and a streak of lightning shot down toward the water from a dark cloud that had quickly approached. The winds began to pick up, and Libby jumped up from the table putting plates on the tray to take back inside. Trevor said he better get back home before the storm got bad. Libby watched him run down the path and along the beach, thinking he should get into track someday. She'd never seen someone run so fast, especially barefoot.

Tassie and Libby made it into the house as large drops of rain began to fall. The dark, heavy clouds looked ominous as the lights flickered and the rain beat down against the windowpanes.

"That certainly came out of nowhere," Libby said, setting the tray on the counter. She began loading the dishwasher, while Tassie sat at the kitchen table, stroking Stella's head.

"You don't think that hummingbird book is still in the house?" Libby asked.

"I think it must be. Otherwise, I don't think Elizabeth would've mentioned it."

"I wouldn't know where to begin to look."

"I'm sure Cecilia would've kept it in a safe place. Someplace hidden, like maybe under one of the floorboards."

"That would take forever to find." Libby wiped her hands on a cotton dishtowel. "What about the attic? That's where I first saw Elizabeth, and there are a lot of boxes and old pieces of furniture up there."

"Could be."

Libby sat down across from Tassie and ran her hand across the smooth weathered oak of the kitchen table. "I don't know. Maybe I shouldn't look for it. I told Josh I would stay out of the whole thing."

"What's the harm in looking for a book?"

From the high vantage point, they saw streaks of lightning shoot across the blackened sky. The only light came from the bare bulbs hanging from the ceiling.

"Here, you sit down on this." Libby felt the thrill of an adventure as she brought over a wooden rocker for Tassie. She brushed it off with a rag and tested it to make sure it was sturdy. "I'll bring the boxes over to you, and we can go through them together."

Libby dragged one of the boxes across the attic floor. She wiped sweat off her brow with the back of her hand and then tore the packing tape off and lifted the top to reveal books. Bingo! Maybe they were in luck. But as they sorted through, they realized it was just old paperbacks and magazines. They moved on to the next one. "I've been wanting to go through all of this, but I just haven't had the time."

There were financial papers and ledgers of household expenditures belonging to the Reynolds. Mixed in with the papers Libby found a photo album. The first page had a picture of John and Cecilia on their wedding day, standing in front of the house. She wondered why Reynolds had left the album behind. More pictures of the Reynolds and even some of Francis Haverford filled the album. Libby turned to the last page, but then stopped and flipped the page back. "Look!" She pointed to a picture of Cecilia seated in a lounge chair on the lawn; she was looking up in surprise at the camera, and in her lap was a book, her hand protectively holding it. "Look at that." She held the book closer for Tassie to see the outline of a hummingbird. "Now we know what it looks like." Libby walked across the room to get another box.

A large clap of thunder shook the house, and Stella ran down the steps out of sight. The lights flickered and then went out, leaving them in darkness.

"Tassie, are you OK?" Libby called out from across the room.

"I'm fine, child."

"I better go downstairs and get a flashlight. Will you be all right 'til I get back?"

"Just wait a minute, child. Give your eyes time to adjust."

Libby stood still. Tassie was right. Objects began coming into view.

"I guess we can't look for the book now. Are you sure you'll be able to make it back downstairs with no light?"

"Shhh...quiet, child. I believe we have company."

"What?" Libby looked puzzled, and then she saw from across the room a shimmering light in the darkness. Slowly the image began to form. Elizabeth was back.

Libby felt her heart racing. She tried to calm her breathing. She heard a humming sound, but she wasn't sure if it was coming from Tassie or Elizabeth. As the humming got louder, the apparition got brighter. Elizabeth's dark blue eyes met Libby's, and she felt a shiver run up her spine. Elizabeth ever so slightly nodded her head. She glided toward the steps and then disappeared.

"Should we follow her?"

Tassie nodded.

Hand in hand, they left the attic, gingerly working their way down the stairs. The next flight of stairs, wider and with a bit more light, was easier to navigate. They followed the glow of Elizabeth's dress as it rounded the corner into the nursery. Libby gripped Tassie's hand in hers as they crossed the threshold.

"I don't see her," Libby whispered. The room lit up as if a giant camera flash had gone off. Seconds later another rumble of thunder shook the house.

Tassie pulled her into the adjoining room, where Elizabeth stood in the corner. Something nudged Libby in the back of the leg. She jumped and screamed. Stella was standing behind her, whining. When Libby looked back across the room, Elizabeth was gone.

"Where'd she go?"

"I think you scared her away."

"Me? I didn't mean to. It was the dog; she scared the hell out of me." Libby held her hand at her beating chest. "Why do you think Elizabeth led us here?"

"I can't say, but this would probably be a good place to start looking for that book."

The phone rang. The sky was brightening as the storm receded. "We probably should go downstairs. I'll look for the book later."

17

Josh hung up the phone. He sat for a moment, staring out the large window of his office to the boats in the harbor. He'd blown it. The conversation hadn't gone the way he'd planned. After what Libby had told him the other night when he got home, he knew he couldn't wait any longer. But he hadn't had the guts to say it to her face.

They'd been in the den watching TV when she told him that Tassie had been over and they'd seen the ghost again. She said she wasn't going to tell him at first, but she couldn't keep it from him any longer. She went on about some book that was hidden in the house, and all she had to do was find it. Then she'd know what the ghost wanted. She spouted off again about Cecilia Reynolds' suicide possibly being a murder. Diana's words had echoed in his head. Libby needed to see someone. He didn't know if it was Tassie's influence or Libby just losing it, but whatever it was, she needed help.

One time when they were living in Baltimore, Libby had gotten it in her head that Mr. Marks, the man who lived in the apartment above them, had been murdered. She said she had noticed some strange men going upstairs one afternoon when she was coming home from teaching. Then, a few days later, she said she'd heard a dragging sound coming from above and a scuffling noise. After that, she said there'd been no sign of Mr. Marks. She'd even gone up to his unit several times and knocked on his door, but no one answered. Josh had told her to forget about it.

The next thing he knew, she'd gotten the super to unlock the door, saying she thought something terrible had happened to Mr. Marks. When they entered, Mr. Marks was nowhere to be found. The mystery was solved several weeks later, when Mr. Marks returned from the cruise he'd gone on. The men she'd seen going up to his apartment had been there to give him an estimate to move some boxes to a storage site. They'd come back a few days later to haul them away, and that had been the dragging sound she'd heard. Josh had chided Libby at the time to quit snooping into other people's business, and he'd assumed that was the end of it.

He was worried about Libby. Yesterday, he'd approached a colleague of his whose wife had recently given birth and asked him if his wife had acted strangely when she was pregnant. Maybe what Libby was experiencing was a typical hormonal reaction. His colleague laughed. "Strange" wasn't the word for it, he'd said. Josh was relieved. But the guy went on to tell Josh how if his wife didn't have two scoops of Ben & Jerry's Chunky Monkey before every meal, she'd go ballistic. He'd patted Josh's shoulder and jokingly told him to hang in there; the insanity would go away once the baby was born. Josh had forced a chuckle and thanked him, trying to appear casual, but inside he was thinking if eating ice cream every day was all that Libby was doing, he'd be happy.

That same day, he'd gone to a woman in the firm that handled the firm's expert witnesses. He knew she'd dealt with doctors before to prepare them for testimonies. He'd made up a story about a potential client whose family wanted him deemed incompetent, and he was wondering if she knew any psychiatrists that specialized in delusional behavior. She'd given him the names of two prominent psychiatrists in the area.

Holding the piece of paper in his hands, he studied the names. Finally, he picked up the phone and called Libby. He told himself he was a master at persuading jurors to rule in his favor; he should be able to convince his wife to seek help. Was he ever wrong.

The late afternoon sun coming through the large glass window glinted off the metal sculpture of a boat that sat on top of the credenza. He rubbed his hand along the bleached wood of his Scandinavian-style desk with its sleek lines and glanced around the soft gray walls hung with abstract acrylic paintings of sailboats on the water in vivid shades of blue. All the while, the fiasco with Libby stirred in his head. He hadn't a clue what to do.

Then, he glanced at the folder on his desk and thought about the meeting he'd had earlier that day with Jerry Barrett and his father Mark, the man whose land Reynolds had bought for a song. The way Reynolds had described Mark Barrett, Josh expected some kind of money-grubber, but in actuality, he was a nice elderly man who had lived in the Annapolis area all his life.

The land had been in his family for years, and he sold it because he wanted to move south to be close to his son. Barrett hadn't discussed the sale with his son beforehand; in fact, the land wasn't even on the market when Reynolds discovered it. Reynolds had sought him out and made him an offer he couldn't resist. To the old man Barrett, it was more money than he'd ever imagined having, and he had been perfectly happy with the deal. But when his son found out who had bought the property and what became of it, he felt that his father had been swindled.

Jerry Barrett was in his late thirties, slightly balding, and about twenty pounds overweight. He worked as a night manager at a large wholesale chain in Jacksonville, Florida. Josh could see the dollar signs in his eyes as soon as he sat across the conference room table from him.

After studying all the paperwork Reynolds' people had given him, Josh could understand why the son was pissed. The property, which was located in a section of Annapolis near the water, had become run down. It had been a quasi-industrial area since the early 1900s with several ailing commercial businesses as well. Most of the buildings had closed down or were going out of business. The area, surrounded by low-income housing, had seen an influx of crime over the years, which had contributed to the decline. The location, though, was prime real estate, considering its proximity to the water. When Reynolds had discovered it, he immediately envisioned an upscale community with shops, luxury apartments, and office space. It was just a matter of planning and timing to make it happen.

He did some investigating and discovered that Mark Barrett owned the bulk of the property in the industrial section. After their first encounter, Reynolds knew he could get Barrett to sell; he was an easy mark—an elderly man with no family in the area and no idea of the true potential of his property. That had been six years ago, and now the area had been transformed into everything Reynolds had imagined, and he had come out that much richer in the process.

It had taken some major negotiating and cajoling with the legislature to get the area re-zoned. He even got rid of the low-income housing, using the premise of trying to reduce crime in the city. He wined and dined fellow legislators, convincing them that the citizens of Annapolis would all benefit from re-zoning the area and the use of eminent domain. The tax dollars the up-scaled property would bring in was something they all liked. The state was facing a budget deficit, and the city could use the face-lift.

Reynolds managed it without ever being in the limelight himself. He let the other representatives take credit for it, which they were only too glad to do; what politician wouldn't want to be responsible for lowering crime and cutting the deficit all at the same time? They moved the low-income housing to another part of town—and in such a way that the local townspeople never had a chance to complain. Reynolds researched an area in the northern part of Anne Arundel County and found that there had been a citizens' group fighting for a park in their area. He collaborated with the local politicians, convincing them that they could build the park and, at the same time, set aside some land for subsidized housing. It went off without a hitch. All the politicians came out on top. Those who were up for re-election at the time campaigned on the platform of having lowered crime and building a surplus for the state. It was a win-win situation for everyone, so no one ever thought to look into why Reynolds had pushed the deal in the first place—that is, until Jerry Barrett showed up.

Barrett had been watching a cable news show when one of the anchors mentioned Reynolds running for the US Senate for the State of Maryland; she gave a small blurb about Reynolds' career and displayed his picture on the screen. When Jerry heard the name, he asked his father if that was the same John Reynolds who had bought their property. His father looked up from the paper he'd been reading and squinted at the screen. He said it looked like the same man. Curious, Jerry did some research online and soon discovered what had become of the property. He saw pictures of the high-rises that had been erected. Barrett realized immediately that his father had not gotten what he could have for the property. He wasn't sure if legally he had a claim, but he knew the nature of politicians; the mere mention of a lawsuit was worse than the plague.

Josh sat across the conference room table from Jerry and Mark Barrett. He had prepared a document that contained so much legalese mumbo jumbo, it would take an expert to decipher it. He gave a copy to both men and then slowly spun the tale he had rehearsed. Josh knew the property had been worth far more than what Mr. Barrett had sold it for, but no one twisted his arm to sell. Persuaded, maybe, but not forced. Luckily, neither of the Barretts knew how much Reynolds had eventually made on the deal. Moreover, he was pleased they'd not thought to hire an attorney. This negotiation would be much easier without anyone else involved. The key was to agree upon the right dollar amount to make everyone happy.

The property, which they'd owned since the thirties, brought them a bit of rental income, but other than the land, the family had no other assets. The money they got from the sale was definitely more money than either one had ever seen, but if they realized what they could have gotten, things could change. He spent nearly an hour reviewing the history of the transaction and, in the end, he had spun it so well even the son's eager dollar signs were beginning to fade. Josh rose from the table and excused himself for a few minutes, giving them time to worry as to whether they had any claim at all.

He returned several minutes later with another document and a check for an amount that he and Reynolds had already agreed on. They had come up with a figure that, to the Barretts, would seem extremely generous. To Reynolds, it was more like hush money. Josh sat back down at the table, smiling warmly at the elderly Barrett, mentioning how much he reminded him of his late father. He told them he wanted to do the right thing, even though legally he did not have to. He explained to them both that Mr. Reynolds felt that the original transaction had been properly handled, but he had decided to give Mr. Barrett more money only because he wanted no questions raised in the future regarding the fairness of the situation.

Josh slowly slid the check across the table, setting it right in front of both men. By the look on the father's face, it was clearly more than he ever expected. Even the son seemed pleased with the figure. Josh went on to explain that before they could take possession of the check, they would have to sign an agreement stating they would not make any future claims on the property, nor would they mention the matter to the public. They both agreed readily, and each signed the agreement without hesitation. Josh knew that Jerry Barrett was already calculating ways to spend the money.

Josh glanced at his Tag Heuer watch. 4:25 p.m. He had a meeting with Jenna Thompson, a political speechwriter who had worked on several campaigns. She had certainly made a name for herself. Word around town was that she was one of the best. Reynolds had hired her several months ago to work on his campaign, and he wanted Josh to collaborate with her to draft a speech regarding the land deal that would make him look like a hero. Jenna had agreed to meet Josh in his office, and then they were to go to Dominick's to meet Reynolds and some of his staff to go over the speech.

While he jotted down some notes from the meeting with the Barretts, pleased with the way things had gone, Stephanie buzzed to say that Jenna Thompson had arrived. He told her to send her in and then leaned back in his chair, thinking Reynolds should be satisfied with the outcome.

Josh stood up as Jenna strode into the office with confidence, revealing a self-assured woman. In her early thirties with dark auburn hair swept off her face into a French twist, she wore a cream-colored suit that fit her to a tee. Her five-seven frame was in perfect condition. She carried a mahogany brown, exquisitely tooled Italian leather briefcase in one hand as she extended her other to Josh, giving him a firm handshake. "Hi, Mr. Langston. Jenna Thompson," she said, her smile showing a perfectly corrected set of white teeth.

"Good afternoon, Ms. Thompson, and please call me Josh," he said as he motioned for her to sit in one of the dark gray leather chairs in front of his desk.

"Josh." She nodded and smiled. "Call me Jenna." She sat down and crossed her legs, smoothing her skirt as she did so. She placed the briefcase on her lap and snapped the clasp open, pulling out a pad of paper and a pen. "So, Mr. Reynolds informs me that he would like us to put our heads together and come up with something that will make him sound wonderful. His words, not mine."

"Yes, I'm not sure how much he's told you about this case," Josh said, lowering himself into his chair. "It looks to me like he's done nothing illegal, but not totally kosher either. He wants us to mitigate any damage this thing could cause to the campaign before anything comes of it."

"Why don't you tell me what it is that he did," Jenna said, poised with pen in hand.

Josh leaned back in his chair and placed his hands in front of his face, prayer fashion, as he tapped his index fingers together, thinking how to phrase his next statement. "Several years back," he began, "Reynolds acquired some property at, let's just say, well-below market price." Josh explained the details of the transaction. "So, out of the generosity of Reynolds' heart, he is willing to give Mr. Barrett more money in exchange for his silence."

"If that's the case, then why bring it up at all?"

"Because, as I'm sure you know, nothing in the political arena ever really goes away. The closer this race gets, it would be just a matter of time before someone found out about it. I suggested we preempt them. If Reynolds discloses this now, it would diffuse any future bomb to be dropped."

"It sounds like you know politics pretty well. I'm surprised I haven't heard your name mentioned. Have you done any political work before?"

"No, I just know human nature, and when people get desperate, they'll usually resort to anything they can to get what they want."

By the time Josh and Jenna finished collaborating on the speech, it was time to meet Reynolds at Dominick's. Jenna offered to drive Josh over there; there was no need to take two cars. She would drive Josh back to the office since she had to come back this way.

Jenna's car was parked in the garage below. They got off the elevator, their footsteps echoing as they walked across the brightly lit concrete flooring toward a silver BMW 3 Series convertible. The lights flashed, and the car sounded a familiar beep as Jenna hit her remote to unlock the doors.

"Nice car," Josh said as he slid into the black leather seat.

"Thanks. I do a lot of driving, so I figured I might as well have fun while I'm doing it." She flung her briefcase onto the backseat.

Josh was still driving an old Audi he had bought used when he graduated law school. This would have to be his next purchase, he thought to himself. When he'd lived in the city, a car was never that important to him, but now that he had such a long commute, he deserved something better. He liked the way Jenna thought; why not have fun while you're driving?

On the way to Dominick's, Josh discovered that Jenna had grown up on the Eastern Shore. "Where on the Shore did you live?"

"A little town called Corsica that no one's ever heard of. It's one of those little towns that people drive right by on their way to the beach and never even know it."

"I know it quite well. My wife and I recently moved there."

"You're kidding?"

"No, we moved over there in May. In fact, we bought the Haverford House, John Reynolds' old place, but it was purely coincidental. I wasn't even his attorney then."

"Small world. I can't believe someone actually would choose to live over there. Growing up on the Shore, I couldn't wait to get the hell out of that place."

"Do you ever go back?"

"Only on my obligatory visits to see my parents. My brother and I both left to go to college, and neither of us went back. I have a condo in Alexandria on the water and absolutely love it. I'm only minutes from DC and surrounded by fabulous restaurants." She turned to look at Josh. "What possessed you to move over there?"

"It was my wife's idea actually. She hated living in the city. We never expected to move quite that far out, but my wife fell in love with the place."

"How about you? Do you love it?"

"I gotta say I had my reservations in the beginning, with the commute and all, and the remoteness of it, but I have to admit, when I drive over that bridge, I can just feel myself slowing down and relaxing. It's really growing on me, and I know Libby's happy."

"She's a lucky lady to have a man like you put *her* happiness before his."

Josh smiled and shifted against the leather seat, feeling flattered but somewhat uncomfortable by her comment. He wasn't quite sure how to respond. "I wouldn't say I don't consider my happiness, too. I insisted we live on the water; it was something I'd always wanted."

Jenna laughed. "You don't have to defend yourself. It was a compliment. So many men have their head so far up their own asses that they wouldn't have the first clue what would make their woman happy. It's very refreshing to know that there are still some decent ones left out there."

Jenna shifted down the gears, her hand firm on the gear stick as the engine wound down, and she pulled up to the curb of the restaurant. A valet walked swiftly over to her car and opened the door. She handed the valet her keys, and he handed her a ticket. As she strode over to the door, briefcase in hand, to meet Josh, he noticed her tan, muscular stocking-less legs. This was a powerful woman, he thought to himself, in more ways than one.

Josh held the door for her, and they walked into the restaurant together. Reynolds and his group were seated at a large table in the back of the restaurant. The six men and two women around the table were heatedly involved in a discussion when Josh and Jenna approached. Reynolds glanced up, saw them, and immediately stood up. "Finally! Sit down. Let's hear what the geniuses have come up with," he said in a broad voice, giving Jenna a kiss on the cheek and pulling out a chair for her. Josh sat in the empty chair next to her. The discussion came to a stop, and all eyes were on Jenna and Josh. Jenna spoke first.

"Josh and I have come up with a speech that would make even Bernie Madoff sound like a Boy Scout. Not that I'm saying you're like Bernie." Jenna patted Reynolds' hand. Josh waited for Reynolds' reaction, thinking he would not take too kindly to the Madoff reference, but Reynolds just smiled at her. She continued, "Let's face it. The public is jaded when it comes to politicians. I mean, you're basically guilty until proven innocent in this game. They are expecting you to be dishonest or shady, but after this speech, they're going to think of you as another Mother Teresa."

Everyone laughed. Josh thought picturing Reynolds as Mother Teresa was pretty far-fetched.

"Hey, what's so funny? I'm a nice guy; you all know that," Reynolds said, hitting himself on the chest. Everyone agreed, nodding his or her head in unison. Josh observed the group, thinking Reynolds' minions would probably do anything he asked them to do.

Jenna ignored the banter and continued in her businesslike tone. She went over the key points of the speech and then handed everyone a typed copy in its entirety. Everyone at the table was silent as each read it, including Reynolds. Afterward, they all wanted to hear what Reynolds had to say first. Reynolds appeared to be taking longer than anyone else to finish reading. He wore half-glasses down on the end of his nose as he read. He flipped the pages back and forth, re-reading different paragraphs. Josh was beginning to get worried; maybe he didn't like what they had come up with.

Finally, he set the papers down. He removed his glasses and placed his palms firmly on the table. "Excellent, Jenna. You have outdone yourself again."

The group let out a collective sigh.

Jenna smiled, but when Reynolds reached under the table and squeezed her thigh, the smile quickly disappeared. Her eyes flashed at Reynolds with a look that said she could break him in two. Josh noticed the exchange and figured she'd dealt with this before, politicians with inflated egos on power trips. But he didn't think Jenna had any problem playing in the big league. She looked like someone who wouldn't be taken advantage of.

The rest of the evening's conversation centered on the speech and when and where it should be delivered. Josh discussed with Reynolds the events of the meeting with the Barretts, and Reynolds was pleased with how Josh had handled it. By 9:30 p.m., everyone started to leave. As Josh stood and pushed his chair back, Reynolds came over and patted him on the shoulder. "Fine job today." He leaned in close to Josh and whispered in his ear, "You deserve a little fun now, if you know what I mean." Reynolds winked and nodded toward Jenna, who was talking with another woman on Reynolds' team. Josh gave a quick smile and shook Reynolds' hand.

As a businessperson, he admired Reynolds, but he wasn't sure if he liked his attitude toward women. He couldn't let that bother him, though. What Reynolds did with his personal life was none of Josh's business.

Jenna and Josh waited out front for the valet to bring the car around. The stars were barely visible in the night sky, diffused by the bright lights of the city. The heat of the day still lingered in the air. Jenna looked over at Josh. "It's a beautiful night." She breathed deeply with a sigh and then added, "I think everything went well."

"Yeah, I think so, too." Josh inhaled the musky smell of her perfume. He felt something stir inside him, and he didn't like it. He wanted to tell her he would take a cab back to his car, but he knew that would sound strange. The two drinks and very little food were making him feel light-headed. He loosened his tie, feeling suddenly warm. Standing this close to her, he felt her energy like an animal magnetism, something he was sure she wasn't even aware of.

The valet pulled up with the car. Jenna slid onto the leather seat as Josh got in on the passenger side. She clasped the lap belt across her and then stepped on the clutch, putting the car in gear. She pulled away from the curb with the conviction of a racecar driver.

When several blocks down she pulled to a stop at a red light, a drunken man staggered into the street and placed his hands on the hood of her car. Instantly, Jenna pushed the window button and yelled out at the man to get the fuck off her car. Her words shot out like venom, and the man jumped back, almost knocking himself over, continuing his disoriented path across the street.

Josh was shocked at the level of her vehemence. He stared at her profile as she accelerated with the green light. Her hands quickly maneuvered the gears, moving in unison with her foot on the clutch. By the time she reached third gear, she glanced over at Josh. "I'm sorry if I surprised you back there, but I can't stand drunks."

"No, that's fine. I don't really care for drunks either." Josh let out a short laugh. "I think you may have sobered that guy up; he looked like he'd seen a ghost." Josh looked out the window at the brick row houses whizzing by. "I sensed a little pent-up anger."

"Yeah." Jenna snorted. "I guess that's what you could call it. My father's a drunk, and I spent too many years watching him act like an ass. I have no tolerance for that kind of behavior."

"I'm sorry. I didn't mean to pry."

"No, I don't mind talking about it. After years of therapy, I've gotten used to talking about it. If you haven't experienced growing up with an alcoholic parent, it would be hard for you to understand."

"I guess so. My parents were more like Ozzie and Harriet Nelson. They couldn't have been more boring."

"Boring can be good. Believe me, I used to dream of having boring, ordinary parents when I was a kid. Living with my father, I saw how he ate away at my mother, belittling her, taking away her self-esteem. I knew I didn't want that to happen to me, so the first chance I had to leave the farm, I left and never looked back. The only reason I go back is to see my mother. She's a good woman."

"Sounds like it was pretty rough."

"I survived." She pulled up to Josh's office building. He thanked her for the ride, and she said good night before revving the engine and taking off down the street.

He watched the red taillights as she turned the next corner and drove out of sight. Josh shook his head; he'd never met anyone quite like her before.

18

Libby pulled the car to the curb. She'd just gotten off the phone with Josh, and she was having trouble breathing. Her world suddenly turned upside down. One minute, she'd been driving into town to buy groceries, singing along with the radio, and the next her husband was telling her she should go see a psychiatrist. "He thinks I'm crazy." The words silently played in her head.

After she'd told him the other night about her encounter with Elizabeth, learning about the diary, and her belief that Cecilia may have been murdered, she'd been surprised at his apparent acceptance. She'd expected some kind of resistance from him. She hadn't liked keeping any of it from him, and she thought if she got it out in the open, maybe she'd convince him to see her point. But he'd been mostly silent that night, not saying much of anything. She realized now that what she'd seen as acceptance actually had been his mind racing with ways of having her committed.

She still couldn't believe he wanted her to see a doctor. And when he told her that her mother felt the same way, it had been a blow to her gut. Had they been plotting behind her back? She didn't know who Josh was anymore. Tears streamed down her face. She had to get out of the car, suddenly feeling claustrophobic.

She strode down the sidewalk. Where she was going, she hadn't a clue; she just needed fresh air. The flowers along the square melded together, blurred by her tears. She swiped the tears with the back of her hand, snuffling her nose. The sound of an engine rumbled, and she saw a car slowing down along the curb beside her. She glanced over. It was Will's patrol car. He leaned over toward the passenger seat and said out the open window, "Need a lift?"

She forced a smile and shook her head.

He saw the tears in her eyes. "Everything OK?"

She shrugged.

He reached over and opened the passenger door. "Get in."

Libby hesitated on the curb for a second and then slid into the car.

He pulled away from the curb. The two sat in silence while Libby stared out the side window. He stopped the car in front of the sheriff's station. "Sit tight. I'll be right back." He jumped out of the car and ran inside.

Libby wondered what she was doing. Why had she gotten in the car with him? He probably thought she was crazy, too. Did everyone think she was crazy? A minute later, Will headed back out with something in his hand. He hopped back into the car, and she saw he had two beers. She gave him a puzzled look.

"I was thirsty," was all he said. They headed out of town. Libby wondered where he was going. As if reading her mind, he said, "There's a place I want to show you." Will turned up the radio, and they drove without speaking.

About ten minutes later, he turned onto a dirt lane lined with trees. Libby's curiosity was aroused. Where were they? The car bumped and weaved over the uneven track. When they came to a clearing along a creek, Will stopped the car and turned off the engine. He opened the door, grabbed the beers, and said, "Follow me."

Libby did as she was told, wondering what he wanted to show her. They walked along the edge of the creek, and then Will stood back and said, "Ta-da!" He gestured with a flourish toward a large rock that hung over the water. "Your rock."

Libby gave him another puzzled look.

"I found this spot the other day, and when I saw this rock, I thought of you. Remember in the diner how you told me about the rock you used to sit on as a child? It was your favorite place."

Libby laughed. Temporarily forgetting her troubles, she slipped off her sandals and walked over to the rock. Heat permeated through the soles of her feet. The afternoon sun shone onto the water, spotlighting a swarm of gnats that hung above the surface. The sound of crickets chirped in the distance.

She sat down, pressing her palms against the rock and feeling its smoothness. She tilted her face back and closed her eyes, drinking in the warmth of the sun. She opened her eyes to see Will standing next to her. He lowered one of the brown bottles into the cool water, and wedged it between two rocks. Twisting the cap off the other one, he drank a long gulp, and then sat down next to her. He removed his shoes and socks and then rolled up the cuffs of his pants.

"So, you want to talk about it?"

Libby smiled. She stared out at the water, watching two ducks, probably mates, bobbing along with the current. "Did you ever feel really alone? Like in the pit of your stomach. That hollow empty feeling."

"Yeah." Will picked up a small stone and tossed it into the water. It plopped and disappeared under a circle of ripples. "Why do you feel so alone?"

"Josh thinks I'm crazy."

Will chuckled.

"No, I'm serious. He really thinks I'm crazy. He even suggested I see a doctor."

"What?"

"It's the whole ghost thing. If only he would see the ghost, then he'd believe me." She stopped and looked over at Will. "You probably think I'm insane, too."

Will took another swig of beer. "I must admit when you first told me, I thought it was pretty odd. But I can tell when people are lying. I don't think you're making it up."

"But do you think I'm delusional?" A flash of Cecilia Reynolds ran through her mind. Had Cecilia been delusional, or had it been her husband making that up because he was having an affair? Was Josh having an affair? Was he trying to make her think she was crazy? He had been spending a lot of time in Baltimore, not coming home all night.

"You don't seem delusional to me. Josh is probably just concerned about you."

"I don't know what's happened to my marriage."

"I hear you."

Libby looked over at Will. His comment had surprised her. She thought he and Julie were the perfect couple. "You and Julie?"

Will nodded. "Things haven't been good lately. In fact, she left with the kids to go to her mom's for a few days. I don't know what's going on."

"Relationships. Why do they have to be so complicated?"

"Beats me." Will finished off the beer and grabbed the second one out of the water. He opened it, but before he could take a sip, Libby snatched it from him and drank a big swallow. The cool liquid was refreshing. She rationalized in her head that the doctor had said a few sips of wine was okay, so why not a beer? They shared the bottle. Will picked up another stone and threw it across the creek. It skimmed along the surface and then fell in.

"I remember skimming stones when I was a kid," Libby said. "We used to have contests to see who could skim it the farthest." She jumped up and gingerly stepped with her bare feet along the edge of the creek lined with rocks. The water was cold, but it felt good. The few sips of alcohol had relaxed away her tension. "You just have to find the right rock." She bent down and searched through the stones. "Here's one!" She flicked her wrist and sent the rock dancing over the surface of the water. "Five hops! Beat that one." She laughed.

Will joined her along the edge where she was collecting more rocks. He gathered some, too, and then they stood side by side skimming them across, trying to outdo each other. The smell of honeysuckle hung thick in the air. A crow cawed in the distance. They ran out of rocks and began their search again.

Libby spotted the perfect rock, but Will got to it before her. "Hey, that's mine!" She tried to grab it out of his hand, but he held it up above his head. She jumped trying to reach it. He then dangled it in front of him, taunting her. She laughed and lunged at him, and they both lost their footing, stumbling backward. They fell to the ground onto the damp grass with Libby on top of Will, their faces inches apart.

They both froze for a second, and then Will reached up and brushed back Libby's long hair that had fallen in her face. He placed his finger under her chin and then leaned in and kissed her, slowly and softly. Libby's head spun as a surge of warmth shot through her body. The kiss intensified as their tongues explored the depths of their mouths. They rolled on the grass, their clothes smeared with dirt, leaves clinging to Libby's tangle of curls.

Their lips remained locked while their hands grasped at each other, pressing their bodies together. An overwhelming desire engulfed Libby. Blood coursed through her veins, but then she suddenly drew away. What was she doing? Will pulled her back, but she resisted, pushing her palms against his chest. She sat up, brushing the grass off her blouse. Maybe she *was* insane. Her lips and cheeks felt raw. She exhaled deeply. What had she just done? She was married, expecting a child. Her heart was racing, and she felt it pounding against her chest. Will sat up beside her and stared out at the water for several minutes. He glanced over at her and picked the leaves out of her hair.

She faced him and said, "We can't."

"I know."

"I—" He put a finger to her lips and shook his head. Then he stood up and extended his hand. They both adjusted their clothing. Will picked up the two empty beer bottles in one hand and then took her hand in his and led her back to the car.

19

A dark cloud hung over Haverford House, even though it was a gorgeous sunny day. Libby hadn't slept well. Three days had passed since her life tumbled out of control. Will and she had vowed to never speak of what they'd done, neither one wanting to ruin their respective marriages. Facing Josh afterward had been awkward. Guilt had swirled in her head along with anger at him for not believing in her. She told herself he'd driven her to do what she did.

They'd barely spoken for two days, and then last night they finally talked. The conversation had gone long into the night and had ended with Josh apologizing for doubting her. He'd told her he would try and spend more time at home, and she'd promised to leave the murder theory alone. But neither one had told the truth. Josh knew he was still going to work long hours, and he worried about her sanity. And Libby knew she wasn't going to be able to let Cecilia's death go. But they'd kept their hidden thoughts to themselves.

It was already half past nine when Josh shook Libby awake. They were going on the Reynolds yacht today. Instead of getting up, she rolled over, covering her head with a pillow. "Do we have to go?"

"Lib, we've already gone over this. I'm sorry I didn't tell you sooner, but I did mention that Reynolds wanted to take us out a while ago. Look, it's a beautiful day; you're always saying we never do anything together. Come on, please," he pleaded, sitting on the edge of the bed.

Libby rolled onto her back and moved the pillow. "I *do* want to do things with you. I just wish you'd discussed it with me before committing us."

"Why do you hate him so much? You don't even know him. Just do it for me, OK? He's my client, and this is all part of the game."

Libby propped herself up against the pillows, running her hand through her mass of curls. "*Part of the game?*" she repeated, not masking her sarcasm. "Ever since you made partner, you've been acting differently. You're even dressing differently. All those new suits? You didn't even ask my opinion on them. And then you tell me the other night how you want to get this sports car. Where did that come from? It's as if this game that you're in is all about material things. I feel like that's all that matters to you now. Like you're so impressed that he has this big yacht and we get to go out on it. You don't even care if the guy is a scumbag."

Josh got up from the bed and walked across the room, running his hands through his hair. He then turned and faced her. "I don't know what you want from me. I'm doing all this for us. You want to stay home with the baby, fine, but someone has to make the money. You wanted to move over here, so we moved over here. I got this house for *you*. Now my career is taking off, and you're mad because I don't spend more time with you. It's all about you!"

Tears stung Libby's eyes. Why were they arguing again? After the past few days of tension, she didn't want to fight. She missed Josh, and she wanted their time together to be good, but lately her intentions went awry. His words had hurt. "You make it sound like I'm the only one who decided that I should stay home with the baby. You agreed that was the right thing."

"I didn't mean it like that." Josh jammed his hands in his pockets and paced the floor. "Of course I want you to stay home with the baby, but that also means I'm the only one bringing in the money, so I don't know why you're holding it against me if I want to do a good job."

Libby knew what he said was true, and maybe she was being selfish. "I guess I'm just tired." Libby pushed back the covers and walked over to Josh, putting her arms around his neck. "I promise I'll try to have a good time today. Let's not fight anymore, OK?"

He smiled and kissed her.

"I love you," she said.

"I love you, too." He smiled a devilish grin. "You know, we have a few extra minutes before we have to be ready."

They pulled into the Reynolds' driveway past large, black, wrought iron gates that sat open for them to enter. Driving up a curving lane past an immaculately manicured emerald-green lawn, bordered by magenta-blossomed crepe myrtles and over-flowing beds of flowers, they circled a fountain and parked near a wide expanse of brick steps leading up to the house. The structure was enormous, over ten thousand square feet of living space. Josh thought how out of place his old Audi looked; next week he was going car shopping. "Nice digs," he said to Libby as he squeezed her hand.

"This place is insane. It looks like a hotel," she replied.

They walked up the steps and rang the bell beside the massive hand-carved, African black ironwood doors. A Hispanic woman clad in a starched uniform opened the door. "Good afternoon," she said in a heavily accented voice.

"Hi, I'm Josh Langston, and this is my wife Libby. We're here to see Mr. and Mrs. Reynolds."

"Si, come inside." She opened the door wider, and they stepped into a mammoth foyer with large black and white marble squares that led to a sweeping staircase. A landing ran across the wide expanse above and joined another staircase, which curved back down into the foyer. A crystal chandelier hung in the center, spanning six feet.

Cynthia Reynolds appeared at the top of the landing. "Hello. We'll be down in a minute. Maria, take the Langstons into the sunroom and give them some lemonade."

Josh and Libby followed Maria down the hall and into a room with floor-to-ceiling windows looking over the Severn River. Tall palms and hanging ferns filled the nooks, along with masses of blooming hibiscus.

Maria motioned for them to sit down on one of the cushioned wicker loveseats, and then she left the room. Before they'd had a chance to take in their surroundings, Cynthia glided into the room. She wore a white silk shirt tucked into a pair of white flowing pants. Her perfectly coiffed blonde hair was swept up with a lapis-blue jeweled clip. Understated gold jewelry adorned her wrist and neck. "So sorry we weren't downstairs to greet you. John's running a bit late, I'm afraid. It's so nice to see you both again." She extended her hand to Josh, and a whiff of an exotic-smelling perfume brushed by them. Josh immediately stood up and shook her hand. "Please sit. Make yourself comfortable."

Libby remained seated as she reached out and shook Cynthia's flawlessly manicured hand.

Maria came back carrying a tray with a crystal pitcher of iced lemonade and four tall frosted glasses. She set the tray down on the large teak coffee table and carefully poured the drinks into each glass. When she was finished, she silently slipped out of the room.

"It looks like it's going to be a beautiful day on the water. We'll be having lunch on the boat. I hope you're both hungry."

Libby studied Cynthia's face. She had dark green eyes and perfectly shaped lips that were shaded with a peach lipstick, the same color as her nails. Libby wondered how John and she had met. Could she have been the woman that he was seeing when Cecilia died? She doubted it, considering that was twenty years ago, and Cynthia didn't look much older than herself.

They were sipping their lemonades when John Reynolds strode into the room. He was dressed in a pair of linen-colored slacks and a teal blue polo shirt that matched his eyes and set off his tan. With his combed silver hair, he looked like he should be on the cover of some travel magazine for the rich.

"Josh, good to see you," he said as Josh stood to shake hands. "And your beautiful wife, Libby." She smiled and nodded to him, extending her hand. But instead of shaking it, he held it as he leaned in and kissed her cheek. "I hear you're expecting. Pregnancy must agree with you, because you are positively glowing, isn't she, Cynthia?"

"Yes, how far along are you?" Cynthia asked.

"About seventeen weeks."

"Well, you've certainly kept your figure so far," Reynolds added.

"Thank you." Libby felt her cheeks getting hot as she reflexively ran her hand over her belly, looking down at her scooped neck sundress and wishing she'd chosen something with a higher neckline. She'd met men like Reynolds before, and they made her feel self-conscious—like women were objects that existed solely for men's pleasure. She wondered if it bothered Cynthia. If it did, she hid it well. Her perfect smile remained plastered to her face.

"So, are you kids ready to head out?" Reynolds led them through the French doors.

The sunroom opened onto a deck that led to the water. The back lawn was as lush and green as the front. Libby eyed the landscaping as they made their way down the sloping terrain to the dock. Judging from her recent dealings with landscapers, this had to cost a small fortune, not to mention the upkeep. She was sure Cynthia wasn't out here on her hands and knees weeding.

A muscular deckhand with bronzed skin dressed in white met them at the pier. His black hair was slicked back, and his eyes were hidden behind dark sunglasses. He took Cynthia's hand as she stepped onto the yacht, letting it linger a second longer than necessary. Libby noticed the way Cynthia returned his gaze and wondered if he provided more than just services for the boat.

The vessel was a sixty-five-foot Westbay motor yacht. The covered aft deck made of teak was polished to perfection. There were several lounge chairs and a linen-covered table set with china, crystal, and silverware. When Cynthia said they were having lunch on the boat, Libby had pictured a picnic basket with sandwiches. She felt like she'd just stepped onto a movie set. She glanced over at Josh to see his reaction, and what she saw disturbed her; he had a look of sheer pleasure on his face, as if this was where he'd always wanted to be.

John escorted them on a tour of the boat, explaining to Josh how he had bought it used several years back from a real estate tycoon from Florida who was filing for bankruptcy. "Timing is everything," he said as he led them into the galley, where the buffed-out deckhand doubled as a chef. A delicious aroma emanated from the state-of-the-art kitchen.

"Something smells wonderful," Libby commented to Cynthia.

"I think Carlos is whipping up some duck a l'orange for lunch. He's truly amazing. He's from Venezuela but going to school here. He works for us part time doing various jobs. You could say he's a jack of all trades." A smile passed over her lips.

"Nice," Libby replied.

"Lunch will be ready in thirty minutes," Carlos said as they exited the galley.

Josh and John went up top on the flying bridge to start up the engines, and Carlos untied the lines from the pier. While John and Josh discussed the power of the 1,000 hp Man diesel engine, Libby and Cynthia headed for the aft deck to lounge on the cushioned chairs. The motor purred low as they began to cruise out into the river.

Carlos placed a covered basket and a dish of butter on the dining table. As he walked back to the galley, Libby noticed he brushed by Cynthia, making contact with her leg. It was very subtle, but Libby was sure it wasn't an accident.

"Carlos, could you be a dear and fix me a vodka tonic, and"—Cynthia turned toward Libby—"what would you like?"

"Ice water would be fine."

Carlos nodded as he left the deck.

"How long have you and John been married?" Libby asked.

"Five years."

"Do you have any children?"

Cynthia gave a slight chuckle. "John and children don't mix. I knew when I married him that if I had kids, I would be on my own. John is too self-centered to have children." Cynthia had put on dark glasses, so Libby couldn't see her eyes, but she detected an edge of bitterness. She then continued in a lighter tone, "Some people weren't meant to have children, which is fine with me."

Carlos returned with the drinks, and as he handed Cynthia her glass, her hand covered his for a split second before he slipped it away.

Libby sensed a hint of sadness that bled through the veneer of Cynthia's perfect demeanor, and the old adage "money can't buy happiness" came to mind.

Libby learned that Cynthia had worked at the State House in Annapolis when she met John. They were engaged within a year. It'd been a whirlwind courtship with them traveling all around the world, and she said he'd literally swept her off her feet, like "a fairy tale come true."

"And fairy tales always have happy endings, right?" Cynthia sipped the last of her vodka tonic.

The men came down from the bridge, and Reynolds dropped the anchor. They had stopped at a secluded cove off the bay. The sky was a cerulean blue with dots of white cumulus clouds scattered about. The water lapped along the edge of the boat as it gently swayed with the current, and a soft breeze blew across the deck. Libby had to admit that this was relaxing.

They gathered at the table just as Carlos swept out from the galley carrying a covered platter. He placed it on the table and removed the top with a lavish gesture before stepping back and bowing slightly.

"This looks fabulous, Carlos. It looks like you've outdone yourself again," Reynolds said.

"Gracias," Carlos replied. "Enjoy!" He bowed again and returned to the cabin.

Reynolds started dishing up the food. The aroma made Libby's mouth water; she was starving. She took a bite, savoring the taste. She'd never tasted anything so wonderful in her life. Cynthia was right; Carlos was good at what he did. "What is Carlos studying in school?" Libby asked. "He certainly knows how to cook. This is delicious."

"He's majoring in business. His plan is to go back to Venezuela and take over his family's coffee enterprise. Cooking is just a hobby of his; he's been doing it since he was a child with his mother," Cynthia said. "John has known his father for years."

The conversation eventually drifted to game fishing. John told Josh about the famous catches he'd had over the years. He even invited Josh to join him for a couple of days in the upcoming Annual White Marlin Tournament in Ocean City. The prize money could be well over a million dollars. It was one of the biggest tournaments on the East Coast. Josh glanced at Libby before answering Reynolds. "I'll have to check my schedule. Can I get back to you on that?"

Reynolds patted him on the back and guffawed. "I know, the better half might not want you away from her," he said as he winked at Libby. "You wouldn't mind if your husband had a little fun with me, would you?"

Libby smiled, forcing down a bite of food. "Josh is his own person; he can make his own decisions on what he wants to do." She looked over at Josh, seething inside.

"Well, that's great. It sounds to me like you can come."

Josh looked back at Libby. She read the battle going on in his head. She knew he wanted to go, but if he had the time to take off to go fishing, why didn't he have the time for her? "Like I said, I just have to check my work schedule. I may have a court date this week. I'm not sure."

"Let me know by Wednesday."

After lunch, Reynolds asked Libby if she would like to go up on the flying bridge. Carlos had pulled up the anchor, and Reynolds had started the engines again. "You get a great view from there," he said.

Libby glanced over at Josh like someone drowning looks at a life raft, but he was busy talking with Cynthia. She didn't want to go, but she didn't know how to get out of it politely.

They climbed the steel ladder on the side of the deck. At the top there were two white leather seats anchored to the platform. Libby sat down on one of the seats, and Reynolds began to steer the boat. He pulled back on the throttle, and the engines purred in response. He slowly maneuvered the boat out of the cove and then accelerated into the open water. A stiff breeze blew across their faces. "Isn't this great!" Reynolds shouted.

It was exhilarating being up on the bridge. The view of the bay was incredible; the sea air was intoxicating; and Libby spontaneously let out a laugh. This isn't so bad after all, she thought. "It's beautiful!" she shouted back over the engine.

Reynolds pointed out various landmarks on the Shore. Jet-skiers rode their wake, flying through the air beside them. Libby closed her eyes and tilted her head back, feeling the warmth of the sun on her face. After several minutes, she felt a hand on her shoulder, and she reflexively jumped.

"I didn't mean to startle you, but I wanted you to see something," Reynolds said. He was standing beside her. "You see that lighthouse over there?" She could feel his breath on her neck. Her eyes followed to where he was pointing. She nodded.

"That's one of the oldest integral lighthouses in the country." The lighthouse, originally a single-story structure, was now a white two-story dwelling with a red cupola and a porch on the front.

"How old is it?" Libby asked.

Reynolds sat back down in his chair, and Libby felt her body relax, not liking how close he'd been.

"It was built in 1830 and is said to be haunted. It served as a civil war hospital and a prisoner of war camp."

Libby thought about Elizabeth and the Haverfords. "Your first wife's family goes way back in this area, don't they?"

Reynolds gave her a puzzled look. "How did you know?"

"I came across an old trunk in the attic, and it had a family album in it from the original owners. James Haverford was a sea captain, but I guess you knew that."

"My father-in-law loved to regale me with tales of his lineage."

"I discovered we're the first owners not to have a family tie to the Haverfords." Libby's hair whipped around, and she brushed a strand from her face. "That family really had its share of tragedy." She studied Reynolds' profile, pausing for a minute. "It must've been very traumatic dealing with your wife's death." Libby waited for his reaction, watching his body language for any clues.

His jaw muscles twitched as he stared straight ahead. "It was one of the hardest things I've ever had to deal with."

"Why do you think she killed herself?" Libby felt the adrenaline pump through her veins, just like when she was a kid, looking for clues.

"I don't know for sure, but she'd battled with depression, and the death of her father took its toll on her." He turned to face Libby. "You know there's something about you that reminds me of Cecilia. Maybe it's your fair skin—no, it's the eyes. You have her eyes, the same blue." His gaze bore into her, and she blinked several times. A chill shot up her spine.

She looked away and then asked, "Did you miss her?"

"What a strange question. Of course I missed her; she was my wife."

She nodded and looked off toward the distant shore, wondering if maybe she'd been wrong about Cecilia. She felt his hand rub across her back, and he was standing right next to her again.

"You're very beautiful," he whispered, his lips brushing her ear. Libby felt the hair rise on the back of her neck as she sat straight up in the chair. What was he doing?

"I'm getting a little chilly. I think I'll go back down and get my sweater."

"Careful going down the ladder; you wouldn't want to slip." His eyes caught hers, and the look cut right to her core. She couldn't explain what it was she saw in his eyes, but it felt sinister, almost evil.

It took all her reserve not to bolt down the ladder as she carefully made her way. She reached the deck and let out a long breath. Then she went over and sat down beside Josh.

"How was it up there? The view is fantastic, isn't it?" he asked.

"Yeah, it was great." Her voice sounded calm, but inside she wanted to scream at Josh to take her home. She spent the rest of the trip glued to Josh's side.

20

Jenna cursed under her breath as she crossed over the Bay Bridge. She was stuck in beach-bound traffic. This was not how she had planned to spend her Saturday, but the phone call she received from her mother at six that morning sounded extremely urgent. She hadn't seen her parents for at least six months and dreaded going back to the farmhouse with all its reminders of the past. She'd had a bittersweet childhood, filled with wonderful memories, but also nightmares that she'd like to forget.

She loved her mother and had tried to convince her to come visit in Alexandria, but her mother hated going to the other side, having left the Shore just a handful of times her whole life. As much love as she had for her mother, she had an equal amount of hate for her father, not caring if she ever saw him again. Alcohol made him repulsive.

Jenna and her brother used to hide in the hayloft to escape their father's drunken tirades. On one of his binges, he was like a tornado, destroying anything in his path. Jenna cringed when she thought of the horrible things that would spew from his mouth.

She had built a completely different life for herself. She loved the friends she had and the lifestyle she lived. To them she never mentioned her past. Instead, she'd reinvented it to reflect what she wished it had been. Her new friends were well educated, worldly, and well connected. She was a rising star of the political "inside the beltway" group. Her name was becoming more and more familiar around town. She hoped working with John Reynolds' campaign would put her over the top with dreams of one day being the White House press secretary.

Jenna gazed down at the water below. Sailboats, scattered about, were gently rocking with the breeze. A beautiful day and she was going to spend it dealing with her father. Her brother was the smart one; he'd moved all the way to Atlanta. Her mother would never expect him to come over at a moment's notice. Oh well, maybe she could get things settled quickly and be back in Virginia by early afternoon, still time to meet up with friends gathering in Old Town later in the day.

Once over the bridge, the traffic picked up. Her mother's voice played back in her mind. She had sounded near hysteria on the phone, crying and telling Jenna that her father was going to kill her. She'd told her mother to calm down and to explain what was going on, even though Jenna already knew; he was on another bender. Her mother insisted this was different, that she'd never seen him so crazy before, and she was hoping Jenna could talk some sense into him. Maybe *knocking* some sense into him would be better, she thought. She'd been tempted to tell her mother to just call the police, but her pleading made it hard for Jenna to say no.

Thirty minutes later, she pulled her car into the gravel drive. Nothing had changed since her last visit; actually, nothing had changed for the past twenty years it seemed. She turned off the BMW and got out. She'd dressed quickly that morning, putting on a pair of old jeans, running shoes, and a faded T-shirt with NIRVANA written across the front. Her auburn hair was pulled back in a ponytail and her face freshly scrubbed with no makeup; there was no need getting fixed up to come to the farm.

The house was eerily silent. Usually her mother would be right at the door, ready to greet her. No one was in the living room, and as she walked down the hall, the only sound came from the floorboards creaking underfoot. She headed into the kitchen. "Mom? I'm here." No answer. The kitchen was empty as well. Instead of soup or stew simmering on the stove and an enticing aroma wafting from the kitchen, she found cabinet doors left open and drawers pulled out.

Jenna walked up the narrow staircase from the kitchen to the second floor. It was warm, and she heard the droning sound of a window fan down the hallway. She passed her room and looked in; it was still as she had left it before going off to college. Ribbons from 4H horse shows and skeet shooting contests hung on the wall along with her lacrosse stick. "Mom?" Jenna called again. Her senses heightened, she walked further down the hall toward her parents' bedroom. She felt her heart pounding against her thin cotton shirt. She heard her breath as it inhaled and exhaled. Something wasn't right.

She stepped into their bedroom, afraid of what she would find. The normally meticulous room was in a total upheaval: a lamp knocked over on the dresser and a broken vase on the floor alongside a framed picture of her grandparents. Clothes were strewn about the floor as well, but she saw no sign of either her mother or her father. She stood in the center of the room for several minutes. A large fly hovered over her head. She swatted at it. Where was her mother?

As she turned to leave the room, her eye caught a glimpse of something out the window. Her mother was running toward the barn, and her father was chasing after her. Jenna flew down the stairs, stumbling at the bottom.

She entered the mudroom off the kitchen, lined with hooks holding work coats and overalls and muck boots neatly arranged on the floor underneath. Without consciously thinking, she opened the gun cabinet, grabbed a shotgun, and then headed out the back door. Her adrenaline pumped as she ran across the yard toward the barn.

As she got closer, she heard raised voices from inside. The barn, which had once housed the horse she'd grown up with, now sat empty except for some farm equipment and tools. She opened the old wooden door made of rough-hewn wood and quietly entered the barn, giving her eyes a second to adjust to the dark. A beam of sun shone through the open door, making visible dancing dust particles and spotlighting a tractor that sat in the middle of the open area. On one side was her father wielding an axe, and on the other was her mother with a pitchfork. Her father was screaming obscenities. Jenna yelled out, "Dad! Put that down!" Both of her parents turned toward her. She stood in the doorway, the shotgun pointed right at her father. Jenna had been an excellent markswoman when she was young, able to shoot a soda can from a hundred yards away. But it had been years since she'd even held a gun.

"What are you doin' here?" her father called out. "Did she call you?"

"Yeah, Mom called me."

"We don't need you around. Just git outta here. I need to teach your mama a lesson. She's got some damn-fooled idea that she can tell me what to do. She probably got it from watchin' that damn television or maybe talkin' to you. No woman of mine is going to back talk me."

"Just shut up, Dad. I'm sick of hearing your fucking bullshit. You're drunk. Mom, come over here; it's OK. He's not going to hurt you."

"Who do you think you're talkin' to? Ada, don't listen to her. You stay right where you are. This is between me and your mother; it has nothing to do with you." Her father weaved toward her, axe in hand. "Did you hear me? I said git out!"

"Jimmy! Stop!" Ada yelled, running over to him. But just before she reached him, he pivoted and swung the axe in her direction. Ada screamed and, at the same instant, a loud *bang* resonated through the barn. Birds fluttered up in the loft, swooping around in circles. Jimmy Thompson reeled backward, the axe falling from his hand, and his body hit the hard dirt floor.

"Oh my God!" Ada screamed. "Oh my God!" She looked up at Jenna, who hadn't moved, the shotgun lowered toward the floor. "What have you done?" Ada knelt down beside Jimmy's body, his arm smattered with birdshot, blood seeping onto his overalls. Jenna knew she'd just grazed her father. If she'd wanted a direct hit, she could have nailed him in the chest with no problem, blowing a hole several inches across. Instead, she'd aimed slightly off to his left, just enough to stun him and knock the axe out of his hand. Still, his breathing was shallow.

"Call 9-1-1! He's still alive!" she heard her mother shout.

Jenna turned slowly, gun in hand, and walked back toward the house. She robotically opened the back door and stepped into the kitchen. She picked up the receiver hanging on the wall and methodically punched the numbers 9-1-1.

"9-1-1, what's your emergency?"

"I've just shot my father; I think we need an ambulance." She gave them the address and then hung the phone back up on the wall. Everything seemed surreal; it was as if time had sped up, yet she was moving in slow motion. She walked back out to the barn, where her mother was crouched over her father's body, sobbing, rocking back and forth.

Jenna stood in the doorway and stared at the scene as if she were watching a movie, wondering why this woman was so upset. The monster had tried to kill her, and now he couldn't hurt her anymore; she should be happy.

Jenna felt no emotion. The smell of hay mixed with the lingering smell of gunpowder filled her nostrils. The sound of wasps, swarming overhead where her father lay, circling their hive, droned in the distance. She stood frozen in one spot and then heard the sirens approaching. She didn't move, couldn't move, as if her limbs were set in concrete, the gun still locked in her grasp. The next thing she knew, the paramedics were rushing by her.

"Ma'am, put the gun down," a man's voice said from behind. She remained frozen. "Ma'am, I said put down your weapon." The voice sounded far off, and it took a few seconds for it to register that he was talking to her.

She slowly set the shotgun on the ground and turned toward the voice. A young-looking deputy with blonde hair was pointing a revolver at her. How bizarre, she thought. She'd somehow become a part of this strange scene. This man was actually pointing a gun at her as if she were a threat. He took two slow steps toward her and picked up the gun, setting it down away from her. He then took her hands behind her back and clasped handcuffs on them. "Did you place the call to 9-1-1 saying you'd shot your father?"

"Yes."

"Ma'am, you have the right to remain silent..." He recited her Miranda rights as they walked to the patrol car. He opened the back door, placing his hand on her head as he helped her into the backseat.

The paramedics brought her father out on a stretcher, an IV bag held by one of them. Still, she felt nothing. Watching her mother walk beside the stretcher, sobbing, was more a curiosity than sadness.

The patrol car waited for the ambulance to pull out, and then they drove over the gravel drive, passing her BMW parked out front. Jenna glanced at the car, and reality began seeping back in. What had happened? One minute, she'd been planning her afternoon with friends, and the next she was being hauled away in handcuffs in the back of a police car.

They rode to the sheriff's office in silence, passing familiar landmarks along the way: the high school where Jenna had been homecoming queen, the houses of friends she no longer knew. They drove through town past the courthouse, the Corsica Bank, Edward's Pharmacy, and all Jenna could think of was the pharmacy had a new sign out front. The old one, she remembered, had been faded for so long that it had read "WARDS HARMA Y."

They pulled in front of the station. Jenna had never been inside the sheriff's office in all the years she'd lived here. Deputy Seevers—she'd noticed the name on his badge—led her through the door. A short woman with big blonde hair sat at a desk inside. She looked up from the papers she was working on, and Jenna immediately recognized her as Maggie Porter, a fixture in Corsica for years. Jenna remembered when she was a child, Maggie, with the same hairstyle, dishing up the food at the potluck suppers they would have at the community center from time to time.

"Why, Jenna Thompson! I haven't seen you in years, child. I'm so sorry about your daddy." Maggie had taken the call from the emergency operator who told her a man had been shot at 923 Foxhall Road. Maggie knew immediately it was Jimmy and Ada Thompson's place, and she naturally assumed Jimmy had been shot. She had passed the news on to Will, who'd been out in his patrol car at the time. As soon as the words had left Maggie's mouth, she noticed the handcuffs on Jenna. "Good Lord, Will, what happened?"

"That's what I'm about to find out," Will answered. Sheriff Tucker was out fishing, and there was no way to get in touch with him, but Will knew he could handle this on his own; he'd handled much worse cases in Baltimore.

Jenna smiled briefly at Maggie, but Jenna's eyes revealed only her emptiness. Will took Jenna into a small room off the main area used for questioning suspects, but more commonly used for holding teens while waiting for their parents to come get them after joyriding in the streets. The room was bare except for a metal table and three metal chairs.

Will seated Jenna in one of the chairs and removed the handcuffs. She rubbed her wrists as she watched Will take his place across from her. A blank pad of paper and pen sat on the table, ready for any information a suspect might reveal.

"So, I assume you're Jenna Thompson." Will held the pen poised over the tablet.

"Yes." Jenna looked down at her hands, rubbing them together in her lap.

"And you're the daughter of Jimmy and Ada Thompson."

"Yes."

"You live in Alexandria, Virginia?"

"Yes." Jenna looked up and gave Will a puzzled look. "How did you know that?"

"I met your mother a few weeks ago, and she told me about you and your brother. He's in Atlanta, if I recall correctly."

"That's right."

Will studied Jenna's face and body language, looking for signs that might disclose her motivation. He stared into her green eyes flecked with gold. He saw a beautiful woman, close to his own age, someone strong and independent. She didn't look like a killer, though. But Will had learned over the years, there really was no such thing. He'd arrested seventy-year-old men that, at first glance, looked like somebody's kind grandfather. Then he'd learn this man had just stabbed his wife to death. But this wasn't a murder, at least not yet. He was waiting for an update on Jimmy's condition.

"So, Jenna, you want to tell me what happened?"

"I shot my father."

"Could you elaborate?"

"You mean why did I shoot him?" Jenna sat back and closed her eyes; she opened them and looked directly at Will. "I shot him because he's a drunken asshole that has no respect for women. I shot him because I lived for years hearing the same bullshit over and over again. I shot him because of the constant abuse he gave my mother." She paused and looked back down at her hands, her lips pursed together as she fought off tears. She lifted her head slowly and stared at Will. "I *shot* him because I thought he was going to kill my mother. I didn't kill him. I could have, easily; I just wanted to stop him."

"Do you have an attorney you'd like to call?"

"Do I need one?"

"It wouldn't hurt. Until an investigation is done, you could be charged with aggravated assault or possibly attempted murder."

"Isn't it ironic? I'll probably go to jail, and he'll be made out as the poor victim." She shook her head. "I was only doing society a favor."

"You can't take the law into your own hands."

"I guess I should've waited until he axed my mother and *then* shot him."

"I'm sure once we talk to your mother and corroborate your story, the charges may be dropped, but in the meantime there are laws we have to follow."

"You said I get to make a phone call?"

"Yeah."

"Then get me a phone."

Will left the room. He seemed like a decent guy, Jenna thought. He definitely wasn't one of the good ole' boys. Thank God. He wasn't bad looking either, but too good-looking to be working in this crap bag of a town, she thought. She noticed the wedding ring on his left hand. The good ones were always taken. She let out a laugh to the empty room. This had to be a dream. She couldn't actually be sitting in a jail waiting to be charged with attempted murder—and sizing up the deputy sheriff. Could things get any more bizarre?

Will returned with a portable phone.

"Thanks."

Maggie popped her head in the door: "Will, the hospital's on the phone."

Will left Jenna alone to make her call.

She wished she had her cell with her; it had all her numbers in it. She stared at the phone, wondering whom to call. There was Steve, she thought, a friend she knew in Alexandria, but he specialized in wills and trusts. Maybe he knew someone. She called information to get Steve's number, but when the operator came on the line, Jenna told her she needed two numbers. She reached across the desk and grabbed the pen. Will had taken the pad of paper, so she wrote the numbers in the palm of her hand.

She dialed the second one first. After several rings, a Hispanic woman answered the phone and told her that Mr. Reynolds was out on his boat. He wouldn't be back for hours. Jenna gave the woman her cell number and told her to have John call her when he got in. She was sure she'd be out of here by the time he got back.

She then called Steve. She exhaled with relief when he picked up. She explained her situation, and he gave her the name of a criminal lawyer he knew, saying the guy had a great track record. He would call him and give him a heads up that she would be contacting him. She wrote down the number on her hand.

Will came back with a grim look on his face that made Jenna uneasy.

"That was the hospital on the phone." He looked down at the table.

Jenna held her breath, wanting to shout, "What! Spit it out!"

"Your father passed away."

Jenna's eyes widened with surprise and confusion. How could he be dead? She'd just grazed him. He *can't* be dead. They must be playing some kind of weird trick on her. This whole thing was some sort of peculiar game. She sat silent as he continued.

"The doctors aren't sure of the cause of death. They're going to perform an autopsy to find out more."

"I need to be with my mother."

"I'm afraid you're not going anywhere right now, except over to the county jail. I've spoken with the prosecutor. There'll be a hearing Monday morning, but until the——"

"This is fucking ridiculous. I didn't *kill* my father!" She needed to get out of the room. Her breath was coming in short gasps. She looked down at her sweating palms. The inked-in numbers were beginning to blur. She buried her head in her hands.

21

"I might as well knit you a pink one, too. I just know she's a girl." The yellow yarn wrapped around Tassie's finger wove its way into a blanket as the knitting needles clicked together. She rocked back and forth while her fingers worked their magic, creating a beautiful pattern. Libby had polished the rich dark wood of the old rocker from the attic and had placed it in the adjoining room of the nursery.

The newly purchased, multicolored braided rug in pastel shades of pink, blue, green, and yellow adorned the center of the room. Libby sat in the middle of the rug sorting through a multitude of baby outfits. Her mother had recently shipped several boxes filled with clothes, miniature watercolors in yellows and greens, and several baby quilts.

"How do you know it's a girl?"

"I just do, child."

"Well, we'll know if you're right in just a few weeks when I go back for my next sonogram." Libby held up a green bunting. "Oh my God! Is this not adorable?"

Tassie smiled and nodded as her needles *click-clicked* with the creak of the rocker.

Libby set the bunting on the floor and ran her hands over the embroidered stitching of a bunny on the front. "I had a hard time bringing myself to call my mother to thank her for all of this stuff. I'm still mad that she went behind my back and called Josh, insinuating I was mentally deranged for seeing a ghost."

"Now, now, child, your mama did it out of love."

"Love? That's a strange way of showing you love someone, to suggest they're crazy."

"Some people have a hard time believing something they can't see and don't understand." Tassie shook her head. "There's one thing that's always puzzled me, though."

"What?" Libby folded the outfits into piles.

"Millions of people have no problem believing in the good Lord, even though they never laid eyes on him, but when it comes to other spirits, they're quick to doubt. I think maybe it has something to do with fear. They know that God is benevolent, but they're not sure about the lesser spirits."

"You're probably right." Libby went into the adjoining room to put some of the clothes into the antique dresser she'd bought last week. Returning she said, "You know, I never did figure out where that hummingbird book is." She tapped her foot on the wooden floorboards along the wall. "I walked all over this floor before I put the rug down, checking for loose boards, but I couldn't find any." She went over to the wall and began tapping. The solid thud of the plaster walls was the only sound. "Why would Elizabeth bring us in here?" She stepped over Stella who lay sprawled out, warming herself in the sun that streamed through the long window. Libby tapped on the sides of a built-in bookcase: *thud-thud, thud-thud*. She reached her arm in and knocked on the back. There was a different sound. Not as low. "Did that sound hollow to you?"

"I believe so."

Libby repeated the knocking. She ran her hand along the wood surface, pressing in various spots. She pushed on one side, and the wood gave way. She looked over at Tassie with a look of surprise. As she pushed farther, the panel popped out. She stretched her arm but could barely reach behind the shelf. She ran out of the room and returned with the dressing stool from her bedroom. She climbed up on it and reached into the hole, blindly feeling her hand around. Aha! Her fingers grabbed onto something. It felt like a book. She pulled it out and held it up. The sun caught the jeweled pattern on the front, casting prisms of light around the room. Dark blue and green crystals formed the shape of a hummingbird. "I found it!" Libby jumped off the stool and ran over to Tassie. She sat down on the floor next to her and opened the book.

The first page contained a poem titled "The Hummingbird" written in a neatly scripted handwriting. Libby read the poem aloud:

> *The new day dawns*
> *The flowers turn their blossoming heads to the rising sun*
> *Their vibrant colors bursting with the glory of spring*
> *The trees shake their arms of green while the baby birds sing*
> *I see you flutter by to the flowers on the vine*
> *I see you hover as if suspended in time.*
> *I wonder do you ever stop or are you always on the run?*
> *Can you come and see me later when you think that you are done?*
> *You are such a tiny creature I would like to see you more*
> *I sit by the window to hear your knock upon my door.*
> *I hope that you can spare a minute from your busy, busy day*
> *And join me in my bedroom so we can sit and play.*

The poem was dated July 16, 1984. Cecilia had been sixteen when she wrote it. It must have been right after her father had given it to her on her birthday; Libby remembered she had been born on July 15, 1968.

The book was quite thick. She must have made many entries over the years. Although most of them were poems, some were about her thoughts on different subjects. Libby skimmed through the pages until she came to Cecilia's writing about first meeting John Reynolds. Her words sounded very much like a schoolgirl with a crush, but from the date of the writings, Cecilia was twenty-one years old. From her words, it appeared to be her first love; she'd probably never gone out with anyone before, Libby thought.

Libby flipped through the pages and stopped at one entry:

John is coming over tonight. I think he is going to ask my father for my hand in marriage. I hope he does. I can't picture living my life without him. I know my father will say yes. He adores John. I will be seated out back on the settee, and I will look surprised when he comes out the back and walks across the lawn toward me. Then he will get down on one knee and take my hand in his. It will be just like in the movies.

"She sounds so childish," Libby said.

"She did live a sheltered life," Tassie replied.

Libby turned to the last few pages in the book, where she found an entry dated April 25, 1992:

My life is crashing down around me. I discovered two days ago that I am expecting. I was waiting for the right opportunity to tell John, since he said we were not ready to have kids yet. Why, I don't know. I have wanted a child more than anything ever since we got married. I knew once I told him the news, he would be as happy as I am, but last night I witnessed something that has changed everything. I was alone waiting for John to come home. I was in the bedroom, and I saw a boat out the window approaching the dock. It scared me at first, as I wondered who would be coming this late at night. There was a full moon so I could clearly make out the images, even at such a distance. When the boat came to a stop, I realized it was John's boat. Then I saw her, the silhouette of a woman. I saw him kiss her. Who is she? I feel as if someone has stabbed me in the heart. My mind has been racing all night. I don't know what I should do. Should I confront him and let him know that I saw him, or should I pretend I don't know and tell him about the baby instead. But what if he doesn't want the baby? What if he loves this woman more than he loves me? How can I go on? All I've ever wanted was a happy family. Now nothing will be the same. I pray that I have the strength to do what is right.

Libby stopped reading aloud and looked up at Tassie. "That poor woman—how sad. But from what she said, it's hard to tell if she committed suicide or not."

"Are there more entries?" Tassie asked.

"Let me see." Libby flipped the page. The next page was dated May 1, 1992:

I did it. I confronted John. I still haven't told him about the baby, but I let him know what I saw. Of course he tried to deny it, telling me that I am crazy. He got so angry that at one time I feared he was going to hit me, but I think that was just his shock of having been caught. I know what I saw, and he will eventually have to tell me the truth. I have decided that if he will come clean and explain what happened, I may forgive him, but only if he promises to stop the affair. Then I will tell him about the baby, and maybe we can still have our happy life. Everyone makes mistakes, and I know the Lord would want me to be forgiving. I'll give him time to reflect, and then I'll bring the subject back up. The only way for us to continue together is to get this out in the open and move forward. I pray that John will do the right thing.

Cecilia wrote her last entry two days before she died:

John is acting very peculiar. He's not arguing with me anymore, but he's been very distant. Yesterday, I decided to tell him about the baby. I thought maybe if he knew, he would come to his senses, but his reaction was one of shock. He said he was not ready for a family, and I should never have allowed myself to get pregnant. He said this was all my fault! My fault!

I can't believe he thinks his unborn child is something to blame me for. He left the house and did not return until late into the night. He slept in the guest room, and when I saw him this morning he barely said two words to me. I don't know what to do. All I know is that I want this baby more than anything, with or without John. I had a dream last night that was so vivid, I thought it was real. I had the baby, and it was a little girl. I had named her Olivia, after my grandmother. She was so beautiful; she had blonde curls surrounding her face and big blue eyes. She looked like an angel. When I woke this morning, I felt so happy until I realized it had all been a dream. But I now know nothing is going to stop me from having this baby. Please, dear Lord, help me to make the right decision.

The rest of the pages were blank. Libby closed the book in her lap and looked over at Tassie. "Well. What do you think of that?"

"I think if I were John Reynolds, I would not want that book to ever come to light," Tassie said, solemn.

"Do you really think he could've killed her?"

"Some people are just born evil. No matter how much kindness is bestowed upon them, it doesn't change their soul. Sometimes a good soul can be damaged, but they can be saved. There's no hope for the truly evil ones."

"What makes you think John Reynolds is evil?"

"I didn't say he was. If he did kill Cecilia, I hope it was because his soul was temporarily damaged and he's repented." Tassie's knitting needles clicked and then stopped. She looked up at Libby. "Because if he was truly evil, he'd have no regrets. There's nothing an evil soul wouldn't do."

Libby felt a shiver run through her. Evil souls, damaged souls. It all sounded macabre. She envisioned a grotesque-looking horned creature rising out of the ground coming toward her.

She jumped as her cell rang next to her on the rug. It was Julie. She said she was in a bind. She couldn't get a hold of Will, and her mother had just called and said they were taking her father to the hospital. He was having chest pains. She wanted to know if she could drop the kids off. Libby said that was fine, not to worry about it. Julie thanked her profusely and said if she ran late, she'd get Will to pick up the kids.

It was getting close to six o'clock, and Josh had called saying he wouldn't be home for dinner. Libby had been upset that he'd gone in on a Saturday and assured her it wouldn't be for long. His schedule was getting worse instead of better.

Sara sat on the kitchen floor folding her doll's blanket the way that Libby had shown her. Smiling, Libby watched Sara carefully wrap up the baby and then hold it to her chest, pretending to nurse it. "This is how you feed the baby," Sara said.

"Did your mommy show you that?" Libby was standing at the stove, making grilled cheeses for everyone.

Sara nodded.

Tassie and the boys were in the den watching a movie. Sara had stuck like glue to Libby ever since Julie had dropped them off. She placed the sandwiches on a tray and headed into the den with Stella and Sara in tow.

She loved the den; it was one of her favorite rooms in the house. Built-in bookshelves and cabinets lined the walls. An Oriental rug partially covered the dark, wide-planked wood floors. She placed the tray on the large square coffee table in front of the leather sofa where Tassie sat. The kids gathered on the floor around the table and ate their sandwiches. Libby plopped down in a big overstuffed armchair. It felt good to sit down.

Within minutes after finishing her sandwich, Sara climbed into Libby's lap and curled her warm body against Libby's chest. Libby smiled, happy that Sara felt comfortable with her. She kissed the top of her blonde head, inhaling the sweet smell of a child. She would have her own soon. A little girl. That is, if Tassie was right. Libby glanced over at the diminutive woman who looked lost in the giant sofa. Her eyes were closed, and she had a peaceful look on her face.

A knock on the door sent Stella barking into the foyer. Libby extricated herself out from under Sara and headed to the door. It was Will. She hadn't seen him since their encounter at the creek. There was a moment of awkward silence, and then Libby stepped back for Will to enter.

"How's Julie's dad?"

"Fine. They say it was a false alarm. Acute indigestion. She's spending the night at her mom's. She didn't want to have to drive back tonight."

Libby nodded. "I fed the kids. Have you had anything to eat?"

"No, but that's OK. I can fix something at home. It's been a long day."

"The kids are watching a movie. I can make you a grilled cheese if you want." Libby was trying to act normal, as if nothing had happened, but she was having trouble breathing. She felt drawn to Will, and she didn't know why. Last week had been a mistake, and it wouldn't happen again. He was her friend, period.

Will followed her into the kitchen. She went over to the counter and got out the bread, then opened the refrigerator door, grabbing the cheese. She felt Will watching her from across the room. She wondered what he was thinking. Was he wishing they hadn't done what they did? They needed time to get it behind them.

"Any more ghost sightings?" he asked.

The butter sizzled as she placed the sandwich in the hot pan.

"That reminds me, I found Cecilia's journal." She told Will about the secret space behind the bookcase. She flipped the sandwich over and got out a plate. Pouring a glass of iced tea for Will, she said, "I think it places more suspicion on Reynolds. Cecilia wrote that she was expecting." Libby brought the tea and sandwich over to the table. "Let me go get it." A moment later Libby came back with the book and sat down across from Will.

"Speaking of Cecilia," Will said, "I wanted to tell you that I spoke with the coroner, and he showed me his notes on the case. He remembered that case very well; he'd just started working as the county coroner when she died, and it was one of his first cases. He wanted to do an autopsy, but the sheriff put the kibosh on it. Some of the evidence didn't jive with drowning, accidental or otherwise, he said. No outward signs indicated that she'd fallen and hit her head, no bruising, so that pretty much ruled out an accident. He also said that usually when someone wants to commit suicide in a bathtub, they slash their wrists and bleed to death or take a lot of pills, inducing them to pass out and drown. But to just go under the water and drown in a bathtub is very rare." Will bit into his sandwich and then picked up the book.

Libby thought, he believes me; he takes me seriously. To him she wasn't some kind of nut for wanting to look into the case.

He continued, "Since the coroner was the new guy in town, he didn't have a whole lot of say in how matters were handled; he wanted to keep his job, so he never really pushed the case. He said it wasn't like there was overwhelming evidence that proved any foul play, but he would've preferred to have been certain, and without the autopsy there was no way of knowing."

"Hmm…I wonder if there's any way we could get the body exhumed and whether it would tell us anything."

Will skimmed through the pages of the book while he ate. "It could probably tell you if she was pregnant. I don't think we have enough to go on to get an exhumation, though. I'll keep searching; maybe I'll come across something." He set the book on the table and took the plate over to the sink to rinse it off.

"Take the book with you if you think it will help."

"What does Josh think about me snooping into this case?"

"Maybe we should just keep it between the two of us for now."

Will nodded. "I have a funny feeling about this case. It happens sometimes with cases, where things just don't feel right."

Libby headed toward the counter to put away the cheese just as Will was turning from the sink. Their arms brushed against each other. He paused and Libby stopped. Then he touched her arm. She closed her eyes, and a warm rush spread throughout her body. Her heart raced. She opened her eyes, and he was staring at her. He leaned in closer and kissed her. A surge of pleasure shot through her. She heard footsteps and backed away.

"Daddy!" Nathan shouted as he ran into the kitchen.

Libby turned and walked to the counter. Her hands shook. What was happening to her?

"Hey, buddy. Go get your brother and sister and tell them it's time to go." Nathan ran from the room.

Libby felt Will standing behind her. Her palms pressed against the counter. After a minute of silence, he said, "Well, I should probably head home." She glanced over her shoulder. He picked up the book and left the kitchen.

22

J ane Michaels had been the county prosecutor for twelve years. She never married, instead having opted for the companionship of two dogs and a cat. She loved her job, and her five-foot-four-inch petite frame belied her true nature as a fighter.

She sat at the long table in the windowless interrogation room of the county jail. It was 9:00 a.m., Monday morning. Will was meeting her there to interview Jenna and her mother before she made a decision on the case. Dressed in her "uniform,"—as everyone at the courthouse referred to her usual attire of a navy blue pants suit with a white button-down shirt (she actually had four suits identical in style: two navy, one black, and one tan)—she examined the notes that Will had taken after questioning Jenna.

The door opened and Will walked in, guiding Ada Thompson by the arm. Ada looked distraught and disoriented. Her eyes were bloodshot, and the skin on her face was blotchy. She had on a flowered blouse over her plump, matronly torso and a pair of polyester slacks. The buttons of her blouse were buttoned wrong, leaving the shirt uneven at the bottom.

Will pulled out a chair for her so that she sat across from Jane Michaels. Ada had a handkerchief tightly balled up in her hand. Will sat down next to her.

"Mrs. Thompson?"

Ada glanced up, her expression one of confusion.

"I'm Jane Michaels, prosecutor for the county. I want to talk to you about what happened on Saturday."

"Where's Jenna?"

"She's here."

Ada nodded.

"Do you think you could tell me what happened? I'm going to be recording your statement."

"It all seems like a blur to me. Everything happened so fast."

"Just do the best you can; take your time and try to remember." Jane hit the button on the small recorder on the table.

"Well, I'd gotten up to feed the chickens, and I noticed Jimmy wasn't in bed. In fact, he hadn't come to bed all night. He'd been drinking heavily the night before, and I figured he'd fallen asleep on the couch downstairs. He does that from time to time. But when I looked in the living room, he wasn't there." She wiped the handkerchief across her nose with a sniffling sound. "I went into the kitchen to get some coffee started before going out to the chicken house, and there he was tearing through the drawers like he was looking for something. I asked him what in the world was he doing, and he turns and looks at me with this crazed look in his eye. I'd never seen anything like it before. It was as if he didn't even know who I was." She paused, turning the handkerchief around in her hands.

Jane prompted her. "Then what happened?"

Ada looked up at Jane as if she didn't understand her. Then she went on: "He said he wanted to know where the money was. You see, I keep a jar of money for emergencies hidden in the house. He'd already rummaged through all the cupboards and the pantry. I asked him what he needed money for, and he told me it was none of my damned business, so I told him I'd never tell him because he'd probably just blow it on alcohol. Well, that got him real mad, and he comes at me screaming. So, I turned and ran up the stairs and locked myself in the bedroom. That's when I called Jenna. I'd never seen him so worked up."

She stared off into space, shaking her head back and forth. The tape recorder kept running. "He starts banging on the door, calling me every name in the book. I sat on the bed and waited for him to stop, and after a little while, he did, so I waited a little longer and figured it was safe to come out. So I quietly walked over to the door and opened it a peek. I looked out but didn't see him anywhere, so I came out of the bedroom and took the front stairs and went out the front door and hid behind my lilac bush in the side yard, waitin' for Jenna to arrive. I heard him inside screamin' again, saying he wanted that money and he would find it. There was all sorts of crashing and banging going on, and I was afraid to think what he was doing to the house. Then it got quiet again, and my legs were cramping. You see, I've got arthritis in my knees." She rubbed her hand on her knees.

"I couldn't wait for Jenna to git there. She used to be able to calm him down when she was little, and I hoped maybe she'd talk some sense into him this time. Then I heard the screen door slam out back, and I knew he was coming lookin' for me. He was yellin' my name and saying all sorts of terrible things. I never been so scared in my life. I ran out from the bush and around the house and down to the chicken house. I waited in there for so long that I thought for sure he must've passed out or left. I musta been in there for two hours, but I was afraid to come out until Jenna got there. But then I heard him open the door. The chickens started a clucking and carrying on when he came in, and I ran out the door on the other end, but he saw me. He started chasing me toward the barn. I ran in and grabbed a pitchfork hanging on the wall." The fluorescent bulb overhead buzzed and sputtered, blinking off and on. "He was right behind me and I said…" She stopped. Her lips began to quiver, and tears filled her eyes.

Will patted her hand.

She blew her nose and then continued: "I said, 'Jimmy Thompson, don't you come near me! You're outta your mind!' But he grabs an axe that was layin' by one of the stalls and starts coming at me, circling around the tractor. I swear I think he'd lost his mind. That's when Jenna came in. Neither of us heard her until she called out to her dad. When we saw her standin' in the doorway, she had a shotgun pointed right at him. She told her daddy to put down the axe and leave me alone, but he wouldn't listen." Ada paused again and dabbed at her eyes.

"It's very important that you remember exactly what happened next."

"Jenna kept the gun aimed at him, and instead of listening to her, he started to come at her. I was so afraid he was gonna try and hit Jenna with the axe, and I ran over screaming, '*No, Jimmy!*'" Ada reached her hand out as if she were reliving the nightmare. "That's when he turned toward me and raised the axe. The next thing I know, the gun goes off, and Jimmy's on the floor." Ada put her face in her handkerchief and then said in a crackled voice, "I feel like this is all my *fault*; if I'd just given him the money, at least he'd still be alive."

Jane looked over at Will. Then she asked Ada, "Do you know where Jenna got the gun?"

Ada shrugged. "I guess in Jimmy's gun cabinet. That's where all the guns are."

"Did he keep them loaded?"

"Some, I think." Ada dazedly stared at Jane Michaels. "What's gonna happen to Jenna?"

"I don't know yet."

"Jenna's a good girl. She'd never hurt anyone." Ada looked at Will. "I just thought she could talk some sense into him is all."

Jane Michaels thanked Ada, and Will led her out of the room.

Later he asked Jane, "What do you think?"

She shook her head. "It looks like self-defense, maybe. I just wonder why she came into the barn with a loaded gun."

"She knew what her father was like."

"There'd never been any charges of violence with Jimmy Thompson. I mean, he was a drunk, but Ada herself said she'd never seen him that crazed before. How would Jenna know what was going on in the barn?"

"I guess you'll have to ask her yourself."

"Go get her."

A few minutes later, Will led Jenna into the room, thinking she looked tired. When he'd gotten her out of the holding cell, he'd noticed the dark circles under her eyes. Her hair was pulled back in a ponytail, but strands had come loose and were hanging limp around her face.

"Hi, Jenna," Jane said as Jenna sat down in the same chair her mother had just vacated.

Jenna's demeanor had changed, Will thought. The anger, now gone, was replaced with uneasiness. He couldn't tell if it was fear or guilt or both.

"Jenna, I know Will's already asked you some questions regarding what happened at the farm, and I've already spoken with your mother, but I'd like to hear what you have to say as well. I'm sure Will has told you. You don't need to talk with us without your attorney. I assume you have one."

Jenna nodded. She'd spoken with the lawyer that her friend Steve had recommended—Jackson Darrow—and he told her he'd meet her today at the detention center. He also told her not to talk with anyone.

"He should be here sometime, but I'll talk." Jenna wanted to explain what had happened. She hadn't tried to kill her father. She had nothing to hide. Jenna sat with her arms folded across her chest.

"OK." Jane looked at Will. "I'm going to tape record your story of events."

Jenna nodded.

"Go ahead."

"When I got the call from my mom, at first I thought it was just another one of my dad's tirades, but she sounded different this time, really frightened. I wanted her to call the police, but she begged me to come." Jenna gave a slight grin. "I was the peacemaker. Ever since we were teenagers, my brother used to get furious with my dad, yelling back at him, and it just made things worse. But I could always calm him down." She brushed a strand of hair behind her ear, and for a moment, Will caught a glimpse of the young girl she'd once been.

"Did he ever physically abuse your mother, or you and your brother?" Jane asked.

"No, it was usually just verbal. He threatened my brother sometimes when he would yell back at him, but as Jack got older, I think my dad was afraid of him. He was on the football team, running back." Jenna paused and pursed her lips, drawing in her breath. "When my dad was sober, he was a completely different man. There were times when he was actually a nice person. He used to take me skeet shooting, and he taught me to ride a horse." Jenna looked down at her hands in her lap and picked at her fingernail. She took another deep breath and wiped the tears from the corner of her eyes with the back of her hand. "So much for years of therapy. I guess I should tell my shrink I want my money back." She forced a laugh.

Jane Michaels remained straight-faced. "Could you tell me what you did when you got to your parents' house?"

"I knew something was wrong the minute I walked in the house. It was too quiet. I searched all the rooms for my parents but couldn't find them. The rooms were a mess. Then I spotted them outside—my father was chasing my mother toward the barn."

"Where did you get the gun?"

"From the gun case in the mudroom."

"So you took a gun with you from the house out to the barn. What made you take the gun?"

"I don't know. I didn't really think about it."

"Did you go out there thinking you were going to shoot your father?"

"No. I don't know. Like I said, I didn't really think at all. When I got to the barn and saw my father with an axe, I pointed the gun at him and told him to drop it."

"Did your mother have anything in her hand?"

"No. No, wait. She had a pitchfork in her hand."

"What happened next?"

"He started yelling at me and telling me to leave. The next thing I knew, he was coming at me with the axe, and then my mother ran toward him. When he turned toward her, he raised the axe at her. So I shot him."

"Did you think he was going to hit your mother?"

"I didn't know, but I wasn't about to wait and find out. I purposefully aimed toward his hand, just to knock the axe out. Believe me, if I'd wanted to kill him, he'd be dead now." As soon as the words left Jenna's mouth, she realized what she'd said. "What I meant was, I'm an expert shot, and I didn't shoot to kill."

23

The small brick post office, built in 1892, sat at the corner of Main and Liberty. There was nothing fancy about it, just a wall of post office boxes, packing supplies hanging on a rack, and a short counter where Mary Alice the postmistress was stationed on the other side.

"Good morning, Mrs. Langston. How are you today?" Mary Alice smiled as Libby walked in with Stella on a leash.

"Fine, thanks," Libby replied. "I need to get some stamps."

"Would you like a book or a roll?"

"I need at least forty, so whichever you think is better."

"I'll give you a roll." Mary Alice pulled open a drawer and set the roll on the counter.

Libby began applying the stamps to the stack of invitations.

"What's the occasion?" Mary Alice asked.

"We're having a party on Labor Day weekend. In fact, maybe you could help me with some of the addresses for a few local people."

"Why sure."

Libby went down the list of names, including Mary Alice's. Mary Alice pulled out a book of addresses and started looking up the missing ones for Libby.

"Why, that's mighty sweet of you to invite me and Herbert. We'd love to come. I think it's wonderful you've opened back up Haverford House. It sat empty for so many years. It was truly sad to see such a beautiful place go downhill."

"Did you visit the house when John Reynolds lived there?"

"No, but I did know Cecilia. We were the same age. I used to go there occasionally when I was a little girl."

"I guess it was quite upsetting for you when she committed suicide."

"Oh, it was." Mary Alice frowned and shook her head. "I remember saying to Herbert that something wasn't right about the whole thing. Cecilia was an unusual girl, but I never would've believed she'd kill herself. I can't imagine how things could've gotten so bad."

"From what I hear, she was distraught over her father's death."

"Oh, that's just an excuse." Mary Alice waved a dismissive hand. "I know Cecilia was very close to her father, but not so close she'd want to die over his death. She always knew her father had a fragile heart. If anything drove her to kill herself, it was that husband of hers."

Libby looked up from the envelopes, a stamp stuck on her finger. "What makes you say that?"

"I always wondered about him." Mary Alice glanced toward the door and then leaned into the counter. "He had a post office box here with just his name on it, and the only thing that ever came was letters from a woman. I mean, why did he need a post office box when his mail was delivered to his house? The only thing I could figure was he was cheating on his wife."

"You wouldn't by any chance remember the woman's name?"

"Oh my, that was so long ago." She chuckled and then tapped her finger to her lips. "Let me think. I can picture the envelopes; they were all the same." She closed her eyes and thought for a minute. "Clara? No. Catherine! Catherine Collins—that's it. I have a photographic memory, have had one ever since I was a child. The return address was from Hollywood, Maryland. I remember that because I used to think it was funny that her name, Catherine Collins, sounded like a movie star's name."

"You do have a good memory." Libby smiled. She placed a stamp on the last envelope. "I guess Reynolds got rid of the post office box when he moved."

"He did, but not for several months. But I do remember that after Cecilia died, the letters stopped coming."

"Hmm." Libby finished filling in the missing addresses on the envelopes and gave the stack to Mary Alice.

Coming out of the post office, Libby noticed a gathering of people around the courthouse. She wondered what was going on. She saw a van parked by the curb with the letters "WBOC TV NEWS 16" on the side. Out of curiosity, she walked over to the gathering across the square. She noticed Mrs. Jenkins from the bakery standing next to Pearl and walked up to them. "What's all the commotion?" Both women turned toward her and smiled. Mrs. Jenkins answered, "It's the Thompson girl, Jenna. They say she's being charged with murder."

"If you ask me, Jimmy got what he deserved," Pearl added. "He was nothing but a no-good drunk. I don't know how Ada put up with him all those years."

Just then, the doors to the courthouse opened, and Libby caught a glimpse of a woman with long auburn hair and dark sunglasses, wearing a charcoal-colored dress with a wide black belt, led out by a man in a dark, expensive-looking suit. She's striking, Libby thought.

She watched the reporters clamor around her and her attorney, trying to get a statement from them. The attorney helped Jenna into a black Lexus parked at the curb, then turned toward the reporters and said that Jenna was innocent of the charges, and it would not be long before the truth was told. He then got in the car, shut the door, and they drove off. The crowd began to thin as Libby took Stella and walked back to her car.

Her mind drifted to Mary Alice's remarks about the post office box. Maybe Cecilia had found one of the letters and discovered that Reynolds was having an affair. After the day on the boat, Libby was even more convinced that Reynolds was someone not to be trusted. He gave off a bad vibe, she felt. She'd given up discussing it with Josh; she was never going to convince him that there was anything wrong with Reynolds.

Perhaps she could track down Catherine Collins in Hollywood, Maryland—that is, if she still lived there after twenty years. What was she doing? What if Reynolds hadn't killed his wife, and all he was guilty of was an affair? She could possibly ruin his chances of winning the election, not to mention Josh's career.

❦

Libby stared at the computer screen for several seconds before picking up the phone again. She dialed the third C. Collins listed on the White Pages for Maryland, but the woman that picked up had never heard of a Catherine.

Libby returned to the Google search page. On a whim, she typed in "Catherine Collins, Maryland" and pressed enter. Several sites popped up, but one in particular caught her eye. The excerpt said, *"Catherine Collins, formerly from Maryland, launches line of women's designer clothing."* It was a clip from an article in the *San Francisco Chronicle*. Libby clicked on the site, and the entire article appeared on the screen. It was dated January 6, 1999. There was a picture of an attractive woman with spiked, platinum-blonde hair and large, captivating eyes standing next to a model dressed in a mod-looking outfit. Ms. Collins, the article read, had exploded onto the fashion scene and would probably be the talk around town this spring. Asked about how she got her start, she was quoted as saying that a generous backer had given her the seed money to develop the line. The rest of the article described the line's fabrics and styles. Could this possibly be the Catherine Collins from Hollywood, Maryland?

❧

"My sister called today."

"Yeah?" Josh replied, scooping another forkful of mashed potatoes off his plate.

Trevor, Libby, and Josh were eating dinner on the back porch. Trevor had shown up a few minutes before dinner and knocked on the kitchen door. He told Libby that his brother, who was in the service, was leaving for Afghanistan in a few weeks. He said his mama was all upset, and his daddy and she had been arguing, so he decided to leave the house for a while. Libby had invited him to stay for dinner, and he'd accepted with very little urging.

Libby filled Josh in on her sister. "Emily said she'd probably not be able to make it this summer with the kids. Their schedules are so busy. She's got them in band camp, sports camps, and some theater group. And then school starts before the end of August. I tell you, kids just don't get to be kids anymore."

"It's a competitive world out there now. You have to start young."

"But what happened to just having fun? I remember summers as a kid, I'd leave the house in the morning and not come back 'til dinner. We used our imaginations. Do you want our kids to be into all that stuff?"

"Like your sister's?"

Libby nodded, taking a sip of water.

"I don't know. Maybe some."

She glanced over at Trevor who was engrossed in eating a fried chicken leg. "Trevor, it's fun being a kid, isn't it?"

He nodded with a mouthful and then licked the tips of his fingers.

"Emily said maybe they'd come after Christmas to see the baby." Looking out at the newly replaced boards of the almost-completed pier, she tried to think of something else to talk about. Geese honked overhead as they flew by in a V formation. She wanted to tell Josh about tracking down Catherine Collins and emailing her from the address that was listed on her website, and her conversation with Tassie, but she couldn't. She hated not discussing it with him. Why couldn't Josh just accept the ghost and the possibility that Cecilia Reynolds was murdered? She felt there was a huge chasm forming between them.

Libby had driven over to Tassie's earlier hoping to catch her at home. She had passed by Tassie walking along the side of the road, amazed that Tassie walked to town at her age, considering she lived almost two miles away.

They'd shared some afternoon tea, deliberating over Cecilia's death and Elizabeth's role in the mystery. Tassie believed that Elizabeth would guide Libby to discover the truth about Cecilia's death. But Libby didn't know if that was possible after all these years. After telling Tassie how frustrating it was that she never knew when Elizabeth would appear, Tassie had left the room and come back with a small wooden box.

She set it on the table and explained to Libby that there were ways to prompt the spirit world into action. Libby watched quizzically as Tassie opened the box and extracted a small mesh bag of herbs. It looked like the potpourri bags she kept in her linen closet. Tassie then removed a tiny bottle of amber liquid.

She expounded on the ability she had to draw spirits, but for the average person, she said sometimes a little help was needed. She explained exactly what to do with it. Afterward, Libby had driven home, the bag and bottle safely stashed in her purse, anxious, but skeptical as to what would happen.

The breeze kicked up blowing a salty smell across the patio. "There was quite a bit of commotion in town this morning," Libby said to Josh. "I was coming out of the post office and the whole square was filled with people and news trucks. Some woman, I forget her name, had been accused of killing her father."

Josh nodded. "Jenna Thompson."

"You know her?"

"She's Reynolds' speechwriter. I had to meet with her to go over a speech for Reynolds."

"You never told me about her."

"There was nothing to tell." Josh took a sip of wine.

"Are you still working with her?" Libby tore a piece of meat off the chicken breast in her hand. Had Jenna had something to do with Josh's overnight stays in Baltimore?

"Not right now. I hear she's staying with her mother until this thing gets resolved. She'll probably get off. They're waiting on the autopsy results." Josh poured some more wine into his glass. "I forgot to tell you— I talked with a security company about getting an alarm system put in here."

"Alarm system? Why?"

"I think it would be a good idea. You have to admit we're pretty remote out here."

"I think Stella's a great alarm system." Libby looked over at Stella who was lounging under her favorite tree.

"It can't hurt to have a little extra security."

Libby shrugged, thinking Josh was being paranoid.

"I told my mama about the book you found," Trevor interjected. "She was real happy. She said she knew Miss Cecilia would be glad it was in good hands." He scraped up the last of his potatoes on his fork. "I also asked her why she thought Miss Cecilia killed herself."

Libby glanced over at Josh. She hesitated and then asked, "What did she say?"

"She don't think she did."

Josh cleared his throat and wiped his mouth with his napkin.

"She remembered the day they had this big fight. My mama heard every word. Mr. Reynolds was tellin' Miss Cecilia that he was going to put her in the nuthouse if she kept making up stories of him cheatin'.

She said Miss Cecilia came to her where she was ironing after Mr. Reynolds had left and was crying. My mama kept ironing, pretending she hadn't heard anything, but Miss Cecilia sat down and told my mama she wasn't crazy, and she knew what she'd seen. Miss Cecilia said she was going to find out who the woman was."

"Did she?" Libby blurted out, so caught up in Trevor's story she forgot about Josh.

"No, cuz, my mama said it wasn't two weeks later she was dead."

Libby stared at the ivy in the small clay pot on the kitchen table. The glow from the lamp next to it reflected onto the dark green leaves. Josh was in the den. After Trevor had gone home, they'd exploded into another fight. Libby had tried to persuade Josh that her probing into Cecilia's death might have merit considering what Trevor had said. But instead of being persuaded, he'd been furious. He told her how this was his career she was meddling with, and he couldn't understand why she didn't realize the damage she could do. He'd said it was ludicrous to even think that Reynolds was a murderer. But his final comment was what had shocked her: What did it matter what happened twenty years ago?

Did he not care that a woman may have been murdered, and he was working for the man who may have been the killer? With her hands intertwined on the table, she rubbed her thumbs together feeling an ache in her gut. Was she putting Cecilia's death before her own marriage? Why couldn't she drop it?

Her cell rang. She looked at the caller ID. It was Will. Her heart skipped a beat. Why was he calling? In the few seconds before hitting the answer button, a roller coaster of emotions washed over her— excitement, guilt, happiness, sadness. She took a deep breath and said hello.

"Julie had the baby."

Libby exhaled and slumped back against the chair feeling slightly deflated. Guilt rose back up inside. "That's great. Did everything go OK?"

"Yep. Caleb James, nine pounds, six ounces. Mom and baby are both doing fine."

"Congratulations." Libby felt the sting of tears in her eyes.

"Well, I've gotta go. Just wanted to let you know."

Libby held the phone in her hands as tears streamed down her cheeks. What was wrong with her? Why was she crying? She loved Josh. And she was happy for Will and Julie. What had she been expecting when he called? What they'd done at the creek was a mistake. They both knew that and had discussed it afterward. But then the kitchen. After Will had left that night, she'd chastised herself, telling herself it was wrong, and it would never happen again.

So why was she feeling—what was she feeling? Disappointment? Envy? Frustration? Her problems were with Josh, not Will. She cradled her head in her hands, suddenly feeling exhausted.

Standing in the doorway to the den, she stared at Josh who was reclined in his chair with his arm behind his head, still dressed in his work clothes, his tie loosened around his neck.

"I'm going up to bed," she said. Canned laughter rang out from the sitcom on TV.

Josh glanced over at her with a quick nod in response. No words. No good night. No I'll be up in a minute. No I love you.

24

⧓

She was drowning, surrounded by black water. She felt her limbs becoming weaker in their effort to keep her afloat. Her head slowly slipped beneath the surface of the cold water, and she struggled not to breathe it in. Finally, she couldn't hold her breath any longer, and she felt the rush of water fill her lungs. Libby bolted up in bed, gasping for breath. Her hands were at her throat.

She glanced over at Josh, softly snoring beside her, unaware of her horrific nightmare. She wiped the perspiration off her brow with the back of her hand as her breathing returned to normal. She sat up. A thin strip of moonlight through the parted curtain shone onto Stella who was lying on the rug beside the bed. Her head cocked at Libby as she gave out a whine. Could she sense Libby's feeling of panic that lingered from the dream? Libby threw back the covers and headed to the bathroom. Then she slipped on her robe and padded out of the room.

She entered the darkened kitchen, dimly illuminated by the light on the hooded range above the stove. After pouring a glass of milk, she sat down at the table feeling calmer, but still somewhat shaky from the vividness of her nightmare. Her purse was lying on the table next to her. She glanced at it, remembering the herb bag and the bottle Tassie had given her the day before. Would it really bring forth Elizabeth as Tassie had claimed?

She reached in and pulled out the bag, turning it in her hands. She brought it up to her nose, sniffing the contents. It had a pleasant smell, lavender mixed with something—What was that smell? She couldn't place it. She fished out the tiny bottle of amber liquid and tugged at the cork top. She raised the bottle and then hesitated. Was it safe to inhale? Tassie wouldn't give her anything that would harm her. She slowly brought the bottle to her nose and took a tiny whiff. She frowned. Almonds? No. She whiffed again and shrugged, unable to pinpoint the smell.

Libby jumped up, went over to the cupboard, and removed a mid-sized mixing bowl. She rooted through the drawers until she found a box of matches, and then she pulled a placemat out of another drawer and brought everything back to the table. She spread the placemat onto the table, set the bowl on it, and then untied the string on the herb bag and dumped half the contents into the bowl. She stared at the bowl and then glanced over at Stella sitting on the floor next to her with a hopeful look that asked, "Is this something I can eat?"

"Sorry, Stell, this isn't dog food." Libby ran her palms together and exhaled. Was she really going to do this? What harm could it do? The worst that could happen was Elizabeth wouldn't appear. She wanted to know more answers and was tired of waiting. This whole thing was consuming her life, and until she got to the bottom of it, she'd never be able to let it go.

She dribbled the thick liquid over the herbs the way Tassie had instructed her and then carefully pushed the cork back into the bottle. She slid open the matchbox, extracted a long wooden match, and held it over the side of the box for several seconds; then she ran it against the phosphorus striker, swiftly igniting it with a sizzling sound. The yellow flame glowed brightly. She lowered the flame to the bowl, letting it touch the coated herbs. In an instant, the bowl was afire and Libby jumped back. But just as quickly, the flames died down to a simmer, eventually leaving only a stream of smoke that wafted up from the bowl.

Libby sat down in front of the bowl. A warm, heady aroma filled the room. She closed her eyes and began a soft hum, again following Tassie's instructions. A part of her wanted to laugh, thinking if Josh came down and found her like this, he'd most certainly have her committed.

Her arms were stretched out on the table, straddling the bowl, with her palms upward. After a few minutes, she heard Stella making a soft whining/growling sound. She felt something brush across her cheek, a subtle feeling softer than air. She opened her eyes, and across the room was Elizabeth, radiantly glowing the way she had in the attic. It worked! Libby's heart beat against her ribs. Now what? But before she had a chance to think of an answer, Elizabeth motioned with her head for her to follow, and she disappeared through the closed kitchen door.

Libby jumped up from her chair, practically knocking it over, and ran over to the wooden door. Unlatching the lock, she opened it onto the warm night air, thick with a damp, marshy smell.

She stepped out onto the porch, Stella at her side, and padded down the cool concrete steps. Rounding the back corner of the house, she saw Elizabeth, dimly illuminated by the crescent moon, standing on the path leading down to the beach. Their eyes met and then Elizabeth turned quickly, vanishing down the path.

Filled with anticipation, Libby followed, gingerly stepping on the sandy, stone-laden path past the reeds where it opened onto the beach. Elizabeth was heading toward the boathouse.

The moonlight glistened off the water as a breeze ruffled her thin cotton robe. Images of her nightmare, the black water, flashed through her mind. She involuntarily shuddered and pushed the thought away.

She tiptoed up the stepping-stones leading to the door of the boathouse and cupped her hands on the glass of the small window, peering into the pitch-black room. It was too dark to make anything out, and the only sound was the lapping of the water as it rose onto the shore.

She glanced down at the old weather-pitted brass knob. Was she being foolhardy? Stella whined at her side as her nose sniffed along the bottom of the doorway. Her rational self urged her to go back to the house, but something stronger compelled her to stay. She gently turned the knob and pushed open the battered door. The rusty hinges creaked loudly. She wished she'd fixed the light that hung from the ceiling or had thought to bring a flashlight with her.

Scanning the room in the dim light, her gaze fell upon the shimmering figure of Elizabeth in the far corner of the room. She didn't want her to disappear like she'd done before, so she slowly tiptoed around the table, making her way to the back of the room. Libby's pulse drummed in her chest, and adrenaline pumped through her veins. She stopped at the end of the table, only a few feet from Elizabeth, waiting to see what she would do. The air was musty and Libby stifled a sneeze. Elizabeth's deep blue eyes looked beseechingly at Libby. She turned her gaze toward the back corner of the room, then back to Libby. Was she trying to show her something? Libby was afraid to speak, afraid she might break the connection.

Instead, she followed Elizabeth's gaze. A large cardboard box and some old paint cans sat in the corner. Libby stepped closer and, at the same time, Elizabeth glided backward, her arm pointing toward the box.

Libby knelt down. She moved the rusted paint cans out of the way and lifted the interlocking flaps of the cardboard box. She turned to see if Elizabeth was still there. Her shimmering image was beginning to fade, but there was a slight smile on her lips.

Stella made herself comfortable on the cool concrete floor, unperturbed by Elizabeth.

Libby turned her attention back to the box, which contained spray cans and bottles. What was it she was looking for? She pulled out one of the cans, barely making out the label that read "Marine Varnish." What kind of a wild goose chase had Elizabeth gotten her on?

Then her eye caught sight of a small brown bottle hidden behind a spray can of insecticide. She pulled it out of the box and tried to read the label, but it was too dark. It was different from the rest of the box's contents. It looked like some kind of medicine bottle.

She quickly turned back toward Elizabeth, but she was gone. Frustrated that Elizabeth wasn't more specific, she studied the bottle. Could this be what killed Cecilia? She stood up, grasping the bottle firmly in her hand, and quickly exited the boathouse with Stella at her heels.

The smoke had subsided from the herb-filled bowl, but the intoxicating aroma still lingered in the kitchen. She turned on the lamp at the table and held the bottle up to the light. The label read "Halothane BP 250 ml." What was halothane? The ticking of the schoolhouse clock that hung on the wall above the table counted off the thoughts in her head. She needed to put the bottle somewhere safe. She glanced around the square-shaped room: the stainless steel refrigerator humming in one corner; the tiled counter, where she kept her bright-colored canisters of flour, sugar, and coffee; or the large windowsill above the deep porcelain sink.

She walked over to the cabinet under the sink and slipped the bottle behind some cleaning supplies. Libby then cleaned up the contents of the herb bowl, washed her hands, and headed down the hall to the den. She turned on the monitor, which lit up the darkened room. She sat down in the chair at the desk and waited while her computer booted up. After logging onto the Internet, she typed "Halothane" in the search box. Libby clicked on the first result: *"Halothane is an inhalational general anesthetic. It is colorless and pleasant smelling."* She skimmed the article. Halothane had been used since the 1950s as a general anesthetic, but there was a dramatic reduction in use by the 1990s, as it was replaced with newer drugs. She continued reading:

"Its properties include cardiac depression at high levels and potent bronchial relaxation." Could Cecilia have been poisoned with halothane? A feeling of dread filled her gut, and she wrapped her arms around her belly. Then she switched off the computer and left the room. She had to tell Will.

She slipped under the covers as Josh stirred beside her. He rolled over and lifted his head off the pillow. "Is everything all right?"

"Yeah, I just got a drink."

Josh rolled back over.

Libby lay her head down on the pillow and closed her eyes. Sleep did not come easily. Her mind raced with different scenarios. Could John Reynolds have committed such a horrible crime? Had he drugged Cecilia and then put her in the tub to look like suicide, or had Cecilia taken it herself? And how would they ever find out the truth?

25

He felt Maggie glancing over in his direction, curious about his reading material. The jewel-studded book stood out, so it was hard for him to conceal it from her. He'd gotten to the office early, hoping to have some quiet time to go through the journal and sort out his strategy on the Reynolds case, but also because he needed to get out of the house. He'd taken a couple of days off to be with Julie and the baby, and he'd enjoyed it, but he was happy when her mother had arrived. The chaos at the house was getting to him, and he wondered how Julie did it every day.

Libby had stopped by the night before to see the baby, and she'd told him about a suspicious bottle she'd found. He hadn't been able to ask her any details; he'd been bathing the kids and getting them ready for bed at the time.

He regretted what he'd done with Libby. He'd never done anything like that before, barely even looked at other women, and he'd found himself questioning, why now? He listed the possibilities in his head: (1) he'd been with Julie since they were kids, and their marriage was in a slump; (2) Julie had been pushing him away for several months; (3) something about Libby sparked something inside him; and (4) he was a jerk. All his excuses were just that— excuses. He felt like a cad. He knew why Julie had been irritable lately. She had three kids and one on the way. She was tired. He couldn't blame her. And just because their marriage had hit a rut didn't mean it was time to have an affair. He loved Julie. He liked Libby, as a friend, and wanted it to remain that way. He hoped Libby felt the same.

He'd been so busy the past week with the kids, the Thompson case, and bringing Julie home from the hospital that he hadn't had time to even think about the Cecilia Reynolds case. The journal had intrigued him, but all he'd done so far was skim through it. But the alone time in the office he'd been hoping for was not what he got. Maggie was already there making a pot of coffee when he'd arrived.

"It's a diary, in case you were wondering," Will said without looking up.

Maggie quickly looked away and then replied, "What was that?"

"The book I have; it's a diary."

"Oh." She giggled. "I hadn't even noticed."

Will resumed his reading and, after a few minutes, Maggie said, "Whose diary would that be?"

"Cecilia Reynolds," Will replied, hiding his grin. He was having fun watching her act as if she didn't really care, but all the while he knew her curiosity was killing her.

"Where did you come across that?"

"Libby Langston found it at Haverford House."

"Hmm…" Maggie sat watching Will as he wrote down notes on a pad of paper. She got up from her chair and walked over to Will's desk. "I couldn't help but notice the cover of the book. It's so unusual. What is that?"

Will closed the book and showed Maggie the jeweled front. "It's a hummingbird."

"How beautiful." She ran her short, plump fingers over the cover. She stood there for a few moments, while Will waited for her to sit back down. Finally, she returned to her desk, and Will continued reading and jotting down notes.

Maggie worked on her crossword puzzle for the next fifteen minutes. Then she put her pencil down and blurted out, "OK, so what is so interesting about Cecilia Reynolds' diary, and why are you writing things down?"

Will glanced up from the book and then closed the cover. He leaned back in his chair and ran his hand across his forehead, brushing back his blond hair that had fallen in his eyes. "This is between you and me, OK? Sheriff Tucker doesn't need to know about this yet." He waited for Maggie's agreement.

She nodded her head and added, "My lips are sealed." She ran a line across her mouth with her fingers and turned an imaginary key to lock her red-painted lips.

Will decided it would not be a bad idea to have Maggie on his side. She had an uncanny way of getting Sheriff Tucker to do whatever she wanted.

"This diary may contain information that could implicate John Reynolds in the death of his wife."

"Oh my God! I don't believe it. What does it say?"

Will relayed the information about Reynolds having an affair and Cecilia expecting a child and how happy she was about it. "I think it's highly unlikely that she would commit suicide so shortly after writing what she did."

"Cecilia was pregnant? I had no idea! What are you going to do with it?"

"I haven't decided yet. I was just checking to see if there was enough information for me to re-open the case."

"Do you think there is?"

"I think so, but I don't know if Tucker will agree. I think I'll do a little investigating on my own before I get Sheriff Tucker involved. You can keep a secret, can't you?"

"Of course! I told you my lips are sealed, cross my heart." Maggie drew an X across her plump bosom. "Listen, hon, I always thought that all that talk around town of Reynolds killing his wife was just hogwash, but if there is evidence that proves otherwise, I would be the first to say go after the man, whether he's a friend of Baynard's or not."

"That's good to know. I may need your help on this."

"Anything you need, hon, I will be there for you."

"Thanks, Maggie."

Will glanced at the clock on the station wall; it read five minutes to nine. He knew Sheriff Tucker would be walking through the door any minute, so he slipped the book in his desk drawer; he wasn't ready to answer any questions from Tucker.

Exactly on schedule, Sheriff Tucker entered the station at nine o'clock. Will was reminded of the movie *Groundhog Day*.

"Good morning, ya'll."

"Good morning," Will and Maggie replied.

"What's new?" Sheriff Tucker asked Will, as he settled his rotund figure into his swivel chair.

Maggie caught Will's eye and gave him a wink on the sly. He smiled at her and replied to Sheriff Tucker, "Nothing much."

"I was over to Pearl's this morning, and it looks like it's going to be another bad year for the crops. Joe Dudley said his beans ain't half what they should be. I tell you, it's just too dang hot and not enough rain to cool things off," he said as he lit up his cigar. "So what's on the agenda for today?"

"Jane Michaels called and wants to come over today to work on the Thompson case," Maggie replied.

"She does, does she? What's going on with that now anyway? Bring me up to speed, Will."

"Well, we got the autopsy results, and it showed that Jimmy Thompson did not die from the gunshot wound. It turns out he had a massive aneurism on his aorta that was a ticking time bomb just waiting to blow. At first, they thought maybe the birdshot had done it, but after further examination, there was no evidence to suggest that. I think Jane is going to have to drop the charges of murder, or at least reduce it to attempted murder. But if you ask me, I think the charges should be dropped all together."

"Jimmy was a mean drunk. I remember when I was just a deputy back in sixty-six, and I had to haul Jimmy into the station. He had been out carousing with his buddies; he wasn't no more than sixteen, and he was drunker than a skunk. All the other boys were scared to death about bein' caught, but not Jimmy. He had a mouth on him, and he was ready to do battle with me. I knew it was just the alcohol talking, but I still thought a night in jail might do him some good. I thought it worked, too; he was a changed boy in the morning.

"I had called his parents the night before and told them what I was going to do, and they agreed it might put some sense into him. When his daddy came to get him the next morning, Jimmy was all apologetic and swore he would never drink again. Some people just can't handle their liquor."

Sheriff Tucker wiped his brow with his handkerchief and then re-lit his cigar. Holding a match to the end, he took small puffs until he had it burning good. He shook out the match and threw it in the ashtray on his desk. Smoking bans did not apply to Sheriff Tucker. After a few satisfactory drags on the cigar, he leaned back in his chair and said, "Jenna was a good girl. She don't deserve to go to jail over this. I remember when she was in the junior skeet-shooting club. She was the best shot in town. She could outshoot all the boys, and boy did that make them mad." He chuckled as he thought back. "She was a tough one, though; she never took any stuff off them boys. I remember having to break up a fight one day after a competition because some boy said she had to be a dyke, because no real girl would want to shoot all the time. She jumped on him so fast he didn't know what hit him. That was when she was about fourteen or fifteen.

"About a year later, I saw her at another match, and things had changed dramatically. She no longer looked like the tomboy she had always been. She had developed into one beautiful lady. She had every boy hanging around her, but I don't think she ever realized how pretty she was."

"She was homecoming queen her senior year. I remember her riding in the parade, all smiling and waving to everyone," Maggie interjected.

"I think she had a rough life with a father like Jimmy. It would be a shame if the prosecutor doesn't drop the charges," Will added.

"Jane sometimes gets a hair up her ass and won't let something go. Maybe you should try talking to her, Will, and see if you can change her mind. She won't listen to me; she just thinks I'm some big old redneck." His belly laugh shook his whole body.

"I'll see what I can do," Will replied.

Jane Michaels walked into the station around half past ten, brief-case in hand, in her navy suit with matching pumps. "Hi, Maggie," she said as she brushed past Maggie's desk and headed toward Sheriff Tucker.

Sheriff Tucker was on the phone with one of his cronies, making his plans for a fishing trip that weekend. Will, upon seeing Jane briskly walking in Sheriff Tucker's direction, immediately jumped up from his desk and blocked her path.

"Jane, it's great to see you," he said, extending his hand.

"Hi, Will, nice to see you, too."

"I hear you want to discuss the Thompson case. Why don't we go into the back room. I've got the file in there."

"OK," Jane replied. Will saw the gears in her mind shifting from her original mission. She followed Will into the interrogation room. A manila folder sat on the desk.

"I was going over the file this morning; we received the autopsy report, which I'm sure you're aware of." Will shut the door behind them.

"Yes, that's one of the reasons I'm here," she replied, sitting down on one of the metal chairs. She placed her briefcase on the table in front of her. As she pressed her thumbs on the brass clasps on the front, the lid snapped open, allowing her to extract some papers.

"I know everyone thinks I overreacted with the charges I brought on Jenna Thompson. I read the newspaper, but what people don't realize is we have to follow the law. I can't make a different set of rules for some people just because we don't like the victim."

"I understand," Will said, "but I'm sure you would agree that now that we have the autopsy results, the charge of murder should be dropped."

"I agree that the clinical cause of death was the ruptured aorta, but we don't know if the gunshot trauma could have brought it on."

"Jane, I know you have a tough job, especially when it goes against public opinion, and I respect the fact that you're not swayed by that, but don't you think you're being a little hard on Jenna?"

"You don't seem to get it. Don't you see that if I drop all charges on her, it just opens the door for any Tom, Dick, or Harry who has a grudge with a family member to go ahead and blow his or her brains out?"

"Jane, come on," Will said, looking her straight in the eye. "You don't really think that's going to happen."

"You never know. Ninety percent of the population in this town owns a gun."

"That doesn't mean they're going to use it on a family member. This was an unusual case, and besides, Jenna didn't blow her father's brains out, even though she could have. She was only protecting her mother."

"I want you to go back out there to the farm and go over everything again with a fine-tooth comb. I want to know if the gun case in the house was kept locked and if there was a pitchfork and an axe in the barn. Ask the paramedics that were on site if they noticed Ada with a pitchfork. I want to know why Jenna had a gun in the first place when she went to the barn."

"Fair enough. I'll go today."

26

Driving the patrol car out to Foxhall Road, Will pondered how quickly someone's life could change. Jenna, who had been a rising star in the political arena, was now facing years in prison. It just didn't seem right. Jenna was charged with murder when all she was doing was defending her mother, and Reynolds gets off scot-free in the death of his wife. Will knew there was no solid evidence so far on Reynolds, but it was looking more and more likely that he had something to do with his wife's death. When he finished at the Thompsons', he thought he would stop by and see Garrett Mosley, the coroner, and ask him a few questions regarding Cecilia. He liked Garrett, he reminded him of a young Jimmy Stewart, and he knew he would be straight with him.

Will pulled into the gravel drive and noticed not only Jenna's BMW but also a black Lexus parked beside it. It looked like Jenna had company. He made his way to the front door and, after several knocks, Ada opened the door clad in her flowered housecoat and slippers. She had aged since Will had last seen her.

"Mrs. Thompson, nice to see you. I was wondering if I could come in; I have a few things I need to go over regarding Jenna's case."

"Why, of course, come on in. I just finished a batch of cookies. They're cooling on the counter." She led Will down the hall toward the kitchen, walking slower than he had remembered her walking before. "Have a seat."

"Thanks, Mrs. Thompson."

"Please, call me Ada."

"Ada, thanks. Is Jenna here?"

"Yes, she's upstairs; do you want me to get her?"

"No, not yet. I have a few things I'd like to ask you first."

"OK." Ada set a plate of chocolate-chip oatmeal cookies on the table in front of Will.

He couldn't resist. He picked up one of the cookies and bit into it. They were as good as her pie had been. He savored the cookie for a minute before asking her, "Where exactly is the gun case located?"

"In the mudroom, right in there." Ada pointed toward the doorway to the room off the kitchen.

"Do you keep it locked?"

"No. I know we probably should, but Jimmy wanted to be able to get to his guns fast if there was some mangy critter outside that he wanted to shoot. He didn't want to have to take the time to go and find the key and unlock the case."

"So the case was always unlocked. And were the guns loaded?"

"I believe so. Again, he didn't want to waste time loading if a fox was after the chickens. I don't know if all the guns were loaded, but I know his shotgun always was."

"One more thing, you had said you had a pitchfork in your hand. Do you remember if you were still carrying it when you ran toward Jimmy?"

"I don't recall," Ada replied. She closed her eyes, trying to remember. "I just can't recall; I think my mind has blacked it all out."

"That's OK. Do you mind if I take a look at the gun case?"

"Why no, go right ahead."

Will got up from the table and went into the mudroom. He noticed the boots neatly lined up along one wall, along with overalls and jackets hanging on hooks. Ada had not removed any of Jimmy's things yet. The tall, wooden gun case stood against the opposite wall. He went over and turned the latch, and it opened right up. Each gun was securely resting in its slot, all except for the shotgun Jenna had used, which was still in the evidence room at the courthouse. He picked up a rifle and opened it to see if there was any ammunition inside. The chamber was empty.

There was a shelf at the top of the cabinet, which housed boxes of various bullets and shotgun shells. He set the rifle back in its slot and picked up a shotgun. He opened it and looked down the barrel; there were no shells in either chamber. Maybe Jimmy had a favorite gun that he always used to shoot at the critters, as Ada put it. Maybe Jenna knew which gun was always loaded, or maybe she loaded the gun before heading out to the barn. If she had just wanted to scare her dad, she could have taken any one of these and not loaded it. He was sure it had not been just a coincidence that the gun she chose was already loaded.

Will popped his head around the door and said to Ada that he needed to go out to the barn and check on a few things. He told her that when he got back, he would want to talk to Jenna. He opened the back door and walked toward the barn. He tried to picture what he would have done in Jenna's circumstance, even though he could never envision his father acting the way Jimmy had acted. If his father was after his mother, would he have reacted the same?

Inside the barn, he waited for his eyes to adjust and then walked over to the axe that still lay on the floor where Jimmy had fallen. The dirt was dark where the blood had pooled under his body. Will searched around for the pitchfork. At first, he didn't see it, and then he spotted it lying partially under the tractor that was in the middle of the barn. He stooped down beside it, picked it up, and turned around, reenacting the scene the way Jenna and her mother had described it, playing the part of Ada. He figured she was standing somewhere near the tractor because Jenna had said her parents were on opposite sides of the tractor when she entered the barn. He took a few steps back and stood facing the doorway where Ada would have turned when she heard Jenna come in. He then ran toward where the blood was pooled in the dirt, throwing down the pitchfork in the process. It landed roughly where it had lain minutes before. He deduced that Ada must have dropped the pitchfork in her rush to stop Jimmy from harming Jenna.

He brushed his hands off on his trousers and headed back to the house. All that he had seen here further confirmed that Jenna reacted in defense of her mother when she shot her father. That she had chosen the only loaded gun in the case really didn't matter; there was no proof that she would have known it was loaded, and even if she did, she could still say she only took it to scare him. He was sure a good attorney could get her off, not to mention the fact that the jury would be on her side anyway. Jane Michaels would be fighting an uphill battle if she took Jenna to court for murder.

As he entered through the mudroom door, the aroma of fresh-baked cookies filled his nostrils. He thought to himself how ironic this whole thing was. On the outside, it appeared to be a nice, wholesome family—the homemade food and farm life—but deeper down there had been a dark side to the picture, one that had insidiously been woven into their daily lives, so tightly ingrained that they didn't even realize how bad it had become.

In other cases he had worked on, when it came to domestic problems, those involved had a tendency to try to continue with the normal activities of life, hoping it would mask what lay beneath. But just like smoldering lava, the pressure would eventually erupt. It was sad to think how many families dealt with abuse and violence—a cycle that was hard to break. In this case, though, Jenna had gotten counseling and, from what he could tell, had lived a normal life. Ada had told him her son had a great life in Atlanta as well. He hoped Jane Michaels would drop the charges and then maybe this family could heal and begin a better life.

Jenna was seated at the kitchen table along with a man who had his back to Will. Ada was nowhere in sight. Jenna looked up. "Will, you know my attorney, Jackson Darrow."

Will reached out and shook his hand. "Nice to see you. Any relation to Clarence?" Will joked.

"Actually, yes, but very distant. Ada tells us you wanted to talk with Jenna?"

"Yes." Will pulled out a chair and sat at the table with them. "I don't know if you've been told or not, but we got the autopsy results."

"No, we hadn't heard," Darrow replied.

"Would you like your mother to be here?"

"She's lying down right now. I'll relay everything to her later."

"It turns out your father died of an aortal aneurism, and from what the coroner said, it looks like the rupture had nothing to do with the gunshot wound."

"Oh, thank God!" Jenna exclaimed as she let out a breath.

"I know, that's great, but you're still not out of the woods. The prosecutor hasn't decided yet if she will be dropping the charges, or maybe reducing them to manslaughter."

"But why wouldn't she? This proves I didn't kill my father!"

"Jenna, calm down. It will be OK," Jackson Darrow said. He placed his hand over Jenna's clenched hands on the table. Will noticed the look he gave Jenna, and it appeared there was more than just an attorney-client relationship going on here. "I'll go to court tomorrow and file a motion to have the charges dropped," Darrow continued. "No judge in his or her right mind would consider having this go to trial."

"Mr. Darrow, I'm not sure where you practice law, but I have a feeling it's not in a small town. You have to understand things run a little differently here. The judge and the prosecutor have a very close working relationship. I wouldn't discount the possibility that the judge backs her up. If you could just wait a few days, I'm going to tell her what I have found after re-examining the scene, and I assure you it is all in your client's favor. I think things will run a lot smoother if you give her the chance to drop the charges on her own."

"I guess a few days won't hurt, if you're sure she'll drop the charges."

"I can't guarantee it, but I'm pretty sure I can convince her to."

"All right." Jackson rose from the table, leaned down toward Jenna, and gave her a kiss on the cheek. "I have to run. I'll call you tonight." He turned to Will and extended his hand. "Nice meeting you. I'll get in touch with you tomorrow and see how you made out."

Will shook his hand and replied, "I'll do my best."

After Jackson had left, Will said to Jenna, "So, is it just my imagination, or is Darrow more than just your attorney?"

"We're good friends."

"Friends?"

The smile on Jenna's face said they were more than that.

"How long have you been seeing him?"

"Actually, I only met him a few weeks ago when I called him about my case. He's a friend of a friend of mine." Jenna grabbed a cookie from the plate and turned it around in her hands. She then broke off a piece and put it in her mouth. Another smile crossed her lips. Will noticed a youthful pleasure on her face and imagined her as a young teenager.

"You seem pretty happy."

"I know this sounds crazy, considering everything that has happened, but I think I'm happier than I've ever been before." She went over to the fridge and poured two glasses of milk, handing one to Will. "I've spent my whole life working to prove myself. I never allowed myself time for any serious commitments. I didn't want anything to interfere with my goals." She dipped her cookie in the milk and then bit into it. "I don't know if it had anything to do with my relationship with my father, but I think subconsciously I was afraid to get too involved with anyone for fear he would hurt me, not physically but emotionally. From the minute I met Jackson, something clicked. He truly understands me without me having to explain anything. Maybe I'm in love—I don't know. I've never felt this way with anyone before." She took the last bite of cookie and then said, "You're married, right?"

"Yeah." Will wiped his mouth of cookie crumbs.

"When you met your wife, did you feel this way? Like you want to burst out in laughter or skip around the room, singing at the top of your lungs?"

Will thought back to when he and Julie started dating. He smiled, thinking of the excitement he'd felt every time she'd walk into a room. "I don't know about skipping, but yeah, I know what you mean."

"You still feel that way? How long have you been married?"

"Going on seventeen years." Will felt a pang in his gut. Did he still feel that way? He couldn't remember the last time Julie and he had shared even a minute together alone. He wanted to get that spark back. "Life kind of gets in the way sometimes, but I still love my wife as much or maybe even more than I did when I first met her." That was true. Watching Julie in the middle of the night, sitting beside him in bed nursing the baby, filled him with joy. He was the luckiest man alive. How could he have almost blown it all?

Jenna sat back in her chair and ran her hands through her thick auburn hair. She smiled at Will and then said, "You know, it's funny. If you had asked me three weeks ago if I wanted to be in a relationship, I would have told you no way. I thought people who were wrapped up with someone else were weak. I couldn't have been more wrong." She chuckled. "Even though I should be scared shitless right now, I wake up each morning excited about the day, and I can't wait until I see Jackson again."

"Listen, Jenna, I'm serious about doing everything I can to convince Jane Michaels to drop the charges. She's just afraid that she'll be seen as soft, or condoning you taking the law into your own hands. But this is a unique case. I don't think she needs to make you the poster child for cracking down on vigilantism."

"I'm hoping she drops the charges, too, but I also feel confident that if it goes to trial, Jackson will get me off."

"Let's hope it doesn't get that far." Will stood up from the table. "I better get back to the station. Tell your mom I said good-bye." He stopped and turned back. "Is she doing OK?"

"I think so. This has been hard on her, though. My brother was up for a few days, and he said he would come back with the kids once this is all settled. That made her really happy. I think once this case is over with and she adjusts to a new routine, she'll realize how much better off she is now that my father is gone."

Will said good-bye to Jenna and then walked back to his car. He sat in the driver's seat and looked through the windshield at the old farmhouse. He thought about Jenna's words, that her mother was better off now that her father was gone. A little voice in his head questioned whether Jenna had wanted to do this all along. Was this just a perfect opportunity for her to kill her father? Had it been something she'd been planning her whole life? But Jenna couldn't have known her father had an aortal aneurism, and without that he'd still be alive. Her mother probably *will* have a better life now that Jimmy Thompson was dead.

27

Libby had been checking her e-mails every day for the past few weeks. Nothing. If Catherine Collins was the right person, she must not want to talk about her past. Sitting in front of the computer, cup of tea in hand, she logged in to Catherine Collins' website and clicked on her photo gallery. She flipped through countless images of models on the runway and on location at the beach, park, and mountains. The models wore flowing gowns, short dresses, and swimwear. Libby then clicked on a box titled "In The News." She scrolled through shots of Catherine Collins at celebrity events, posing with famous people, smiling at the camera. Libby scanned the images quickly and then stopped. She flipped back to the previous picture. It was him—a photo of Catherine Collins standing next to John Reynolds. The caption read "Debut Collection." The year was 1999. She'd found her. But now what? How could she find out more about their connection to each other?

On a whim, she picked up the phone. A woman answered in a throaty voice, "Good Morning, Catherine Collins Fashions."

"Could I speak to Ms. Collins, please?"

"May I ask who's calling?"

"Libby Langston." Libby paused and then said, "Tell her I'm a friend of John Reynolds."

"One minute. Let me see if she's available."

Jazz music played over the line, and Libby tapped the pen against the pad on the table, ready to take down any information, anxious about what she would find out. She felt the familiar rush of adrenaline from unlocking a mystery.

"Catherine Collins." Her voice was soft and smooth.

"Hi, my name's Libby Langston." Libby took a deep breath. "I believe we have a mutual friend. Do you by any chance know John Reynolds?"

There was silence on the other end of the line.

"John Reynolds. Yes, I do. Is John OK?"

"Yes." Libby hesitated. "My husband works with him, and..." She faltered, not knowing what to say.

"Did John ask you to call?"

"Well, not exactly." Libby hesitated again. "This may sound strange, but I'm just going to come out with why I called. You see, we bought the Haverford House. I've been doing some research on the history of the house, and your name came up from the letters that were sent to him."

"You have my letters?"

Libby detected the surprise—or was it panic?—in her voice. "Let's just say I know about your relationship with Reynolds." Libby gritted her teeth, hoping the woman wouldn't hang up.

There was a short laugh on the other end of the line. "You know, it's ironic you should call now. I've been thinking about him recently. For years I blocked him out of my mind. I'm doing a show in Milan soon, and a reporter is doing a bio piece on me. They've been asking me a lot of questions on how I got started. John had a lot to do with it."

Libby heard Catherine exhale. "I don't know what Reynolds has told you about me, but I think he may have been my first love. I was so naïve back then." She laughed again. "I was putting myself through design school and barely had two nickels to rub together, and then along comes John. He was so handsome and charismatic; he literally swept me off my feet."

Libby recalled Cynthia Reynolds saying that exact same line.

❧

Will and Libby sat at the kitchen table. She'd been eager to tell him what she'd learned from her conversation with Catherine Collins. He'd called shortly after she'd hung up with Catherine and said he wanted to stop by to pick up the bottle she'd found.

She'd just finished telling him about how Catherine had been seeing John for several months before she discovered he was married. She said she'd broken it off immediately. But he kept pursuing her, telling her that he was going to leave his wife and marry her. He told her that his wife was unstable, and he worried what she would do if he confronted her. It wasn't until after Cecilia's death that Catherine discovered the whole estate had belonged to his wife. She said she'd always had a nagging feeling in the back of her head about the suicide. But she'd dismissed it, not wanting to believe anything else. Reynolds had wanted her to move in with him at Haverford House, but she was focused on her career. He'd pleaded with her. Catherine said he'd gotten furious with her when she told him she wanted to move to California. She'd never seen him like that.

A couple of years later, she received a check from him, out of the blue. The money had been enough to launch her career. She told Libby that at first she hadn't wanted to accept it, but then she thought, why not? But she'd always wondered why he'd given her the money.

Libby told Will that Catherine sounded surprised when Libby told her that Cecilia was pregnant at the time of her death, not mentioning that it was yet to be proven conclusively. She said Catherine had been silent for several seconds and then muttered, "What a monster."

"I think between Catherine and the halothane we could nail him."

"Do you have a plastic zip bag?" Will asked.

Libby went over to a kitchen drawer and came back with the bag.

Will carefully picked up the bottle by the lid, slipped it into the bag, and then sealed it closed. "Depending on what we find, it may throw suspicion Reynolds' way, but it doesn't put the smoking gun in his hand. Even if I could get an exhumation done, and it showed she had halothane in her system, we couldn't prove it was Reynolds who gave it to her."

"But you have to admit, if you put all of it together, it looks like murder. We have the journal, which shows they argued and she was excited about having a baby—not suicidal. We have Catherine Collins who admits he wanted to leave Cecilia, but not the money, and now we have the halothane. Isn't that enough circumstantial evidence to convince a jury?"

"Remember who we're dealing with. This guy has connections, and if we don't handle it right, he could make us all look like idiots."

Libby slumped back in her chair, feeling dejected. A failure. After reading the journal, she'd felt a connection to Cecilia. She felt she'd been chosen for whatever reason to be her avenger, to get the truth out.

"Don't be discouraged." He patted her hand that was resting on the table. "Even though I'm not supposed to be investigating this case, it doesn't mean I'm going to stop."

Libby nodded.

Will let his hand linger on hers. The two sat in silence for a minute. Libby pulled her hands into her lap, even though his touch felt so good.

"How are things with you and Josh?"

Libby shrugged and felt her cheeks flush. "How about you and Julie?"

"They're getting better. Things are kind of crazy right now with the baby and her mom there, but we're working on it."

"That's good." She felt the sting of tears, but forced them away, inhaling deeply. "The baby is adorable." She looked down at her hands as she picked a thumbnail. She thought about the other day when she'd gone to their house to see the baby, in the bedroom with Julie, who was nursing Caleb. An overwhelming guilt filled Libby as she'd looked around the room. A collage of pictures hung on the wall above the bed. Candid shots of the children in various stages of growth. Two laundry baskets sat on the floor, each piled with clothes.

They were a family, with history. How could she have done something so horrible? A bizarre thought had flashed through her mind— was it Haverford House? Had it put some strange curse on her that made her do what she did? She was desperate for an excuse for her behavior.

Will stood up to go and squeezed Libby's shoulder. "Things are going to get better for all of us. Josh will come around once the truth comes out."

Libby pictured Cecilia's body being exhumed. This was real. It wasn't one of her detective games when she was young. There could be major consequences from this. "What if we're wrong?"

"What?"

"What if Reynolds is innocent?"

"That's not what my gut is telling me. And I've been doing this for years."

Will drove down Haverford Lane and contemplated heading directly over to the lab in Easton. An old friend of his worked at the lab, and he knew he could pull a favor from him. If Reynolds' prints were found on the bottle, it would help the case; Reynolds wouldn't be able to deny having ever seen the bottle. It wouldn't do much more than that, though. But Libby was right; the evidence against Reynolds was adding up. At the end of the lane he stopped. Then he made a left turn and headed toward Easton.

28

He found Maggie alone at the station. Sheriff Tucker was nowhere in sight. Maggie informed him that Baynard had gone out for a spell and might not be back that day. She asked Will how it went out at the Thompsons'.

"Good," Will replied. "From the way things look, I think Michaels needs to drop the charges. Those people need to get on with their lives. They've all suffered enough. Now I just need to convince Jane of that."

"Good luck. Sometimes that woman thinks she's on a crusade for justice, and she forgets to look at the human aspect of things. I know we have laws for a reason, but sometimes you got to bend the rules a little. Everyone knows that Jenna would never have killed her father on purpose."

Will sat down and kicked his feet up on his desk. Then he leaned back in his chair with his hands behind his head. He looked over at

Maggie. "I think that is what Jane Michaels is worried about. What if this was something that Jenna had always wanted to do? For years she's come to her mother's rescue and has tried to defuse her explosive father. What if this was just the last straw and she snapped?"

"You think Jenna shot her father intentionally to kill him?"

"No, I don't, but I think that is the case that Jane Michaels will try to present. The only problem with that theory is that Jenna is such an expert shot; she never would have missed her target from that distance. I just need to convince Jane that it would save the taxpayers a whole lot of money to plead this case down instead of taking it to trial. She could still charge Jenna with aggravated assault or something like that and give her community service—but no jail time. Not to mention the fact that Jenna has a top-notch attorney. I think he would be a formidable match for her."

"All I got to say is you've got your work cut out for you." Maggie set down the nail file she had been using on her merlot-colored nails. "What about the diary? Did you find out anything more on Reynolds?"

"I think I've got enough to talk to Sheriff Tucker about. He has to agree that this new evidence shows that it was highly unlikely that Cecilia Reynolds committed suicide."

"And you think Reynolds had something to do with her death?"

"Possibly."

"But why would he want her dead?"

"Money and lust, pure and simple."

The next morning, Will rehearsed the speech in his head that he would deliver to Sheriff Tucker regarding the diary. He wasn't going to mention the halothane just yet, not until the prints came back. But by nine o'clock, when Sheriff Tucker walked into the station, the look on his face said there would be no need for the speech. Before Will could say anything, Sheriff Tucker marched over to his desk.

"What's this I hear about you wanting to exhume Cecilia Reynolds' body?" Sheriff Tucker's face was beet red from his quick jaunt down the block from Pearl's Diner.

Maggie looked over at Will and shrugged, shaking her head, indicating she had nothing to do with the leak. That left the coroner Garrett, and his assistant, Ashley.

It took Will over an hour to calm Sheriff Tucker. He showed him the diary and the entries regarding Cecilia's expecting a baby. He asked Sheriff Tucker if her words sounded like a woman on the verge of killing herself. Sheriff Tucker just shook his head. Will suggested exhuming the body to find out if she was pregnant at the time of her death, but Sheriff Tucker said he needed to think about the whole thing before they went and did something as drastic as that.

After Will had exhausted all his theories, Sheriff Tucker stood up from his desk and said he needed to go out for a bit. As soon as the door closed behind him, Maggie said to Will, "It wasn't me. I swear I never said a word to him."

"I know. I think I know who did, though."

"Who?"

"I went over to Garrett's office yesterday to ask him some questions concerning Cecilia, and Ashley was there. She was listening to my conversation with Garrett."

"Say no more." Maggie raised her hand. "I guarantee you it was her; she probably didn't wait five minutes after you left to tell her mama, who then probably picked up the phone and called her sister Pearl. I bet Pearl couldn't sleep last night just waiting to spring the news on Baynard."

"Oh, well, it didn't quite go as I had planned, but at least he knows now," Will said.

"I think you did a great job of explaining things to Baynard; you have me convinced John Reynolds was involved in his wife's death."

"Thanks," Will replied.

Sheriff Tucker got in his squad car and immediately punched in the numbers on his cell phone. He waited while it rang. He was ready to leave a message on voice mail when he heard, "Bubby, what's up?"

"Are you busy?"

"I always have time for my favorite sheriff."

"I've got some news you need to hear, and you should probably be alone when I tell you."

"I don't like the sound of that. Give me a second. I'll call you back."

"OK."

Five minutes later, his cell rang. Sheriff Tucker, parked outside of town along the side of the road, picked up the phone on the first ring. "Hello."

"So Bubby, what's this news that's so important?"

"John, it appears that Cecilia had a diary." Sheriff Tucker paused for Reynolds' reaction.

After a brief spell of silence, Reynolds said, "I know my wife had a diary."

"Well, it's been discovered, and some of what she wrote makes suicide seem pretty suspicious."

"Discovered? Where? I searched that house from top to bottom when I got rid of her things, and I never came across the diary."

Sheriff Tucker thought that was an odd response, but he ignored it. "I'm not sure where it was found, but I've seen it, and it clearly was Cecilia's."

"Then I think you'd better send it to me immediately. That was my wife's; therefore, it belongs to me now."

"I'm afraid I can't do that. You see, my deputy has the diary, and he wants to exhume the body. But don't worry. I'm not going to let him do that just yet."

"Exhume the body! What in the hell is going on, Bubby? You do realize I have a campaign going on right now, and I don't need some small-town cop trying to make a name for himself at my expense. You're the boss; tell him to forget about it."

"It's not that easy. You see, Cecilia wrote about things that I think need some answers."

"Bubby, you know me. There was nothing suspicious about Cecilia's death; she had serious mental problems."

"She wrote that she was expecting a baby, and she sounded very excited about it. Why would she want to kill herself?"

Reynolds was silent. Then he said, "She was delusional. She wanted to have a baby so badly that she made the whole thing up. That diary was her way of creating a fantasy life. The whole thing was a work of fiction. Listen, we're only a little over two months away from the election, and I'm ahead in the polls. Do you know what a story like this could do to me? At least hold this off until after the election. Then I'll cooperate fully with whatever questions you have."

"I'll see what I can do. I can try and stall things until then." Sheriff Tucker watched a large turkey vulture swoop down and begin tearing at some roadkill along the shoulder.

"Thanks, Bubby. You know I never forget a friend. I've still got projects in the works for that highway to come to Corsica, and if I get elected, I'll have the opportunity to speed things up. Just think, this time next year, you might have three deputies working for you."

Sheriff Tucker smiled. Three deputies. He would just have to delay Will from any further investigation into the case. He would explain Cecilia's delusions to him, and that should put an end to it.

He started up the engine of the squad car and pulled off the shoulder onto the road. The vulture looked up at Bubby and then flapped its long black wings, flying up into a tree. Sheriff Tucker had an uneasy feeling in his gut. Something didn't seem right, but he had to keep his word, at least until after the election.

29

Will sat across from Jane Michaels in her office on the second floor of the courthouse. Built in 1785, the building was three stories of white-painted brick. Jane's oversized office had floor-to-ceiling paned windows that still had the original glass, giving the outside a wavy appearance. On top of her massive mahogany desk were piles of papers and file folders. File boxes lined the walls. Jane's neat and orderly personal appearance was a sharp contrast to her office. To an outsider, it would seem that she was completely disorganized, but she could put her finger on any case she needed. She was never one to put things back in their rightful place, but she could tell you the exact details of a case that happened three years ago.

"It's not as easy as you make it sound," Jane said, after listening to Will's take on the case.

"It can be. All you have to do is say the word, and the charges can be dropped."

"Did you talk with the paramedics that were on the scene?"

"Yes, and they confirmed my theory that Ada threw down the pitchfork while running toward Jimmy. Ada was kneeling down beside Jimmy, and there was no pitchfork in sight when they arrived. I found the pitchfork lying partially under the tractor, where it would have fallen if she had dropped it when she started coming toward Jimmy."

Will sat back in his chair, running his hands through his blond hair, a gesture that indicated his frustration. He then leaned forward and spoke calmly: "Jane, I understand you not wanting Jenna to get off totally free, but I think the picture her attorney will paint will make the jury very sympathetic to her, and in the long run, after spending a fortune of the taxpayers' money, you will probably lose."

Jane smiled at Will. She liked him. From her dealings with him in the past, she thought he was a decent guy. But she didn't give up cases just because she thought she might lose; she had a duty to uphold for the county.

"Will, I appreciate your advice, but what makes you so sure Jenna is completely innocent? We have a woman who, since the time she was a little girl, had been subjected to abuse at the hands of her father. She watched her mother tormented by him as well. From her own admission, she spent years in therapy trying to cope. How do you know Jenna didn't just snap and shoot her father to end all the suffering they had endured? Maybe technically she didn't kill him, but what was her intent when she went in that barn? I think we can still charge her with attempted murder. And who knows, even though she used to be an expert markswoman, she supposedly hasn't fired a weapon in a long time, and I'm sure her nerves were in play. Shooting your father is a bit different from shooting at skeet. Maybe she wanted to kill him, but missed."

Jane leaned back in her chair and clasped her hands over her stomach. "I'm surprised with all your years in law enforcement you would be willing to give her a free pass so quickly." She released her hands and then moved forward against the desk. "Is there something else going on that I don't know about?"

"I'm not sure what you're insinuating," Will felt his blood pressure rise. Indignation welled inside. How could she suggest he and Jenna were having an affair? He'd never do anything like that. But then the scene at the creek popped into his head. He and Libby, lying on the ground. He felt his face get hot. "*Because* of all my years in law enforcement is the reason I feel she's innocent. I've learned how to tell when someone's lying. I'd bet my career she didn't intentionally try to kill her father."

Will leaned forward his elbows resting on his knees. "Jane, you're in the position to use your judgment in interpreting the law. Even the autopsy report shows that it wasn't the gunshot wound that killed him." He raised his hand before Jane could interject. "I'm sure you can find a doctor somewhere to refute that, but don't you think this family has suffered enough? Jenna's not going to be a threat to society. Let them live their lives."

"Jimmy Thompson doesn't get to live his."

"And he would probably have died soon anyway. He never went to the doctor, according to Ada, and that aneurism was like a balloon ready to burst."

Jane tapped her pen against the blotter on her desk; her lips were set in a firm line as she stared at Will. After a minute she said, "All right, I'll consider reducing the charges, but I'm not guaranteeing it. I'll get back to you tomorrow on my decision."

"Thanks." Will got up and headed toward the door.

"You know, Jenna really owes you. She should be paying you instead of her attorney," Jane said.

"No, I think you would have come to this conclusion on your own anyway; I just pushed it along a little faster."

"I haven't decided anything yet."

"I know, I know." Will nodded as he turned and left the office.

The Corsica Pub was crowded for a Thursday night. Laughter and the hum of voices mingled with an Alan Jackson song that played in the background. Will, Julie, Josh, and Libby were eating pizza, with Caleb sleeping peacefully in his infant seat beside them.

Julie had called Libby the day before and asked her if they'd like to get together. She'd gotten a sitter for the older kids, telling Libby she desperately needed some time out of the house.

Julie was animatedly recounting a tale about Milo digging up a pile of bones in the woods where Wyeth and Nathan had been playing a game of hide and seek with the dog. Wyeth was trying to teach Milo to be a search and rescue dog after watching a show on Animal Planet. "They came running in the house with this bone, shouting some fantastic story they'd concocted about a wolf tearing apart someone in the woods and then burying them."

"What kind of bone was it?" Libby asked.

"I couldn't tell. I thought maybe a deer leg, but they said there were more bones back in the woods. I told them to wait for their father to come home before they could go back there.

"I'm not sure what kind of stories he reads to these kids at night," Julie pointed in Will's direction, "but they have some pretty wild imaginations. Going on about a giant wolf that had terrorized the town and dragged the people out to the woods where he devoured them and then buried their bones." She paused to take a sip of her beer.

"Did you find out what kind of animal it was?" Libby asked.

Julie looked over at Will, who continued with the story, "Well, the boys were right." He paused.

Libby stared at Will with raised eyebrows, waiting for him to finish.

"They were the remains of a human that had been eaten by a wolf."

"*What?*" Libby said in astonishment. Then quickly realized Will was joking, when she saw him wink at Josh.

"You brat! You had me going," Libby shouted at Will.

Things were different between them now. It was as if a switch had been flipped inside Libby. Her yearnings for Will had dissipated. Maybe it had been her hormones; she didn't know.

Over the past few weeks, she'd been spending time with Julie. They'd gotten together a couple of times, meeting at the park in town, while the kids played. The first time, they'd run into each other unexpectedly. Libby had been sitting on a bench in the park with Stella, when Julie had shown up with her brood. She'd told Libby her mom had just gone back home.

Libby had felt awkward at first, as if what she and Will had done was plastered all over her face. Shame was making it hard for her to breathe. She listened to Julie talk about her life, the problems she'd been having with Will, and how things were finally getting better. Julie had told her how she knew most of it had to do with the pregnancy, and she knew she'd taken it out on Will.

Libby listened in silence, wishing she could turn back the clock, erase what had happened. She liked Julie and wanted to be friends. She needed a friend. There were times she felt desperately alone. Driving home that day, she decided to lock the memory of Will away. Everyone makes mistakes. She knew Will loved Julie as much as she loved Josh. They needed to bury what happened and start anew.

"Actually," Will continued, "they were the remains of a wild boar."

"A wild boar!" Libby blurted out.

"Supposedly there were boars around here years ago. I took some of the bones over to the coroner; he has books on all kinds of animals' bones. They matched up perfectly with the boar."

Josh was making a joke about a client of his that reminded him of a wild boar, when Jenna and her attorney, Jackson Darrow, walked in. She saw them and waved, changing her direction as she walked over toward their table.

"Hey, Jenna," Josh said. He stood up and hugged her.

"Hi, Josh." She motioned toward Jackson, "This is my friend *and* attorney, Jackson Darrow." Then she said to Jackson, "Josh is an attorney also."

Both men shook hands. Josh asked if they'd like to join them.

They sat down, and Jenna told them how she and Jackson were celebrating.

"What's the occasion?" Libby asked.

Will was the only one at the table who already knew the answer.

"All charges have been dropped. I'm a free woman again!"

"Fantastic!" Josh said. "How'd that happen?"

"I think I have this guy to thank for it," Jenna said as she motioned toward Will.

"A round of drinks are in order," Josh waved down their server. He ordered beers for everyone.

"So, tell me how all the charges were dropped. Last I heard, they had you for murder, which I thought was ridiculous," Josh said.

"These past few weeks have been so surreal. I couldn't believe the murder charge either, but thanks to Will's backing and Jackson's brilliant defense skills, the prosecutor figured it wasn't worth the fight."

The Tiffany-style pendant light over the table cast a soft light onto Jenna's face. Libby studied her, thinking how beautiful she was. There was a seductive quality about her. "I can't imagine what you were going through," Libby said.

"I like to look on the bright side. If it wasn't for all of this, I never would have met Jackson." Jenna leaned over toward Jackson and squeezed his arm.

"You've got to tell me how it all went down with Jane. She is one tough nut to crack," Will said.

"I got a call from her saying she wanted to meet in her office to discuss the charges with me. She wouldn't elaborate. I assumed she'd decided to reduce the charges. But Jackson wasn't taking any chances; he went in there loaded for bear."

Jenna related the meeting with Jane Michaels, telling them how Jackson had cited precedent cases, some even in Maryland, where escalated force was allowed in self-defense or the defense of another. "You could just see the look of defeat on her face. She knew she was beat." Jenna smiled at Jackson. "This guy was awesome!" She leaned over and kissed him hard on the mouth.

Libby felt a pang of jealousy. She visualized Josh and Jenna, alone together, working late. Had he been tempted by this dynamic woman, whose eyes sparkled flecks of gold? She felt she paled in comparison.

"How's your mom holding up?" Julie asked.

Jenna frowned. "She's doing OK. We're taking things one day at a time. I guess even with all the abuse my mother took, she still loved the man. I can't understand it."

"Maybe she's remembering the good times," Julie said.

"Maybe. I've arranged for someone to take care of the animals for a while, so my mom can go down to Atlanta and visit my brother. I think that'll really help her heal."

"What are your plans? Has this affected your career at all?" Julie asked.

"I don't know. I'm hoping it'll all blow over, and I can pick up where I left off."

"Have you talked with Reynolds?" Josh asked.

"I tried calling him this afternoon to tell him the news, but I couldn't reach him. I'm hoping I still have a job." Jenna laughed.

"I think you'll be fine," Josh replied.

Libby interjected, "I was wondering if you received the invitation to our Labor Day party?"

Jenna nodded. "Things were kind of up in the air, so I hadn't RSVP'd.

"No, I understand. I just wanted to let you know we'd love for both you and Jackson to come."

After a rousing round of darts with the men against the women, where the women trounced the men, the group sat back down at the table. Caleb had woken up, and Julie began to nurse him.

"How old is he?" Jenna asked.

"Four weeks and two days," Julie replied.

"You look great. Is he your first?"

"No! I have three others at home."

"Wow, four kids!" Jenna turned toward Will and smiled. "You really are the family man."

"I guess you could say that." Will kissed Julie on the cheek.

Libby glanced over at Josh who was looking at Jenna.

"A friend of mine just had a baby," Jenna said. Then she added, "In fact, I feel like I'm the only one left who has yet to have one." She laughed. "Not that I'm ready!" She held her hands up.

Julie joked about never really being ready for kids. "I think the sleep deprivation is the worst part." She reached over to Libby, placing her hand on her arm. "That reminds me, I was up in the middle of the night with Caleb a couple of days ago and a show came on TV about paranormal activity. Has the ghost been around lately?"

Libby glanced at Josh, who gave her a look that said, "Please don't go there."

"Wait a minute," Jenna interjected. "Your house is haunted?"

Libby nodded.

"That's wild! Josh, I can't believe you didn't mention that before." Jenna paused and then held up her finger. "Wait, didn't you tell me Reynolds used to own that house?"

Josh nodded.

"I wonder if Reynolds ever saw the ghost," Jenna said. "Tell me about it," she added enthusiastically. "I love ghost stories."

Libby briefly explained the encounters with Elizabeth, hoping Josh wasn't getting mad.

"I can't wait to see this house. Do you think the ghost will show up at the party?"

❦

"Do you think she's pretty?" Libby brushed back strands of hair that blew in her face from the open car window.

"Who?" Josh was fiddling with the radio as he pulled out of the pub parking lot.

"Jenna."

"I don't know. I guess." He hated these kinds of questions. "Why do you ask?"

"Just wondering." Her gaze focused on the streetlamps along the road. "I feel so mediocre," Libby said after minutes of silence.

"Mediocre? What makes you say that?"

"I don't know. Everyone seems to have such exciting lives. I haven't done anything that's worth remembering."

"Are you kidding? What about all those inner-city kids you taught? I'm sure you made a huge impact on their lives."

"I doubt it. They probably don't even remember my name."

"What about the baby? You're about to take on the most important job in the world." He reached over and grabbed her hand. "You're going to be the world's best mom."

30

The house sparkled like a debutante on her coming-out day. There had been a flurry of activity all morning in preparation for the guests who were to arrive around half past four.

Libby had her hair swept up with a few curly tendrils around her face. Her blue eyes glistened, and her cheeks had a rosy glow. There was no mistaking she was pregnant now. It was like Jiffy Pop, she thought.

Her prayers had been answered; the temperature hovered in the upper seventies with low humidity. By 4:30 p.m., cars were lining the circular drive. Libby, along with Stella, greeted guests at the door and directed them onto the patio where Josh was manning the bar, stocked with everything from mint juleps to mojitos. An hour later, most everyone had arrived, and the patio was crammed with people talking and mingling about. The smell of barbequed ribs and chicken wafted through the air. Smoke rose from the large, black iron grill set up on the far side of the tent.

Even Tassie had come; she had ridden over with Mary Alice and her husband Herbert. Trevor was there, too, dressed in a collared shirt tucked into a nice pair of dress pants and polished loafers. He had told Libby that his mother made him wear his church clothes to the party. He said he felt silly all dressed up when Julie's boys were wearing shorts and T-shirts. Libby told him he looked handsome and that he should never worry about being dressed too nicely. Then she said, if he wanted to, he could take off his shoes and run around with the other kids. He smiled at her, kicked off his shoes and socks, and ran out onto the lawn to join Wyeth and Nathan.

She stood at the edge of the patio watching the guests interact, her eyes scanning the yard. What a transformation, she thought. The overgrown weeds replaced by an explosion of color from the blooming knock-out roses, vincas, and impatiens. She smiled feeling proud of all that she'd accomplished over the long, hot summer. Will appeared beside her. Leaning toward her, he whispered, "We need to talk."

Libby's smile faded, and she felt a tight knot in her stomach. Julie found out about the two of them. Did Julie hate her? Would she tell Josh? The thoughts flipped through her mind like an old newsreel. She swallowed hard, feeling her legs weaken beneath her.

"What's going on?" Her voice cracked.

He guided her by the arm onto the lawn away from the crowd. "I got a call from my friend at the lab in Easton yesterday. He said he got a couple of clear sets of prints off the bottle; one of them may be yours since you were handling it."

Libby exhaled. He'd wanted to discuss the case. Relief washed over her, and she let out a laugh.

Will paused, looking puzzled.

"I'm sorry, go on," Libby said, waving her hand at him.

"We were hoping that Reynolds' prints were already in the system, but they're not. So, I thought this could be the perfect opportunity to get his prints. All we have to do is get him to hold a glass of something, which shouldn't be hard; the tricky part will be to get the glass away from him without getting the prints smudged up from someone else touching the glass."

"This is exciting!" Libby's eyes lit up. She loved this kind of stuff. A rush of excitement ran through her. "I can help get the glass away from him."

"We have to be careful. We don't want him to get suspicious."

"Don't worry. I've got an idea." Libby patted Will's arm and took off across the lawn.

Will watched from a distance as Libby walked up to Reynolds and his wife. He noticed Reynolds already had a drink in his hand and wondered how Libby was going to get it away from him. After several minutes of talking, she stepped away from them and then returned with a drink wrapped in a napkin. She said something to them, and they all laughed. Then she handed the drink to Reynolds, keeping the napkin in her hand. He took a sip and then handed it back to Libby, who carefully took the glass by the rim and then set it in the palm of her hand, holding the bottom of the glass with the napkin. Sheriff Tucker joined the group, and Libby stayed for a few more minutes talking with all three. Then, she glanced over at Will across the yard, tilting her head for him to follow her.

He made his way across the patio, saying hi to people along the way, squeezing past them to the side of the house and into the kitchen. The muffled sounds of laughter and talking filtered through the screen door.

"Ta-da!" Libby said, holding up the glass in the palm of her hand. "I did it! And I don't think he suspected a thing." She carefully set the glass on the counter. "Now what do we do with it?"

Will looked around to make sure no one was coming into the kitchen. "We need a Ziploc bag."

"Sure." Libby reached into the kitchen drawer.

He unzipped the bag and held it open. "Pick up the glass around the bottom, the way you were holding it, and dump the contents into the sink. Then slip it in the bag." Libby did as she was directed, and Will sealed the bag. "How'd you get him to take the glass?"

"I asked him what he was drinking, and he said bourbon and water; so, I told him he had to try Josh's specialty drink. I wiped down a glass at the bar with a napkin, making sure it didn't have any prints, and then poured a mojito into it. I told him the true test of any good politician is that he pleases the hostess, and nothing would please me more than to get his opinion of Josh's mojito mix. It worked!" Libby clapped her hands together. "He took a sip, but said he'd stick with his bourbon."

"You'd make a great detective."

Libby smiled. "It was fun!"

Will chuckled. "One more thing. I think it would be a good idea to get your prints as well, since you touched the bottle. That way we can eliminate them. Mark said there were two sets on the bottle."

Libby opened up the cupboard and took out a glass. She wiped it down with a paper towel and then grabbed the glass firmly. Will held out another plastic bag and she slipped the glass inside.

"Thanks. I'll take these out to my car. I don't want anything to happen to them." Will headed for the door and then turned back to Libby. "I'm glad—I mean, I..." Will paused.

"What?" Libbie looked puzzled.

"Are things OK with you and Josh?"

She nodded and smiled. "And you?"

"Yeah." He held the bag up. "Hopefully, we'll have some answers soon."

Josh was on the pier with some of the guests, showing them the new boat that had arrived the day before. He was telling the group how he was going to take his maiden voyage tomorrow. Jenna, with a drink in hand, sauntered down the pier and joined the group that had gathered around Josh. As soon as she spoke, it was obvious she'd had a few too many mojitos.

"So what's going on down here? Are we going for a boat ride?" She grinned wide, her eyes half closed, as she weaved slightly.

The other guests began to disperse, leaving Josh and Jenna alone. "I think you've had enough of these," he said as he tried to take the glass from her.

"Hey, don't take that! I love these. I love you, too," she added in a slurred voice as she put her arm on Josh.

"Where's Jackson?" Josh asked.

"I don't know. I think he's mad at me."

"Jenna, have you had anything to eat? Why don't we go back, and I'll fix you a plate of food."

"Let's go out on the boat!"

"Not right now." Josh took her arm and guided her back down the pier.

"Do you think I'll ever make it in Washington? My career is probably ruined now. No one will want to hire a murderer."

"You're not a murderer. What happened was an accident."

"Was it?"

"Maybe not an accident, but you were only defending your mother."

"I *hated* that man. I used to wish he'd die. And now he is! Voila!" Jenna threw her arms out to the side, her drink splashing out onto the pier.

"He sounded like a horrible man."

"He was." Tears welled in her eyes.

Josh put his arm around her and squeezed her shoulder. "Hey, don't beat yourself up. You've been through a lot these past few weeks. Your life will get back to normal soon."

"I hope so. I hope Reynolds takes me back. I tried to set up a meeting with him, but all I got was his secretary. She said she would have him call me, but he hasn't yet, and he hasn't said two words to me today."

"He will. Just give it time." A gust of wind swept by, splashing the bay water against the pilings. The boat rocked on its moorings.

Jenna threw her arms around his neck and then kissed him on the cheek. "You're a nice guy, you know that?" She smiled at him with her long auburn hair blowing around her face. He smelled the alcohol on her breath.

"Yeah, yeah. Come on, we're gonna get you some food." Josh released her arms and led her down the pier and up the stone path.

Libby was on the patio talking with Mrs. Jenkins and Julie about organic versus non-organic foods when she caught sight of Josh and Jenna on the pier. She fixed her gaze, wondering what they were doing out there. Then she saw Jenna wrap her arms around Josh's neck and kiss him. She felt a tap on her arm, and she glanced back to see Mrs. Jenkins staring at her. "I said, have you been to the new bookstore in town?" Libby's pulse quickened. What was going on between Josh and Jenna?

"Libby?" Julie was frowning at her. "Are you OK?"

"What? Oh, yes, I'm sorry. What did you say?" She looked back at Mrs. Jenkins, who repeated her question. Libby shook her head saying she hadn't had a chance to get to the bookstore yet. Her mind raced with visions of Josh and Jenna together. Meeting at a clandestine spot in Baltimore. How could she get upset? She'd done the same thing. But that was different. It had been a momentary lapse of her senses. She didn't love Will.

One of the caterers came up to her and asked her a question about the food. She excused herself and followed the caterer over to the food tent. They discussed when to start putting out the desserts. When she finished with the caterer, she searched the crowd for Josh but didn't see him.

Another guest came up to her to compliment her on bringing Haverford House back to life. She smiled and chatted with the woman, but her mind kept picturing Josh and Jenna on the pier. She felt a nagging unease in her gut.

Reynolds was deep in conversation with the mayor, when Jenna crossed the lawn with a purposeful stride. The mayor saw Jenna and reached out, giving her a hug along with condolences for losing her father. He didn't mention the shooting. The three talked for a few minutes, and then the mayor walked away, leaving Reynolds and Jenna alone.

"I've been calling you. Has your secretary been giving you my messages?" Jenna asked Reynolds, a bit more sober after eating the plate of food Josh had fixed for her. Jenna rarely drank more than an occasional glass of wine, worried she'd be like her father. But once she got started, it was hard for her to stop. She'd picked up another mojito before heading over to Reynolds, downing a gulp for liquid courage.

"I've been very busy lately," Reynolds replied. He was scanning the crowd, not looking at Jenna. He took a sip of his drink and said, "I hear all the charges were dropped."

"Yes. I'm a free woman!" she shouted, throwing her head back and spreading her arms. Realizing her nerves were making her overact, she tried to tone it down. She didn't like the fact that Reynolds held her future in his hands. She hated groveling, but she needed reassurance that she still had a job. "So how does it feel to be back at your old house?"

Reynolds shrugged. "It's been a long time."

She sensed Reynolds giving her the cold shoulder, as if a wall were between them. Jenna continued trying to keep the conversation going. "I remember when your wife died. The whole town was in shock."

"It was very tragic." Reynolds' eyes were focused toward the patio, as if he had already mentally dismissed Jenna, ready to move on to someone else.

She felt desperate. He wasn't going to take her back. She knew if he walked away, her chances were over. "Did you ever see the ghost when you lived here?"

"Ghost?" He raised his eyebrows and finally looked at her.

"Josh and Libby tell me the house is haunted. Some woman has been appearing in the house, leaving cryptic messages for them to 'save her' or something like that."

Reynolds huffed. "Ghost stories are hardly something I'd take cre-dence in." He flashed his politician smile at her as he began to step away.

A breeze blew the salty air across the lawn, and Jenna brushed a strand of hair behind her ear. "Maybe it's your wife; maybe she's trying to tell them something about her past." A distant voice in Jenna's head told her to stop, but the alcohol wouldn't let her.

Reynolds' eyes bore into her. "I think speculation is a dangerous thing. You should stick to things you know."

Jenna hated his dismissive tone. She became angry. "But what if it *is* your wife? Wouldn't you be interested in what she wanted?"

"I don't believe in people communicating after death. There is no hereafter."

"How can you be so sure?"

Several children raced around the lawn beside them, screeching with delight. One of the boys bumped into Reynolds' leg, laughed, and then ran on.

Reynolds brushed the leg of his pants. "I live in the here and now. To me, life is about getting everything you can while you're here."

"That's kind of sad." Jenna looked out at the afternoon sun glis-tening on the peaks of water.

"It's not sad to me. I think my life has turned out pretty well."

"It's sad because you place yourself above everything else." Jenna knew what she was saying was professional suicide, but she couldn't stop herself. She hated his smugness. "You worship material things, and when and if you ever lose them, you're left with nothing."

Reynolds chuckled. "Aren't you the philosopher? First off, I don't plan on losing anything I have; and second, worshipping tangible things, I think, makes a whole lot more sense than worshipping things you can't even see." Reynolds held up his drink as if toasting to Jenna before turning to walk away. He stopped after a few steps and turned back. "I'll call you sometime this week. I'm afraid I've had to go with another speechwriter while you were tied up with your crisis. But there may be something you could do for me."

Jenna wanted to slap him, to rip the self-assured look off his face. She was good at her job and didn't need to beg at this man's feet.

Her drink still in hand, she walked over to an Adirondack chair and sunk down, staring at the bay. The anger slipped away, replaced with depression. Her life seemed to be falling apart rapidly. She'd gone from a rising career to shooting her father, being charged with murder, losing her job. She took a sip of her drink, feeling sorry for herself. She watched a buoy that bobbed in the water, appearing to be moving freely but never actually getting anywhere. A shadow fell across her chair. She looked up to see Jackson standing beside her. She gave him a hollow smile.

"Are you sorry you came with me?" she asked.

"No." He sat down in another chair beside her.

"I know I was acting pretty badly earlier. I get that way when I've had too much to drink. I guess I'm no better than my father."

He picked up her hand and held it in his. "I think you're too hard on yourself. I love the whole package, sober or drunk." He leaned over and kissed her cheek. Then he added with a laugh, "I *prefer* sober."

"I don't deserve you." Jenna's eyes clouded with tears.

"Yes, you do; you are a brilliant, beautiful woman. I'm a lucky man."

"Do you still want me even if I'm out of a job?"

"What do you mean?"

"I think I just blew it with Reynolds, although he'd probably already made his mind up to let me go. He was just enjoying stringing me along."

"There are other politicians out there. You'll bounce back. Just give it some time."

"I love you." It was the first time she'd ever uttered those words to a man.

Maggie was perched at the table on the patio finishing her third helping of barbequed ribs. It was her favorite food. She meticulously sucked off the juice from each stubby finger. Sheriff Tucker sat beside her, puffing away on his cigar. "Those are some of the best ribs I've ever had," she said as she wiped a napkin across her chin. She glanced over at the food table. "Did you get any pie, Baynard?"

"No, I didn't, but I sure would love a piece."

"I'm just going to run inside and freshen up, and I'll bring you back a slice."

"Why, that would be very kindly of you."

Maggie picked up her plate—laden with rib bones picked clean—and headed toward the house. A few minutes later, John Reynolds walked over and sat down in her chair.

"So, Bubby, do you have everything under control?" He leaned toward the sheriff with his hands on his knees.

Sheriff Tucker glanced around to see if anyone was within earshot. "I had a talk with my deputy and told him to put the case to rest for now." He nervously played with the edge of the white plastic tablecloth.

"Did he agree to that?" Reynolds fixed his eyes on Bubby.

Sheriff Tucker tugged at his belt, feeling uncomfortable under the intensity of Reynolds' gaze. "What else could he do? I *am* the boss." He snorted a short laugh and then cleared his throat, averting his eyes from Reynolds. "You know, John, I can't keep this hanging forever. After the election, we're going to have to follow up on this."

"Absolutely. I told you I would cooperate one hundred percent. I just don't want false allegations to ruin my chances of being elected. You can't un-ring a bell."

"I understand," Tucker replied.

"Have you heard any other talk about my wife, about the journal?"

"Will never told me where the journal came from, but Maggie tells me that the Langstons and the Seevers are good friends. Maybe they're the ones who found it in the house somewhere."

Reynolds rubbed his chin, looking off into the distance, and then he slapped his hands on his knees. "If you hear anything else, keep me informed. Remember, I don't forget a favor." He winked at Tucker.

Maggie returned with a plate of pie in each hand. "Hello, Mr. Reynolds."

"Maggie." Reynolds gave a short nod with his head and stood up, pulling out the chair for Maggie. "Here, sit down. I was just leaving."

"Why, thank you." She sat back in her seat.

Libby was in the kitchen with Tassie seated at the table, discussing the benefits of composting. Several of the guests had said their good-byes. The room was filled with a golden light from the little lamp, the sun having dipped close to the horizon. Crickets chirped outside as the screen door opened and John Reynolds strode into the room.

"Why there you are, pretty lady," Reynolds said to Libby. "I wanted to compliment you on a wonderful party."

"Thank you." Libby glanced over at Tassie. She introduced them and told Reynolds that Tassie was Corsica's oldest living resident.

"How do you do?" Reynolds bent down, extending his hand to Tassie. "It is truly a pleasure to meet you. I do recall hearing your name when I used to live here."

Tassie reached out her spidery black hand and slowly placed it in Reynolds'. As she grasped her fingers around his palm, she closed her eyes. Reynolds gave Libby a perplexed look. She just smiled and waited. Seconds later, Tassie's eyes popped open wide, and she pulled her hand back from Reynolds.

"Are you all right, Miss Jackson?"

"I'm a little tired is all."

"I can understand that. I'm sure this has been a long day for you." Reynolds then turned to Libby and said, "You haven't by any chance come across anything that belonged to my first wife since you moved in?"

Libby felt her cheeks get hot. His question had caught her off guard. She glanced over at Tassie, who was slowly shaking her head as if to say "don't say a word."

Libby shook her head. "Nothing that I recall." Libby knew she didn't lie well, and her voice shook slightly as the words came out. She could tell Reynolds knew she was lying from the look on his face.

He said in a quiet but firm tone, "Well, if you do happen to come across anything, I would appreciate it if you let me know." He gave her a strange smile.

"Of course," she replied.

"It was nice meeting you, Miss Jackson." He gave a slight nod with his head toward Tassie. "If I can find my wife, we will be taking off. I have a very busy schedule tomorrow with the campaign."

"Thank you for coming," Libby said as she stood up. Her stomach was churning inside.

He sidled close to her and said in her ear, "Be careful with that baby; you wouldn't want anything to happen to you while you're pregnant." He then flashed a big grin and left the room.

Her knees were shaking as she sat back down next to Tassie. Libby's arms were protectively wrapped around her stomach. "Did you hear that?"

"I sure did, child. I'm telling you, that man is pure evil."

"I think he just threatened me. Do you think that was a threat?"

"Whether it was or not, you need to stay away from him. In all my born days, I have never felt such wickedness. When I touched his hand, it was as if my body was filled with a horrible plague."

"I think he knows about the hummingbird book."

"He knows something."

Just then, Julie came into the kitchen with Caleb in her arms. "I've got to sit down. My feet are killing me," she said as she pulled out one of the kitchen chairs and slipped off her sandals, rubbing her feet with her free hand.

"Let me hold that baby," Tassie said, taking Caleb from her.

"He's all yours," Julie replied with a smile. "Will and the boys are playing horseshoes with Josh and Trevor." Julie glanced over at Libby. "What's wrong? You look like you've seen a ghost." Her eyes got big and she added, "You didn't see the ghost, did you?"

"No, but I think I was just threatened."

"Threatened? Who threatened you?"

"Reynolds. I think he knows about the journal I found."

"What? How could that be?"

"I don't know, but he asked me if I had come across any of his wife's things, and I don't think he believed me when I said I hadn't. He told me that I should be careful with my baby, that I wouldn't want it to get hurt—or something like that."

"Oh my God! Libby, you've got to tell Josh and Will about this."

"I can't say anything to Josh right now. He doesn't know I've still been looking into Cecilia's death, and if he finds out what I did behind his back he'll be furious."

"But Reynolds threatened you!"

"Will is working on the case. If there's any truth to the journal, they'll be able to arrest Reynolds. And besides, how can he hurt me? I'll just stay away from him until the case is solved. No more boat rides."

"What do you think, Tassie?" Julie asked.

"I think we are dealing with the devil, and we better be careful."

Libby laughed. "He may be a scumbag, but I don't think he's the devil."

"The devil can come in many forms. Just like God is in many, so is the devil. I had to hold this child so's I could be filled with love again after touching his hand."

Libby shifted in her seat, looking over at Julie, as an ominous feeling seeped into her gut.

The last guest left a little after 10:30 p.m. The caterers had packed up their supplies an hour before, returning the next day for the tables, chairs, and tent. Josh was out on the patio collecting stray glasses and trash scattered about the tables. The tiki torches set up around the patio still burned, along with the twinkle lights that sparkled in the trees. A warm breeze blew from the water and a bullfrog croaked in the distance. Libby crossed the patio with a glass of ice water and sat down in one of the chairs.

"I'm exhausted," she said, putting her bare feet up on the chair next to her. She reached up and removed the clip from her hair, and her blonde tendrils fell about her face. She rested her head on the back of the chair. "I think the party was a success, don't you?"

"Yeah, it went really well. You outdid yourself," Josh replied. He walked over to where she was seated, lifted her feet up off the chair, and sat down, lowering her feet onto his lap as he gently massaged them.

"Oh, that feels wonderful." Libby closed her eyes.

"It was an interesting mix of people, but I think everyone got along really well. Josh told her about an exchange between his boss, Robert Peterson and Bruce Tompkins from the hardware store over whether #4 shot or #5 shot is better for hunting pheasant. "The next thing I know Bruce is inviting Peterson over to his farm."

Libby laughed. "I can't picture Peterson dressed in camouflage." She stared out at the pier. The moonlight shimmered on the water. "I saw you and Jenna talking earlier. What was that all about?"

"I think the whole crisis had caught up with her, not to mention the drinks she'd had. She's trying to figure out what to do with the rest of her life."

"But all the charges were dropped. Can't she go back to working for Reynolds?"

"He's decided she had too much baggage attached to her, and he needed to play it safe. From what I hear, he's already hired a guy from New York to be his speechwriter."

"That's sad, but it doesn't surprise me. That guy has no heart. What's Jenna going to do?"

"I don't know, but I'm sure she'll do fine. She's great at what she does. I don't think she'll have any trouble getting work."

"Are you attracted to her?"

"What?" Josh wore a puzzled frown.

"Oh, come on, you have to admit she's beautiful."

"Not anywhere near as beautiful as the woman right in front of me." He leaned forward, cupping her face in his hands, and gave her a slow kiss on the mouth. "How would you like to go for a little night ride on the boat?"

"Right now?"

"Why not? It's a gorgeous night."

Libby hesitated, wondering if she was up to it.

"Come on, we haven't done anything exciting for a long time." He grabbed her arms and pulled her out of the chair. His dark hair glistened in the moonlight, and Libby could smell the spicy scent of his aftershave as he rubbed his face against hers. Warmth radiated out to her limbs and down her belly. She no longer felt tired.

31

Maggie spent the morning gossiping about everyone that had been at Josh and Libby's party. Will listened halfheartedly as he filled out some routine paperwork that had piled up on his desk, glancing up every so often and giving her a smile or a short response. He was preoccupied with the glasses sealed in plastic bags that sat in his desk drawer. He'd dropped them off at the station Saturday night on his way home from the party, locking them in his desk drawer.

Sheriff Tucker made his usual nine o'clock appearance but stayed only for a half hour before heading back out. He had promised Joe Dean at the party Saturday night that he would come out to his farm and check on the problem Joe had been having. Tucker told Will that, according to Dean, someone was stealing his eggs out of his henhouse; Dean was sure of it. For the past several weeks, when Dean went out in the morning to collect his eggs, there was only one or, at the most, two. Normally his hens produced between sixteen to twenty-four eggs a day. Dean said there was no way all of his hens stopped producing at the same time.

Will suggested setting up a camera in the henhouse to catch the thief in the act. Sheriff Tucker said that sounded like a better idea than the one Dean had. He laughed, his jowls jiggling, and said, "Dean wants to stake out the henhouse with his thirty-ought-six."

The sheriff stood up from his desk, hiking up his pants around his rotund girth, and headed for the door, shaking his head and muttering to himself that it seemed mighty strange that someone would take the trouble to steal a dozen eggs every night.

After the sheriff left, Will glanced over at Maggie, who was talking about Mrs. Parson's new perm and how awful it looked, while she performed her daily ritual of applying a fresh coat of polish on her nails. Will chuckled inside, thinking Maggie was one to talk about hairstyles with her hairspray-encrusted beehive.

He was trying to figure out a way to get the glasses out of his drawer without Maggie catching sight of it. He didn't feel like explaining to Maggie why he had two glasses inside plastic bags in his drawer. He wanted to keep this under wraps until he had more evidence. He leaned down and opened the drawer, but before he could reach in, she glanced up from her polishing and said, "Do you agree?"

Will looked up and replied, "Sure," not having a clue as to what he just agreed to.

Maggie's red lips formed a big smile. "I think you are about the only man who would." She screwed the top back on the bottle of polish, holding her fingers splayed.

A thought popped into his head. "I could really go for a honey bun right now." Will had noticed a box of pastries sitting on the lunch table when he had arrived that morning.

"Would you like me to get you one?"

"That would be great, but I can get it," Will added, knowing full-well Maggie would insist on getting the honey bun.

"No, you stay right there. I'll get it," she said, getting up from her desk and blowing on her nails.

"Thanks." He watched her walk to the back of the office, and then he quickly removed the glasses from the drawer and placed them in a thermal lunch bag that he had under his desk.

She returned a minute later with a glistening, sugary-coated honey bun on a small paper plate, along with a plastic fork and a napkin. "Here you go."

"Thanks, Maggie. You're a doll."

She gave him another big red smile.

After eating the pastry and commenting on how good it was, he told Maggie he would be back in a bit after running some errands. He stood up, making his exit, lunch bag in hand.

Will eased the patrol car into a space out in front of the forensic lab, anxious about what would show up. He entered the lab and greeted the young receptionist at the desk again.

"Hi, Will. You're becoming a regular around here." She flashed Will a big smile.

"Seems like it. Is Mark around?"

"I'll ring him." She buzzed through to Mark Gonzalez, who said he'd be up in a minute.

Will leaned against the counter.

"Did anyone ever tell you, you look kinda like Brad Pitt?" The receptionist leaned forward at her desk, looking up at Will.

"No, can't say that they have." Will laughed and moved away from the counter a bit.

"So what have you got for me?" Mark asked, coming through the door. Will had called Mark on his way over to give him the heads up. Will raised the thermal lunch bag. "Come on back." Mark motioned for Will to follow. They went into Mark's office, and he shut the door.

"Two perfect set of prints, I believe." Will removed the glasses from the paper bag. He had labeled the bags with Reynolds and Libby's names.

"If you've got a few minutes, I can run them right now and compare them to the ones from the bottle."

"That'd be great."

"Have a seat; I'll be back in a few." Mark took the glass from Will and left the office.

Will sat in the chair facing the desk and looked around the office at all the files and folders stacked up everywhere. He realized Mark was doing him a huge favor.

He contemplated his next move if the prints on the glass matched the bottle of halothane. He had researched halothane online and found the same information that Libby had given him, and he'd also discovered that when given in a high dose, it could cause temporary paralysis and even death.

If he could exhume Cecilia's body and determine whether halothane was in her system, they'd have another piece of the puzzle. Yet, it wouldn't prove Reynolds gave it to her. But if his prints were on the bottle, it would sure help. First, he had to find out if halothane could still be detected after all this time.

If Reynolds tried to claim she poisoned herself, Will thought, he could use the journal to show Cecilia's state of mind.

Will thought about the woman Libby had talked to—Catherine Collins. If she would be willing to come forth with the things Reynolds had said to her, it may be enough to sway a jury, but he didn't want to get ahead of himself. He didn't even know if the prints would match up yet.

The other issue he faced was confronting Sheriff Tucker and convincing him that they couldn't wait on this. Tucker had made it perfectly clear to Will that the investigation had to be stopped until after the election. If he told the sheriff that he had still been investigating the case, he had better have some darn good evidence against Reynolds to back him up.

After a little more than a half hour, Mark came back in the room, shutting the door behind him. "Well, we've got a definite match. The two sets of prints on the bottle are the same two on the glasses."

"That's great! And you're sure there were no other prints?"

"Nope. Just the two."

"Thanks, Mark, I really appreciate this."

Mark handed Will the bottle and the two glasses, all in sealed forensic bags. Will placed them in his lunch sack and stood up. "I've got to get back to the station. I hate to run, but I know you're busy, too."

"Anytime, man. I owe you," Mark said. Will knew he was referring to Mark's kid brother, who Will had gotten off on a trumped up drug charge in Baltimore years ago.

"Not anymore," Will said. Then he asked, "Would you testify in court as to the accuracy of the print match?"

"Absolutely. Just tell me when and where and I'll be there."

"Thanks." Will placed his hand on the knob to open the door.

"Hey, dude," Mark called out to him, "Be careful."

"Don't worry. I'm going to have everything airtight before anyone knows about this."

"Good luck."

Driving back to the station, Will picked up his cell and called the coroner's office. He talked to Garrett, and they arranged to meet at 2:30 p.m. at a truck stop on 306 just outside of town. He didn't want Garrett's loose-lipped assistant anywhere around when they talked.

He spent the next couple of hours catching up on more paperwork at the station before heading to the truck stop. The summer heat had risen again, and the sun beat down on his head as he walked to his car. Sweat dripped down the back of his uniform.

The truck stop at the intersection of Routes 306 and 311 had large bays for pumping gas to accommodate the constant tractor-trailer traffic that traveled up and down Route 311, heading north or south. Next to the gas station was a diner run by a couple, Yancy and Hazel Schuman, who had owned the diner for over forty years. It had earned a reputation among the trucker set for having some of the best comfort food along the East Coast. The Schumans didn't believe in low fat, and the term "light cuisine" was not in their vocabulary. But they were certainly not hurting for business either.

Will arrived first and took a seat at one of the booths. He glanced around to see if anyone from town was there, but it looked to be only transient diners. A woman dressed in a pink and white uniform that had seen better days came up to the table with a menu and a glass of water, which she placed on the table along with a paper placemat.

"Do you know what you want?" Her voice matched the weathered, hard look of someone who has had a tough life and smoked at least two packs a day. She pulled a pad of paper from her apron pocket and removed a pencil from behind her ear.

"I'm meeting someone. Could I get a cup of coffee for now?"

"Sure."

Will perused the menu as his stomach began to rumble, and he realized he hadn't eaten since that honey bun Maggie gave him earlier. He decided to order the cheeseburger with fries when the server returned with his coffee. She brought another placemat and menu for Garrett, who had yet to arrive.

After about ten minutes, Will saw Garrett's navy blue Subaru SUV pull into the parking lot. His tall, lanky frame stepped out of the car and sauntered over to the diner. He slipped into the vinyl seat across from Will. "So, what's going on?"

Before Will could answer, the less-than-happy server came over to take Garrett's order. "I'll just have a lemonade." She nodded her head and took the plastic-coated menu off the table.

"I'm still working on that case involving Cecilia Reynolds. I've been able to obtain some more information, but it all has to stay under wraps. You can understand how sensitive this is, considering Reynolds is running for office, and Sheriff Tucker wants to please Reynolds at all costs. But I think if I have enough evidence, the sheriff will have to go along with me to exhume the body."

"What did you find out, other than she might've been pregnant?"

"I think she may have been drugged. We came across a drug called halothane at Haverford House, and John Reynolds' prints are on the bottle."

"Halothane?"

"Yeah, it's a drug that was used as an—"

"I know what halothane is; I was just curious as to why they'd have it in their house."

"That's what I'd like to know, too. If Reynolds poisoned his wife and then drowned her in the bathtub, would the drug still show up in an autopsy now?"

"I'm pretty sure it would, if it was administered shortly before death."

"Before I went to Tucker, I wanted to be sure the drug could be detected."

"I can't make any guarantees. Like I said before with the pregnancy, until I know the state of the body, it's hard to say for sure. What I can say is that under good conditions we should be able to take samples to test for the drug."

Will took a big bite of his cheeseburger, while Garrett sipped on his lemonade.

"You know that stuff will kill you," Garrett said, pointing to Will's half-pound of ground beef.

"I know, but it sure tastes good," he replied, wiping the grease and ketchup from his chin.

"Let me know when you want to do the exhumation, and I'll get the paperwork ready."

"I was hoping that as few people as possible would know about it," Will said.

"I think we can work that out." Garrett began to pull his wallet out of his pants' pocket.

"It's on me," Will said. "Thanks for meeting me. I'll call you in a few days."

After Garrett left, the server asked Will if he wanted dessert. The chocolate cream pie behind the glass case at the counter was calling to him, but he knew he'd better stop with the cheeseburger. "Just the check."

She pulled out her pad, tore off Will's bill, and set it on the table. "Pay up at the counter."

32

Two weeks had passed since the Labor Day party, and Josh was still heavily immersed in work with what seemed no end in sight. He was in the middle of reviewing some documents from a new client when the words on the page blurred together. He set the papers down on the desk and swiveled his chair around, gazing out at the Inner Harbor.

He stood up and walked over to the window, staring down at the people twenty stories below. He could pick out the lunchtime crowd as they scurried along the pavement, hustling to get back to their jobs; and then there were the tourists strolling along the harbor, feeding the ducks. A large schooner, anchored in the water, rocked back and forth, its sails billowing in the wind.

He longed to be sailing; he had taken the boat out only once since he got it. He wondered if all the hard work was worth it. What was the point in acquiring things if you never had the time to enjoy them? His thoughts drifted to the night on the boat with Libby and he smiled. He missed her; they'd hardly seen each other since that night. Maybe he would tell Peterson he was going to take some time off, just a few days, after the Sanders case was finished.

Stephanie's voice came over the speaker: "Mr. Reynolds is on the line."

"Put him through." Josh turned from the window and sat back down at his desk.

"Mr. Reynolds, how are things going?"

"Great. Listen Josh, I was wondering if you could meet me after work this evening. I'm going to be in Baltimore giving a speech to some local union heads, and afterwards I thought we could get together and go over a few things I need taken care of."

"Sure, when and where?"

"How about seven? Meet me at the Renaissance Hotel. I have a suite booked there. Just come up to room ten-seventeen."

"OK, see you then."

He started to pick up the phone to call Libby but then changed his mind. He'd tell her later. He really didn't have to call her at all; being late was now the norm.

The Renaissance was only two blocks from Josh's office, located at the center of the Inner Harbor on East Pratt Street. The lobby was open all the way to the top with a labyrinth of glass-enclosed skywalks connecting the floors; plants and trees filled the center of the ground floor reaching up toward the twelve stories above.

Josh headed over to the bank of elevators and pushed the "UP" button. Within seconds, the doors slid open and several people got off. Josh stepped to one side and then made his way on to the empty cubicle. He hit the number ten button and waited as the doors closed in front of him. Glancing over at his reflection in the mirrored walls of the elevator, he smoothed back his hair with his fingers, wondering what Reynolds needed.

The elevator stopped at the tenth floor, and Josh stepped out onto the plush burgundy carpet. A gold plaque on the wall opposite the elevator gave the directions of the rooms, and he followed the arrow pointing to the left that indicated rooms "1001 thru 1025." He stopped at room 1017 and knocked. He heard soft music coming from the room. A few seconds later, a tall blonde wearing a skin-tight sheath dress opened the door. Josh checked the number on the door, thinking maybe he was at the wrong room, but then he heard Reynolds' voice inside. Was he having a party?

"Hi, come on in. You must be Josh." Her syrupy southern accent couldn't be real, he thought.

He glanced around the room. Two of Reynolds' minions that Josh had met before were seated on a plush sofa; a brunette with legs that went on forever was nestled between them. Reynolds sat in a large wing chair sipping a bourbon and water.

"Josh! You made it. You remember Wally and Joe, my assistants," Reynolds said, waving his hand in their direction. "And this is Melinda." Reynolds patted the blonde on the rear. "And Sabrina." He nodded in the direction of the brunette.

Josh shook Wally's and Joe's hands and said hello to the women.

"Have a seat." Reynolds motioned toward an upholstered chair next to his that faced the couch. "What do you want to drink? Scotch, was it?"

"On the rocks."

"Melinda, can you fix Mr. Langston a scotch on the rocks, dear?"

"Sure," the tall blonde answered.

"The boys and I were just wagering on whether the Ravens will go to the playoffs this season. I said, they probably have a better shot than the Redskins. I tell you, that team has gone downhill ever since Snyder took it over. I remember back in the eighties—now that was a team—Riggins and Monk, those boys could play."

Melinda handed Josh his drink in a crystal-cut glass. She then sat down on the ottoman next to Josh's chair. Josh felt uneasy. Why had Reynolds wanted to meet him here, and who were these women?

"How did your speech go today?" Josh asked.

"Fine." Reynolds sipped his bourbon. "Those union bosses haven't got a clue about the way things are. They think they can just keep giving their guys raises and benefit hikes, and the work will still be there. I tried to tell them how the market is changing; it's not like the old days when they ran the show. There are contractors out there that pay good wages and provide benefits, but they don't have to fork over the big bucks to the union. They're taking over the job market, making it harder and harder for union contractors to compete. I had to play it soft, though. I need their support. In the end, I told them what they wanted to hear." Reynolds threw his head back and bellowed a laugh.

"What did you need to see me about?" Josh asked.

"Business—that's what this guy's about," Reynolds said to Wally and Joe as he pointed to Josh. "Relax, we'll get to that. Did you know Melinda here is a dancer? She can take her leg and put it straight up against that wall. Isn't that right, sweetie?"

"That's right," Melinda giggled.

"Why don't you girls put some good music on and do a little dancing for us?"

Melinda and the long-legged brunette went over to the stereo across the room.

Wally and Joe were in an animated discussion on the best team in the NFL. Reynolds leaned over to Josh and said, "That was a great party you had. The food was terrific."

"Thanks, we enjoyed it." He thought Reynolds had business to discuss. He wasn't here to chitchat and watch women dance, but he figured he'd have to wait it out for a few minutes.

"How's Libby?"

"She's fine."

"I've been meaning to ask you, I heard mention at the party that you and your wife have a ghost in the house? Do you really believe in that stuff?" Reynolds frowned at Josh.

Josh was taken by surprise. He stammered for a second and then said, "My wife thought she saw a ghost, but she'd just found out she was pregnant, so maybe her hormones were playing tricks on her. It's really nothing." Josh felt heat rising under his collar, and he pulled at his tie.

"That's good to know. I really don't understand these nuts that go around saying they can talk to spirits and such. It's all a bunch of malarkey if you ask me."

"I agree," Josh replied. Had Reynolds thought he was one of those nuts? He wondered how he had found out about the ghost.

"I was asking Libby, at the party, if you all had come across any of my wife's things."

"I haven't come across anything. What did Libby say?"

"She said she didn't recall seeing anything either. One thing I would really like to find is my wife's journal. She wrote in that thing every day. I was never able to find it after she died. If you ever come across it, I would love to have it." Reynolds paused for a minute and then leaned in closer, lowering his voice. "You see, my wife was a troubled soul, and she liked to express some rather vivid fantasies in her diary. I would hate for someone else to read it and take things the wrong way. Besides, it would mean a lot to me to have it, since it was so special to her."

"I can understand that," Josh replied. "I'll ask Libby about it, but as far as I know she hasn't come across it."

Reynolds leaned back in his chair and studied Josh's face.

Josh was uneasy. Was that why he'd asked him here, to find out if they had his wife's journal?

The girls had put on some sultry dance music, and the two were across the room grinding on each other. Wally and Joe had stopped their sports discussion. Josh saw them salivating as they watched the women dance.

"I think there's a lot of work to finish before tomorrow's speech at the VFW," Reynolds said, looking at Wally and Joe. "I'll see you two tomorrow, and we'll go over it then."

The two men reluctantly stood up and left the hotel room. Josh didn't like the way things were going. He felt his palms sweating as he rubbed his hands together.

"Mr. Reynolds, if you don't mind, I really would like to get to the reason for me being here. I thought you had some business to discuss."

"Forget about work for a while and just enjoy yourself. You know what they say, all work and no play…" Reynolds stood up, chuckling, and gave Josh a slap on the shoulder.

Josh hadn't eaten lunch, and the scotch was going straight to his head. He was feeling light-headed and slightly woozy. He smiled at Reynolds, but inside he felt anxious and uncomfortable as his mind raced with thoughts of how he could get out of there.

Reynolds walked over to the women and joined in on the dancing. Josh wondered if this was some kind of test with Reynolds. Was he trying to see if Josh could play with the big boys? And if he didn't, would he ditch him as an attorney? Nothing good was going to come of this evening if he stayed. He got up from his chair and had to balance himself for a second. His heart pounded in his chest. He wasn't sure what to do. Melinda, the blonde, came dancing over to him and began to grind on his side. She ran her hands up his back and then nuzzled her face in his neck. He could smell the heavy scent of her perfume. It was intoxicating and at the same time frightening. Her full red lips made their way to his mouth, and she slipped her tongue in his mouth before he even knew what hit him.

"Do you like to dance?" she whispered into his ear.

"I really have to go." He extricated himself from her hold. "I'm sorry, Mr. Reynolds, but it's getting late. I really need to go if there's no business to discuss."

"What are you talking about? It's the shank of the evening. Don't tell me you don't like Melinda? Come on, are you a man or what?" The brunette was wrapped around Reynolds, and her leg was rubbing up and down his side.

"I'd rather just stick to business." Melinda wound her arms back around Josh's neck as she swayed her body back and forth, rubbing up against him. He was having difficulty breathing. "I'm sorry, I really have to go." He pulled her hands off again, this time more forcefully. He looked over at Reynolds. "Call me tomorrow at the office if you have any business to discuss."

"Suit yourself. Your loss is my gain." Reynolds gave out a low laugh as Melinda worked her way over to him.

Josh walked to the door with measured steps. The heavy door closed behind him, shutting out the music from inside. He took several deep breaths, and by the time he reached the elevator he felt his pulse returning to normal. He got on the elevator and again was alone. He leaned his head back on the wall and looked to the side. The face looking back at him in the mirror was not one he recognized. Red lipstick smeared his face. He took his handkerchief out of his suit pocket and wiped his mouth and cheek. His hands were shaking. The elevator dinged and stopped at the fourth floor. Josh stood up straight, feeling self-conscious, as if they knew where he'd just been. It was a couple with two small children. They smiled at Josh as they entered the elevator and then talked to the children about where they would be going to dinner.

All his life he'd had dreams of being rich and powerful, but deep down inside he was a simple man. He loved his wife, and he wanted a family; those things meant more to him than anything else in the world.

Libby had warned him about Reynolds, and he'd refused to see, but she was right. The man had no morals. Josh loved his job, but he didn't have any desire to be a part of that world. Maybe Reynolds wasn't the right client for him. And then he thought, maybe after tonight, Reynolds had already made that decision.

He stepped out into the late summer evening air. The sun had almost set, but the city was alive with people busy to get to their destinations. He strode down the sidewalk eager to get to his car in the parking garage two blocks down. Pulling his cell phone out of his pocket, he punched in the speed dial number for home and waited as it rang six times. He was about to hang up, thinking Libby must have gone out, when he heard her voice breathlessly say hello on the other end of the line.

"You're there!"

"Josh, sorry. I was outside when I heard the phone ring. Are you done with your meeting?"

"Yeah, I'm heading to my car now."

"Great, I'll see you when you get here. Have you eaten?"

"What?" He stopped on the sidewalk as people brushed past him. He wanted to tell her how good it was to hear her voice, how much he missed her and wished he was with her right now, but he was afraid she'd wonder what had gotten into him.

"Dinner, have you eaten anything?"

"Should I pick up something on my way home?"

"I made a risotto and a salad. There's plenty left over."

"Sounds great." Josh hesitated and then added, "I love you."

He put his phone back in his pocket and entered the parking garage. He slid into his old Audi. The Porsche he'd almost bought the other day still sat at the dealer. He hadn't made up his mind which car he really wanted.

He started the engine and glanced in the rearview mirror. A faint streak of red was still on his cheek. He took out his handkerchief again and rubbed his cheek hard. He looked at the white cloth in his hand, now streaked with red, and then rolled down the window and threw it out, wanting to rid himself of any remnants of the night.

He leaned his head back against the seat and closed his eyes. He pictured the tall blonde, her tongue forcing its way into his mouth, and he was filled with an overwhelming guilt. Just last week they'd found out they were having a girl. He'd been with Libby when she'd gotten the sonogram. When the doctor told them it was a girl, Libby's eyes welled with tears of joy. That's all that mattered to him now.

33

The information jotted down on note cards now needed to be transferred to a timeline, laying it out pure and simple for Tucker to see. Will pulled up to the station determined that today he would confront Sheriff Tucker with all the evidence he had on the Reynolds case.

The past few weeks he'd had to put the case on the back burner. Nathan and Wyeth got strep throat, and then the baby came down with the croup. He and Julie had been up most every night with Caleb, so Will had spent his days driving the kids to the pediatrician and helping Julie around the house in between going to work. This was the first day that both of the older boys had gone back to school, and Caleb was finally sleeping through the night again. Thank God, Sara had never gotten sick. Order had returned to the house.

A touch of fall was in the air as Will walked toward the station, thinking after such a steamy summer, autumn was a welcome relief.

Maggie was already at her desk. He wondered what time she got to work. He had yet to beat her in to the office, no matter how early he got there.

"Good morning, Will," Maggie said as he walked by her desk.

"Good morning, Maggie," Will replied. "It looks like it's going to be a beautiful day. Even a little nip in the air."

"I noticed. I had to put a sweater on this morning before I left the house. Don't let the weather fool you, though. There have been late Septembers when it was ninety degrees."

"I know."

"How are the kids? Is the little one doing OK?"

"They're fine, now. I'm sure Julie could use a vacation. I don't know how she does it every day."

"I'm sure it helps having a husband like you."

Will smiled.

"Guess what I heard yesterday?" Maggie asked, waiting for Will to reply.

"I have no idea. What did you hear, Maggie?" Will poured himself a mug of coffee.

"Remember Dean's missing eggs?"

"Yeah."

"Well, Baynard solved the mystery."

Will headed to his desk and raised his eyebrows at Maggie, waiting to hear how the mystery was solved.

"He and Joe Dean set a trap on the henhouse door. And bingo, if it wasn't a darn pig sneaking in there and stealing the eggs." She laughed. "I'd like to have seen a video of that."

Will nodded and then went back to his work, laying out a large sheet of paper and drawing a timeline across the bottom. He spread all his notes out on his desk and organized them in chronological order. Maggie continued chatting as Will half listened to her, nodding occasionally in response.

"…I just think they should keep their opinions to themselves, don't you?" Maggie chattered on.

"Mm-hmm," Will replied. He glanced up at the clock; he had less than an hour to get everything together before the sheriff arrived at nine. He needed to concentrate.

The phone rang, and Will hoped whoever it was would keep Maggie occupied for a few minutes so he could finish.

He started with Reynolds' affair with Catherine Collins, writing down— Reynolds wanted to leave wife. Further down the line, he wrote "April 25, 1992, Cecilia pregnant, suspects John of affair." He then made a notch on the timeline and jotted down halothane; he referenced Reynolds' prints being on the bottle and the effects of halothane. The next entry was "May 12, 1992, two days before her death, Cecilia confronts Reynolds," and then added how Cecilia said she wanted the baby no matter what happened between her and John.

He sat back in his chair and studied the timeline. Granted, there was no smoking gun, but when you put it all together, the evidence definitely pointed to John Reynolds. He just hoped Tucker would see it the same way.

Maggie, who was now working on her crossword puzzle, looked over at Will. "What are you working on so intently over there?"

"Just a case."

"A case. I didn't know we had any cases right now?" Maggie paused and tapped her pencil on the table. "Don't tell me you're still working on Cecilia Reynolds' case. Do you like your job? If Baynard finds out, he will blow a gasket."

"I think when Tucker sees it, he'll have to forget that he told me to stop looking into it. There's just too much evidence, I think, that points to John Reynolds. And besides, we were going to look into the case anyway; Sheriff Tucker said he just wanted to wait until after the election."

Will swiveled his chair toward Maggie. "Think about it. Do we really want someone who possibly murdered his wife becoming our Senator? If we can exhume the body quietly, without anyone knowing, and the evidence shows Cecilia was drugged and pregnant, Tucker's claims that the journal was probably just fantasy written by a delusional woman would be false."

"It sounds risky to me. I don't know if Baynard will agree with your analysis on the situation. He and Mr. Reynolds are pretty good friends."

"I'll take my chances." Will looked at the clock; Sheriff Tucker would be walking through the door any minute. He was feeling a little nervous. He hadn't thought he would lose his job over this, but listening to Maggie made him wonder just how good of friends Reynolds and Tucker were. He may be stepping into something that could risk his whole career in this town.

A few minutes later, Sheriff Tucker stepped into the office. Will noticed a sprinkling of powdered sugar on Baynard's uniform, evidence that he had stopped at Pearl's to have his morning donut. Will folded up the ledger sheet and glanced over at Maggie, who held up her hands and raised her eyebrows as if to say "you're on your own in this."

"What's new today, Will?" Tucker asked, walking past his desk.

This was his chance. "It's funny you should ask, Sheriff Tucker, because I have something I want to show you."

"And what would that be?" Tucker sat himself down in his old swivel chair and leaned back facing Will at his desk. Will got up and walked over to him with the ledger paper in hand.

Driving home, Will replayed his conversation with Tucker. Overall, things had not gone too badly, he thought. He hadn't wanted to bring Libby into it, but Tucker had caught him by surprise.

When he presented all the evidence to him, at first Tucker just sat there, rubbing his chin and not saying anything. Then, he got out one of his cigars and lit it up. Will held his breath, waiting to see what Tucker would say. Would he be out of a job for disobeying orders? After a few puffs on the cigar, Tucker picked up the timeline and studied it. He then leaned back, his chair creaking from his weight, and looked Will in the eyes. "I hope you know what you're doing, son, because it looks to me like this is just your theory of how things happened. I don't see any concrete evidence here, and we're talking about possibly ruining a man's career."

"You have to admit that when you piece it all together, Reynolds looks pretty suspicious," Will had replied.

Maggie had gotten up when their conversation started and headed for the storage room, claiming she had some files to straighten—although she kept the door ajar so that she would not miss any of the dialogue. Will was definitely in this alone.

"Just tell me one thing," Sheriff Tucker had said, leaning forward in his chair. "How did you come across all this evidence? Did that Langston woman have anything to do with it?"

"She discovered the halothane in her boathouse, and she's the one who contacted Catherine Collins."

"Sounds like Mrs. Langston has been a very busy woman."

"She actually wouldn't have made a bad detective. I promised her I would look into the case when she came to me with the evidence she'd found."

"There's quite a bit of stuff here, but like I said, we have to be very careful how we handle this. We can't just go willy-nilly and open this whole thing back up," Tucker said, staring at the timeline.

"I understand, which is why I was hoping we could get Garrett Mosley to exhume the body and run some tests on Cecilia very quietly. If the autopsy reveals she wasn't pregnant or that she didn't have any drugs in her system, then we put the body back, and no one has to know about it."

Tucker puffed on his cigar, shaking his head. "I don't know. I tell you what. Let me think on this tonight, and I'll give you an answer in the morning."

Tucker left the office that evening pondering the situation at hand. He didn't like this kind of thing. He liked the status quo, and Will had put him in a very uncomfortable position. As he headed out of town, he picked up his cell and punched in the number he had memorized. He waited for an answer.

"Hello?"

"We've got to talk."

"Hey, Bubby, what's up?"

"Things are not going too well over here with our little situation. I really need to discuss something with you."

"I thought you had this all taken care of?" Reynolds' hissed.

"Well, some more information has arisen, and I don't know if I can make this thing go away."

There was a slight pause on the line, and then Reynolds replied, "I'm at a fundraiser right now in Calvert County. I'll probably be tied up here for another few hours. I'll call you when I leave."

Tucker was seated in his recliner, eating a Stouffer's meat loaf dinner and watching *Wheel of Fortune* when his cell phone rang. He wiped his chin with the napkin he had tucked into his shirt and moved the tray out of his lap to answer the phone.

"Can you meet me around nine o'clock?"

"Where?"

"There's a church off the first exit from the Bay Bridge heading west. Pull around to the parking lot in back. It's pretty secluded there. And don't bring the squad car; we don't need anyone spotting you over on this side of the bridge."

Tucker looked at the clock beside his chair. It was 7:15. He could definitely make it by nine. "All right, I'll see you then."

At nine o'clock sharp, Baynard Tucker pulled into the deserted church parking lot and slowly drove around to the back. It had started raining heavily as he crossed the Bay Bridge, and the winds had picked up. He parked his gray Taurus in a darkened section, far from the two pole lights centered in the lot that cast off a giant circle of light. He shut off his engine and killed the headlights, waiting for Reynolds to arrive. The trees surrounding the church lot swayed violently as the wind swirled.

He mentally rehearsed the questions he wanted to ask Reynolds. He wanted to know if Reynolds had really had an affair with someone named Catherine Collins. He also wanted to ask him why there was a bottle of halothane with his fingerprints on it in the old boathouse. How Reynolds answered these questions would help Tucker decide how he was going to handle the investigation.

He was a loyal friend to Reynolds, but friendship only went so far. He was not about to ruin his reputation in town just because he had promised Reynolds he would wait on the case.

Just then, he saw headlights rounding the corner of the church. Reynolds pulled up next to Tucker in a black Mercedes CLS550 sedan. He motioned for Tucker to join him in his car. Tucker got out and hurriedly waddled his heavy frame, hunching down to fight the rain, over to the passenger side and slipped into the charcoal leather seat.

"So what is so urgent that you had to see me tonight?" Reynolds asked.

"My deputy has discovered some more information in the case."

"I thought you told him to stop the investigation until after the election!" Reynolds shouted.

"I did! Let me finish." Sheriff Tucker waved his hands down in a gesture to ease the tension. "He found a bottle of something called halothane with your fingerprints on it. From what he tells me halothane does, it seems pretty strange you would have it."

"I don't understand how this is happening. Don't you have any control over your deputy?"

"Well, I also found out it isn't just my deputy who's doing the investigating. It turns out that that Langston woman has been stirring this whole thing up. She's the one who discovered the drug bottle, and she's been supplying Will with all the evidence." Tucker felt that this would at least help explain why he didn't seem to have any control over his deputy. "What about the halothane? Why was it in the boathouse?" Tucker asked.

"*I don't know!*" Reynolds shot back. "There's tons of junk I left in that boathouse. Who knows, maybe it was something Cecilia had gotten when she wanted to commit suicide. Do you think if I had used it on her, I would have left the evidence behind?"

Tucker had to admit that did seem odd. Why not just throw the bottle away somewhere? "That's not the only thing; he also said there's a woman named Catherine Collins who says she had an affair with you around the time of Cecilia's death, and that you told her you wanted to leave your wife for her."

Tucker strained to see Reynolds' reaction, but the darkened car made it difficult. He could see the muscles in Reynolds' jaw clenching. The only sound in the car was a rhythmic thump as the windshield wipers slapped back and forth.

Finally, Reynolds replied, "This whole thing is absurd! Just because some woman wants to claim she had an affair with me almost twenty years ago, and that I wanted to leave my wife for her, doesn't mean it's true. If what she said was true, then why didn't I end up with her after my wife died? Don't you see, Baynard? There are people out there who would love to see me destroyed. I'm now ahead in the polls, something Jamison's people never thought would happen, and they will do anything to try and find dirt on me."

"Are you saying you've never heard of that woman?"

Reynolds stared out the windshield for a minute before replying. "Look, everyone has a past, and I do admit I have done a few things in my past that I am not proud of, but it's ancient history. I may have had a short fling at one time, but you have to understand what I was going through. My wife had severe mental problems, and she had a hard time being close with anyone. I'm sorry, but I had needs of my own. It wasn't the right thing to do, but I was very discreet about it. I never wanted to hurt Cecilia, and I certainly would've never left my wife for that woman."

Baynard nodded his head, sympathizing with Reynolds. What Reynolds said made sense, but he had an uneasy feeling about the whole situation. He still didn't know how he was going to handle this.

He decided to keep Reynolds thinking he would wait on the investigation no matter what he ended up doing.

"All right, I'll have another talk with my deputy and explain it the way you put it to me."

"Don't tell him we spoke," Reynolds said with urgency.

"No, I won't mention having spoken to you at all."

"Good. These next few weeks are going to be critical for me. We're getting into crunch mode in the campaign, and I don't want anything screwing this up."

"OK, don't worry." Tucker raised his hand up. "I'll keep things quiet on my end."

"Thanks, Bubby. I knew I could count on you. And just remember, we're getting closer and closer to getting that access road to Corsica. I see big things in your future."

Bubby gave him a nod and then opened the car door, fighting his way back to his car through the driving rain, getting soaked in the process.

As Baynard Tucker pulled out of the church parking lot, the sky lit up, illuminating the large cross on top of the steeple, and a clap of thunder resonated in the air. He shuddered, partly from being drenched with rain and partly because he was a God-fearing man. Had that been a sign? He felt as befuddled as ever. Was God trying to tell him what to do? Instead of feeling excited about the prospect of the new road coming to town, he was beginning to wonder if what Reynolds promised him was more of a bribe to keep him quiet. Maybe Reynolds' version of the events was true, or maybe he was being snowed by Reynolds—he wasn't sure. But one thing he'd learned from all his years in law enforcement: when a case started smelling fishy, it was usually because there was something rotten to be found.

34

According to Dr. Crawford, the baby was right on track for a December delivery. Standing in her bedroom naked in front of the cheval mirror, Libby looked down at her skin stretched tightly over her protruding stomach. She rubbed her hands over her belly and smiled. "Hey, little girl, what should we call you?"

Ever since she'd found out it was a girl, she'd been running through baby names in her head: Taylor, Lydia, even Diana, after her mother. But none of them felt right to her. She had only spoken to her mother a few times since Josh had confronted her about seeing a doctor. Neither of them had mentioned the subject, and Libby felt a wall had gone up between them. It hurt. She loved her mother and missed their conversations, especially now that she was expecting. She knew she should let it go, but her stubborn streak wouldn't let her.

She thought back to a few weeks ago when she and Josh had gone for the sonogram—and the look on Josh's face. The love she'd seen in his eyes made her believe he was finally feeling a connection to the baby. Hopefully, by the time the baby arrived, he'd be thoroughly involved.

She grabbed a short-sleeved blouse and a jumper from the closet. Her plan was to pot some fall flowers out back. She missed Trevor helping her in the yard; she'd enjoyed spending time with him, listening to his stories. He was back in school and had been around only a few times. He said his mother needed him more at home.

Lately, her days consisted of straightening the house, going to the grocery store, reading books, and sleeping, which she never seemed to get enough of. Rarely was she able to stay up past nine.

She breathed in the clean, crisp smell, sitting at the wrought iron table out back. Autumn was in the air. A strange feeling came over her, as if she were in limbo. She loved this time of year, not only the weather, but as a teacher, it represented a new beginning, like a clean slate. She'd stand in front of her classroom full of students fresh from their summer break, eager to fill their brains with her new lesson plans.

In a few months, she'd have her hands full with the baby, but right now she felt purposeless. Excitement mixed with anxiety rose up inside. She was going to be a mother. Her life was going to change forever. She thought of Julie and her sister. They'd done it, but could she? Doubts began to creep in. Would she know what to do with a baby? She could handle a roomful of twelve- and thirteen-year-olds, but the thought of a tiny infant scared her. Would she be all alone, only getting brief minutes with Josh here and there during the week? She pictured her life with just the dog, the baby, and Elizabeth to keep her company. She would probably end up one of those eccentric women who wore hats with birds on them and had tea parties with imaginary friends.

The past few weeks she'd been alone most of the time. Julie's kids had been sick, so they'd hardly seen each other. She'd driven over to Tassie's a couple of times for tea, but other than that, she'd had no contact with anyone, not even Elizabeth. Had Elizabeth given up on her?

Libby took another deep breath and brushed back her hair. She looked down at the To-Do list in front of her. She pushed thoughts of Elizabeth out of her head and checked off the line "pot chrysanthemums." The next thing on the list was "library—return books." She'd read at least eight books over the summer. One she'd just finished reading had been about a woman who finds out her husband was cheating on her, and she leaves him and starts a brand new life without him. She wondered what she would do if that happened to her. Her mind drifted to Cecilia. How terrible it must've been for her to find out she was pregnant, while at the same time discover her husband was having an affair. In the book, the woman at first ignores the signs of her husband's infidelity, the changes in his behavior, not wanting to believe it. It made Libby think how peculiar Josh had been a few weeks ago.

She remembered the night he'd come home from work late, as usual, but this time he'd acted so differently. He'd been extremely solicitous, asking her how she was feeling and wanting to know if there was anything he could do to help her. The attention was flattering but at the same time suspicious. Why was he all of a sudden being so attentive? Was it a guilty conscience? Could he be having an affair? Or was it her own guilty conscience driving her suspicion? A melancholy lingered over her.

She stared out at the water; a breeze blew ripples across the surface. She loved the tranquility of the steady motion. It calmed her, easing her doubts about being a stay-at-home mom and about Josh. The long, reed-like legs of a blue heron carefully stepped into the water, intent on catching a fish, and then stood statuesque for several minutes. She watched closely, waiting to see how long he would stand so still.

"Hello," a voice behind her called out.

Libby jerked around and saw John Reynolds standing on the patio. Stella, who'd been lying under her favorite maple tree, picked her head up, gave out a low woof, and then came running over, barking and wagging her tail at the same time. Great watchdog, Libby thought.

"You startled me." Libby laughed nervously as she looked up at him, placing her hand over her brow to block out the sun.

"I knocked on the front door, but I guess you couldn't hear me. I saw your car, so I figured you must be out back. I hope you don't mind. I took the liberty of walking around the side yard. It's funny, since this used to be my house, I feel more at home here than I guess I should." Reynolds, casually dressed in a pair of khaki pants, boat shoes, and a polo shirt, leaned down and rubbed Stella's neck.

"What are you doing here?" She hadn't meant for her words to sound so rude, but he'd surprised her with his unexpected visit.

"I guess I should have called first. I've been thinking about my wife's things ever since the party, and I know I asked you if you'd come across anything, and you told me that you hadn't, but there's one thing in particular that I'm interested in. You see, my wife kept a diary, something that was very special to her. It had a jeweled bird on the cover. It would be hard to miss if you saw it."

Libby's heart pounded in her chest. She felt the hairs on the back of her neck rising. He knew about the journal. Did he think she still had it? She remembered his threatening words at the party.

"I told you I hadn't come across anything, and nothing has changed since then."

"I'm afraid I don't believe you."

"You can believe anything you want. I don't have your wife's book." Libby was trying to sound forceful, but inside she was shaking. She didn't like him looming over her. She wanted to stand up and run inside, but she was afraid to move.

"Maybe you don't have it in your possession right now, because you gave it to your deputy friend." Reynolds smiled with a look that made Libby snap back in her seat. He continued, "Is there some reason you want to destroy me?"

Her mind raced. Why hadn't Will told her Reynolds knew about the book? The last time she'd spoken to Will was when he called to tell her the prints on the bottle were a match, but he'd never mentioned talking to Reynolds. "I have no idea what you're talking about, but I'd appreciate it if you would leave. I assure you, we don't have anything that belonged to your wife." Libby stood up, her legs shaking. She strode past him toward the house, but he grabbed her arm.

"I don't think you understand." Reynolds' words shot out at her.

She stopped. Her breath halted as she stared straight ahead, afraid to make eye contact.

He continued, "I know you've stirred up a whole investigation about me regarding my wife's death. I didn't kill my wife. I *need* that journal." His grip tightened on her arm but then loosened. "My wife had mental problems and said things that could be misconstrued. Don't you see you're going to ruin my career with your ridiculous accusations?"

Libby realized he must know about everything. Her voice shook as she replied, "If you did nothing wrong, then you have nothing to worry about."

"You *stupid* woman!" His words spat out through clenched teeth. "Don't you realize I'm in the middle of a political campaign? Just the hint of something like that could ruin my chances!"

"That's not my problem." Libby pulled her arm away from him and continued walking toward the house, wanting to break into a run, thinking all she had to do was get inside and lock the doors.

"Don't walk away from me!" Reynolds ran in front of her, blocking her from the house. He had a look of fury in his eyes. She pushed past him, and he grabbed both her arms. She screamed, struggling to free herself from his grasp.

She wriggled out of his arms and turned, running in the opposite direction, not thinking where she was running. Adrenaline coursed through her veins, signaling her to flee. She ran down the stone-laden path toward the water, hearing his footsteps behind her, along with Stella's barks and then a growling sound. She heard him curse something, but she was afraid to slow down and turn to see what was happening.

She made it to the beach and ran out onto the pier. She needed to call someone; maybe the boat had a radio, if she could make it there.

Her feet hit the boards, and within seconds, she heard his heavy footsteps behind her. She realized she was never going to make it all the way down to the boat. Halfway down the pier, her breathing became labored, and she felt her stomach tightening. She wrapped her arms around her belly and slowed down, gasping for breath.

He came up behind her, and she turned and screamed. Stella was at his leg, tearing at his pants, growling furiously. Reynolds kicked at the dog, trying to release her from her grasp.

Libby ran down the pier again, but he caught up to her and whipped her around to face him. "Why don't you just *listen* to me! You need to stop all of this!" His face was beet red, and his eyes looked crazed. Libby fought back, punching wildly at him, clawing at his face. She felt his blood on her fingertips.

Reynolds grabbed his face and then looked at the red smear on his hand. His eyes opened wide with a look of pure evil, and he swung his hand back with a pounding blow to Libby's head that sent her flying off the pier. She hit the water with a splash, and then her body disappeared under the surface into the black liquid below.

35

Reynolds stood on the pier glancing around furtively, making sure no one had witnessed what had just happened. He drew in deep breaths of air, leaning over with his hands on his thighs. There were no boats on the water, and not a soul could be seen on the shore. He waited several minutes and then went to the other side of the pier to see if she had surfaced. The dog was circling in the water, whining. He walked to the end of the pier and looked in the boat.

After ten minutes with no sign of her, Reynolds walked back down the pier. He'd not planned for this to happen; he'd only wanted to talk to her and convince her to tell the stupid deputy to stop his investigation. Why did she have to put up such a fight? It was her own fault, he thought.

He headed back around the yard to the circular drive and stood beside his Mercedes, brushing off his pants. He ran his fingers down the side of his face and felt the welts that had risen to the surface. He had to get out of there, fast. On Haverford Lane, he hadn't passed any cars, and hopefully, he could get out the same.

He got into the car and clicked his seatbelt in place as he methodically ran a scenario in his head: By the time her body was discovered, he'd be back in Annapolis with an alibi for his whereabouts that afternoon. The police would rule her death an accident. She'd been walking on the pier, tripped, hit her head, and had fallen into the water. The only witness was the dog. He glanced down at his pant leg that was ripped to shreds. He lifted up the torn material and saw two puncture wounds. That damned dog had bitten him good. He would destroy the pants. He examined his face in the rearview mirror. She had done a number on him. There were streaks of dried blood down the side of his face. He glanced in the back of the car; a golf towel lay on the floor. He gingerly wiped away the blood, thinking once he washed up and put a little makeup on it, he'd be fine. The police wouldn't suspect him anyway. Why would they? What good would it have done him to kill Libby Langston? Things were going to be fine.

He pulled down the drive and looked both ways at the end, making sure there were no other cars on Haverford Lane. The two-lane road was empty. His senses were heightened; he wouldn't feel safe until he was back on the other side of the bridge.

As Reynolds hit the major highway, merging into the sea of cars on the road, he eased back in his seat; everything would be OK. A feeling of calm took over, but then an uneasy feeling crept back in. He still needed that diary.

36

He ran wildly through the reeds, not stopping until he came all the way to his front porch. He flew through the door, slamming it behind him.

"Trevor? Is that you, child?" His mother's weak voice called from the bedroom.

Trevor didn't answer; he couldn't speak.

"Trevor, why you home from school so early?"

He ran into his room and shut the door. He lay on his bed weeping into his pillow. He had played hooky from school that day. He didn't know why, but he just didn't feel like going, so instead, after walking down the lane in the morning to catch the bus, he turned off into the woods and went exploring. He spent the morning sitting on a log, watching two squirrels race around a tree together, but then he got bored. He decided to walk down to Miss Libby's house; he hadn't seen her for a long time. He was walking along the shoreline, approaching her house, when he heard raised voices. He stopped and crouched down, not wanting to interrupt Miss Libby and Mr. Josh if they were having a fight. He slipped into the reeds and slowly stood up just high enough to see the backyard, but it wasn't Mr. Josh. It was another man, and he was arguing with Miss Libby. Then he saw them running down the path toward the water.

Trevor clutched his pillow, pressing his face into it, trying to block out what he'd seen. Miss Libby had fallen into the water. He'd wanted to run to her, but he was frozen to his spot in the reeds. He'd watched the man just walk away; he hadn't tried to save her. He knew Miss Libby must be dead. He was so scared, he'd taken off running all the way back home. He sobbed into his pillow, thinking he should've done something. He should've tried saving her. He wanted to tell his mama what had happened, but he knew she'd be furious with him for skipping school, and also for not saving Miss Libby. He couldn't tell anyone what he had seen. He might even get arrested if they knew he'd been there and not helped her.

He rolled over on his bed and stared at the ceiling, thinking of Miss Libby. She had always been so kind to him; he loved her and now she was gone. He cried for a long time before he finally got up and went to the bathroom and washed off his face. He heard his mama calling him again, so he went to her room.

"Trevor, I thought that was you. What's wrong, boy? You look terrible."

"I wasn't feeling good, so I came home from school."

"How'd you get home?"

"I got a ride from a friend's mom." Trevor hated lying to his mama.

"Come here, child; let me feel your head."

Trevor walked over to his mama's bed, where she spent most of her days now, too weak to get up. She put her warm, soft hand on his forehead. Just her touch sent Trevor into another bout of tears. "Child, what's wrong? Do you feel that bad?"

He lay down on the bed next to her, and she put her arms around him. "You're shaking; you must be coming down with the flu." She stroked his head and whispered into his ear that everything would be all right. No, Trevor thought. Things would never be right again.

37

She fell into a deep, dark abyss, disoriented from the shock of the cold water. And then everything came flooding back. Her first instinct was to swim to the surface, but she knew he'd be looking for her. The murky waters made it hard for her to get her bearings, and she was determined not to panic. She reached her hands out in front of her and began to swim. Suddenly her right hand hit something hard. She ran both hands around the wood of the piling. If she judged it right, she could come up for air under the pier out of Reynolds' sight.

Her lungs were reaching their limit; she couldn't stay down any longer. She rose upward toward the light and silently popped her head out of the water. Her lungs wanted to gasp for air, but she forced herself to breathe in softly without a sound. She had lucked out and come up under the pier. She saw Stella in the water frantically searching for her. She dipped back down under the water, not wanting the dog to give her away.

Reynolds' face was etched in her mind, the look of a sheer madman. She needed to find a way out of the water without Reynolds seeing her.

Using the pilings as her guide, she slowly swam down the pier, periodically coming up for air. Reaching the T-shaped landing, she swam along the far side of the boat docked at the end. Searching down the shoreline, she spotted an overturned canoe bobbing up and down in the water not far from the shore. It was on the other side of the boathouse about twenty-five yards from the pier. Could she make it in one breath? The water was cold and her body shook, not only from the chill, but from fear. If Reynolds spotted her, would he kill her? If she could make it to the canoe, she could hide under it and then work her way onto the shore hidden from view by the boathouse. She took two deep breaths and then went under, swimming as fast as she could toward the canoe.

Out in the open water, she had no directional clues to guide her. She hoped she was staying on the right course. After what seemed an eternity, her body screamed for oxygen. Her legs felt weak, and her lungs felt like bursting. A dark object came into view. With two more swift strokes, she dived down under the overturned canoe, rising out of the water into the small pocket underneath and gasped in huge gulps of air.

She began to shiver uncontrollably, so she waited several seconds before diving back under, this time coming up on the far side of the canoe, away from the pier. She crouched in the water that was now only up to her waist alongside the canoe, peering over the top. The boathouse shielded her sight of the shoreline. She crept out of the water and fell onto the beach, knowing she couldn't stay there out in the open. But her legs were too weak to move. Slowly, she dragged herself along the sand into the tall grasses along the shore. Once she had hidden herself in the grasses, she stopped; her body could go no further. She lay shaking and sobbing, instinctively holding her belly, hoping her baby was safe.

She waited. The heat of the sun beat down on her, enveloping her body like a warm blanket. The adrenaline that had propelled her through the water was replaced by exhaustion. She felt drugged and, within minutes, drifted off into a dreamless state.

She awakened to a warm, wet tongue licking her cheek. She opened her eyes to Stella standing over her, wagging her tail and whining. Libby moved her head, and she felt a sharp pain along her temple. She slowly sat up, surrounded by tall grasses. Her body ached. How long had she been lying here? She hugged Stella as tears streamed down her cheeks. Then she searched the shoreline for any sign of Reynolds. Was it safe to get up? She rolled onto her side using her arms to push herself to a seated position, and then she rose to her feet with great effort. Her jumper, still damp from the water, clung to her body. Her head was throbbing from the blow Reynolds had given her. She gradually worked her way over to the boathouse, whispering to Stella to stay behind her.

She crept along the wall, her body snug against the warm weathered wood of the boathouse. As she got to the corner, she slowly peered around the edge toward the dock. There was no sign of Reynolds. She snapped her head back around the corner, standing with her back against the wall, thinking about what to do next. Stella softly whined at her feet, wondering what sort of game they were playing.

After hearing no sounds, she decided to chance it and make her way to the house. She followed the path, hoping Reynolds wasn't lurking in the reeds, ready to jump out at her. She reached the patio and broke into a run, flinging open the French doors, and raced into the kitchen. She grabbed the phone off the wall.

Her first instinct was to call Josh, but then she changed her mind and called Will. Her fingers trembled as she hit the buttons, having to redial it several times.

"Will Seevers."

With the sound of his familiar voice, she lost it and began sobbing, unable to form a coherent word.

"Hello? Libby?"

She managed to sputter, "Will, I…" And then she broke into tiny incomprehensible sounds.

"Libby? What happened?"

She took a deep breath, forcing the words out. "Please come. I've been attacked."

"Attacked? Libby, are you OK?"

"It was Reynolds."

"Are you at home?"

"Yes."

"I'll be right there."

Libby sank like a rag doll into the kitchen chair, still clutching the phone in her hand as if it were her lifeline. She knew she needed to call Josh, but she didn't think she could go through explaining everything. Instead, she just sat motionless at the table, trying to comprehend what had transpired.

Fifteen minutes later, she heard the front door open. Footsteps echoed through the foyer, and then she heard Will's voice calling her name. Her voice responded with a whisper, as if they were the first words she'd ever spoken. "I'm in here."

Will entered the kitchen. "Libby." He rushed over to her and pried the phone out of her grasp, hanging it back on the receiver. "I've been trying to call you back. I even tried your cell. You had me worried when I couldn't get through." She looked bewildered, and her hair was a tangled mass about her head, with bits of grass sticking out.

"What happened?" He sat down at the table next to her.

She shook her head slowly, staring off into space. After a few seconds, she said, "It was like a dream. I don't know. One minute, I'm sitting on the porch, and the next I'm being knocked into the water."

"What was Reynolds doing at your house?"

"He just showed up. He said he wanted Cecilia's diary." She turned her head and looked into Will's eyes. "He knew you had the diary."

"What? That's impossible..." Will paused. He then remembered his conversation with Sheriff Tucker. He'd told Tucker that Libby had been the one who'd given him the evidence. Tucker must have gone to Reynolds to warn him. He had no idea Tucker was that deep into Reynolds' pocket. "Oh my God, Libby, I'm so sorry. It must've been Sheriff Tucker who told Reynolds. I never thought..." Will reached out and held Libby's hand. "Tell me what happened."

She closed her eyes and sat back in her chair, taking a deep breath, and then she recounted everything that had happened. Her face grimaced as she recalled the details. She shook her head. "It all happened so fast." She looked down at Stella lying at her feet and smiled wistfully at her as she wiped the tears from her eyes with the back of her hand. Stella cocked her head to one side. Libby snuffled her nose and then continued, "It was as if he'd snapped. He kept shaking me, saying I had to stop what I was doing to him. I never..." She paused for a minute with her hand up to her mouth.

Will leaned forward, placing his hands on her knees. "It's OK. You're safe now." He handed her a tissue.

She nodded and blew her nose.

Will reached up and gently touched the side of her head. "You've got a nice-sized knot there. We should probably get you to a hospital to get checked out. Have you told Josh?"

"Not yet. I'm OK."

"I still think you need to get looked at; you're in shock."

"Can you call Josh? I don't think I can talk to him right now, but be sure to let him know I'm OK."

Will went over to the sink and poured Libby a glass of water. She took small sips of the water and recited Josh's work number to Will, but Josh's secretary told Will that he was out at a client's. He called Josh's cell, but that went straight to voice mail.

"I'll keep trying him on the way to the hospital. Why don't you go get changed into some clean clothes. Can you make it up the stairs?" Will stood beside her chair.

"I'm fine."

He helped her to stand and then waited for her to come back downstairs.

She got a thorough examination from the emergency room doctor at Easton Memorial. He told her the baby's heart rate sounded normal, and all her vital signs looked good, but she should probably take a couple of days of bed rest, just in case she had a concussion.

The double glass doors swooshed open as they walked back out to the parking lot. "I got a hold of Josh just before you came out. I told him the doctors said everything looked good, and he said he'd meet us at the house as soon as he could."

"Did he sound mad?"

"Mad?" Will frowned. "He sounded worried."

"I probably should've told him what I was doing."

On the drive back home, they talked about the case.

"You know, even though Reynolds said Cecilia was mentally ill, I don't believe it. Her writings in the journal sounded naïve, but they were rational, not like they'd been written by someone deranged," Libby said.

"I think this just proves our case," Will replied.

"How do you know for sure? What if what he said was true? That he didn't kill his wife, and the only reason he snapped was because of the election. I mean, that's what he kept saying."

"If Reynolds was innocent, he wouldn't have done what he did. I've dealt with suspects before who just snapped and killed someone. Husbands who've discovered their wives were cheating on them. Frustrated employees who felt they'd lost everything. I don't think he snapped just because he's desperate to win the election; there was more to it than that. I think you hit a nerve with him. He thought all these years he'd gotten away with the perfect crime. Kills his wife, gets all her money, ends up a huge success.

And then, along comes Libby Langston, who blows the whole thing wide open."

Libby stared out the car window, wondering what she'd done. When she was young and played imaginary detective, things always worked out; no one ever got hurt. It had seemed fun and exciting in the beginning, searching for clues about Reynolds, but she'd never imagined anything like this. Maybe she should have left well-enough alone.

By the time Josh arrived, Libby was lying on the couch in the den, wrapped in a blanket, with Stella curled up at her feet. Will had made her a cup of tea, and he was seated in the overstuffed chair next to the couch, keeping her company.

Josh rushed into the room dressed in a dark suit and burgundy tie that was loosened around his neck. His hair looked disheveled, as if he'd been pulling at it. He sat down on the edge of the couch next to Libby and brushed her hair away from her face. "Are you OK? Is the baby OK?"

"I'm fine and she's fine," Libby replied, rubbing her belly.

Josh turned toward Will, noticing him for the first time since he entered the room. "What the hell happened?" he asked him. "None of this makes sense."

"Josh, I'm afraid I'm partly to blame. I had no clue that Sheriff Tucker would've warned Reynolds as to what we were doing. I'm telling you, Reynolds is a dangerous man."

Josh turned back to Libby. "Why didn't you tell me about any of this? I thought you'd stopped all that snooping around."

"I'm sorry. I should have listened to you. And I didn't tell you because I didn't want to put you in an awkward position since Reynolds was your client."

Josh stood up and paced around the den, running his hand through his hair again. "Reynolds asked me the other day about a journal and if we had found it. I had no idea what he was talking about at the time." He stopped pacing and turned to Will. "I still don't understand why he would attack Libby over it."

"The journal has some incriminating evidence. I think he knows it could implicate him in his wife's murder," Will said.

"He kept saying how this was going to ruin his career, like that's all that mattered," Libby said to Josh.

"What good would it have done for his career if he'd killed you?" Josh asked.

"I don't think he came over here with that in mind. I think he thought he could intimidate Libby into dropping this whole thing. I don't think he expected her to not give in," Will said.

"You could've been killed, *and* the baby." Josh looked frustratingly at Libby.

"I know. I'm sorry." Tears filled her eyes. "It was stupid of me to have gotten involved." She put her hand over her eyes.

Josh came back over to her. "It's all right. I'm just glad you and the baby are OK." He leaned down to hug her. They sat silent for a few minutes, and then Josh said to Will, "So, what happens now?"

"One thing we have to assume is that Reynolds has no idea that Libby's alive. I'm going to contact the state boys to bring him in for questioning. Don't worry; we've got him now."

38

Crossing over the Bay Bridge in the back of the olive green and black Maryland state trooper car, Reynolds tried the cell number of attorney Maury Silverstein for the third time. Maury was one of the area's finest criminal attorneys and a good friend of John Reynolds. He heard it going to voice mail again. Where was he? A few minutes later, his cell rang. "Maury, I've been trying to reach you."

"I see that. I just noticed I had three missed calls from you, and I figured it must be something urgent. This better be good. I'm on the eighteenth green, and if I sink this putt, Craig will owe me another fifty."

"I really need you right now. Can you meet me in Corsica on the Eastern Shore at the sheriff's office? It's a big misunderstanding, and I could really use your help."

"No problem. It'll take me a few minutes to get off the course, but I'll be there."

"Thanks."

"In the meantime, whatever's going on, my advice is to keep your mouth shut."

"OK." Reynolds sat back in the patrol car, looking out over the bay. He wasn't worried. Between Maury and Sheriff Tucker, he would be home in no time.

While Detective Sgt. Cummings and Trooper Washington were tracking down Reynolds, Will had gone back to the station to discuss the events with Sheriff Tucker. He was seething inside, thinking how close Libby had come to getting seriously injured, or even killed, and it was all due to Tucker's good-ole-boy system. Well, that was going to stop. He'd had enough of trying to appease Tucker.

He stormed into the station and looked around. "Where's the sheriff?" Will asked Maggie abruptly.

"He ran down to the drugstore to get some more cigars. He'll be right back. Will, is everything OK?"

"No, everything's *not* OK."

"What happened?" Maggie's eyes were open wide with concern.

"You'll find out soon enough, when Tucker comes back." Will didn't mean to be short with Maggie, but he didn't want to have to go through the story twice. He sat down at his desk and waited. He caught Maggie's sidelong glances. Her curiosity was killing her.

A few minutes later, Tucker walked through the doorway. "Will! There you are. I've been wondering where you've been all day. I wanted to talk to you about that case. I did a lot of thinking last night, and I think—"

"I don't want to hear it."

Tucker was shocked. "Excuse me? What did you just say?" He placed his hands on Will's desk, leaning over him, his massive belly hanging down like a giant beach ball, the buttons on his uniform straining to free the enormous girth. Tucker's cheeks flushed a deep shade of crimson as he breathed smoke-laden breath in Will's face.

Maggie sat frozen at her desk.

"I said I don't want to hear what you have to say. I've just spent the past few hours at Libby Langston's house after I received a call from her that John Reynolds tried to kill her. He told her that he knew all about the investigation and that she had been the one to provide me with the evidence." Will's words were slow and deliberate. He paused for a minute to let his words sink in.

Tucker took a couple of steps backward, visibly stunned.

Will continued, "Now since I told no one about Libby's involvement in the case except you, it's pretty ironic that the very next day *after* I told you, Reynolds comes after her. And if it *was* you who told him, then that would mean you've been obstructing justice. And I don't think I have to tell you what that means."

Sheriff Tucker fell back into his chair, his legs buckling under him. "I…I can't believe John would try to kill that woman." Tucker stared bewilderingly across the room.

"So, are you admitting that you spoke with Reynolds yesterday?"

Sheriff Tucker took several minutes before he turned to Will with a blank look. "Are you sure it was Reynolds?"

"Of course I'm sure. I've already been to the state police, and they're bringing Reynolds in now as we speak. I told Detective Cummings that I want to be involved in the questioning, and he's already said he'll turn Reynolds over to me once he gets him. I want you to know that *I* will be running this case, and whatever I say goes; otherwise, I'll have to let the state boys know you had a little chat with Reynolds. In fact, I think it would be a good idea if you weren't even around when Reynolds gets here."

Sheriff Tucker nodded slowly, looking every bit of his sixty-eight years. He sat hunched over at his desk, shaking his head. "I never knew. I never meant for anyone to get hurt."

Maggie stared down at her desk.

A few minutes later, Sheriff Tucker stood up, collected a few things off his desk, and walked out of the station.

39

Will told Maggie to go home for the day, even though she insisted she didn't mind hanging around until the state troopers got there, just in case he needed her assistance. Will knew that Maggie really wanted to stay because she didn't want to miss the excitement. As she was walking out the door, he stopped her and told her that she was not to breathe a word of any of this to anyone. She nodded, but he was pretty sure that by tomorrow it would be the buzz around town.

At 6:35 p.m., Trooper Washington parked the police car in front of the station. Will glanced out the window and then checked his notepad on his desk, quickly scanning what he'd jotted down while waiting for them to arrive.

Will's beach-boy surfer look deceived quite a few people into thinking he was younger than he was, and more naïve than he was. It was something that worked in Will's favor most of the time, especially when questioning suspects, who tended to let their guard down. And that could be an advantage during interrogations.

As the three men entered the station, Will stood up from his desk. Cummings came through the door first, followed by Reynolds, and then Trooper Washington. Will picked up his notepad and led the three men to the small room adjoining the office. The metal chairs grated against the tile floor as the men took their seats around the worn, wood-grained laminate table.

"Mr. Reynolds, do you know why you've been brought in here?"

"I think this is a case of mistaken identity."

"Were you at Haverford House today?"

"No, I was in Annapolis all day. I've already told the troopers this. I'm telling you this is a mistake." Reynolds' voice had an edge to it, not of fear, but of exasperation. "Where's Sheriff Tucker?" he asked.

"Sheriff Tucker won't be working this case." Will's eyes were on his notepad in front of him.

"I want to see Tucker. We can get this straightened out in no time."

Will looked up from his notepad. Reynolds sat back in his chair, looking as if the whole matter was already settled.

"I'm afraid that's not going to happen," Will said. "Some pretty serious charges have been brought against you, so I think cooperating with me would be the smart thing to do. Could you tell me your whereabouts starting with this morning?"

Reynolds rolled his eyes as if to say this was a big waste of his time, but when Will didn't budge and continued to stare at him, he sat forward and began to relate his already thought-out explanation of his day's events. He told the officers how he had met Wally and Joe early that morning around ten at the city dock, and they walked around for a couple of hours discussing their campaign strategy.

Will interrupted him. Why, he asked, did they choose to meet at the dock and not his campaign office?

"We wanted privacy. The office gets a little crazy sometimes, and I think more clearly if I'm out in the fresh air."

Will leaned in closer. The fluorescent light glared down on Reynolds' face. "What happened there?" Will pointed toward Reynolds' left cheek.

Reynolds reached his hand up to his face and then smiled and said he'd slipped with the razor that morning.

Will nodded, tapping his pen on the notepad. "So you met outside at the dock. Then what did you do after that?"

"We had lunch and then headed over to headquarters around one-thirty. We were there all afternoon."

"Where'd you have lunch?"

"Outside. We got sandwiches from the farmers' market at the dock."

"What did you have?"

"Excuse me?" Reynolds frowned.

"For lunch, what kind of sandwich did you eat?"

"I don't see how that matters." Reynolds was taken off guard. He hadn't expected this kind of questioning. He'd assumed Sheriff Tucker would have been the one to interrogate him. This Deputy Seevers was like an annoying gnat that just wouldn't go away. He'd just have to go along with it until Maury got there.

"Just answer the question."

Reynolds popped out the first thing that came to mind: "Corned beef on rye."

"And the others, what did they get?"

This is getting ridiculous, Reynolds thought. None of this was going the way he'd planned. Where was Maury? He should have been here by now. He felt his blood pressure rising. This small-town cop thinks he's Columbo, and he just won't stop. "How should I know what they had? I don't remember!"

"OK," Will replied. "Did you run into anyone else in town that could verify your being at the dock this morning?"

"No, but Wally and Joe were with me the whole time. Ask them."

"We will. One other thing, would you mind lifting up the legs of your pants?"

Reynolds' eyebrows shot up with an indignant look. "I most certainly will not! This is a violation of my rights. I'm telling you, I was in Annapolis all day, and I have witnesses to prove that." Reynolds spoke through a clenched jaw, and each word shot out like a bullet across the table. "My attorney is on his way here. He should be here any minute. Until then, I think this conversation is over."

"You've already called your attorney?" Will glanced over at Cummings, who just shrugged. He then looked back toward Reynolds.

"I know how you people work. I am not going to have some Barney Fife ruin my career on a trumped-up charge. You do realize that I'm running for the US Senate. A story like this could end it all. I'm not taking any chances on this. When Maury Silverstein gets here, we can get this cleared up."

"Fine, I'm not going anywhere. Let's wait for Mr. Silverstein." Will leaned back in his chair and placed his hands behind his head, fixing his eyes on Reynolds.

Reynolds began to fidget in his chair. Things were not going as he'd expected, but he could still beat this. He had Wally and Joe. They would back him up. He'd told them exactly what to say. They were used to covering for him. Usually it was because he was in a hotel room enjoying one of his trysts, but whatever the reason he knew he could count on them to cover for him. He hadn't expected it to happen this fast, but he also hadn't expected the Langston woman to still be alive. This definitely put a snag in things. But it was her word against his, and since he had an alibi, there was nothing this two-bit deputy could do to him.

About ten minutes later, they heard the front door to the station open. "That's Maury," Reynolds said.

Will got up, walked out of the interrogation room, and greeted Maury, a tanned, salt-and-pepper-haired man in his late fifties, wearing a pink polo shirt and white golf slacks. He was a small man, only about 5'7" and weighing about 130 pounds soaking wet, but perfectly proportioned. His prominent nose, strong jaw, and slightly hooded eyes gave him a look of intelligence and authority. Will suspected Mr. Silverstein was very good at his job.

"If you gentlemen don't mind, I would like to have a moment with my client," Maury said in a soft yet commanding voice as he entered the interrogation room.

The two troopers stood up, and Will replied, "We'll wait outside." He followed the troopers out and shut the door behind them. "Can you do me a favor?" he said to Cummings.

"Sure, what?"

"Do you think you could track down the so-called witnesses that Reynolds referred to and get a statement from them? Maybe you can get them to slip on their story."

"Not a problem. We've already met them. They were with Reynolds when we picked him up at his campaign headquarters. We already got their names and addresses." Cummings hesitated for a moment and then continued, "Are you absolutely sure Reynolds is the guy? What if we're barking up the wrong tree? It's kind of crazy for someone like Reynolds to just go attack a woman out of the blue."

Will didn't want to explain why Reynolds had been at Libby's, so he ignored Cummings' comment.

He knocked on the door of the interrogation room and then opened it. "How's everything going in here? Have you had enough time with your client, Mr. Silverstein?"

"Yes, thank you, Deputy Seevers. After going over the events that transpired this afternoon, it sounds to me like you have the wrong man."

"I don't think the woman he attacked would feel that way," Will replied. "I know your client says he has an alibi, but we need to get that confirmed. One thing we could do right now, which I've already asked your client to do, is take a look at his calves. I really don't see the harm in that if he is as innocent as you say. You see, the victim's dog attacked the assailant, and whoever that was probably has some scratches or bites on his leg. What's the harm in letting me take a look?"

"Well, I guess you're forgetting my client's rights. Until you have probable cause, other than one person's word over another's, my client doesn't have to show you anything. Just because he may have a cut on his leg—and I'm not saying that he does, but if there was one—it still would not prove he got the cut from this dog. Tell me, Deputy Seevers, do you have any physical evidence my client was at this woman's house today?" Before Will could respond, Silverstein continued, "I thought not. Since my client has witnesses to back up his whereabouts today, and there's no physical evidence, I think we are finished here. I'll give you my card. Please contact me if you need anything else from my client. Thank you." Maury Silverstein stood up and then motioned for Reynolds to stand. "Is there anything else?" he asked Will.

Will clenched his jaw, trying to remain calm. He'd let his closeness to Libby cloud his vision on how he'd handled things. He never thought Reynolds would have an alibi with witnesses for that morning. He must have bribed them or something to get them to lie. Finally, Will responded, "Nothing else for right now, but I suggest you stay in the area. This is far from over."

Maury chuckled. "Deputy Seevers, I don't think you realize who my client is. He happens to be a very prominent, upstanding citizen, not some low-life criminal without any ties to the community. Not to mention, he's running for office. I don't think leaving town would be something he would consider with the election so close. Did you ever think that maybe this is some ploy by David Jamison's group to try and discredit my client? I'm sure you've thought about the repercussions to your career if it turns out this was all a hoax." Silverstein smiled at Will and then continued, "As I said before, if you need Mr. Reynolds for anything further, please do not hesitate to call me." He stuck his hand out to Will who reluctantly shook it. Reynolds walked by him, a self-satisfied smirk on his face. Will was certain that if Reynolds had been ten instead of fifty-three, he would have sung "*Nah, Nah, Na-Nah, Nah*" on his way out.

Will stood in the empty office, staring out the window as he watched the black Lincoln pull away from the curb with the two men inside. Reynolds was not going to get away with this. He was determined now more than ever that he would nail this guy, not only for the attack on Libby, but for the murder of his wife as well.

The sun had begun to set, leaving a golden glow over the town square outside the office. He ran his hand through his blond hair that had fallen on his forehead, pushing it back from his face, and then he rubbed the back of his neck. It was getting late, and he should be getting home to Julie and the kids. Nothing else would get accomplished that night. He would just have to wait to hear back from Cummings. He hoped one of Reynolds' aides would tell the truth so he could get Reynolds locked up by morning. He didn't want to have to tell Libby that Reynolds was still a free man.

Will threw his cell phone down on the small plastic table. He tucked his arm behind his head, lying back in the lounge chair in the backyard, looking up at the sprinkling of stars in the night sky. Cummings had just called and told him that they didn't get much from Wally and Joe. They were sticking to their story, corroborating Reynolds'. He said Wally had acted nervous, though, especially when he'd asked him what kind of sandwich Reynolds had for lunch. Instead of saying he didn't remember, which had been Joe's answer, he'd stammered and blurted out tuna fish.

The kids were already in bed, and Julie was putting Caleb down. He'd stayed at the station for an hour after Reynolds had left, trying to devise the best strategy. He sipped on his beer. Frustration brewed inside as he thought how Reynolds might get away with it. The trouble with the law was that he had to play by the rules. But Reynolds didn't.

Julie came out wrapped in a sweater with a flannel in one hand and a beer in the other. "I thought you could use this." She handed Will the shirt.

He smiled and thanked her. She always knew what he needed. His thin T-shirt wasn't enough in the cool night air. He sat up and put on the flannel. She snuggled down next to him in the lounge chair.

"I went with Tassie to see Libby after I talked to you earlier," Julie said.

"How was she?"

"I think she's feeling guilty. Once Josh left the room, she kept talking about how she should've listened to him and left the whole thing alone."

"What's done is done."

Julie smiled and then chuckled.

"What's so funny?" Will tilted his head down at her.

"Nothing. I was just thinking what a unique woman Tassie is. I mean, she's gotta be close to a hundred or maybe older." Julie took a sip of her beer. "I got Katie to babysit so I could take a pizza over to Josh and Libby's, and when I got to Billy's to pick it up, there was Tassie, sitting at a booth eating pizza. I sat down with her while I waited for the pizza, and I told her what had happened to Libby." Julie wrapped her arms around her chest. "After I told her, she closed her eyes and sat motionless for a few minutes. I wasn't sure if the news had done something to her, and I was beginning to get worried, but then she popped open her eyes and said that all day she'd had this terrible feeling, and that's why she'd finally walked into town. She said she needed to be around other people."

"She is different," Will said. He drank his beer and adjusted his arm around Julie.

"I'll say. Then she went on to tell me how Reynolds is the devil. And she said it with such certainty. I mean, here's this tiny woman, no bigger than a minute, sitting up so straight in the booth, her little hat on her head, talking about the devil as if he were real." An owl screeched loudly over the hum of crickets, and Julie flinched. "When most people refer to someone as the devil incarnate, you don't think they really mean it. But I got the feeling Tassie wasn't using it as a figure of speech."

"I just hope I can nail him."

"Why wouldn't you?"

"It's not as easy as you think."

"If anyone can, you can." Julie wrapped her arms around him tightly and nestled her face against his chest. "I have complete confidence in you."

Will wished he felt the same.

40

L ibby had persuaded Josh that he should go to work. He hadn't
wanted to leave her alone in the house, even though she knew
he had a mountain of work waiting for him.

She was surprised that she felt as good as she did, considering less
than forty-eight hours ago, she'd been attacked and almost drowned.
She still couldn't believe it. Other than the bruise on her temple, which
Josh had already documented with his camera, she had no physical ail-
ments. But she'd promised Josh she would take it easy and stay in bed.

They'd spent the previous day watching old movies in the den together.
Josh rarely left her side, bringing her snacks, making her lunch. They even
played backgammon, something they hadn't done for years. She'd almost
cried when she watched his car head down the long drive this morning, but
things had to return to normal, and she told herself she'd be OK.

She sat at the kitchen table, drinking her orange juice and eating a
bowl of cereal, wondering if Will could fully open Cecilia's case now.

She'd been feeling guilty about getting the whole thing started and putting her life and her baby's life in jeopardy, but if Cecilia's murder was solved because of it, then maybe it had been worth it.

She looked down at Stella curled up at her feet; she'd stayed even closer to Libby, if that was possible, ever since the incident, following her from room to room. She'd fought for Libby, tearing at Reynolds' leg. Libby reached down and stroked Stella's sleek fur. Stella whined and looked over at the kitchen door, wondering why they weren't doing the normal routine.

Even though Libby had convinced Josh she was fine, she couldn't bring herself to sit out back on the patio like she'd done every other morning. Hopefully, in time, she'd be able to.

She loved being outside, especially in the early morning, hearing the birds sing, the water lapping on the shore, breathing in the salt air, but instead she sat inside with the doors and windows shut and locked; she even activated the alarm system that had been installed weeks ago, which she hadn't used until then.

The phone rang on the wall next to the table, and Libby jerked in her seat. Maybe she was fooling herself in thinking she was OK.

It was Will calling to see how she was.

"My nerves are still a little on edge, but physically I'm fine."

"I wanted to let you know what's been going on. I'm afraid the news isn't so great right now. We've been unable to detain Reynolds. It turns out he has an alibi for that time."

"*What!* How?"

"I half expected something like this from him. He got a couple of his lackeys to say they were with him all day."

"But you know that's not *true*! Can't you arrest him on what I told you?"

"It's not that easy, but believe me, Libby, we're going to get him. His alibi won't hold up. If we put enough pressure on those guys, one of them is sure to break. I'm sorry it's not better news."

Libby's hands gripped the phone with an intensity that matched the anger building up inside her. Reynolds better not get away with what he had done to her.

"Are you going to be OK? I can drop by a couple of times a day, if it would make you feel safer."

Libby chuckled. "It's funny. I think I was more afraid before you called, but now I'm just furious."

"You've got my word. I'm going to put this guy away."

Libby placed the phone on the receiver and sat back down at the table. She wondered what Reynolds must have been thinking when he left her house yesterday. He had to have assumed she was dead. He probably thought he had gotten away with another murder. It must have shocked him to find out she was still alive.

She glanced around the kitchen—the bright peach walls, the white and blue-tiled counters and white cabinets, and the warm sunlight streaming through the window above the sink. The room usually made her feel happy, but an ominous feeling crept over her. Should she be afraid? She was the only witness to what had happened. Would he come back and try to finish the job? She glanced down at her hands clenched together on the table. Her palms were sweating, and her heart pounded in her chest.

She'd been practicing hypno-birthing from a book her mother had gotten her, a technique for managing her labor. It taught meditation exercises. She felt her heart rate return to normal as she inhaled and exhaled in measured breaths, concentrating on her breathing. She thought about calling her mother but then changed her mind. She didn't want to hear, "I told you so."

The phone rang again, and again she jumped in her chair. She needed to do something constructive to get her mind off this.

It was Josh checking in on her.

She told him about Reynolds' alibi. He tried to allay her fears, but she heard the underlying tension in his voice. This was hard on him as well, she thought. She asked him how this was going to affect his work, and he told her not to worry about it.

Josh hung up the phone and stared out at the tall buildings. His hands gripped the arms of his chair tightly; he wanted to find Reynolds and strangle him with his bare hands.

Stephanie brought his mail into his office and told him that Peterson had just buzzed her and wanted Josh to meet him in his office. He nodded, not making eye contact with her. He hadn't told her what had happened. He figured it would be better to wait and see what transpired.

She left the office and Josh tapped his fingers together, wondering what to say to Peterson. Josh had planned on meeting with Peterson first thing this morning to tell him about the incident, but Peterson had been tied up. Had he been talking with Reynolds? And if so, what had Reynolds told him?

He slowly rose from his chair and stood at the window. The exhilaration he normally felt when he looked out at the magnificent view was replaced with anger. Anger at Libby for not listening to him and almost getting herself killed; anger at himself for not realizing what a monster Reynolds was; but mostly anger at Reynolds for almost destroying everything that mattered to him.

He headed down the hall toward Peterson's office, his footsteps silenced by the thickly padded carpet. He hesitated at the large mahogany door before turning the gold handle. This could possibly be the end of his career here. The firm wouldn't want to lose Reynolds as a client.

He opened the door and walked into the reception area of Peterson's office. Peterson's secretary glanced up from the notes she was transcribing and gave him a nod to proceed into the next room. He went through the second door to find Peterson standing behind his desk with his hands in his pockets, looking out at the sights below, just as Josh had been doing several minutes before in his own office. He turned when he heard Josh enter.

"Josh." Peterson glanced back out the window. "You know, I never get tired of this view. The harbor is like the heartbeat of the city; all the energy pumps in and out through the streets. He turned back around and motioned for Josh to sit in one of the leather armchairs that faced his desk.. "Have a seat." Josh obeyed. "You probably know why I called you in."

"I have a guess."

"I just got off the phone with Reynolds."

"I wanted to meet with you earlier, to explain."

"Well, let me tell you what he told me, and then you can explain." Peterson's six-four frame and broad shoulders gave him a commanding presence; he could intimidate most people with his size alone.

He sat down and leaned back in his chair, studying Josh, with his hands folded over his chest. After several seconds, which seemed like hours to Josh, Peterson sprang forward in his chair. "He says your wife has become fixated on the death of his first wife twenty years ago. That she's claiming to have seen a ghost in the house who's telling her that John murdered his wife." He paused with his eyebrows raised.

Josh sat silently in his chair, his mind racing. Peterson was waiting for his rebuttal, but there was no point in interjecting. What he'd said so far was true; it just sounded worse when spoken aloud.

Peterson continued, "He said he found out that your wife had discovered a journal in your house that had belonged to his wife, and when he asked her about it, she denied having it. He said she was acting very strange at the time. Then, out of the blue, he says that two state troopers come to his headquarters and accuse him of trying to murder your wife. He swears he was working all day on his campaign, and he even has witnesses to back it up. He's very concerned about your wife and why she seems obsessed with trying to destroy him." Peterson leaned back in his chair. "Under the circumstances, he also said that he would not be able to have you as his counsel any longer, but he did say that if you and your wife were willing to drop this whole mess, he would continue to be a client of the firm, as a courtesy to me and our longtime friendship."

Josh nodded, fuming inside. The bastard is going to come out the victor, and Libby's going to look like she's insane.

Peterson continued, "I want you to think about this, Josh. You do know how much this account means to the firm. Are you absolutely positive what your wife is saying is true?"

It took all of Josh's restraint to answer Peterson in a controlled manner. He wanted to jump out of his chair and yell at the top of his lungs: "I don't give a damn how important the account is! My wife was almost killed by this lunatic!" But he knew that would just make him look crazier, so instead he calmly replied, "What you've said is partially true. My wife did discover some things in our house that led her to wonder about the circumstances of Reynolds' first wife's death. She also claimed to have seen a ghost. I know it all sounds crazy, and I didn't believe her in the beginning either.

In fact, I tried to discourage her from pursuing it, but I was with my wife right after she was attacked. I saw what she'd been through, and there is no doubt in my mind that what she is saying is the truth. I don't know if Reynolds purposely set out to harm my wife, but that's what happened. You can believe what you want." Josh's eyes scanned Peterson's face, searching for an expression that would clue him in on what he was thinking, but Peterson remained poker-faced.

Josh continued, "Did you ever consider that maybe he did have something to do with his wife's death and was getting nervous when he found out she was on to him? As to his suggestion that Libby and I drop the accusation, you can forget that. We're not letting this go."

"I understand how upset you must be, Josh." Peterson's tone was that of a placating father to a small child. "I know if my wife told me a story like that, I would be troubled as well. Try to look at this rationally, Josh. You've been working long hours. And I must say, when I saw your house, I was quite surprised you would want to be in such a remote area. My wife would be going stir-crazy if she couldn't get to a mall or one of her social clubs. Not to mention Libby's pregnancy. Have you thought about getting medical attention for her, maybe if she could talk with someone…"

Josh adjusted his position in the chair, feeling heat rise under his collar. What could he say? Yes, I thought my wife was crazy, too. "My wife loves living where we live; in fact, it was her idea to move there in the first place. And after working with Reynolds, my estimation of him has gone down considerably. And if you want to continue having him as a client, then maybe this isn't the firm for me."

"Think about what you're saying, Josh. You have a tremendous opportunity with this firm. You don't want to throw it all away so lightly."

"I know exactly what I'm saying. When the truth comes out, and it will, do you really want to be associated with someone as treacherous as Reynolds? I don't think the other partners would regard that as good PR for the firm." Josh stood. "I think maybe both of us should take some time before either of us makes any decision."

Peterson remained in his chair, clearly flummoxed by Josh's outburst. He cleared his throat and said, "That may very well be the case, but for right now I am taking over the Reynolds account personally. I'm sure you have enough work to keep you busy, and if you would like to take some time off to spend with your wife, that would be fine, too."

"Is that just a suggestion?"

"Of course, I think if what you said is true, your wife probably needs you right now."

"Thank you for your concern. I'll think about it." Josh walked out of the office.

His pulse raced as he stormed past Peterson's secretary. Voices in the hallway sounded muffled as he made his way to his office. His temples throbbed, and he pressed his finger to the side of his head.

He breezed past Stephanie's desk and said to her, "Hold all my calls." The expansive glass across one wall shook as he slammed the door behind him. He paced back and forth, running his hands through his dark hair. He felt like his life was spinning out of control. Yesterday, his main concern had been Libby and her safety, not thinking into the future. Driving to work this morning, he'd played a scenario in his head. He'd pictured telling Peterson what had taken place, but things had gone very differently in his mind. He should have known Peterson would take Reynolds' side.

He was furious. Everything was crashing down around him. This wasn't fair; he'd worked too hard to lose it all, but Libby and the baby were his true concern. Reynolds had almost taken both of them away from him, and it made him sick every time he thought about it. He needed to remain calm; not make any rash decisions.

After several minutes of repetitive steps back and forth across the carpet, he eased himself into his chair and stared at his desktop. A folder that he had been working on lay in front of him. He picked up his pen and proceeded to finish where he had left off; work was his panacea.

41

It had been twelve days since the attack, and there was still no word from Will that Reynolds had been arrested. Libby restrained herself from calling him. She'd already phoned him twice over the past ten days, and each time he told her they were still working on it. Will, along with two detectives, had come out to the house scouring the backyard area and pier, searching for clues that Reynolds had been there, but nothing panned out. Libby was beginning to think Reynolds would get off scot-free again. She had to do something, but what that was she had no clue.

She had yet to leave the house, except to go to the grocery store; keeping busy, baking and going through baby books. It took all her concentration not to dwell on what had happened. With each passing day, the attack became more surreal. There were times she even questioned her own sanity. What if Reynolds really did have an alibi?

What if she had imagined the whole thing? But it *had* happened. She wasn't crazy.

Straightening up the den, she came across a slip of paper with a number on it and the name Catherine Collins. She held the paper in her hand for several seconds, just staring at the number. Libby thought, if Catherine told her story to the prosecutor, maybe it would be enough to get Cecilia's case re-opened. She hated thinking Reynolds was going to skate on everything. A voice in her head said to drop it. This is what got her into trouble in the first place. But what harm was there in a phone call?

On impulse, she picked up the phone in the den and punched in the San Francisco phone number.

"That sounds rather cryptic," Catherine said after Libby told her she needed her help.

"I'm not really sure where to begin, so I guess I'll just start with telling you that I was attacked by John Reynolds recently, but the police haven't been able to arrest him because he has a trumped-up alibi. And until they find some evidence to prove he wasn't where he says he was, he's going to get away with it."

"Why would John attack you?"

"I think I was getting too close to what happened regarding his wife's death."

"You think John had something to do with it?"

"I do."

"I'm not sure how I can help you."

"I was thinking maybe if you came out here and told the story you told me to the prosecutor, it might be enough to get his wife's case opened. I remember you told me how Reynolds brought you to the house by boat one night and told you that the house could be yours one day. Don't you think he had a plan to kill his wife? He shouldn't be allowed to get away with murder."

There was a moment's silence, and Libby thought that maybe she'd lost her, but then Catherine spoke: "Libby, I appreciate what you're going through, but I'm afraid I can't help. I've been doing a lot of soul-searching, and I really would prefer to keep that part of my life in the past. Not to mention, you've caught me at a really bad time; I'm leaving tomorrow for Paris. I'll be gone several weeks." Catherine continued, "If you want my advice, I think you just need to let it go. John uses people to his own advantage. I'm sorry you were attacked, but just be glad you're alive and move on. I have."

Libby replied, "That's easier said than done." She felt as if a weight was pressing on her shoulders as she slumped back in the chair. "I'm sorry I bothered you. I just didn't know what else to do." Libby's voice cracked as she tried to hold back tears of desperation.

"Hang in there; just remember time heals all wounds, as they say. I hate to cut you short, but I've got a million things to do to get ready for the trip."

"Of course."

Libby dropped the phone on the desk and buried her head in her hands. The tough façade she'd kept in place was finally cracking from the weight of frustration. Ever since the incident, she'd been getting up each morning, telling herself she was OK, she was strong, and that it was just a matter of time before she got that phone call from Will telling her it was all over. Now it seemed that day would never come.

A few days ago, Will told her he wasn't going to be able to get Cecilia's body exhumed. It turned out that Reynolds had convinced the state's attorney, whose wife happened to be a close friend of Cynthia Reynolds, that the opposition was trying to discredit him by implying he had something to do with his first wife's death.

It wasn't right; Reynolds was going to get away with one murder and the attempt of another, and probably win the election. And if she kept pursuing the case, she'd end up looking like some kind of fanatical nut.

Libby lifted her head and wiped her tears with the back of her hand. She had a choice: either, succumb to the hatred she had for Reynolds, and allow it to destroy her life, or let it go, like Catherine had said, and move on.

Inhaling deeply, she squared her shoulders and thought, she was going to have a baby soon; that was the most important thing in her life right now. She needed to forget Reynolds and the whole sordid mess. Today would be her new beginning and she was no longer going to be a prisoner in her own house.

She went around the house opening up the windows, letting in the fresh, salty air. As she unlatched each window and pulled up the sash, it was like liberating her soul. She was free to enjoy life and forget about ghosts and murders.

Punching in the number to deactivate the alarm at the kitchen door, she thought it really was more trouble than it was worth. Stella liked to jump up on the door handle and open the door, a trick she had mastered to Libby's dismay, and was constantly setting off the alarm.

The crisp air rejuvenated her senses as she stepped out onto the back porch. It made her feel alive again. She set about with her garden snips, clipping flowers and pulling up weeds.

He had come to Haverford House several times since that day, sitting down by the water's edge and crying, thinking it was his fault that he had lost her. He hadn't done anything to save her.

Trevor had watched the news each night and combed the papers, but never saw anything about her death. He was afraid to ask his mother, because then she would start questioning him as to how he knew.

He would get off the school bus some days, and instead of going straight home, he would walk in the other direction, through the woods, and down toward the water.

The house looked empty and quiet from his vantage point, and the gardens appeared to have lost their vigor, as if they, too, were mourning her death.

Today he got off the school bus and decided to go visit her watery grave. At night when he was having trouble falling asleep, he would have visions of walking down the beach and finding her lifeless body washed up on the shore. This was his pain that he had to endure for the rest of his life. He wondered if this was his punishment for not doing all the things his mama had told him to do.

He was making his way through the tall marsh grass, when he heard a noise over by the house. He ducked down and slowly peeked up through the reeds. He caught a glimpse of Stella running through the yard, heading for her ball. He smiled. Maybe Mr. Josh was home.

Stella picked up the ball and ran back in the direction she had come from. Trevor followed her path with his eyes, and what he saw astounded him. Standing by the stone path leading from the patio was Miss Libby. He blinked several times and rubbed his eyes. Was he imagining this? Had he wished so hard for her to come back that his mind made him actually see her?

Then he heard her voice, that wonderfully sweet voice: "Good girl! Go get it!" He watched her throw the ball again and heard her laugh as Stella jumped through the air to catch the ball.

Trevor stood frozen, feeling as if he were watching a movie, and they were in another dimension, one that he couldn't enter. He stood for several minutes observing the scene, and when it didn't fade away, he decided to move forward. Maybe God had answered his prayers and brought her back to life.

He made his way up the stone path. She had her back to him. He didn't want to scare her, so he softly said, "Miss Libby?"

She quickly spun around, and when their eyes met, her face brightened up with a huge smile. "Trevor! I haven't seen you in so long. How are you?"

He stood in the path, his mouth hanging agape. Finally, he whispered, "You're alive."

"What did you say?" Libby frowned.

"I thought you were dead," he said louder.

"Why did you think—?" Libby's eyes lit up. "Trevor, did you see what happened on the pier, with Mr. Reynolds?"

He nodded.

"Oh my God! Where were you?"

"In the reeds. I'm sorry, Miss Libby, I didn't know what to do. I thought for sure you had drowned."

"It's OK, Trevor. There was nothing you could've done. I'm OK." She saw the pained expression on his face, realizing the torture he had put on himself. She wrapped her arms around him. Trevor hugged her back tightly, breathing in her familiar scent.

"I sure am glad you're not dead. I cried every night thinking I would never see you again."

"I'm glad I'm not dead, too." Libby chuckled. Suddenly it dawned on her what this meant. If he had witnessed it, then it wasn't just her word against Reynolds'. This was the break they needed. "Trevor, there is something you can do, something that would be a really big help."

She leaned her back against the front door after Will left with Trevor to go to the station and get his official statement. She felt as giddy as a kid in a candy shop. She wanted to jump up and down and run about the house shouting, "Yes!" A joyous bubble rose up inside her, spilling out with a smile and a laugh. It would all be over soon. She punched the numbers in the keypad to set the alarm, and a dose of reality set in. She shouldn't get too excited yet. Nothing was certain until Reynolds was behind bars, but things were definitely looking up.

She went straight to the phone to call Josh, but she got his voice mail. She knew by the gaunt look on his face the past few days that the whole thing was taking its toll on him. He'd lost the vigor he used to have getting ready for work each day. It hurt seeing him like that, and she wished she could make it better for him.

Libby found herself in the nursery; she wasn't sure how she got there or why. She'd been wandering around the house, trying to find things to keep her busy until Josh got home. The anticipation of what was about to happen was making her antsy.

The room was empty except for the antique dresser. The buttery, cream-colored walls mixed with the late afternoon light that streamed through the tall windows filled the room with cheery warmth.

She pictured the cradle her father was making sitting in the corner. As the sun fell lower in the sky, the light through the window changed to an amber-orange, giving the illusion that the room was aglow. The colors of the walls became abnormally intense, the dimensionality crystal-clear as if she were looking through a child's viewfinder. Stella, who was lying on the floor, gave out a small whine and thumped her tail. Libby assumed Stella was dreaming about something, which she did often, running in place on the floor and making little yipping sounds. But when she looked at her, Stella's head was cocked, and she was staring at something across the room.

Libby turned in the direction of Stella's gaze and saw Elizabeth standing in the far corner of the room. She was wearing the same outfit, the embroidered blue and green silk shawl draped over her shoulders. But this time, her face looked different. She no longer had that pleading look in her eyes; rather, she was smiling, and her eyes were lit up in a way that surprised Libby. It had been so long since she'd seen Elizabeth; she'd thought maybe she was gone forever. Libby studied her face. Had Libby finally given her what she had come for?

"Elizabeth, do you know…" Libby spoke softly, hoping to get some answers, but the image began to flicker and fade. "Please, don't go." She reached out toward the fading shape and then closed her eyes. She tried to convey her thoughts telepathically. A surge of warmth enveloped her like a hug, and an overwhelming feeling of peace swept through her.

Slowly she opened her eyes and the vision was gone, but she sensed Elizabeth was still there, watching over her.

42

Will stopped by Jane Michael's office on the way to the station after taking Trevor home. He had gone over everything that had transpired and wanted her opinion. He told her that Detective Sgt. Cummings was on his way now to revisit Wally and Joe, hoping that if they knew there had been a witness to Reynolds' actual whereabouts that morning, maybe they would change their story. He also gave her the background on Cecilia's case, and how the state's attorney wasn't allowing them to exhume the body. He mentioned the connection Reynolds had to the state's attorney.

Jane's jaw was firmly set as she mulled over everything. She stared out the window for a minute and then told him that if Reynolds' men denied being with him that morning, she wanted Reynolds charged with assault and attempted murder.

He hadn't expected the second charge, but he wasn't going to complain.

As he strode down the sidewalk from the courthouse, he shivered from the autumn breeze. He shoved his hands in his pockets, thinking he'd have to start bringing his jacket to work. The leaves on the trees had turned a bright golden yellow. A scattering of dried leaves made a rustling sound as they scurried across the walkway in front of him.

He loved the change in season ever since he'd moved from Southern California and experienced it for the first time. The air became cleaner, the colors sharper, all of which invigorated him— even though he knew it was a precursor to the brutal winter winds.

As Will stepped into the station, he was surprised to find Sheriff Tucker still seated at his desk, a rare sight at six o'clock in the evening. Maggie had gone for the day, and the only light in the office was a lamp lit on Sheriff Tucker's desk that cast a shadow across his face.

"Hi, Will," Tucker said in his raspy cigar voice.

"Hello." Will had barely said two words to Tucker since the incident with Libby, partly because Tucker had made himself scarce whenever Will was at the station. "What's kept you here so late?" Will asked.

"I wanted to talk with you, before all the commotion starts. Maggie told me you had that Clay boy in this afternoon giving a statement. If what I hear is true and he did witness what happened to Mrs. Langston, then I want you to know I am behind you one hundred percent. I have no ties to Reynolds, and I don't want you to think I'd try and impede your investigation in any way. Just because me and Reynolds go way back doesn't mean I would try and cover for him." Tucker leaned back in his chair, the buttons of his shirt near popping.

The sheriff knew which side of the fence to be on when push came to shove. He was no dummy, Will thought; he liked being on Reynolds' good side when it served him well, but he wasn't about to go down with him when things went badly.

Will sat down at his desk. He'd been surprised that no word had leaked about Reynolds' being brought in for questioning a couple of weeks ago. Maggie had done an exemplary job of staying quiet. "I appreciate you telling me that. I can use all the support I can get. This is going to be one tough case, and I know Reynolds is not going to make any of it easy."

Detective Cummings and Trooper Washington tracked down Reynolds at Cresthaven Country Club, an exclusive golf club in northern Anne Arundel County. Dark wood paneling lined the walls, along with pictures of former club presidents and previous tournament winners. As they approached the wide-open doorway, they heard men's laughter. They turned the corner and entered the lounge. Six men were seated at a large round table of dark polished mahogany. Cigar smoke hung in a cloud above their heads. One man was dealing out a deck of cards. Glasses filled with ice and various scotches and whiskeys surrounded the edge of the table.

The men glanced up simultaneously, looking quizzically at the two officers dressed in their tan and brown uniforms. Their shiny black holsters strapped with a gun, handcuffs, and baton appeared incongruous in the lounge setting. The only one who didn't look bewildered was John Reynolds; he recognized the officers immediately and knew something was up. Instead of surprise, Reynolds had a look of disdain, thinking, what now? He couldn't believe they'd actually tracked him down at the club; didn't they have anything better to do than to harass him?

The man dealing smiled at the officers and said, "Hello, gentlemen. Is something wrong? If you're here to arrest us on smoking in public, you can forget it; this is a private club." The others around the table chuckled like schoolboys.

"No, we're here to speak with Mr. Reynolds," Cummings replied tersely, silencing their humor. All eyes turned toward Reynolds.

Reynolds smiled and set his cigar down in the ashtray next to him. He stood and said, "You know how it is, men. The closer we get to election day, the crazier things get." The men laughed, easing their curiosity. "If you'll excuse me for a minute, play this hand without me."

"I think you may want to cash in," Cummings said. "You're going to need to come with us." Cummings took pleasure in asserting his authority over Reynolds' arrogant posturing.

"Let me give you my attorney's number, gentlemen. I'm sure anything you have to say you can run it by him first." Reynolds began to reach into his trouser pocket.

"Mr. Reynolds, please don't make this difficult. I'm afraid you don't understand. We are not here to discuss anything; we are here to arrest you." There was a wave of astonishment around the table as some of the men began to mumble under their breath to each other. None of them made eye contact with Reynolds.

Reynolds inhaled deeply with his hands clenched at his sides, his bravado slowly chipping away and being replaced with an intense anger. How could they arrest him? He'd already contacted James Mallory, the state's attorney. He thought the whole thing had been settled.

"Sir, if you could come with us… There doesn't have to be a scene."

"A scene? Do you know what you're doing? I'll go with you, but just wait until I get a hold of Mallory; both of you will be out on your asses." He turned toward the table of men and said, "Jamison is at it again. I told you things were getting crazy; the opposition will do anything to win."

The men nodded, their jovial demeanor now subdued.

Reynolds grabbed his sports jacket from the back of his chair, and the three men left the lounge.

As soon as they had rounded the corner, the table was abuzz. No one noticed a young man, who'd been sitting at the bar, slip off his stool and head outside the lounge. He waited in the parking lot, watching them place Reynolds in the back of the Crown Victoria. He then slipped into his Toyota and pulled out behind them.

Things went differently for Reynolds with his second visit to the Corsica station. Maury Silverstein, who arrived shortly after the troopers and Reynolds, demanded to know why his client was hauled back into the station. Once he read Trevor Clay's statement, and Wally and Joe's recanting of the events, he advised Reynolds to keep his mouth shut. There was no way that they were going to let his client off this time, and he didn't want him to mouth off about anything that could possibly incriminate him further.

The two troopers were hanging around the station, just in case they were needed for anything else. Cummings had laughed when he told Will how Reynolds' two minions had caved faster than a house of cards. He said when he'd told them there had been a witness to the assault, and if they didn't come clean they could be charged with obstruction, they were falling all over themselves saying that Reynolds had told them to lie.

Cummings stationed himself in a chair right outside the interrogation room, wanting to hear every word. Trooper Washington, not caring as much as his senior partner about the arrest of Reynolds, decided to go outside for a quick smoke.

He stepped out onto the concrete walk in front of the station and lit up a cigarette. The sun had set, and a chilly breeze blew across the square. He took in a long drag and let it out slowly. The burning ember glowed with each puff as he shifted his weight back and forth trying to keep warm.

Across the square, a man parked in a nondescript Toyota got out of his car. Dressed in a pair of khaki pants and a leather jacket, he came up to Trooper Washington and asked for a light.

At seven-thirty that evening, John Reynolds officially was charged with assault and attempted murder. Will told Reynolds and his attorney that he had arranged a special bond hearing for the next morning, but he would have to spend a night in the county detention center until then.

Maury calmed Reynolds down and assured him he would be home before noon. Reynolds' rage toward Will was like a rocking valve on a pressure cooker ready to blow. Reynolds couldn't believe any of this was happening. It wasn't supposed to be like this. If that damn Langston woman had just kept her yap shut about Cecilia. The woman was insane; she couldn't leave well-enough alone.

His mind ticked off how things would go. Maury would get him out on bail tomorrow, and he'd be home before anyone caught wind of what was going on. The only ones who knew he'd been arrested was the group at the club. He could easily spin it; it was just a mis-understanding. Then, if Maury could do his magic to keep it out of the press and stall things until after the election, things may not turn out too badly. After that he could easily make everything go away for good.

He still couldn't believe Wally and Joe had turned on him. What happened to loyalty? He wanted to fire them right away, but it would be better to keep them employed, keep them under his control, so he could ensure they stayed quiet about the whole thing. And this other witness, whoever he was, had to be dealt with. He wondered how much money it would take to shut the person up. Everyone had a price.

Maury made it clear to Will that if anyone leaked anything to the press, he would have their jobs. He also requested a closed-bond hear-ing, explaining how irreparable damage could be caused if this got out, before even proving Reynolds was guilty. Will assured him there would be a tight lid on it.

On his way home, Will made the phone call he'd wanted to make for quite a while. He punched in Libby's number and waited for an answer.

43

J osh drove across the Bay Bridge on his way to the office. He
thought about the phone call Libby received last night. Things
would finally get resolved. He hoped that soon their lives would
return to normal, if he could even remember what normal was. It
was a chore going into the office each day, noticing the hidden glances
his colleagues gave each other as he passed by, knowing that their
unspoken thoughts were ones of derision.

He had committed a cardinal sin in their eyes. The client was
always paramount, especially one of Reynolds' caliber. Most of them
believed Libby had gone off the deep end and made the whole story
up. Some felt sorry for Josh's having to deal with a psycho wife, while
others were just downright mad that he'd allow his wife to jeopardize
the firm, pitting it against one of their most influential clients.

Now that Reynolds was arrested and they had built a solid case
against him, it wouldn't be long before everyone found out the truth.

He debated whether to go to Peterson and tell him the news or to wait until it finally came out in the press. He eventually decided to let Peterson find out on his own. He wondered how long before the story broke.

The gold elevator doors opened directly onto the reception area of the law firm. The receptionist, seated behind the large, curving, mahogany half wall with the gold letters Abbott & Peterson across the front, looked up as Josh got off the elevator. She gave him a big smile and then added, "Good morning, Josh."

"Good morning," Josh replied, thinking he couldn't remember the last time she'd seemed so cheerful to him. He headed down the hall to his office, and, on the way, he passed by Rick Morgan, another junior partner. Instead of the usual averted eyes of late, Rick looked him straight in the eyes and said, "Hey Josh, how's it going?"

He continued down the hall to his office wondering if he'd gotten off on the wrong floor. Stephanie hung up the phone as Josh neared her desk. "Josh, how are you?" Stephanie had a concerned look on her face.

"I'm fine." Josh frowned. "Is something going on in the office that I don't know about?"

"I guess it's because of the article. Everyone's been talking about it all morning."

"Article?"

"You mean you haven't seen it? I thought for sure…"

"What article?"

"The one on the front page of the *Sun* about Reynolds' being arrested." Stephanie reached down on the floor by her desk and handed Josh the paper. There was a file photo of Reynolds taken at a fundraiser where he was standing at a podium with his arms raised and his mouth open wide in the middle of a speech, making him look slightly crazed. Above the photo was a headline in bold black letters that read **Senatorial Candidate John Reynolds Charged With Assault**.

Josh was amazed this had already hit the press. He wasn't expecting anything for at least a couple of days. He quickly scanned the article, which pretty much said what he already knew.

Stephanie watched Josh as he read the paper. "I believed you."

Josh looked up. "What?"

"I believed you from the beginning. I know a lot of people here doubted your story; in fact, they were saying some pretty nasty things behind your back, but not now. You should've heard them this morning. They've jumped ship on Reynolds so fast, they're climbing over each other to say they always suspected him of being dishonest."

"Have you seen Peterson this morning?"

"No, but I talked to Sheila, and she said Peterson has been in his office with the doors closed all morning with Abbott."

"I can't believe this."

"Didn't you know he'd been arrested?"

Josh nodded. "The deputy called us last night, but I figured it'd be a couple days before the press got ahold of it." Josh stared off into space and then asked, "Do you mind if I hang on to this paper for a little bit?"

"No, go right ahead. You can keep it."

"Thanks." Josh headed into his office and shut the door.

He sat down and placed the paper on his desk. He read the article all the way through and then read it again. He noticed Libby's name wasn't mentioned, which was a good thing. He glanced over the line in the paper that said "and according to sources, he left the victim for dead." He pictured the whole ordeal all over again—Reynolds knocking Libby into the water. He couldn't imagine his life without Libby.

A few minutes later, Stephanie buzzed him and said that Peterson wanted to see him.

He walked into Peterson's office to find Peterson and Abbott seated on a long leather sofa against one wall. Peterson motioned for Josh to sit down in the wing chair across from the couch.

"Josh, good to see you. Charles and I have been discussing the article in this morning's paper, and in light of events, we think it would be best for the firm to terminate Reynolds' relationship. We also know how awkward it would be for you, for the firm, to keep him as a client. Our main concern is with our employees. We want you to know that we're here for you in anything that you need. And just to make things clear, in case there was any confusion, your standing as a partner has not changed in any way."

Josh nodded, but inside he felt contempt. Just a week ago, Peterson had practically accused Libby of fabricating the whole story, and now he acted like he'd been supporting him the whole time. Were these the people he wanted to be associated with? They didn't care about him or Libby.

"If you don't mind, I have a stack of papers I need to sort through on the Palmer case. Unless there was something else you wanted to discuss?" The false compassion was more than he could stand.

"We just wanted to be clear that we're behind you." Peterson spoke in his booming courtroom voice. He stood up from the sofa and shook Josh's hand, his large frame towering over Josh.

Abbott, who was much smaller than his partner, with a slim frame and a penchant for style, remained seated; his expensive gray trouser leg, crossed over his other leg, was raised slightly to expose matching silk gray socks and Italian leather shoes that probably cost more than most families brought home in a week. His hand rested nonchalantly on his knee. He exuded an air that came with money and status, a cool confidence that Josh had always yearned for but at this moment only made him sick. He told Josh that he wished the best for his family in the coming months. Josh thanked them both again and left the office.

Walking back down the hall, Josh shook his head thinking how fickle people were. Everyone in the firm was out for themselves; there were no true friendships here. It was all about the money. Maybe this wasn't the life he wanted. Almost losing his wife and child had made him re-evaluate his priorities.

44

Reynolds stepped out onto the pumpkin-lined courthouse steps to find a crowd of reporters clamoring around. White vans with satellite antennae on the roof were parked around the square. Every news organization in the area was in Corsica. The normally quiet town had been transformed into a hubbub of media personnel mixed with curious townspeople passing through to see what all the commotion was about.

The temperature was a crisp fifty-five degrees, and a slight breeze blew a hint of leftover breakfast smells emanating from the exhaust fan at Pearl's Diner across the way. The dappled sunlight filtered through the large oak trees that had stood on the square since the turn of the previous century, witness to many a scene, but this would be one that was told over and over in the coffee shop and diner for years to come.

A reporter shouted above the crowd, "Mr. Reynolds, what do you have to say about the allegations? Is it true what the paper said—that you assaulted a woman?"

The hearing had been sealed off to the public, so the media knew only what had been printed in the *Sun*. News traveled like wildfire in the press, from the minute the paper had hit the stands, every news outlet was on it, sending their reporters over to the Shore to see what was going on.

Silverstein jumped in front of Reynolds, shielding him from the press. "My client has been wrongly accused, and it is just a matter of time before he is fully exonerated of these charges. Now, if you will excuse us, Mr. Reynolds has a campaign to get back to." He made his way down the steps, pushing microphones out of his face in the process. Reynolds was behind him as they dodged their way toward the car parked at the square.

"Mr. Reynolds…Mr. Reynolds…" Reporters, one after the other, shouted in their faces, microphones stretched outward, vying for his reply.

A young woman reporter slipped her way in between Reynolds and Silverstein, blocking John Reynolds' path. "Mr. Reynolds, could you shed some light as to why someone would accuse you of assault?"

Maury turned around and tried to move the woman away to let Reynolds by, but John stopped and smiled at the woman. "That's a good question, and the only answer I can come up with is that Jamison does not like to be trailing in the polls. This vicious canard is absurd."

"Are you suggesting that David Jamison's campaign is behind this?" the reporter asked.

Maury Silverstein quickly stepped in, grabbing Reynolds' arm before he could answer. "We have no further comment at this time. Thank you," Maury said, steering Reynolds toward the car as the throng of cameras followed.

Standing on the far corner of the square, slightly hidden by one of the big oaks, Jenna Thompson watched the melee from a distance. She'd been driving into town to drop off some things for her mother, whom she was visiting for a few days, when she saw the uproar.

She parked her car and got out just as Reynolds walked out onto the steps of the courthouse. She hadn't seen the paper that morning and didn't know what was going on. She got close enough to hear the shouts from the reporters about an assault. What had Reynolds done? she wondered.

The scene brought back memories of her own arrest and she shuddered; she still woke some nights in a cold sweat, thinking how close she'd come to spending her life in jail. Curiosity got the better of her, though, and after Reynolds and his attorney drove off in their car, she went over closer to a reporter who was talking in front of a camera. She listened in.

"Minutes ago John Reynolds left the courthouse here in Corsica, Maryland, and told reporters that his opponent in the Senate race, David Jamison, was behind the allegations that Reynolds assaulted someone. Reynolds has been rising in the polls over the past several weeks, and if what he said is true, this could make for a very nasty campaign. The hearing was closed to the public, so we have very little information to go on at this time, but we are working on finding out exactly who Reynolds allegedly attacked and why. We'll stay on top of this story and give you up-to-the-minute news as it unfolds. For WGCT Channel 8 News, I'm Melanie Hanson."

Jenna stood watching the news crews pack up their equipment. She had no sympathy for Reynolds; he could rot in jail for all she cared. A smile crossed her face as she turned in the opposite direction, leaving the media frenzy behind. She took a deep breath, savoring the rich smell of the fallen leaves, admiring the bright colors of the red and yellow chrysanthemums that surrounded the square, thinking how much her life had changed.

Two months ago, she never would've noticed the flowers, or the smells, or had the time to stop and watch a squirrel scurry across the lawn collecting nuts. Last week, Jackson had proposed to her and she'd accepted. They had yet to set a date for the wedding, but neither was in a hurry. She hadn't found a job yet, but Jackson had encouraged her to start a blog about overcoming abusive relationships.

It proved to be very cathartic, and each day she heard from more and more women raised by abusive fathers or married to abusive men. They all had similar stories. Jenna was surprised in this postfeminist era that so many men still dominated women—in the workplace and in the family. It had been a hundred years since the suffragist movement, and it would probably be another hundred before things were right.

She now spent her time divided between Alexandria and the farm. She loved the farm, now that her father was no longer around. She'd never realized how much she had loved it.

Her mother, through Jenna's encouragement, had started selling her baked goods in town. Jenna had asked Pearl if she would like to offer her mother's pies and cookies as an added item to the menu. Pearl said she'd be willing to give it a try, and so far they'd been a big hit.

That was the reason she was in town today; she was dropping off four pies and three batches of cookies at Pearl's coffee shop. At least it was keeping her mother busy and helping her heal. She headed back to the car to get the boxes of baked goods with a lightness to her step that made her feel like a child again.

Maury was on the phone the minute he pulled the car away from the square. Reynolds was shouting in his ear, demanding to know how the press had found out about the hearing. Maury called his assistant and told him to contact the detention center that had held John and find out the names of everyone there last night. One of them must have ratted to the press. He was livid; he had explicitly told them not to utter a word about Reynolds' arrest.

Reynolds continued his ranting, and Maury had to hold the phone down in his lap and say to Reynolds, "John, please. I cannot take care of this situation with you yelling. If you would just be quiet for a minute, I can get to the bottom of this."

"It sure as hell doesn't look like you know how to take care of anything! The whole damn world knows about this now!" Reynolds' face was deep red, and the veins stood out on his neck.

Maury continued with his assistant, ignoring Reynolds' tirade. "What was that, Chuck? I couldn't hear what you said."

Reynolds got quiet. Reading Maury's face, he could tell something was going on. "What, what's he saying?" Reynolds barked.

Maury held his hand up, motioning for Reynolds to be quiet. Then he replied to his assistant, "What was the reporter's name?" There was a brief pause and then, "Calvin Jones? And it was in the *Sun* this morning? How could...?" Maury stopped for a second but then continued, "It had to have been someone on the inside. They must've called the reporter last night. Get on the phone now, and get the names of each person at the detention center last night. I want some answers fast."

Maury told Reynolds about the article in the *Baltimore Sun*. They were driving by a convenience store on the outskirts of town, when Maury whipped into the parking lot. He jumped out of the car before Reynolds could even ask him what he was doing. A few minutes later, he came out of the store holding a paper. He got back in the car and said to Reynolds, "I wanted to read this for myself, just to see how much information was in the article."

He held up the paper over the steering wheel, and both men saw the front-page picture of Reynolds along with the startling headline. Maury began to read the article aloud. When he'd finished, pausing several times throughout to quiet Reynolds' interjections, he said, "Well, they don't have very many details. At least it doesn't reference the attempted murder charge."

"I bet it was that damn Langston bitch. She's out to destroy me. I'm beginning to think she *is* some kind of operative for Jamison."

"John, get serious. Did you or did you not go over to her house that day?"

"That's beside the point. The point is, she's been trying to dig up things about my past. Why would she do that unless someone was putting her up to it?"

"That very well may be the case, but until we have more proof of that, you need to be careful what you say to the press. If you go accusing Jamison of being behind this whole thing, and he had nothing to do with it, it's going to make you look bad."

Reynolds sneered at Maury. "It's all a matter of perception in this game, whether Jamison had anything to do with it or not. We plant that seed into the public's mind, and it may be enough for them to consider it. Give them some sympathy for me."

Maury chuckled.

"You find this amusing?"

Maury shook his head. "I was reminded of a Rolling Stones song. Look, John, let's take this one step at a time. You get your PR wizards to do some magic on this, and I'll work on the legal aspects. We can only do the best we can."

Reynolds stared out the car window, his jaw clenched tightly, his vision of the passing cars on the highway blurred by his intense rage. Never before had he lost control of a situation. It was all because of the Langston woman, he thought; she'd driven him to do what he did. Everyone should agree that the woman brought it on herself. If she had only given him the diary in the first place, none of this would've happened.

The more he thought about it, the more he convinced himself the woman was a plant for Jamison. She had to be. Who else would want to ruin his chances of winning more than Jamison?

Reynolds had called Cynthia the night before and told her he wouldn't be home. He said something unforeseen had come up, and he'd explain in the morning, not expecting the press to blast the story so soon. Last night, he thought there was a possibility it could all go away quietly. He just needed to grease a few palms.

Maury pulled up the drive to the estate. Reynolds' Mercedes sat parked in the circle; Maury had phoned one of his assistants the night before to go pick up the car from the club.

"If you want, I can handle the media for you. It would probably be better if we came out with an official statement soon, before too much speculation gets stirred up," Maury said.

"Fine. Call Jason Hardwicke on my staff; he's a genius at spin. Just run by me what's going to be said before anything goes out."

Maury nodded. "We'll get through this, John. Just remember to keep your cool."

Reynolds found Cynthia seated in the sunroom. She was dressed in a silk Dior pantsuit with what appeared to be a Bloody Mary in hand. It wasn't even noon yet; this was early even for her, Reynolds thought.

She glanced up as he entered the room. Her body stiffened as their eyes met. She stared coldly at him without a trace of sadness or anger.

"I assume you saw the paper," Reynolds said.

Cynthia gave a short laugh and gazed out the large window overlooking the water. She took a sip of her drink. "No, I haven't seen the paper, but if you're referring to what is being said about you, yes, I've heard. The phone's been ringing all morning. I finally had to tell Maria to take it off the hook.

"After Jacqueline called this morning, asking me what was going on and me feeling like a complete idiot because I had no idea what she was talking about, I turned on the news, and your face was plastered over every channel. How wonderful to find out your husband's been arrested for assault." She'd been staring out the window, not looking at Reynolds. Then slowly she turned her head toward him and said, "You know when you called last night and told me something unforeseen had come up and you wouldn't be home, I immediately thought you were sleeping with one of your bimbos. How simple that would have been."

She stood up and walked past him toward the window. Reynolds inhaled the scent of Chanel.

She continued, "I should've suspected something when those officers came to the house the other day, but no, I trusted you when you said it was just part of the campaign heating up."

"That is *exactly* what's happening," Reynolds said. "It's *Jamison*; he's trying to discredit me."

She turned around and faced him. "John, do you really expect me to believe that? Maybe you can fool some people with your lies, but you forget, I'm married to you. I know what kind of temper you have. So tell me, was this one of your floozies that threatened to go to the press, so you had to rough her up to shut her up?"

"Cynthia. There aren't any *floozies*." He went over and reached out to her. "I love you." She immediately pushed him aside.

"Don't touch me." Her cold, seething eyes stared hard at him.

"This has nothing to do with a woman," Reynolds said, keeping his distance. "At least not in the sense that you mean. If you would just let me explain. It's that Langston woman, Josh's wife. She's crazy."

Cynthia's cold gaze turned puzzled.

"She's made up some cockamamie story about me killing Cecilia." Reynolds snorted as he rubbed the back of his neck. "I'm telling you the woman is either insane, or she's working for Jamison and trying to stop my chances of winning."

"Cecilia committed suicide. Why would she say that?" Cynthia looked bewildered.

"I know. That's why I say she has to either be insane or a plant."

"What are you going to do?" Cynthia's body had softened.

"I'm not sure. Maury's getting with Jason to come up with a release for the press. We need to get ahead of this before too much damage has occurred."

Reynolds called for Maria, who came so quickly she had to have been around the corner of the sunroom, and he asked her to fix him a bourbon. He needed something to calm him down.

"Did you assault her?"

"What?" Reynolds turned back toward Cynthia.

"The Langston woman—did you assault her?"

"It's complicated. I went over to Haverford House because I'd found out that she was stirring up all sorts of rumors about me, and that she'd discovered a diary of Cecilia's that was left in the house. I just wanted to talk some sense into her, but she wouldn't listen."

"So you hit her?"

"It wasn't like that. She went crazy on me and scratched my face, so, as a reflex, I swung out and hit her, and she fell into the water."

"She fell in the water?" Cynthia frowned.

"We were on her pier. Look, none of that matters. What matters is winning this election. I need you by my side now more than ever."

"This is all rather confusing. Wasn't her husband your attorney? Why would they be working for Jamison?"

"I don't have the answers right now, but it's all going to work out. I just need to know I have your support." Reynolds' supplicating look was something rarely seen.

"I feel a migraine coming on. I need to lie down. We'll discuss this later." She walked away, her heels clicking on the cold tile floor.

45

Libby folded the last towel from the laundry basket, spreading her hand over the soft terry, trying to keep her mind focused on something mundane. The media frenzy was unending. It wasn't long after the paper had broken the story that her name hit the press. She'd woken up one morning last week to the phone ringing. It was both her parents on the line, stunned that she hadn't told them about the attack. They'd seen it on the news in Connecticut. Libby was thankful her mother hadn't gloated about telling her to stay out of the whole thing; instead, she'd just sounded worried. Her father said that they were coming to Maryland, but Libby had insisted she was fine. She would love to see her parents, but her life was so confusing right now, she didn't think she'd be very good company.

The doorbell rang and Stella went flying from the bedroom. Libby looked out the window on the upstairs landing and saw an unfamiliar car parked in the circle out front. Probably another reporter.

Reporters had been knocking at her door and calling the house. So far she'd managed to avoid them, but it hadn't been easy. Every time she turned on the television, another talking head was speculating about whether this was just political backstabbing. Some were even painting her as deranged.

The poll numbers for Reynolds had dropped sharply right after the news hit the stands, but since then, his campaign had been putting out information that insinuated Libby had a connection with Jamison's camp. The latest poll showed he had actually risen a couple of points.

She peeked through the side window of the front door and was shocked. She quickly punched in the alarm code and opened the door. Her mother was standing on the brick step, a suitcase beside her and an overnight bag in the other hand.

"Elizabeth." The only time her mother called her by her given name was when she was mad or worried.

"Mom? What are—How did—?"

"I flew in this morning and rented a car."

"Come in." Libby stepped back.

"You didn't think I could just sit up in Connecticut, did you?"

Tears welled in Libby's eyes. Seeing her mother brought forth all the emotions she'd kept buried. The hurt, the embarrassment with everything that was being said about her. She hugged her mother and felt the tight grip of her mother's arms around her as she breathed in the familiar scent of White Shoulders, her mother's favorite. "Where's Dad?"

"He wanted to come, but we've got workers at the house finishing up the renovations on the kitchen. I told him if things were really bad when I got here, he could hop on a plane then."

"Mom—"

"Don't even say it." Diana held up a hand. "I want to apologize for speaking to Josh behind your back. I was worried about you. And I know you think I want to say 'I told you so,' but I don't. All I care about is your well-being and my grandchild's."

Libby felt as if her mother had read her mind.

Diana stood back. "Look at you; you're positively glowing. Listen, I know things must be crazy right now. I've seen the news, but I thought I might be able to take your mind off it by painting that mural we talked about."

"Really? Oh, Mom, thanks."

"And don't worry, I'm not moving in. It shouldn't take more than a week."

Libby laughed. "You can stay as long as you like."

"If I'm gone any longer, your father will be wandering the halls, unable to find his socks or something."

Diana walked into the kitchen wearing a paint-covered smock with a bright yellow band holding back her auburn hair. "I was beginning to think lunch had been canceled." Diana laughed.

"I'm sorry, Mom. Emily called, and I guess the time got away." Libby felt the days had flown by since her mother had arrived, compared to the past few weeks. In between Diana's painting, they'd spent the time looking through decorating magazines together, going to antique stores, and talking about kids, gardening, horses, anything but the ordeal. Libby hadn't realized how much she'd missed spending time with her mother. "I'll have the chicken salad ready in a minute."

"I was just kidding. I was so engrossed on the mural, I didn't even notice the time had gone by until my stomach started talking to me." Diana washed her hands at the kitchen sink. "What did your sister have to say?"

"She saw the news pieces about the attack and wanted to know how I was handling being in the spotlight."

Libby was chopping celery and placing it in the bowl with the cut-up chicken; her mother came over and began making the dressing for the salad. "Have you decided if you're going to talk to the press?"

"I don't know; maybe I should. According to Emily, the show that she saw made it seem like I was some kind of political kook that had been harassing Reynolds." She glanced up at her mother. "You know he's climbing in the polls again."

"You should do whatever makes you feel better. There's nothing wrong with talking to the media, as long as it's not more stressful for you."

Reynolds switched off the television set with the remote and then threw it across the bedroom, but instead of crashing to the floor and breaking apart in bits of broken plastic, it landed silently onto the rose-colored carpet. Cynthia sat quietly in the chintz-covered chair behind him, having watched the broadcast in stunned silence.

At 6:45 that morning, Reynolds got a call from Maury Silverstein, informing him of a news piece about the case on Channel 11. Maury thought he might be interested because supposedly Libby Langston was going to talk.

"That woman! She's out to destroy me!" He shouted with such vehemence that Cynthia shuddered in her chair.

"John, is what she's saying true?"

He swung around as if seeing her for the first time in the room. He stared at her for several seconds and then said, "She's *lying!* The woman's a lunatic!"

"She sounded pretty believable to me. Why would she say such things if they weren't true?"

"How should I know?" He paced in a tight circle at the foot of the bed.

"What was in the journal?"

"I don't know."

"Then why did she give it to the police?"

"To destroy me! Can't you see that?" He looked at Cynthia with such rage, she cringed against the back of the chair. "I've got to call Maury." He stormed out of the room and headed down the winding staircase.

Cynthia stared out at the perfectly landscaped lawn, her eyes falling on two swans circling together in the man-made pond on the side corner of their property.

46

Libby's interview on television was like a firestorm, spreading to other media outlets that speculated on why Reynolds had wanted the journal. Her phone hadn't stopped ringing, and the answering machine was filled with messages from reporters wanting to interview her. She'd thought after giving the interview she'd be left alone, but the opposite had happened.

Her parents had called her from Connecticut to say they'd seen clips of her on *Fox News*. They also wanted to know if she was aware that Reynolds' new polling numbers had dropped drastically. This time the talking heads were speculating that his Senate race was over. With the election only a week away, they'd be surprised if he could recover.

Libby couldn't wait for the whole nightmare to be over. At least now she felt people weren't looking at her as if she were crazy. In town everyone she ran into seemed to be on her side. She'd invited Julie over for lunch the next day, wanting things to get back to normal.

She was on her way to Tassie's house to invite her for lunch as well. She passed by the high school where the football team was out on the field practicing. Farther down the road, tractors ran through the dried brown soybean fields, harvesting the crops. She exhaled, letting out the tensions from the past few weeks. Things were going to get better. Once the election was over, all the hubbub would be yesterday's news.

She pulled down Tassie's curving drive through the woods. The brightly colored autumn leaves hung on the trees and blanketed the ground like scattered chips of gold. The broken-hinged gate squeaked in protest as she pushed it open. Tassie's garden was still full of color, filled with chrysanthemums, asters, and flowers Libby didn't know by name. She knocked on the arch-shaped front door, expecting Tassie to open it right away as she usually did, sensing Libby's arrival before she came. But this time there was no response. Libby knocked again, slightly harder this time. Still no response. She looked around the yard; maybe Tassie was outside.

She went around to the back of the house and peered into the kitchen window. No sign of Tassie. Had she gone into town? She went back around to the front. Looking in the window to the living room, she could see a lamp lit on a small table, and the cat was curled up in her usual spot on the chair.

Libby wasn't sure what to do; she knocked on the front door even louder. Nothing. She hesitated for a second and then turned the knob; the door wasn't locked, so Libby walked through and peeked her head inside.

"Tassie?" she called out. The cat lifted her head up from the chair, blinked several times, and then laid her head back down. Libby stepped into the living room. "Tassie, it's me, Libby. Are you here?" she called again, a little louder.

The miniature house was in perfect order, and the only sound was the ticking of the little cuckoo clock hanging on the wall. Off to the right was a short hall that led to what Libby assumed were the bed-rooms. Her heart skipped a few beats as she walked down the hallway. What if something had happened to Tassie? She was well into her nine-ties, maybe even older. Libby told herself if she'd passed away, at least she'd had a good long life. But that didn't help calm her nerves. She silently prayed that everything was OK.

She reached the first door to the right of the hall, which was sit-ting ajar. She pushed it and said in a soft voice, "Tassie?" She entered the small room. Lying atop a white heirloom quilt on a dark spindled bed was Tassie, in one of her flowered shirtwaist dresses and black shoes, her hands neatly folded over her stomach. Her eyes were closed, and Libby couldn't tell if she was asleep or dead. She walked over to the bedside and watched closely to see if she was breathing, holding her own breath in anticipation. She stood beside her for sev-eral seconds and finally saw Tassie's chest move ever so slightly as she inhaled. Libby let out an audible exhalation of relief.

At that same moment, Tassie opened her eyes and Libby flinched, but Tassie wasn't the least bit startled to see Libby standing over her. Tassie smiled.

Libby reached her hand out to her. "Tassie, I was worried about you. I knocked and when you didn't answer, I came in to see if you were OK. Is everything all right?"

"Yes, child." Tassie slowly sat up in the bed. "I needed to lie down. I wasn't feeling well."

"What's wrong?"

"It's just one of those feelings I get sometimes."

"What do you mean?"

"It's only happened a few times in my life, but when I get these feelings, I just know something terrible is going to happen. I thought maybe if I lied down it would go away." Tassie held Libby's hand. "Seeing you here helps take my mind off it. Would you like a cup of tea?"

"You want me to fix it? Why don't you stay in bed, and I can bring the tea in here."

"That's very sweet of you, child, but I can get up. In fact, doing something with my hands will make me feel better." Tassie slowly got up from the bed and headed into the kitchen with Libby in tow.

While Tassie put the kettle on the stove, Libby sat down at the kitchen table. "You said you'd had this feeling before. What happened then?"

"The last time I had this feeling was years ago. It was back in '58. I remember waking one night in a terrible sweat, and I had this horrible feeling of dread. I couldn't stop it even though there was no reason I should be feeling that way. It lasted for two days, and then I got the news that my cousin Thomas had been shot. We'd been very close as children; he was only two months younger than me and lived right down the street. We used to play every day together, but when he grew up, he moved away. He was livin' in Roanoke, Virginia, and I hadn't spoken to him in probably twenty years." Tassie brought two empty cups over to the table. "We drifted apart after he married; his wife was a nasty woman." She frowned and shook her head. "We all wondered why he ever married her in the first place. I think she drove him to drink. From what I heard, he ended up spending most of his time in the local pool hall, just to get away from her.

"Then one night he was hanging out in the pool hall and a fight broke out. Some of Thomas' friends were fighting with some strangers that had come into the hall. Thomas joined in, trying to help his friends out when, out of the blue, one of the strangers pulls out a gun and starts swinging it around. That made everybody stop fighting. Thomas walked over to the man, trying to calm him down and telling him there was no need for any weapons, and without any warning the man shoots him. From the way I heard it, everyone was shocked. Thomas had done nothing wrong; in fact, he hadn't even been involved in whatever started the fight. The man with the gun and his buddies all ran from the pool hall, but they didn't get far. The Roanoke police caught them on their way out of town."

"What about Thomas? Did he survive?"

"No, he died before they even got him to the hospital."

"Oh, how sad."

Tassie sat down at the table with the pot of tea. "The day I got the phone call, I knew that was why I'd been feeling so badly."

"Well, maybe this time it won't be anything. Maybe it's just the change in the weather. It's getting pretty chilly at nights."

"Maybe, child," Tassie said, patting Libby's hand with her gnarled fingers. Her touch was dry and warm. "So what brings you here today?" She poured the tea into the cups.

"Well, I ran into Julie in town, and we decided to get together for lunch at my place tomorrow, and I wanted to know if you could come."

"That would be lovely."

"Julie said she could pick you up. I thought we could eat around noon."

"Maybe I'll make a batch of my homemade brownies; they say they are the best in town."

47

eynolds paced the floor of the headquarters conference room while several of his key staff members discussed strategies to try to bring the poll numbers back up. He ran his fingers through his silver hair in frustration, watching his hopes for the US Senate seat slip through his fingers. All the hard work he'd done to get to this point was for nothing. There was nothing he or his staff could say or do to stop the rapidly declining poll numbers.

His blood pressure had risen off the charts from his fury; he deserved to be senator. No one had the right to stop him. "I'll be back," he said abruptly as he stormed out of the room.

Reynolds drove his Mercedes out of town. He didn't know where he was going; he just needed to drive. His mind was racing. He thought about Cynthia; ever since the Langston woman's interview on television, Cynthia had been keeping her distance from him. She seemed cold and remote. When he tried to discuss what was going on, she said she didn't want to talk about it. He felt like he was losing her.

Maury had told him they had set another hearing date for the end of November. He said that things didn't look too good. With the witness statements, they couldn't deny what had happened. He'd joked about a temporary insanity plea, but Reynolds hadn't thought it was funny. Maury assured him he would work something out so there would be no jail time, but none of that mattered now.

Everything was ruined. Nothing was going the way it should. He drove aimlessly through back roads, pushing the Mercedes to its limits. He raced the machine through curves at a reckless speed, not caring what was around the corner, not even noticing the pavement in front. The only thing etched in his brain was the face of Libby Langston.

❧

Libby added the final seasonings to the soup that was simmering on the stove. The blended aroma of carrots, celery, onions, and broth filled the kitchen along with the smell of home-baked bread. She'd become an expert in bread-baking over the past few weeks. The only thing left to do was set the table and finish the salad of romaine, dried berries, nuts, and goat cheese.

It was chilly when she woke, and after going through her closet and drawers, she realized she needed to shop for warmer clothes. Everything she owned was too tight across the belly. She'd ended up putting on one of Josh's cashmere cardigans over a long-sleeve T-shirt and a pair of jeans that she left unzipped, covering the top with a belly-band.

On cue from Stella's barking, she hit the keypad on the alarm to deactivate the system and let Tassie and Julie in the house. Libby gave each of them a hug, then shut the door and hit the keypad again.

"Will's been trying to talk me into getting one of those," Julie said.

"I hate it. We've had so many problems with Stella setting it off. I've gotten used to it, though, and it makes Josh happy." Libby took the women's coats and then said to Julie, "You know, you look fantastic. I can't believe how fast you lost the baby weight."

"Thanks, but it wasn't intentional. Running after three kids and taking care of a baby doesn't leave you much time to eat. They really should market it as a new weight-loss fitness program," she said with a laugh. "But I'm kidless today! Katie's going part time to the community college and needs extra money. I ran into her yesterday, and she said she could watch Caleb today. Something smells divine in here." Julie held her nose up toward the kitchen.

"Thanks, I made some bread and vegetable soup for lunch."

"We can also have some of these brownies for dessert,"Tassie said, holding up a tin she had in her hands.

Libby's eyes widened, and she smiled a devilish grin. "I can't wait."

The three went into the kitchen.

"So Tassie, how have you been feeling since yesterday? Any more bad feelings?" Libby asked.

"A little. I'm beginning to think that maybe I'm just getting old."

"What are you all talking about?" Julie asked.

Libby told her about her visit to Tassie's and the story Tassie had told her about her cousin.

"Tassie, you know, you are one interesting woman. I think you should write a book about the adventures of your life. Wouldn't that be a great idea, Lib?" Julie asked, picking a dried berry out of the salad bowl on the counter and popping it in her mouth.

Libby nodded as she stirred the soup. Stella waited by the kitchen door, whining and scratching.

"Can I let her out?" Julie asked.

"Sure." Libby glanced over her shoulder. "Wait a sec. I have to turn off the alarm." Libby went over to the kitchen door and punched in the numbers.

"You have to do that every time you let the dog out?"

"I know it seems like a pain, but you get used to it." Libby opened the door for Stella, and she took off running. "Stella has discovered the geese that have arrived this fall, and she's obsessed with watching them land in the water."

Libby arranged a tray with the bowls of soup and salad, asking Julie to bring the basket of bread into the dining room. They rarely ate in the dining room, but it was such a beautiful room overlooking the water, it seemed a shame not to use it.

"This looks wonderful!" Julie exclaimed.

"Thanks."

Julie asked Tassie to tell them more of her stories. She said one day they would have to tape record Tassie telling them so they could compile them into a book. "I'm not joking; I think we could do this."

Tassie chuckled. "I never thought my life to be that interesting that anyone would want to read about it."

"Oh, but they would."

The remainder of the lunch, Tassie regaled them with stories from her childhood. Libby and Julie sat mesmerized, listening to Tassie's lilting voice tell a tale about a time when she was around twelve and took the family horse into town for the first time.

"You see, instead of walking, like I usually did, I decided I would ride Nightshade, who was a dark bay Morgan my daddy used to plow the vegetable garden. He was one strong horse, our most valuable asset aside from our land. I could barely wrap my legs around his large belly." She smiled. "I was always begging my daddy to let me ride the horse, but he always had an excuse. But this one particular day, my daddy was real busy working in the shed out back of the house, and my mama needed me to go to town to pick up some flour and sugar, so she could bake a cake for my Aunt Bessie's birthday. He gave me a long lecture, though, about how I had to be real careful and stick to the roads and come straight back after goin' to the store. I swore to him that that was exactly what I planned on doing, and he would not have to worry one iota about me." Tassie pulled out an embroidered handkerchief from the pocket of her dress and wiped her nose.

"I headed down our lane riding bareback with two saddlebags across his back out onto Millers Road, which was just dirt back then. It was a beautiful summer's day." Tassie closed her eyes. "I remember the birds were singing in the trees, and the honeysuckle lining the road filled the air with such sweetness." She opened her eyes and looked at Julie and Libby. "We made it into town with no problem, and I took my time walking around the town square, showing off, hoping to run into one of my friends so's they could see me on the horse. But none of them were around. The town back then looked different than it does now. Of course, the courthouse and the square were there, but there were only a few shops surrounding the square." Libby pictured the square so many years ago, imagining the dirt-lined streets filled with old-time cars and buggies.

"One of them was Callaway's General Store; Mr. Callaway had everything in that store, from food and clothing to shotgun shells. I loved going in there. It smelled of coffee and spices and made me feel all warm inside. There were wooden shelves floor to ceiling, crammed full of everything under the sun, and Mr. Callaway knew where everything was. I tied Nightshade up to the hitching post out front and went on in, swinging open the screen door. Mr. Callaway looked up from the counter, wearing his white apron he always wore and said good morning to me. He asks me what I needed, and I told him about my mama's cake for Aunt Bessie. He was helpin' Mrs. Carson and told me he'd help me in just a bit."

Tassie's fingers played with the handkerchief, turning it in her hand. "So, I decided to look around. I loved the back section, filled with books and magazines. I went back there, pulled a book off the shelf, sat down on the old wood-planked floor, and started reading about far-off lands. I got so engrossed in what I was readin', I had no idea how long I'd been in there, until Mr. Calloway comes around the corner and says, 'Miss Tassie Jackson, I didn't even know you were still here. I thought you came here to get something for your mama.' I told him I got *sidetracked*. Sidetracked was a new word I'd just learned in school from my teacher who said my problem was I was always getting sidetracked. I didn't know what that meant, so I looked it up in the dictionary and found out it meant to be abstracted from your task. And I started thinking maybe I did get sidetracked a lot because my mind was always straying from where it was supposed to be."

Libby's gaze drifted to the large windows that lined the back wall of the dining room. A sailboat coursed by on the bay, it's red sails puffed against the wind. Tassie's soothing voice filtered back.

"...'That's quite a load for such a little skinny girl like you to be carrying all the way home,' he told me. And I told him I wouldn't have to carry them today because Nightshade was going to do all the carrying for me. 'Well, aren't you a lucky girl,' he says.

"I left the store feeling real lucky until I looked at the hitching post and Nightshade was gone. I looked up and down the street and around the square; he was nowhere in sight. It wasn't like Nightshade to just wander off. He'd stand in the field for hours when he was plowing for my daddy. Here I had two sacks under each arm, and my life was flashing before my eyes, thinking about what my daddy would do to me when I got home without Nightshade. There was no point in even goin' home, so I just sat down on the curb and started crying.

"I hugged my knees with my arms and laid my head down on top of them, wishing that the sidewalk would just open up and swallow me whole. I don't know how long I sat there, telling myself over and over, if I hadn't gotten sidetracked and read the book, Nightshade would probably still be here. Then out of nowhere, I feel this big hand on my shoulder and this deep voice asking me what was the matter. I lifted up my head, and I see this burly man with a big red beard standing over me."

Libby and Julie exchanged glances, thoroughly engaged.

"He was dressed in fancy clothes, the kind I had only seen in magazines. I told him about Nightshade. And he asked me if I'd like to ride in his car to look for him. Believe me, I was quite perplexed." Tassie shook her head and rubbed her lips together. "I had never even sat in a car before, much less driven in one around town. I stood up and gathered the sacks, and the big man walked over to a shiny black automobile and opened up the passenger door. I looked around to see if anyone was watching. I felt like I was dreaming or something. He asked me my name, and when I told him, he asked if I was Sally Jackson's daughter. I nodded and he said he was Benjamin Haverford. My mama worked at Haverford House, but I had never met him before. Here he was, the richest man in town, and he was going to drive me around to find my horse. I had to pinch myself to make sure I was awake. I was sittin' real straight, looking out the window as we drove down the street, thinking that this was even better than riding a horse and hoping my friends would see me now. Mr. Haverford drove real slowly as we went down the side streets of town looking between all the houses. My biggest fear was that Nightshade had walked back home without me, and my daddy already knew.

"Well, he starts asking me about my family, and I told him I had a brother and two sisters. And he tells me how he and his wife didn't have any children. He said they'd tried for many years but had never been blessed. So, I told him about my grandma and how she had all kinds of concoctions to make people well or help them have a baby, and then I caught a glimpse of a black tail swishin' behind a shed out in back of one of the houses.

"Mr. Haverford pulled to a stop, and I jumped out of the car, running down the alley between the two houses calling out, 'Nightshade!' I got to the edge of the shed and went around the corner, and there was Nightshade, grazing on some grass in the yard. When he saw me, he just picked up his head for a second, as if to say, 'well there you are,' and then he went back to grazing. He still had the saddlebags across his back, thank God. The reins were still intact, just dangling down on the ground, so I went over to him, picked up the reins, and walked him back out to the street. Mr. Haverford had gotten out of his car and was standing in the street, watching me bring Nightshade back up the lane. He helped me get the sacks out of the car and put them in the saddlebags. I thanked him for helping me find Nightshade and told him that I was going to work real hard from now on not to get sidetracked.

"He looked at me with a puzzled expression on his face. And I told him how I got sidetracked in the store and started readin' the books in back. Then he reached into his pocket and pulled out a silver dollar and handed it to me and told me he wanted me to have it to buy one of those books. Then, he helped me climb up onto Nightshade. I asked him if he didn't mind not telling my mama about this, and he said it could be our little secret. He got back in his car and drove down the street. I looked down at the silver dollar in the palm of my hand, marveling at it. I had never held a silver dollar before, and it felt warm and heavy. I still have that silver dollar to this day." Tassie finished her story, her small, spidery fingers turning the embroidered handkerchief in her hand.

"I remember you telling me your grandmother taught you about herbal medicine. And that you helped her with Annabelle Haverford getting pregnant. Was that his wife?"

"Yes, it was," Tassie nodded.

"So your grandmother actually gave Mrs. Haverford something that made her get pregnant?" Julie asked.

"That's right. She taught me about all the herbs and wanted me to take over for her someday, since I seemed to have the gift, as she called it. She used to laugh and tell me that the gift must skip a generation because my mama sure didn't have it."

"That is so amazing!" Julie said. "You see what I mean? This is another thing we could put in the book. I'd love to learn more about your herbal medicine stuff."

"You should see her garden," Libby said.

"Anytime you want to come over, I can show you the journals my grandma kept that are full of all sorts of remedies for anything from hangnails to hernias."

"Libby, wouldn't that be fun! We have to go over there," Julie said.

"I agree." Libby put the last bite of her second brownie into her mouth. "I must say, these are the best brownies I've ever tasted."

"Why, thank you. That was my mama's recipe. She may not have had the gift, but she sure knew how to cook."

"Speaking of moms, my mother finished the mural in the nursery. I've got to show it to you guys. I love it!"

Libby entered the room, sweeping her arm out in a dramatic gesture toward the mural. "Voila!"

Both Julie and Tassie stood in silence for several seconds, admiring the finished product. Julie spoke first. "Oh Libby, it's beautiful! Your mother's so talented."

The mural ran floor to ceiling along one wall. Diana had decided on a nautical theme. The top quarter of the wall consisted of a blue sky scattered with small, puffy white clouds and flying seagulls. The midsection displayed a boat sailing on the water, similar to the boat Josh had just purchased, the masts billowing in the breeze and dolphins jumping into the air in unison ahead of it. The lower section of the wall was a kaleidoscope of colorful sea life under the water—starfish, clownfish, stingrays, an octopus, and coral.

"My, my, that is the most beautiful thing I ever did see," Tassie said as she walked slowly toward the wall. "It looks as if it is about to come to life any second."

"My mother never ceases to amaze me. She did this in little over a week. I wish I'd inherited her ability. I can hardly draw a straight line. Maybe it skips a generation, like your grandmother said." Libby pointed toward her belly. "Maybe *she* will have all the talent."

Julie went over to the antique rocker. "I love this, too, Libby. When did you get this?"

"It had been in the attic. All I had to do was polish it."

Tassie walked over to the rocker and sat down slowly; she closed her eyes and began rocking back and forth, humming a melodic tune.

"Hmm..." Julie said. "I think we may have just discovered the baby whisperer."

Tassie's soft humming was interrupted by a loud blaring sound.

"Oh my God! What is that?" Julie said, holding her ears.

"It's the damn alarm again," Libby said. "It's probably Stella. I left her outside, and she probably pushed the door open again. I'll be right back. I have to punch in the code to turn it off, but I'm sure the alarm company is going to call."

Just as she was leaving the room, the phone began to ring. "What did I tell you?" she said as she walked out.

"I think this is one more reason I don't want an alarm," Julie said to Tassie.

Libby went down the wide staircase as fast as she could and punched in the code on the pad by the front door to deactivate the alarm. Then she headed into the kitchen to answer the ringing phone. "This is operator forty-seven from Noah Systems. We have a report of trouble."

Libby told them everything was fine and gave them the passcode. As soon as she hung up the phone, she turned toward the kitchen door to shut it, but stopped in her tracks when she realized the door wasn't open. "That's weird," she said to the empty room. She looked around for Stella but saw no sign of her. She must've opened the French doors in the dining room. She pushed the swinging door that connected the kitchen to the dining room. "All right, girl. Come here. Where are you hiding…"

Upstairs Tassie was telling another story, when suddenly she sat up in the rocker and said, "Something's wrong."

"What do you mean? Are you feeling all right?" Julie looked worried as she went over to Tassie and touched her arm.

"I feel it in my bones. Something's happened to her." Tassie stared straight ahead.

"Who?"

"Libby."

"But she just went downstairs to turn off the alarm." Julie smiled. "She'll be back up any minute."

"No, we have to go find her." Tassie said it with such urgency that Julie didn't question her again. They headed downstairs. Julie entered the kitchen, calling out Libby's name. There was no answer, and Libby was nowhere in sight. She frowned and turned to Tassie, but she was gone.

Julie went back down the hall and found Tassie standing in the dining room at the glass-paned doors, staring out back, shaking her head, "No…no…"

"What, what is it?" Julie rushed over to Tassie's side. She followed Tassie's gaze and gasped. Down by the water was John Reynolds dragging Libby onto the pier.

"Oh my God!" Julie stood transfixed for several seconds. "I have to call Will!" She ran into the kitchen, grabbing the phone off the wall. Her fingers were trembling as she punched the numbers. After telling Will what was going on, she ran back into the dining room, but Tassie was no longer there. Julie flew over to the doors and saw Tassie walking toward the pier.

Julie opened the door and started running. She raced down the path, passing Tassie, but as she got past the reeds, she stopped and looked around. A large shovel was leaning against the wall of the boathouse. She ran across the pebbled path, her feet stumbling and grabbed the shovel, heading back to the pier. When she got to the edge of the pier, Tassie was already standing on it, and Reynolds had spotted her. He then turned his gaze toward Julie. Julie, with shovel in hand, stopped abruptly.

"Don't come any closer!" he shouted at them. "I mean it! Stay back or I'll break her neck!" He had a crazed look in his eyes. A transformation had taken place; the handsome politician had been replaced by a maniacal-looking madman.

Julie took a step closer to Tassie, who was standing very still with her eyes closed. Tassie was making a low humming sound.

"Please let her go. You don't want to do this. The police are on their way," Julie pleaded.

Reynolds and Libby were about thirty feet from the two women down the pier. "I don't have a choice! She's ruined my life!" Libby strained to free herself from his grip.

Like a flash out of nowhere, something whizzed past Julie's leg and bounded down the pier. It was Stella. As she got closer to Reynolds and Libby, her barking changed to a low growl with her teeth bared.

"Get that dog out of here!" Reynolds shouted, kicking out at the dog as she went for his leg. "I swear, I'll kill the mutt if you don't call it off!" he yelled.

Tassie's humming increased in volume to the point that Julie had to look over at her to make sure the sound was actually coming from such a tiny person. The winds picked up, rustling the reeds and causing the water to lap heavily against the pilings of the pier. Seagulls circled overhead, cawing loudly. Stella was lying down on the pier now, and the growling changed to a whimpering.

Reynolds backed up a few steps.

Slowly an apparition began to form about ten feet in front of where Reynolds and Libby stood.

Reynolds shouted something incoherent and reeled backward, stumbling in the process, losing his grip on Libby. The two fell to the pier. Reynolds began crab walking backward, while Libby rolled to her side with her hands instinctively wrapped around her stomach.

Reynolds shouted, "What the fu—" but before the words had left his mouth, the apparition began moving toward him. He scrambled as fast as he could to get up, slipping several times and falling on his rear. When he finally made it to his feet, he ran backward, afraid to take his eyes off the apparition. He was close to the end where the pier formed the top of a T shape. His foot hit a metal mooring hook that stuck up from the edge of the dock, causing him to careen backward. His head struck hard on the edge of one of the metal-capped pilings and propelled him into the water with a loud splash. He disappeared as quickly as he had fallen, the dark water enveloping around him, the lapping current settling back down, as if he'd never been there.

Libby was still curled up on the smooth planks of the pier, breathing in the smell of the wood, while Julie, having dropped the shovel at her feet, had both hands pressed to her mouth in shock. Tassie, her humming ceased, slowly opened her eyes. The apparition was gone. The winds had stopped.

After a minute, Julie whispered, "What just happened?"

"The devil just met his due," Tassie replied softly.

Libby began to sit up slowly as Stella frantically licked her face. Julie ran down the pier toward her. "Lib, are you OK?" she called out.

"I think so."

Julie knelt down beside her and put her arm around Libby's shoulder. The two women sat on the pier, rocking back and forth for a minute, and then Julie helped Libby to her feet. They looked over the edge of the pier, expecting a body to surface at any second, but the inky liquid gave no sign that a body had ever entered.

Julie and Libby walked slowly back down the pier with Stella in tow, as they heard the sirens pulling down the drive. Within minutes, Will was running around from the side of the house and down the stone path; two state troopers followed behind him. As soon as he saw the women huddled together at the end of the pier, he slowed down, gulping in deep breaths. He jogged up to them, and Julie ran over, hugging him tightly, breaking down in tears.

"Is everyone OK? Where's Reynolds?" Julie couldn't lift her head off Will's shoulder, so he looked over at Libby, who pointed toward the water.

"He's in the water?" Will looked puzzled.

Libby nodded.

The other officers caught up with Will, and he began giving them directions. "We've got a man in the water. Call DNR and get some divers and a boat over here ASAP. The paramedics are already on their way; they should be here any minute. Also comb the shoreline, and see if you see anything." He then turned toward Libby and asked, "Are you sure all of you are OK?"

She nodded again, unable to speak.

"Why don't we go back up to the house, and you can tell me what happened."

48

The paramedics were standing down at the water's edge, waiting to see if they would be needed once Reynolds was found. They'd checked Libby's vital signs even though she said she felt fine. The two troopers that had come with Will were searching the shoreline for any sign of his body.

One of the troopers came up to Will and told him something about the direction of the currents. Libby heard them talking, but their words weren't registering. She felt numb. Everything had happened so fast, but at the same time, she felt it had elapsed in slow motion.

"Libby."

A familiar voice brought her back to reality. She looked up to see Julie standing beside her with a glass of water in her hand. "Are you OK? You looked like you were in a trance."

"I'm fine." Libby took the water from Julie's hand, and Julie sat down next to Will at the table on the patio.

Will and the trooper finished their discussion on the tides and currents, and then the trooper went back down the path to the water. Will opened up his notepad, took a pen from his breast pocket, and said, "Libby, can you tell me what happened?"

She nodded and inhaled deeply, closing her eyes for a second. She told him about the alarm and thinking it was the dog. "I went through the doorway into the dining room, and a man grabbed me from behind and put his hand over my mouth, pulling my head backward. I knew right away it was Reynolds; I could smell him. It was strange, though. I didn't panic. I remember thinking, 'you're not going to do this to me again.' I tried to turn around, but his hold was too tight. I even tried to bite him, but his hand was smashed against my face. I could hardly breathe. I was kicking as much as I could, but he had such a grip on me, pinning my arms down, there wasn't much I could do. He started dragging me backward toward the French door. He let go of me with one hand to open the door, and that's when I grabbed the doorjamb. But he was too strong." Libby's chin started to quiver.

"I could feel my fingers giving way, and then I lost my grip. Once we were outside, I realized he wanted to kill me. I stared at the back of the house, willing Tassie and Julie to come. I'd never been so scared. I remember screaming so loudly, but only a muffled sound came out. He dragged me down the path to the water, and the whole way he kept telling me how I had ruined his life, that because of me he'd lost everything, and now I was going to get what I deserved." Libby's voice cracked, and tears came to her eyes. Julie handed her a tissue, and she wiped away the tears and blew her nose.

"You're doing great, Libby. Why don't you take a second and relax."

He turned to Julie. "What did you all see?"

Julie looked over at Tassie and then to Libby. "We saw Reynolds on the pier, like Libby said. And then things got kind of weird."

"What do you mean *weird*?"

But before Julie could answer, they heard the sound of a boat engine roaring around the Point. The DNR boat came into view.

"Just one second." Will got up and headed down to the pier.

The three women watched as Will instructed the divers what to do. Within minutes, two men in full scuba gear dove off the boat and disappeared under the water.

Will was talking to the captain of the boat, when the handlers with their tracking dogs came around to the back of the house. The women directed them toward Will. Libby held onto Stella's collar, as she whined in protest wanting to follow the other dogs.

Tassie looked over at Libby and said, "It's over now, child. No more worries; things are going to be fine." She patted Libby's hand.

Libby smiled at Tassie. "I hope so. I feel like this is never going to stop. When they find Reynolds, I'm going to have to face him all over again at the trial."

"You don't have to worry about that."

"What do you mean?" Libby frowned.

"I felt the weight lifting off me several minutes after he fell in the water. He won't be troubling anyone anymore. The good Lord has seen to that."

"I want to believe you, but I'll feel a lot better once they find his body." Libby looked off toward the pier. "Tassie, did you make Elizabeth appear? I don't think I ever saw her so vividly before."

"I helped her a little, but I knew she was close by the whole time, so it didn't take much to convince her to show."

"This all seems so crazy. I still can't believe what I saw," Julie said.

"We may never see her again. She got what she came for: justice. Her soul can rest in peace now."

"I wonder why it bothered her so much; I mean, she never even knew Cecilia," Libby said.

"Elizabeth had a tragic life, what with losing her daughter at such a young age and then taking her own life. Maybe there was something in Cecilia that reminded her of her own daughter, and since she hadn't been able to save her own daughter, she wanted to be able to at least clear Cecilia's name and let the truth be known."

"How are we going to explain how Reynolds fell into the water? Don't you think it's going to sound crazy?" Julie asked.

"We all saw it. We can't all be crazy," Libby replied. "I think we need to tell Will what happened and let him decide how it should be handled."

"That's a good idea. He'll know what to do."

Josh came rushing out through the French doors. He ran over to Libby, leaning over and giving her a hug. Then he knelt down beside her chair with a stricken look on his face.

"I'm fine, really." She stroked his hair and kissed him on the cheek.

Will returned to the group. "So, where did we leave off?" He picked up his pen and checked what he had written so far. "That's right—you said things started to get weird. What did you mean by that?"

Julie glanced at Libby, who nodded her head, and then Julie began. "It was as if the air was filled with electricity. My skin felt like it was tingling, and the hair on my arms was raised. At first, I thought a storm was coming, and I noticed that Reynolds sensed it, too. He started looking around, and then—now, don't think I'm crazy, but—a woman appeared."

"What do you mean a woman appeared?" Will asked, puzzled.

"It was Elizabeth," Libby added. "We all saw her, even Reynolds." Libby glanced over at Josh, trying to read the expression on his face and wondering if he thought they were making the whole thing up.

"Really, Will, I know it sounds insane," Julie continued, "but there was a ghost standing on the pier, plain as day. It totally freaked Reynolds out." She explained how Reynolds had been running backward and hit his head before falling in the water.

"Did he resurface at all?"

"Not that I could see," Julie said. She looked at the other women, who shook their heads.

"What about the woman?" Will asked.

"She was gone. Once Reynolds fell in the water, she disappeared as quickly as she came."

"How hard did he hit his head?"

"Pretty hard. He was moving fast, and when he tripped, he kind of spun around and hit the side of his head on the piling. It's hard to tell from where I was standing, but it looked like it could have knocked him unconscious at least."

Will stared down at his notepad, tapping his pen on it. He then threw the pen onto the table and leaned back in his chair, rubbing his chin with his hand. After several minutes of contemplation, he said, "All right, this is what we're going to do." He came forward in his chair, placing his elbows on his knees and leaned in toward the table. There was an imperceptible movement toward him from the others around the table. "I wouldn't normally encourage witnesses to change their story, but I'm not sure how the ghost thing will go over with the PA. We all know what Reynolds had in mind when he came here, and I don't want him getting off because somebody thinks you all have concocted some bizarre story for whatever reasons. When you begin talking about ghosts, you lose your credibility. Why don't we just leave the part out about the ghost?"

"How are we going to say he fell in the water?" Libby asked.

Will looked down toward the pier and thought for a minute. Everyone stared at Will, waiting for a response.

After a few seconds, Julie piped up with, "I've got it!" They all turned their attention to her. "We could say that Stella started attacking him, and he panicked and ran backward, tripped, and hit his head, just like he did."

"That might work," Will said. "The less we change the actual events, the better."

"We have to be careful," Josh interjected. "You all have to be on the same page. All it would take is for one of you to slip up with the story, and it would make you all look suspicious. We don't want this to turn around and have it look like he was the victim."

"You mean we could be blamed for Reynolds' death, if he is dead?" Julie asked.

"Probably not, but nothing's certain. Since there were three of you, though, that helps, as long as everyone has the same story."

"We will," Julie said with confidence. "Right?" she looked over at Libby and then toward Tassie. Both women nodded in response.

"Now if Reynolds is still alive, I don't think you'll have as much to worry about. Reynolds will be the one with all the explaining to do," Josh said.

"He's not alive." The soft voice was almost unheard. Everyone turned toward Tassie.

"What did you say, Tassie?" Josh asked.

"I said, he's not alive, so's you don't have to worry."

"How do you know that?" Will asked.

"Some things I know, and this is one of them." Tassie's cryptic answer left Will at a loss for words.

"Deputy Seevers! I think we've got something!" the young trooper called out as he ran up the path from the shore. Will and Josh were the first to jump out of their seats and take off down the path. Libby and Julie followed with Stella in tow, while Tassie remained seated at the table, with a smile on her face.

They got to the shoreline and saw the divers about fifty yards down the shore, dragging something out of the water. It was clearly a body. They all jogged down toward the divers, except for Libby and Julie who walked behind, somewhat reluctant to get too close.

By the time Libby and Julie reached the group, the divers had pulled Reynolds' body up on shore and laid him on his back in the sand. They all gathered around him, and Will knelt down beside him and checked his pulse. "He's gone."

Libby stood at a distance from the rest, staring at Reynolds. His eyes were open, and he appeared to be gazing up at everyone. Other than his blank stare, it was hard to tell he was dead. Libby shuddered, and she hugged her arms around her chest, suddenly feeling chilled.

49

T he snow fell against the panes of glass—big, fat flakes, like something out of a storybook. The forecast called for just a light dusting, but it was already beginning to stick to the grass.

Libby put the final touches on the Christmas tree in the den while she waited for Josh to arrive with Tassie. It was Christmas Eve, and she'd invited Tassie, Will, Julie, and their kids for a small afternoon gathering. Her parents had gone to Chicago to be with her sister's children for Christmas. She missed being with her family, so this was the next best thing.

Her family was supposed to arrive next week to see the baby. The doctor told her that if the baby didn't arrive on her own by the end of the month, they'd induce labor, something Libby was dreading.

Having put the last decoration on the tree, she plugged in the lights, waddled over to the chair across the room, and eased herself down with her legs apart to make room for her enormous belly. She stared at the tree, admiring her work. Josh and she had gone to a tree farm and cut down a long needle pine that stood about nine feet tall. It filled the room with a rich pine scent that reminded her of Christmases as a child. She closed her eyes and breathed in the fresh, earthy smell.

Stella, who'd been lying by her feet, jumped up and went over to the window, whining and wagging her tail. "Have you never seen snow before?" Libby got up and followed her to the window that faced the water. She stared out at the monochromatic landscape. The water had turned from a teal-green to a grayish-black against a leaden sky dotted with white snowflakes that disappeared onto the gray bark branches of the bare trees. It looked cold and austere, a strong contrast to the cozy den with its crackling fire in the stone fireplace.

The dark water moved languidly back and forth against the pilings of the pier. Libby marveled at how much the water could change, not only in color, but also in the feel. How it could swallow someone up without even a struggle. She closed her eyes, and her thoughts went back through the past two months to that dreadful day.

After the paramedics had zipped Reynolds up into a black body bag and placed him on a stretcher, the rest of the day became a blur to Libby. There was a flurry of activity all around her, but she couldn't really remember what had been going on.

The media frenzy that ensued was more than she could ever have imagined. The story ran on the front page of every newspaper and was the lead story on all the networks. She appeared on different television shows, until finally she refused to speak to anyone about it anymore. She wanted it behind her, but it seemed that was never going to happen. She listened to the talking heads speculating as to why Reynolds would have done what he did, and was it really an accident or not. Eventually she stopped watching the shows and reading the papers. She knew what had happened, and that was all that mattered.

The autopsy report came out the day after the election, and the coroner ruled his death as an accidental drowning. The district attorney decided not to bring any charges against anyone since Libby, Julie, and Tassie all relayed the same accounts of what had happened.

Jamison won the election easily, considering his only opponents were several write-in candidates that no one really knew. Reynolds' name had still appeared on the ballot, and he even received some votes, but the majority of voters had already turned against him.

Libby kept hearing his words in her ear, about how she had ruined his life, ruined his chances of winning the election. Part of her began to wonder if maybe she'd done exactly that; she wondered if he had been innocent of his wife's death, and she'd driven him over the edge with her accusations.

It wasn't until Will came to her about a month after Reynolds' death that her worries were put to rest. He had been able to convince Jane Michaels that there was enough evidence, through the journal entries and Reynolds' subsequent behavior, to exhume Cecilia's body and perform an autopsy.

The findings proved that Cecilia had been ten weeks' pregnant at the time of her death, and there were traces of halothane found in her body, enough to have paralyzed her at the time of her death. After reviewing the results, the coroner changed the cause of death from suicide to homicide. Since most of the evidence pointed toward Reynolds as the killer and he was already dead, the prosecutor decided not to re-open the case, but instead gave a statement saying that Cecilia Haverford had not committed suicide, but had been tragically murdered and that, due to the death of her former husband, the case was not going to be re-opened.

A local reporter was given access to the journal, and from that, she wrote a long article on the life and death of Cecilia Haverford. The article dispelled the rumors that Cecilia was unbalanced or mentally disturbed. She contacted Catherine Collins, through Libby's suggestion, and wrote about the strange behavior of Reynolds before and after his wife's death, suggesting he may have had something to do with it. The article went on to say that since there were no more direct descendants of the Haverford estate, the majority of the estate, which consisted of mostly land holdings, had been passed down to Reynolds' second wife, Cynthia.

Libby watched the snow as it continued to fall, feeling she could finally put the whole ordeal behind her. Stella perked up her ears and began to bark, running from the room. Libby heard Josh's voice in the foyer; he was back from picking up Tassie. Looking at the brightly colored lights on the tree, she smiled, feeling happy. Her thoughts of Reynolds were pushed aside as she went out to greet them.

The whole group was gathered around the Christmas tree as Libby passed out gifts to Wyeth, Nathan, and Sara and then handed another brightly wrapped package to Julie. "This one's for Caleb. You can help him open it," Libby said with a laugh.

"Libby, you shouldn't have! You didn't have to get the kids presents."

"I know, but that's what Christmas is all about, the children. In fact, I had a lot of fun picking out their presents."

"Thank you so much," Julie said after opening Caleb's present. She held up a stuffed toy with brightly colored appendages for teething and shaking. Julie dangled it over Caleb, who was seated in his infant seat on the floor, and he immediately started flapping his arms and legs trying to reach for it. "I think he likes it."

The other children had already torn through their packages and were playing with their new toys. "Kids, what do you say to Libby and Josh?" Julie asked.

"Thank you!" they all three shouted.

The adults moved over to the sofa and chairs around the fire, while the children amused themselves by the tree. Josh passed around glasses of eggnog. They'd already eaten a smorgasbord of food: Julie's macaroni and ham casserole; Tassie's famous biscuits, brownies, and Christmas cookies; and Libby's homemade bread and vegetable soup. Everyone felt sated and relaxed.

The group had seen very little of each other since the ordeal. The whole media circus following the incident had made them want to hibernate until it had blown over. They caught up on little things that had happened in town, and with the kids, and finally the conversation somehow made its way to that day. They were all glad it was behind them, and they could finally move on.

Will said, "Oh that reminds me. I have something for you." He got up and went over to the diaper bag. He came back with the journal in his hand. "I thought you might like to have this," he said to Libby as he handed it to her. "We no longer need it for evidence, and since there are no Haverford heirs left, I thought it really belongs with this house."

"Thank you," Libby said as she ran her fingers over the jewel-covered front that sparkled with the firelight. There was silence for a minute, and then Libby said, "I hope Cecilia can now rest in peace along with Elizabeth."

"Speaking of Elizabeth, have you seen her around lately?" Julie asked.

"No, not since that day. I guess she finally got what she came for. Now people know the truth." Libby opened the journal and turned to the last entry. She skimmed through the words and then read aloud the last passage:

I don't know what to do. All I know is that I want this baby more than anything, with or without John. I had a dream last night that was so vivid I thought it was real. I had the baby and it was a little girl. I had named her Olivia, after my grandmother. She was so beautiful; she had blonde curls surrounding her face and big blue eyes. She looked like an angel...

She closed the book and said, "We did the right thing." She looked over at Josh. "I know you thought I should've left well-enough alone, but now that it's all over, I'm glad we were able to clear her name and Reynolds got what he deserved."

"Since we are all here together, I have an announcement to make. I was going to wait until tomorrow and tell Libby, but I think I would like to share this with all of you. You're like family to us now," Josh said.

Everyone looked at Josh with quizzical expressions, especially Libby. She couldn't imagine what he was about to say.

"What? What is it?" Libby's curiosity was piqued.

"Well, ever since this whole mess blew up, I've been doing a lot of reflecting, and one of the things I've come to realize is that nothing is more important to me than my family." He glanced over at Libby. "I've been consumed for the past few years with work and becoming a full partner. I wanted to be the youngest full partner in the firm's history, but now all of that seems irrelevant. So, I've decided to make a change." He paused, holding up his glass of eggnog with everyone staring at him intently. "Starting in a few months, I am going to set up practice here in town. It won't be all the glitz and glamour of Abbott & Peterson, but it will keep me close to home, and it will be all mine."

"Josh, that's great!" Will said, standing up and shaking his hand. "I guess we'll be seeing a lot more of each other."

"Have you told them yet, at Peterson?" Libby asked.

"I'm going to tell them right after the holidays."

"A toast," Julie said, as she held up her glass of eggnog. "To new beginnings!"

A ruckus broke out over by the tree, the children's voices getting louder as they fought over one of the toys. "It's my turn!" "No it's *my* turn!" "Mom! Nathan won't share!" Sara said with a whine.

"OK, kids, break it up," Will said. He walked over to where they were and stooped down beside them. "You do realize that this is Christmas Eve. Santa has his elves out keeping a close eye on all little boys and girls to make sure they're good. If he finds out about the way you two are behaving, he may just decide to fly right over our house and not bring you anything this year."

"Will!" Julie replied from across the room. But his words got an immediate response from both children. They stopped their fighting and pleaded that they would be good.

Will came back over to the sofa. "What? It worked didn't it?"

"I don't know if threatening them with imaginary people to get them to do the right thing is the best way to handle things. They should learn that sharing is a good thing, and fighting over their toys isn't."

"Look, you can do all the psychological mumbo jumbo you want to on them. I just know it worked for me when I was a kid, and it still works now."

"We really need to get them home. It's getting late." Julie got up and walked over to the kids. "Come on, guys, gather up your things. It's time to go." She looked out the window. "It's still snowing; I hope the roads are safe."

"Don't worry, we've got four-wheel drive. It can get us through anything."

Will and Julie bundled up the kids into their winter gear and then said their good-byes to Josh, Libby, and Tassie. Julie asked Tassie if she would like them to give her a ride home, but Libby told her that Tassie was spending the night.

After the Seevers left, Josh and Libby began straightening up. Tassie insisted on helping even though both of them told her to sit down and relax.

"I can do that anytime. I need to keep these old bones moving, or they just might petrify in one position," she said in her soft voice.

Libby took a tray of glasses into the kitchen, while Josh and Tassie straightened up the den. Suddenly a loud crash came from the kitchen; Josh looked over at Tassie and took off running. Tassie followed behind at a much slower pace. When Josh rounded the corner to the kitchen, he saw Libby bent over, clutching the kitchen table, the tray of glasses broken in bits on the floor in front of her. "Libby! Are you all right?" He had run over to her side, placing his hand on her back.

"I'm fine, I'm fine. I just had a doozy of a contraction." Her words were broken with deep breaths in between.

"Oh my God! Is this it? Are you in labor?"

"It's OK, Josh. Calm down."

Tassie rounded the corner. Josh turned to her and said, "Libby's in labor! We have to get her to the hospital!"

"Hold on, child. There's no rush; just calm down," Tassie said in a soft, soothing voice.

"That's what I told him, but I don't think he's listening."

"Why don't we get you someplace comfortable," Tassie said.

"OK," Libby replied.

"Do you want to go upstairs and lie on your bed? It might be a good idea to change into some comfortable clothes," Tassie suggested.

"Yeah, that sounds good," Libby said. Josh helped her up the stairs even though she kept insisting she was fine. "I've been having contractions all day, but they were very mild. I kept ignoring them, thinking they were just false labor. In fact, I've been having them off and on all week."

"Why didn't you say anything?" Josh asked.

"I don't know. I guess I didn't want to make a big deal out of nothing."

They got to the bedroom, and Libby got her nightgown out of the dresser. Then she headed into the bathroom to change.

Josh ran his fingers through his hair as he paced the floor, waiting for her to come back out.

"You need to conserve your energy, child. This could be a long night," Tassie said.

"What?" Josh looked at her as if she'd been speaking in a foreign language.

"I've birthed many a baby over the years, and it can be a long process, especially with the first. You may be up all night, so you don't want to wear yourself out now making a hole in that carpet there."

After a few minutes, Libby came out of the bathroom dressed in a loose nightgown. "I just had another one of those doozies. I thought I had to go to the bathroom, but nothing happened, and then I threw up. Maybe it's not labor; maybe I have food poisoning or something."

"Child, it sounds to me like you may be transitioning."

"Transitioning? How could that be? I haven't been in labor that long."

"Every woman's labor is different. If you don't mind, I could check to see if you're dilated."

"OK." Libby lay down on the bed, and Tassie gently lifted her nightgown up, and with tender hands she stroked Libby's legs.

After examining Libby, Tassie stood up and said, "Well, I don't think we need to be making a trip to the hospital."

"Is it false labor?" Josh asked.

"No, it's not false, but she looks to be about ready real soon. I don't think you want to risk having that baby on the side of the road."

"You mean she's going to have the baby here!" Josh looked like he was about to explode with panic.

"It's OK, son. I've delivered many babies at home. Having a baby is the most natural thing in the world; everything is going to be all right."

"This is crazy. I'm calling an ambulance."

"Josh, stop!" Libby's tone got his attention. "Look at me. Listen to Tassie; everything is going to be fine. Remember all those women that had home births from the hypno-birthing classes, and everything went fine?"

"That was them; I never expected we would be doing it ourselves."

"Just relax. Let's focus on what we learned in class."

"I can't remember what we learned."

Tassie realized that she needed to get Josh under control. She'd dealt with husbands like this before, and she knew just what to do. "Josh, I need your help. Go find me some old sheets."

"Old sheets?" he looked puzzled.

"There are some in the bathroom across the hall in the linen closet, the ones with the pink flowers," Libby said.

Josh stood there for several seconds trying to process the information, and finally Libby shouted out, "GO!" just as another contraction came on. He ran out of the room.

Libby closed her eyes and tried to picture her body as a flower petal opening up, trying not to fight the pain but to go with it, and let her body do the work it needed to do.

Tassie had gotten a cool cloth and gently stroked Libby's forehead, while she hummed a soft melodic tune. Libby could feel the soft notes move through her body, relaxing every nerve as it went. Within a few minutes, Josh came back with a bundle of sheets in his arms. "I wasn't sure which ones you meant, so I just brought them all."

Libby smiled, thinking he looked like a scared little boy—this man who commanded a courtroom. "I said the ones with the pink flowers on them."

Tassie helped Josh sort out the right sheets, and then she told him to spread them out underneath Libby, several layers thick. Once he had finished that task, she told him to go find some receiving blankets, diapers, and to boil some water. He listened intently, nodding his head with each task, and then he walked with purpose from the room.

"Boiling water? Do you actually use boiling water for delivering the baby?" Libby asked.

"No, but I figured he could make me a cup of tea to keep him busy."

Libby chuckled and then grimaced with another pain.

"Just breathe, relax, and breathe," Tassie said soothingly, stroking Libby's arm with her warm, spidery fingers. "This little girl wants to come out. I think she knows that Santa is coming tonight, and she doesn't want to miss him." Tassie went back to humming her soft tune, sitting by the bed.

Josh came back in with several receiving blankets and some diapers. "The water is on; it should be at a boil soon. Do you want me to bring the whole pot up here?"

"No, but you could pour some in a cup with some tea, and bring it up to me."

Josh did a double take as he was about to run from the room. "You're just keeping me busy, aren't you?"

"No, I really would love a cup of tea."

Josh nodded. "You're not fooling me." He went over to Libby and kissed her on the forehead. "How are you feeling?"

"I'm OK, hon."

"What can I do?"

"Get Tassie her tea, and then you can sit with me."

By the time he came back to the room with the steaming mug of tea, Libby was sitting up in bed slightly bent over, and Tassie had her hand on Libby's back. "That's right, just breathe with it, don't force the push, just let your body do it all." Tassie saw Josh out of the corner of her eye, and said, "Oh good, you're back. Set the mug down, and come over here where I'm standing."

Josh did as he was told and took Tassie's place by Libby's side. Tassie moved down the bed and lifted Libby's nightgown. "You're doing great. I can see the head. It won't be long, just a few more pushes."

Libby took another deep breath in, and then let out a slow shushing sound.

"That's it. Here she comes; just wait for the next one."

Libby relaxed a little and looked up at Josh. She had sweat across her brow, and he wiped it away with the cloth. He then leaned down and kissed her head, whispering, "I love you."

Before Libby could answer, she took in another deep breath and repeated the same low shushing sound.

"Here she is."

Josh looked down and couldn't believe his eyes. There, sliding out into Tassie's dark hands, was a little blonde head. And within a few more seconds, a whole body appeared. Tassie looked her over and then placed her on Libby's abdomen. Libby stroked her back.

"What about the cord? Don't you have to cut it or something?" Josh looked at Tassie with a worried expression.

"Not yet. It's best to wait until it stops pumping. She's fine for a bit."

An hour later Tassie had cleaned everything up, with Josh's assistance, and she'd deftly swaddled the baby in a tight little cocoon of receiving blankets. The baby was now nursing greedily. "She's an eager little eater," Libby said, propped up against the pillows.

"That's good. You just want to be careful in the beginning and not nurse too long each time; otherwise, you're going to be painfully sore tomorrow." Tassie was seated in the armchair next to the bed.

"I don't know how to thank you. You're amazing."

Josh came into the room with three steaming mugs of tea on a tray. "I made you another cup, Tassie, since the other one got cold, and I thought you might like one too, Lib."

"Thanks. Just set it on the nightstand." Josh sat beside Libby at the head of the bed and put his arm around the top of Libby's pillows, looking down into the baby's face. She was lying in the crook of Libby's arm, contentedly looking up at both of them. Her big blue eyes were taking everything in.

"She's so beautiful," Josh said. The soft light of the bedside lamp cast a glow on the baby's face. "Those blonde curls make her look like an angel."

Libby looked down at her, studying her face. She had a cute little button nose, two perfectly formed lips, and when Libby gazed into her violet-blue eyes, she felt as if she were looking into an old soul, as if she'd known her for a long time.

"Have you two picked out a name yet?" Tassie asked.

"No, not yet," Josh replied.

"Well, I think I have. That's if you like it, too," Libby said.

"What?"

"I was thinking we could name her Olivia Grace." She looked down at the baby's blue eyes. "Cecilia had dreamt about her baby and wanted to name her Olivia, but never got the chance. It really is a beautiful name, and Grace could be her middle name, after your mother."

"I like it," Josh replied. "Hello, Olivia, welcome to the world." He leaned down and kissed her cheek.

Epilogue

L ibby was outside the storefront assisting Josh in hanging the dark green sign with gold lettering that read **Joshua P. Langston** and underneath *Attorney at Law* in an Old English script. She waved her arm to the right as Josh stood on a ladder, trying to get the best position. Olivia sat in the stroller, her big blue eyes watching the procedure. The office, located along the square, was set to open next week. Tulips, daffodils, and petunias were in full bloom, filling the courtyard with color. The new green leaves of the tall oaks danced in the warm spring breeze.

"Move just a little bit more to the right," Libby said.

"That looks wonderful! Very professional," a voice called out.

Libby turned. "Julie! How's it going?"

"Been pretty busy lately working with Tassie." Julie parked Caleb's stroller next to Olivia's.

"Tassie said business was pretty good," Libby said.

"You need to come over sometime and see what we've been doing. We're thinking of setting something up at the farmers' market. Oh, let me show you." Julie reached into the diaper bag slung on the stroller and pulled out a pale blue pamphlet with a drawing of herbs on the front, along with the name "Natural Necessities" intertwined through a vine. Inside on one page was a listing of a variety of herbal concoctions and what they treated—things like "Bug Buster" for colds and flu and "Energy Lift" for building stamina. The opposite page listed various herbal teas.

"This looks very impressive. Have you tried any of them?"

"Absolutely. They really work. You wouldn't believe the orders we're getting for things. I've learned so much from Tassie and the book her grandmother had. It's amazing! Who knows, if this really takes off, we may be setting up a shop in town, too."

Libby smiled at Julie's enthusiasm and excitement.

Josh came down off the ladder and gave Julie a hug. "Well, if you need any legal advice for the business, you know where I am."

"I like it." Julie nodded toward the wooden sign now swinging on two black chains from the eaves. "So when do you open?"

"Next Monday. I've already got a few clients."

Caleb was sitting forward in his stroller trying to reach toward Olivia. "It won't be long before these guys'll be playing together," Libby said, watching the two babies interact.

"We need to do lunch together soon," Julie said. "Well, I've gotta run and pick Sara up from pre-school." Julie started to push the stroller and then stopped. "Oh, you're not going to believe this. I was talking to Sue Appleton; she works at Corsica Realty."

Libby nodded.

"Well, her son is in the same nursery class as Sara, and she told me about this farmhouse she sold about a month ago to a young couple from out of state. After they bought the house, they decided to do some renovations, and when they were tearing out one of the walls in the kitchen, you're not going to believe what they found."

Libby's brows were raised in anticipation.

"Two hundred thousand dollars!"

"What!" Libby stared wide-eyed at Julie.

Josh, who was back up on the ladder adjusting the sign, turned his attention to the conversation.

"Yeah, it turns out the farmhouse used to be owned by this guy named Carmichael. He was big into raising steer for beef and had property all over the county. Supposedly, he didn't believe in banks or the IRS and kept money hidden all over his property; some of it was even buried in the barn. Sue said, when he died, they found some in the freezer inside ice cream containers. Anyway, they think that's what got him killed. He was shot to death on his front porch several years ago, and they've never been able to solve the case. There was speculation at the time that one of his grandchildren shot him for the money."

"That's horrible!" Libby exclaimed, holding her hand over her mouth.

"According to Sue, he had children scattered all over the place, but they never had enough evidence to arrest anyone. Anyway, the new owners discovered some correspondence he had with one of his granddaughters who lived in Florida, or was it Georgia?" Julie squinted. "I'm not sure which, but she had written to him saying she wanted to come visit him. The letters were dated just a few weeks before he was killed. And Will just told me this morning that the FBI is involved, and they want to re-open the case."

"That's crazy!" Libby said. "I wonder where the granddaughter is now."

"Libby, don't get any ideas. Your detective days are over," Josh said, tilting his head at her and giving her a look of warning.

Libby waved her hand at him and laughed. "Don't worry. Solving one murder was enough." She then smiled at Julie and gave her a wink.

"I'll keep you updated," Julie said, winking back, and then she headed down the street.

Josh came down off the ladder and said, "What do you think?" He stood back and looked up at the sign.

Libby slipped her arm around him and kissed him on the cheek. "I think it's perfect."

Made in the USA
Charleston, SC
15 July 2013